FLOUNDER

ZACHARY DOWNING

BEGGIEBOOKS

Cover design by Luisa Galstyan
Interior design by Nicole Hayes

Library of Congress Control Number: 2021922847

ISBN: 978-0-578-32080-9
eBook ISBN: 978-0-578-32081-6

Beggie Books
Website: zdowning.com
Contact: zdowning@beggiebooks.com

For my mom and her dad:
the lineage of my love of reading.

Passage 1:

End of Senior Year of High School

Chapter 1: Easter

I wonder when they'll bring it up; I wonder if they'll bring it up. At first glance, it seems like a normal Easter supper, but underneath the surface, our family dynamic is shifting. Don't get me wrong, Mom and Dad are the same, Abigail still comes by for the big holidays, and Grandma's still kicking, but the unspoken stuff is coming to a head. And unspoken is how it's likely to be left. So, as the implicit dinner itinerary dictates, we put on our little show. Fresh food, stale script. But I don't mind too much. For once, I get a little more stage time, although I'll probably be second fiddle to Abigail. First grandchild beats college acceptance.

Now that Abigail is showing, Mom's downright giddy whenever Stephen and she arrive. Those old photos prove that Abigail's a carbon copy of Mom's pregnant aesthetic, except for the influence of her adolescent-90's sensibility, compared to Mom's 60's/70's upbringing. I immediately have to hear all about her second trimester, morning sickness, gas, exams— things a brother never wants to know about his sister. The rest of them just nod, like she's revealing some holy, eternal wisdom, while Stephen nods along, playing the dutiful, willfully-unconcerned-about-your-own-receding-hairline husband. Mom and Abigail look over our baby books, while Dad finishes up making the dinner, an occurrence that's both uncommon and entertaining. He's doing a decent job, but you can tell he's a bit out of his element with how much he's checking the food, pushing up his glasses from the edge of his nose, and glancing out the side of his eye, to see how much his own mother is silently criticizing him. Luckily for him, Grandma's also assigned herself the job of umpiring how Stephen and I set the table. I hear another book close, and can tell Mom is getting a little restless.

"Almost done in there, honey?"

Dad momentarily panics, but then sizes up the ETA. "Uh, the ham's just about done, but we're still two-for-two with kids."

"I'll get Dee," volunteers Abigail, as she walks upstairs to Diana's bedroom.

"Are you sure?" beckons Grandma, with a worried look. She ain't that pregnant, Grandma.

Abigail calls back, "Yeah, it's fine," and Grandma relents a bit. The pregnancy has stolen some of the doting attention from Grandma, but she gets it back in full stride when Dad ushers her to and from the nursing home.

Dad shoots a look at me. "Where's your brother?"

"He said his shift ends at four."

"Did you tell him we were eating at four-thirty?"

"I did." I withhold the knowledge that Gerry is probably blazing, to both "unwind" after work, and also give himself some munchies before the big dinner. Everyone except for Grandma and Diana will probably be able to tell, but Dad doesn't need to wonder if he's driving at the same time. Hopefully, there's no coke in his system; he only does that once in a blue moon.

"Can someone call him?" Mom shouts from the other room.

Dad takes the potatoes out of the oven. "Why don't we all take our seats, and I'm sure he'll be in soon." For some reason, not eating until everyone is at the table is a big deal in our family. We're not formal in other ways, but this rule always reigns unbreakable.

Mom walks into the kitchen, does a smiling sniff to the aroma and sits down next to Grandma. She shifts her plate and napkin slightly, looks up, and smiles again. I give Stephen a knowing smirk, informing him that we did a good job setting the table, but also could have done marginally better. Abigail walks in, with Diana a few steps behind, sporting her trademark ponytail and trendy glasses, her mind still in her bedroom.

"Look who I rescued from some Algebra," announces Abigail. She's already sounding like a mom.

Diana releases a deep breath and sits next to Dad's seat. "Where's Ger— "

Before she can finish asking, the front door swings open, and I see him walk briskly to our bedroom. "Our." We always shared it growing up, but for a brief moment it was just "my" bedroom. I know that I'll have a roommate in a few months, but it would be nice to have a space to myself for some amount of high school. It's just that once it became "mine," I didn't expect to be downgraded back to "our" in less than two months.

Mom's head pops up as he passes by. "Gerald, we're ready for the supper."

"Yeah, one sec," he calls back without stopping.

"Now," Dad commands. "We're waiting on you." Gerry's upstairs, but shouts something indistinguishable back.

"What did he say?" Mom asks.

"He said he's changing his shirt," Diana and I say in unplanned, choppy unison. We have the youngest ears, so we're usually translating for the rest of the family when they're having conversations across different ends of the house.

"Well, everyone else can sit down," Dad says. We sit in our usual seats for the holidays, and by the time Dad puts all the food on the table, Gerry has come down, given Grandma a kiss, scratched his scruff over the food, and sat next to me. As I wait for the okay to dig in, I observe the lamb-shaped mold of butter that's starting to soften and change form. Mom always found it gross, but it's an Easter tradition we carry on for Grandma.

"Mom, would you like to say grace?" Mom asks Grandma, as if she'd let anyone else attempt.

Grandma smiles. "Yes, that would be nice." We lower our heads, and hope it won't be too long. "Lord, thank you for this wonderful food, for our family and for bringing us together. Thank you for the new addition that's coming. Please help guide Abigail in learning to become a nurturing and caring mother. Please help Stephen learn to become a diligent and supportive father. Lord, look after me as my gastroenterologist exam approaches. And please be with my friend, Rose, as she's suffering from shin splints. In Jesus' name we pray…"

"Amen," we join in.

"Alright, let's eat," Dad says as he takes a sip of wine. I look at the table as Mom starts making a plate for Grandma: ham, potatoes, a vegetable medley and bread. These are the Easter staples, though not everyone's favorite. We stick to the menu, because Grandma wouldn't have it any other way. Maybe, once Grandma's no longer around, we could switch it up and ditch the ham; maybe the grace could go, too.

When it seems like everyone has had their first serving in front of them, and the plate passing has died down, the performance begins. Mom starts us off. "I guess next year we'll have to add a highchair to the table."

"We'll have to do that for Thanksgiving first," Dad adds.

"Have you given any more thought to names?" Mom asks the expecting couple.

"Since Friday night?" Stephen chirps.

"I just thought you may have some more ideas," Mom says. "What are some of the male names on your side?"

"Well, there's my uncle Salvatore."

"Oh," Mom reacts with disagreement. "Who else?"

"Mom, we'll have some updates for you Memorial Day Weekend," Abigail says, saving her husband.

"You're not coming for Mother's Day?"

"We'll probably be with his side."

"Your first Mother's Day?"

"I won't be a mother yet."

"It still counts."

Dad jumps in to play his part. "Abbie, how's the job? Did you have to take tomorrow off?"

"Yes, but the office will be pretty quiet. A lot of people are away."

"When will you work until?" Mom jumps in.

"Probably a few weeks before the due date, and then I get eight weeks off. But I might take six months. We'll see." Mom already knows this, but she wants everyone to hear her asking and hear the answer.

"And Steve, how's work for you?" Dad asks, using a nickname that may or may not be preferred by Stephen.

"Semester's going well. I'm teaching one less class, so I can go with Abbie to some appointments."

"And what about August?" Mom jumps in again.

"I may be able to take some time off if need be, but I'm planning on working the Fall semester just the same."

"Well, we're always able to help out." Keep on sowing those seeds, Mom. "Since it is your first." Nice reinforcement.

"Steve, you'll have to give Alex some pointers," Dad says.

Stephen looks at me out of the corner of his eye, but keeps talking to Dad. "Yes, we were speaking a bit before, while setting the table. It's an exciting time for him." You'd think that this would be a pivot for the conversation to turn to me, but I know it's not my turn yet. We haven't even gotten through Abigail's wrap-up yet. At a holiday supper, you need to know when and how to take the spotlight, and when you're a background player. We learned at an early age to not have side conversations, while Mom and Dad are steering the flow. So, Gerry, Diana and I just eat quietly, and pretend to find all of it new and interesting. Grandma just smiles, listens and struggles with her peas. I imagine she was the conversation conductor years ago, but probably passed the torch onto her daughter-in-law, when she felt Mom had earned it.

Mom lets out a proud exhale. "Well, just enjoy sleeping now. That's all I can say." That's the pivot. Usually, we stick on Abigail a bit longer, but maybe they ran out of material. Dad also hasn't bantered with Stephen as much. There's only so much you can ask an economics professor while still understanding what he's talking about. Dad usually just says, "Can you believe the stock market?" or brings up credit card fees. The big question is who's up next. Abigail is always first up because she's first born. You'd think it would go, Gerry-me-Diana, but it's really anyone's guess.

Dad takes the shifter. "Diana had her last volleyball game earlier this week." First born to last born.

"How did it go?" asks Abigail. Normally, we wouldn't be able to interject because it runs the risk of derailing the story Mom and Dad are weaving, but Dad's statement was conversation bait. He could have said to Diana, "Tell them about it," but setting one of us up yields the same result.

"We won the game, but we didn't have a good record for the season, so we didn't advance," Diana recounts. After Abigail asks another volleyball question and Diana answers, something about drills I think, Mom takes the cue to bring up Diana's glowing progress report. This is sizing up to be a long act. Being the youngest isn't enough; Diana has to steal the attention in other ways, too. Not only is she an overachiever, but she's probably the brightest of the four of us. I would say Gerry's a pace or so behind her, and maybe Abigail and I are tied for third. For the next ten minutes we nod and listen as Mom and Dad set Diana up to talk about school, cello, ballet, spring soccer, getting confirmed, graduating middle school and which honors classes she got into for high school. Stephen is even already catching on with Mom and Dad's questions. When Mom brings up Diana's math grades, he jumps right in and talks about his favorite geometry topic.

I do have to hand it to Diana. All that praise from Mom and Dad must come with added pressure, but Diana seems poised enough to handle it. When it comes to my friends, Mark has always been an overachiever as well, but it's never really affected how often we chill. He just had to drop some extracurriculars in high school to stay afloat. I'm sure Diana will do the same.

Finally, I hear the pivot. "She's got a bright future ahead of her," Dad concludes. Who will it be next? I take some more ham to divert any eagerness on my part. "How was work today, Gerry?" Dad asks. Looks like I'm up last.

"Fine," Gerry says.

"Anything interesting happen?" Mom adds.

"No, just a normal day selling electronics," Gerry answers.

"Oh, you made a sale today?" Dad asks, feigning intrigue.

"Two, but I was in the stockroom most of the shift."

"Your arms show it," Abigail says. "You're bulking up, bro." Gerry gives an obligatory "thanks," and then continues to give short answers for the few, remaining questions.

This is better than Thanksgiving and Christmas, when Mom and Dad didn't even inquire about him at all. Thanksgiving was still kind of the initial sting for them, and during Christmas, there was so much of Stephen's family around. Uncle Clark momentarily brought it up, but Mom quickly shut him down and changed the subject. As awkward as it was for them at the time, they didn't have to share a room with him again. I guess being only a year apart inherently breeds a too-close-for-comfort relationship, but when he came back from college, things got especially tense because it happened just as I was applying. Abigail and Diana never had to share, but Mom and Dad say that's because they're over ten years apart. I just wish I protested a bit when Abigail's old room became Dad's office. Really the worst of it comes from having to share the third car again. But things are looking brighter now that my senior year is winding down. I just hope that now that it's my time, he doesn't ruin it for me.

"So Alex, why don't you tell everyone the story of how you got in?" Dad says. Just like that? No concluding statement for Gerry? Ouch. I steal a glance at Gerry, who notices, but is also glad his turn is over.

"I received my acceptance letter two weeks ago," I say. Another piece of information everyone at the table already knows, thanks to Mom and Dad. They just want me to narrate it the way they want me to.

"Start at the beginning! Where and why you applied, the requirements, how you decided, c'mon!" Mom encourages.

"Well, we checked out Belston last summer after we dropped off Gerry…" Damn. Gerry shoots me a quick look. I didn't think that one through. To recover, I just brush through the greatest hits: liking Belston when I visited, getting a recommendation letter, applying last fall, finding out I got in and saying yes. Mom and Dad embellish and pose more questions throughout, but we get through it without any more Gerry faux pas. When my turn has run dry, everyone's pretty much full, and we all pitch in cleaning up. Diana hums that James Blunt song again, to which Abigail rolls her eyes. It makes me laugh because I distinctly remember one lake vacation where she herself sang "Waterfalls" non-stop. I'd bring it up, but am still figuring out how much you can pester a pregnant woman. Gerry and Diana retreat upstairs, and the rest of us settle in the den, passing around a basket of Easter candy while watching *Reba*.

It's taken me seventeen years to realize that my family likes to overindulge on achievements, but ignore, conceal and avoid addressing blunders. The problem with sweeping things under the rug is that they still exist, everyone can see the bump, and sometimes they trip on it. I don't blame Mom and Dad for the way they police our holiday conversations. They don't even talk about themselves. I think it's just their way of showing they're proud of us. Not just to Grandma, us or themselves, but in a way, to life. Growing up, it was so rare for all six of us to be sitting down eating dinner together. Even if Mom and Dad were both home from work, one of them was usually taking one of us to an activity, putting Diana to bed early, or on a work call. Those dinner conversations, with only half of us, were more normal. We joked and talked about everyday things, interrupted each other, argued, had side conversations. It was always different. Different combinations of different family members on different days of the week. I think Mom and Dad like to control the holiday conversation because it represents a consistency for them. We're all together, we're all happy, everything in life is good. But change is coming down the pike, and soon I'll be off to college.

Chapter 2: Late April

My pocket buzzes and I look around to see if anyone is watching. We're not supposed to take calls or text during work, but I've seen other employees do so in the past. Carla will totally call you out on it, but I guess that's what a manager is supposed to do. I constantly remind myself to be sneaky because usually it's only us working. Tonight's one of those nights. I guess there's not many people interested in buying a pet on a rainy Monday, so it's really just me cleaning fish tanks. Inside and out. Truthfully, there isn't much time to check your phone when you're draining water and scrubbing fish crud off the glass, but every now and then, you need a break from that ever-so-important task. I'm just waiting for a tank to refill, so now's as good of a time as ever to steal a quick glance.

Mark says he's going over Pete's after dinner, so I ask for a pick up from him, if he can wait a bit. I check for Carla again before opening a text from Mom.

Am I picking you up at 8:30? I knew I forgot something.

No, I'm going to Pete's house.

How are you getting there? Typical response, but with an untypically quick response time.

Mark's picking me up.

I wait.

Do you have an umbrella?

It's okay, I'll just run to his car.

Can you be back by 11? Dad and I want to talk to you about something.

Shit. What could this be about? Maybe because I cut Gym last week? I've been getting along alright with Gerry. Or maybe they found my porn again. I could have sworn I cleared the cookies.

Sure, see you later.

As I slip my phone back into my pocket, I see Carla coming. She gives me a suspicious look, but I know she didn't catch me.
"How many tanks do you have left?"
"Just two. I'll be done before the end of my shift."
"You're here 'til…"
"Eight-thirty."
"Alright. Can you bring up that new tank from the basement before you go, too?"
"Sure." She seems satisfied, and I don't see her for the remainder of the night. The rest of my shift flies, and as I'm putting down the new tank, I can see Mark idling in his car outside. I grab my jacket and shout goodbye to Carla. It's not raining too hard, but I run to Mark's passenger side door, to find that it's locked. I tap the glass and he gleefully takes his time unlocking the door, before I jolt inside.
"Thanks for the urgency," I gripe.
"Beggars can't be choosers," he says, inspecting the length of his all-seasons crewcut in the mirror.

"Whatever," I say as I shake off the rainwater. "Can we leave by 11?"

"Yeah, I've got some Calc to do anyway."

"Cool." We drive around and I think of how different this is from freshman year: I have a job, Mark has a car, and we're out late on a weeknight. We're still going to Pete's to play video games, just like we did since elementary school, but now it somehow feels cooler. Even Mark is a bit more relaxed. He would never put off homework, before, but now that we're both accepted into colleges, I guess he's less concerned. He's always been the brightest of the three of us, but I have to admit, he also works really hard. Not that I don't, but his work seems to get him further. Last year, we both took an SAT Prep class, and he got a 1510, while I just did okay. But Mark and I were never competitive. In elementary school, he'd help me with math when I didn't understand something, but when he joined honors classes, I had to fend for myself.

We roll up at Pete's house and sprint to his front door, hopping over puddles. Pete's mom opens the door as usual and offers a quick, "You know where he is." We run up the stairs to find him in his bedroom, mouth agape, eyes transfixed on "Splinter Cell," while his hands are clasped on the video game controller. He momentarily makes eye contact with us under his shaggy dog hair, and then snaps his eyesight back to the screen, his fingers moving rapidly.

"Hey," Pete murmurs. We know that's his way of saying, "Welcome, come in." As I sit in his armchair, Mark moves to Pete's half-made bed, making sure to block Pete's vision along the way. "Dude!" Pete shouts. We laugh, and after Pete saves his game, Mark and I grab the spare controllers for some multiplayer. The three of us play mostly in silence, save for shouts of frustration or triumph at each other. Years ago, Pete's mom would be alarmed by the commotion and pop her head in the doorway, but now she's used to it. Pete isn't just a video game nerd. He's actually pretty artistic and is in the school plays. He convinced me to audition for one sophomore year, but I couldn't really carry a tune or dance. Mark and I still support him and see the productions. His mom works for a non-profit, something environmental I think. Mom always called them "hippy," but I never really noticed. I guess the one out of the ordinary thing is Pete is deferring college for a year, and his mom is cool with it.

"How are you going to survive without Xbox for eight months?" Mark asks after losing the round to Pete.

"That's why I'm getting my fill now," Pete says.

"Well, I'll be able to beat you when you get back from Paraguay."

"Chile."

"Like the food?"

"No, like the country you know nothing about." We keep playing a few more rounds before Mark and I head out. The rain has pretty much stopped, and when Mark drops me off, I head straight to my room, pulling off my work shirt, as I walk.

I guess I don't see them as I'm passing by, but I'm halfway to my bedroom when I hear Mom call for me.

"Alex, are you home? Can you come down here?"

"Oh yeah," I say. "Let me just change."

"I think Gerry's asleep." I know that's her way of telling me to not go into my own room right now.

"Okay," I say as I leave my work shirt on my doorknob and walk down the stairs.

I find them in the kitchen, Mom sitting down with perfect posture, and Dad standing in his work clothes, leaning his hand on Mom's chair, yawning over a pile of papers spread across the table. Mom motions for me to sit in the empty chair across from her.

"Did you have dinner?" she asks.

"I got a burrito during my break," I answer as I sit down.

"Why are you just wearing an undershirt?"

"There's fish piss on my uniform. That's why I wanted to change."

"I don't care for that language." I roll my eyes.

"Alright," Dad says. "Alex, we need to talk to you about college." I look down to all the papers facing Mom, and realize that this is a serious talk. It's something that both of them need to talk to me about, or else Dad wouldn't be awake right now. Dad points to three separate piles of papers. "These are your loan forms, these are your financial aid forms, and these are your scholarship forms."

"Easy honey, one step at a time," Mom says to him, slowing him down. He pauses for a second.

"You know you'll have student loans, right?" he asks.

"Yes," I answer. "And I filled out the other forms."

"You filled out some of your aid forms."

"Okay, did I miss something?"

"No, a parent had to complete the rest."

"Then what's the problem?" Dad pauses. Mom takes this as a cue to speak.

"Alex, you know college is very expensive, right?" she asks.

"Yes," I answer without thinking. Then my heart sinks. "Can we still afford for me to go away?"

"Yes," Dad says slowly, trailing off. Mom picks up the torch.

"You know that college will be difficult?" she asks carefully.

"Yes," I counter, slowly.

"More difficult than school, now," Dad adds. Now I pause. They're walking on eggshells and I don't know why.

Mom cuts the silence. "We just want you to take it seriously."

"Why wouldn't I?" I ask, perplexed.

Mom takes a breath. "There's not going to be anyone to make sure you do your work." I suddenly realize that this talk isn't really about me. It's about Gerry. They want to make sure that I'm not just a carbon copy of my brother, but they won't come out and say it. I sigh and Mom continues. "We want to make sure that you attend all your classes."

Dad chimes in. "And that should start now, too. You shouldn't be slacking just because you're accepted into college."

"I'm not cutting class," I defend myself.

"But it's late on a school night," Dad says.

"I worked and then saw friends for like an hour!"

Mom changes course. "Let's focus on what we want to show you."

I look down at the papers. "Go ahead."

Mom flips a page towards me and points to the middle paragraph. "In order for you to keep your scholarship, you need to maintain a minimum 3.0 GPA."

"Alright." I say, vaguely remembering reading it.

"You'll make sure you do that?" she asks.

"Yes."

"We just want to make sure that you understand college's worth," Dad says.

I contemplate this for a moment. Worth it for me or worth it for them? I get the feeling they're looking at me like I'm a potential waste of money. Maybe I'm getting the talk they regretted not giving to Gerry. I focus back on them and realize that neither of them has said anything else. I can tell Dad is exhausted.

"I understand what you expect of me," I say, knowing this is what they want to hear. I sense them taking that in and relaxing a bit. "I'm pretty tired. I'm going to go to bed."

"Ok, I'm glad we had this talk," Mom says. She stands up and comes towards me, and I know she thinks a cathartic hug is called for. As I get up to comply, Dad yawns, collects all of the papers from the table, and starts putting paperclips on the separate piles.

"Goodnight," I say to both of them, after escaping the overlong hug.

"Goodnight," says Mom. "Try not to wake Gerry up." I nod and head back to my room, opening and closing my door slowly. Gerry seems fast asleep, but when I collapse into bed, the bounce of the springs makes him rustle a bit. I stare at the ceiling for about fifteen minutes. I was tired, but now I can't conk out because I'm pissed off. I turn and look at Gerry, and wonder about Abigail and Diana, too. I was too young to comprehend college for Abigail, but she always seemed like she knew what she wanted. She got married early like Mom and Dad, and is having kids young, too. Maybe they didn't have to worry about her, and that's why they were blindsided by Gerry.

I look at him sleeping. I feel like I only got three-quarters of the whole story, and just in pieces. Mom, Dad and Gerry don't like to talk much about it, maybe for different reasons, but Diana and I got the gist from Abigail: Mom and Dad got a call from Gerry's RA about some vandalism, and when they came up, I guess they figured out he wasn't going to class either. They didn't give Diana and me a warning. Gerry was just back home one day, and we got the sense we weren't meant to ask questions. Gerry and I were close when we were younger, but in high school we drifted apart. We never ran in the same circles, but I know kids whose older siblings would talk to them about drinking, parties, dating, give them rides. Maybe we could have had that if Gerry hadn't come back home.

I think of Diana and whether Mom and Dad will give her a talk about taking college seriously. Probably not. She's got Gerry's brain and Abigail's drive. They probably won't have to worry about her. Gerry is so naturally smart. Abigail says he may have not been able to adjust from not studying in high school, to having to try in college. Mom and Dad probably think that I'm the same risk as Gerry, but more dumb going in.

Chapter 3: May

School and work stay about the same throughout May. I stay up on my homework, even though it's thinning out. I don't skip any classes, not even Gym, just to keep Mom and Dad off my back. Mark is busy for a week taking AP tests, but afterwards catches a serious case of senioritis. I guess he figures that now he's been accepted into college, and has taken his last important exams, he can just mail it in. He used to be so disciplined about doing his homework, that I'd only see him on weekends. Now it seems he wants to go to Taco Bell or see a movie every other weeknight.

Mother's Day is kind of an Easter repeat. Mom guilts Abigail into celebrating with us, and we take a lot of photos of the two of them. Diana is as busy as ever with her extracurriculars. I go to one of her travel soccer games with Dad. She's pretty competitive in everything she does, and is aiming to maintain all-honors classes throughout high school. Gerry is still working a lot at the tech store. Sometimes we'll watch TV together, but it's mostly quiet between us. The main point of contention is who gets to use the third car. When Abigail got her license, Mom and Dad let her use one of their cars before she went off to college, and I guess they were able to juggle everyone else's schedules in the interim. But when Gerry started driving, they figured things were going to be too tricky with their work and Diana's budding hobbies, so they bought a third car. They didn't buy Gerry a car, they bought the family a "third car." The assumption was that when Gerry went off to college, it would be mine to use, and when I went to college, it would be Diana's. And that's the way it was for a month and change. But when Gerry came back, it basically became his car again. Mom and Dad probably didn't want to make it an issue, because he started needing it for work. I get to use it, too, but it feels like it's mainly his.

Mark, Pete and I never really talked about going to prom, and it seemed like we missed our opportunity once everyone in our class started pairing up. Everything changes when Pete tells us he's asked one of his theatre friends, Nicki Toller, to go with him. Mark, Pete and I do everything together, so much that we refer to each other as MAP, for Mark, Alex and Pete. People who overhear get so confused because even though there's three of us, we talk about MAP as if it's one person, like "MAP is going to the movies later." If Pete's going to prom, MAP figures MAP needs to get on board.

Mark and I start scrambling to see if there are any more girls in our class who don't have dates, but come up pretty dry. Luckily, Pete sets us up with some theatre girls who are juniors. He tells us that he thinks Nicole Bryant and Jessica Connors would be interested and Mark and I look at each other, trying to determine who gets who. I shared a bus with Jessica in middle school, so Mark doesn't mind when I call dibs on her. Mark and I are both pretty nervous, but Pete has Nicki give them a heads up. As soon as I ask Jessica, she says, "Sure!" and I walk off without much more conversation. From what I gather, it went about the same for Mark. The way Pete put it to us, it will be fun for them to just go to the prom as juniors, sharing a limo with their friends. It's a week later that I realize that I have to talk to Jessica again to coordinate our outfits. Mom says I should treat Jessica to the prom ticket because often girls' dresses are more expensive than guys renting tuxes. Jessica appreciates this and says she'll pay for her share of the limo. That's when the money aspect clicks for me. I'll have to pick up more hours at Pets Unlimited to foot the bill. I found out from Pete that we're in a limo with Marshall Kinley and Madison Solomon. They aren't the most popular in our grade, but they'd been dating since sophomore year, so not only was the "Cutest Couple" yearbook superlative in the bag for them, they've also been gunning for Prom King and Queen for the past three years. Once I find out that they're basically in charge of our group's prom schedule, I know it's not going to be a low-budget night.

A rumor goes around that Dave Sebb is throwing a party at his house on Friday night. There haven't been too many parties this year, or at least ones that I've heard about, so this is news. MAP has drank a little, but it's mainly just been us three in Pete's basement. Admittedly, it's not the coolest for three dudes to be drinking by themselves in a dimly-lit room without any girls, but we told ourselves we were getting drinking experience. Plus, I was able to get the not-being-able-to-handle-your-liquor phase out of my system. I only vomited once from drinking, which is probably a credit to my genetics. Uncle Clark once said that Rybacks have Sobieski running through their veins, but Mom's etiquette mandate always prevented that high tolerance claim from being tested at family functions. While Mark and Pete were still puking out their guts, I quickly discovered how to maintain my buzz with minimal hangover. The one downside to being a heavyweight is our stock usually runs dry before I can get hammered. I wonder if that's why Gerry moved onto harder stuff like coke.

Now that Mark has a car, and we actually know about it beforehand, we can find out what these parties are all about. The day of the party, all us seniors are talking about it in whispers, and Dave himself is both pumping his chest and trying to play it cool. He starts telling people they have to bring beer or pay five dollars to come. MAP tries to think of a way to get beer to bring, but each of our parents either only have hard liquor or not enough beer to bring for three people. We don't want to arouse their suspicion, so we just settle on paying. Dave says the party starts at nine, but we agree that we'll show up nine-thirty, so we don't come off as desperate.

As we approach his house, it doesn't seem like there's a party, but at his front door, we can hear some music. Mark knocks, and when Dave pokes his head out of the door, he seems half-harried, as if he lost all of his bravado from earlier in the day.

"Oh hey," Dave says, as he's scanning our faces. "I invited you guys?" Whoops. We didn't plan for this scenario. We assumed it was an open party and didn't consider getting turned away.

"Yes," Pete answers, thinking on his feet.

"Alright," Dave says. "Do you have beer?"

"No, but here's fifteen bucks for the three of us," I say, handing him the money.

"Okay," he says, letting us in. "There's not much beer right now, but we're going to get some more." We walk in, and all somewhat freeze, figuring out what to do next.

Someone shouts, "Dave, your toilet is clogged."

"Shit!" Dave yells, as he brushes past us to his bathroom.

"I guess let's get some drinks?" Mark suggests. Pete and I nod, and we all walk to Dave's kitchen, to find it packed with people, hunting for alcohol. Pete offers to get drinks for the three of us, so Mark and I explore the rest of Dave's house. His dining room has a stereo blasting and a beer pong game going. Other than the four people playing, most are just standing around, watching, whooping for good shots, and waiting their turn. We observe that Tony Spiranti is sporting an outfit that screams "trying too hard," and has deemed himself the DJ of the party, skipping through songs on his iPod, after they've played for thirty seconds. Entering the living room is like being a fish in a fishbowl, with its inhabitants hoping that the new entrants can energize the room. Mark and I stroll through to Dave's den, which is just two guys arm-wrestling. Fearing that we might be pressured to challenge the winner, Mark and I about-face to the living room, where Mark gets a wave from Emily Hatterford. Emily is definitely in the top-ten of our grade, and I get the sense she's finally letting loose like Mark, because she's wearing makeup and showing loads of boob. Mark sits on the armrest of her chair, while I stand, trying to maintain eye-contact with her. Pete returns with some Bud Light and Beck's for us to somehow all split, and we start sipping.

As the night goes on, more people show up, Dave gets more alcohol and the party starts to liven up. I think someone revokes Tony's DJ duties because even the music gets better. Pete and I wait our turn for beer pong, Mark keeps talking with Emily, and Lou Alvarez flaunts his six-inch-flame lighter. In line for the bathroom, I start talking with Stacy Silver, about when we were in Home Economics together, and Pete yells at me that we're on deck for pong.

"I think we can win," I shout back.

"We better," says Pete, slightly less articulate than me. "C'mon, let's go." I nod and we make our way to the dining room. I check my phone and see that it's past one in the morning. A sudden realization hits my memory and kills my buzz: I have to be at work at 7:30 tomorrow morning, or to put it more accurately, this morning.

I turn to Pete. "Sorry, man, I've got to go."

"Don't overthink, bro. It's just a game," he reassures me. I explain my situation and watch as a wave of disappointment washes over his face.

"Maybe you can be partners with Lou," I suggest.

"We're playing *against* Lou!" Pete shouts comically.

He must have been eavesdropping, because Tony Spiranti pops out of nowhere and tells Pete, "I can be your partner." Pete looks at me, looks at Tony, and sighs.

"Alright," he relents to Tony.

"Thanks, man. I'll catch you later," I say to Pete as I bro-hug him goodbye. I can't believe I have to bail as soon as the party is getting good. I head back to the living room to see if I can get Mark to give me a ride home, hoping that he's sober enough. He's nowhere in sight, so I ask some girls if they've seen him.

"I think he's with Emily," says one of her friends.

"Great! Where are they?" I ask.

"Um, wherever they are, I don't think they want you interrupting them," she answers. It takes me two seconds, but I slowly grasp her insinuation. Shit, I can't screw over Mark if he's with a girl. I try to think of who else I could ask for a ride, but then imagine how polling the party would affect my cred for the rest of the year.

"Okay. Thanks," I answer, as I head out the door. I have a general idea of where in town I am, figuring that I'm only a few miles from home. I start to walk to the main road and check the time again. If I'm lucky, I'll get three, maybe four hours of sleep. As I walk, I wonder how beer pong is going for Pete and am happy for Mark and his potential romance. Six months ago, coming to a party like this didn't seem possible. Mark was studious as ever and Pete was rehearsing non-stop for one of his plays. Now that high school's almost over and we have less to worry about, a night like this is always possible. It almost feels earned. I guess everyone in our class feels that way on some level.

I try to concentrate and stay on the sidewalk as I walk home, and find my way to the outskirts of my neighborhood. As I approach a telephone pole, I look at the metal brace between the pole and its support wire. As a kid, I always tried to run, jump and touch that brace, but always came up short. I haven't thought about it in years, but figure I can do it now. I quicken my pace, and after a few strides and a hop, not only do I touch it, but end up swinging from it. While I'm hanging, I decide to do two pull-ups, and then drop back to the ground. I don't land as gracefully as I thought I would, and end up half-twisting my ankle and scratching my palms. I wallow in agony for about a minute, but then get up, wipe off the dust and cross the street.

When I get home, I open the backdoor as quietly as possible and tiptoe to the bathroom. I wash up and look at my hands, which will be a little raw for a day or so. I turn out the lights and sneak into my room. I'm extra careful before I realize that Gerry isn't in the room, and crash onto my bed with all my clothes on.

A few hours later, I'm awoken by a knock on my door and sunlight pouring through a bent segment of my blinds.

"Alex, don't you have work in a half-an-hour?" Dad asks through the door. I look at my phone and see that it is indeed seven in the morning. Every ounce of my body wants to stay in bed and call in sick, but I know that I need the money for prom, and that Mom and Dad will get on my case if I bail.

"Yeah, I'm coming," I mumble, as I will myself upright, and slink to the shower. I turn the handle to cold and count to ten, as the frigid water beats down on my head. Semi-self-rectified, I turn the faucet to warm and finish my shower, now mostly awake. I change into my work clothes, down a glass of orange juice and grab a banana in under five minutes, before Dad drives me to work. I see him eyeing me as he drives, and I scarf down my banana. I think he knows I was out late last night, and whether or not I'm able to make it to work today will determine if he gives me a lecture.

"Pick you up later," he offers as I jump out, leaving him the banana peel. Made it with thirty seconds to spare. Carla has me do some inventory in the basement, where a few times I doze off while standing up. The rest of the morning is slow and at my lunch break, I go out and buy a burger and two energy drinks. I gulp the first, but only make it through half of the second. This keeps me coherent for the rest of the day, although I barely comprehend my conversations with customers.

When Dad picks me up, I can tell he's gauging me again. At home, Mom and Dad let me sleep before dinner, and when I wake up groggy, they don't make much of a fuss. I just listen to them talk to Diana, as my body tries to contend with my sleep deprivation, the energy drinks in my system, and Mom's tuna fish casserole. I can tell that I've passed some sort of test, that they're alright with me partying as long as I keep up with my obligations. The following morning, Dad wakes me up bright and early for some yardwork. Correction: Now I've passed their test. In the afternoon, MAP gets tacos and I hear about the rest of the party, like Lou lighting his arm hair on fire, Hector Allen mooning everyone, everyone singing along to "Lean wit It, Rock wit It" and Stacy Silver making out with Hector.

On Monday, the party is the talk of our grade for most of the day, with Dave gloating about his party-throwing skills, while also commiserating that he overbought on beer. I'm still kind of pissed that I had to miss the part of the party that was most fun, but it's whatever. I guess Gerry heard about it through the grapevine, because even he asks me about it while we're in bed that night. I talk about it vaguely, unsure what he'll do with the information.

Chapter 4: June

Weather is getting warmer, graduation is in sight, and school is a joke at this point. Most of the teachers just show movies or let us just talk during class. Some offer a paper or project in lieu of a final exam, so I only have three finals I actually have to show up for after classes end. If Mark had senioritis before, he is suffering from senioritis gigantus now. Now and then he's MIA from MAP, too, which we infer is time spent with Emily.

Every day, it feels like I get a new update on our limo's schedule for prom. Marshall and Madison have decided every detail of what we're doing down to the hour, and Jessica gives me a fuchsia swatch of her dress, for me to get a matching tie at the tux rental place. I hand the clerk a good chunk of my recent earnings, and figure I'm barely solvent.

On the Friday of prom night, it's all that our grade can talk about. Most girls skip the day or leave early for hair appointments, and Mom says I have to get a corsage for Jessica because she'll have a boutonniere for me. She doesn't let my silence linger too long before filling me in on what they both are, and I wonder why the guy would want a flower in the first place. MAP picks up our corsages and when I get home, I change into the tux. I'm almost out the door, when Diana says she'll see me at the pre-prom party. I groan to myself. This means Mom's coming, too.

MAP shows up, and Marshall and Madison's parents greet us with plastered on, ear-to-ear smiles, holding snack plates, cameras dangling around their necks. We make our way to the backyard and I see Mom and Diana talking with Jessica's parents. I spot Jessica with her auburn hair done up, and we give each other an awkward hug, while Madison's mom snaps away. We pose for a few more, non-voluntary photos and Diana laughs at my very apparent apathy. The longer I stand next to her, the more I get used to Jessica's bright, pink-purple dress. I have to admit, she does look beautiful.

Eventually, Mom shepherds Mark, Pete, Nicole, and Nicki over, and the parents take photos of MAP with its dates. Marshall waits and sways by the side with an extra fancy tux that I'm sure Madison made him get. I feel bad we don't invite him to be in some of the MAP photos, but I think he's waiting for Madison, who I haven't seen yet, even though it's her house. I overhear Nicole and Nicki whisper that she still must be getting ready, and the moment our photo group breaks, Madison appears on her parents' back porch. It seems like the rest of the party instinctively turns to look at her, and all the girls and moms start clapping, as if to say that her appearance was worth the wait. When Madison's dad starts tearing up and clapping, too, the rest of us guys join in and clap, although I don't really understand what the fuss is about. Madison is standing there, smiling and taking in the attention, in a lime green dress with fluffy shoulder pads, and a frilly bottom. I hear one of the moms say that she looks stunning, but I think she looks like an unripe artichoke. I look around and lock eyes with Jessica, who smirks, knowing we're on the same page. Marshall walks over to Madison and they share a big kiss, which apparently calls for more clapping. After their performance, and now that Madison is ready, it's time for more pictures. I can tell Pete is caught off guard as well, because I see him scarfing down the rest of his plate of appetizers and wiping off an unfortunate spill from his pant leg. The parents shoo us all up to the porch, and the six of us join Marshall and Madison, along with the other two couples.

One is the sporty Tyler Chen and Kelly Donner, and the other couple is Monica Salazar and Courtney Richkowski. They won most of the art awards on Senior Night, and people always had suspicions, but they only came out a few weeks ago. Madison's mom must have given the other parents a "heads up," because I see her nodding along to another mom when they pass by. The six couples are made to pose in every imaginable shape and combination: all twelve of us, just guys, just girls, guys holding girls' waists from behind, guys one-leg-kneeling with girls sitting on their thighs, all of our arms around each other, our arms raised in the air. Some of the poses are awkward for Monica and Courtney, but they seem to have a good laugh about it. Luckily, it creeps closer to eight, and we have to leave for the venue. I give Mom, Diana and Jessica's mom a goodbye hug, and as we slip into the limo, we all see Madison's dad slip the limo driver a fifty to make sure we don't stop and pick up alcohol. Marshall and Tyler are one step ahead, and assure us that there will be plenty when we head back to Tyler's house after prom. As we head out and blast the radio, the driver sighs and rolls up the divider.

On the way, we mostly talk about getting drunk later, college and high school gossip. Adhering to Madison's decree, we arrive at the venue fashionably late, and walk in to find most of our class lining up for the buffet and dancing on the dance floor. Jessica and I start gravitating to an open table, before we realize that we're still bound to the groupthink of our limo.

"Hey guys, I think Madison sees a table for us all over here," Marshall offers while gesturing. Jessica and I share another look, and concede. We stand around the empty table for about fifteen seconds before Madison instructs us all where to sit. Tyler asks the group, "Should we get in line for food?" Marshall's head does a 180 from listening to Tyler to bowing to Madison, awaiting her governing suggestions.

"We just had some snacks at my house. Let's dance for a bit," she prescribes. We all offer a nonverbal and mandatory acquiescence, and head to the dance floor. Jessica and I sort of just face each other, smile, and rock to the beat. I wonder if I should grind with her, but I'm not sure if she'll be into it, and Dean Onk is standing along the wall, observing all the students.

He talks to one guy who keeps grabbing his date's ass, so I figure I best not try anything. All the girls in our limo start dancing with each other in a clump. Not knowing what to do, but knowing we won't be forming a guy clump, MAP just cheers them on. They eventually beckon us over, and the guys form a circle around the girls.

After a few minutes, two of the chaperone teachers, Mr. & Mrs. Johnson, dance their way over. They're well-liked teachers, and both probably in their mid-twenties, so when they dance with us, they kind of feel like other students instead of chaperones. I get the feeling that they were chosen by the PTA to be the friendly, safe-fun ying, to Dean Onk's strict, no-nonsense yang. Mrs. Johnson is pretty hot, and all the girls seem to like Mr. Johnson, so it feels a bit edgy for them to be letting loose with their students. I gather that the PTA moms see them as harmless because they're newly married, but when Mr. Johnson dances with Jessica and Mrs. Johnson takes Marshall's hand, I figure they could just as easily be swingers looking for jailbait.

I get a tap on my shoulder, and Marshall lets me know that Madison and he are getting in line for food. Our limo shuffles off the dance floor while fanning ourselves, and while we eat our rubbery chicken and mushy vegetables, I see Marshall and Madison off to the side, speaking in hushed tones.

As the prom winds down, it seems our whole class is on the dance floor at once, and it feels very unifying. We're all bouncing, singing along, and all popularity and cliques fade away until the Prom King & Queen are announced. The moment of truth comes, and Mr. & Mrs. Johnson announce the winners, which Marshall and Madison easily take, to no one's surprise. Even if they hadn't been coaxing votes since sophomore year, I'm sure Madison's parents are in cahoots with the PTA. They get crowned to everyone's cheers, and Madison tears up. Ethan Wright and Farah Martinez reluctantly clap, who hoped there was a chance for them to eke out a win, but I guess just like Cutest Couple, everyone just thought of them as runners-up.

The ceremony concludes and everyone starts dancing again. There's still a good forty-five minutes left, but some limos seem to be leaving early, presumably to start the after-prom drinking.

The DJ changes the music to some slow jams for a few songs. Mr. & Mrs. Johnson jump at the chance to slow dance with each other, but some of the kids in our class find it a bit awkward at first. Jessica and I catch each other's eyes, and agree to give it a shot. We stand facing each other for a second, before I place my fingertips on her waist, and she puts her fingertips behind my shoulders. We initially avoid eye contact, but then eventually get bored of the floor, look at each other, and let our palms rest in place as well. The eye contact feels so intense, so I decide to strike up a conversation.

"Are you having fun?" I ask.

"What?" she asks back, leaning her head closer to my ear. I tilt forward as well to help the communication.

"Are you having fun?" I repeat.

"Oh, yeah definitely," she says.

"Did you take the SAT yet?"

"Can we stop talking about schoolwork while we're at Prom?" My heart sinks and I scramble for an apology. Jessica laughs to let me know that she's half-joking. "It's alright. You're just killing my fun."

"Noted." After that, the conversation feels more natural. We talk about our summer plans, movies, and the last musical she was in. The ballads end, and the DJ announces that he wants to end our prom with some "bangers." He starts blasting loud, anthemic dance songs, like "Ridin'," "S.O.S," and "Crazy." Everyone in our limo finds each other, as we jump and bounce in a circle. The only ones missing are Marshall and Madison. I figure they're busy taking photos with their crowns, but everyone has their own theory.

"Now that they've won Prom King and Queen, they're probably planning their wedding," Monica jokes.

"No, they're probably banging in the coatroom," Tyler says. We laugh and keep dancing. By the last song, we're giddy, exhausted, and one of the only limos still on the dance floor. There's still no sign of our missing cohorts, so Tyler texts them that we'll meet them outside at the limo. Our driver is just as clueless as we are, and we wonder if they're still inside the hall. Eventually, we see Marshall come out through the front door, with Madison a pace behind him. We all notice that one of the employees promptly locks the door once they leave, and that Madison's eyeshadow and mascara are smudged above her cheeks.

"Everything good, man?" Tyler asks Marshall as he approaches.

"Uh, yeah. Sorry for the hold up," Marshall sighs unconvincingly.

"Hey," Nicole coos to Madison.

"Hey," Madison replies meekly. We all enter the limo and sit in silence, aware that something is off.

As Tyler gives the driver his address, the rest of us steal glances at Marshall and Madison who are sitting next to each other, but looking in opposite directions. After a few more minutes, Madison finally speaks up.

"I want hard cider." We all look at her in silence.

"What?" Marshall feels obligated to ask.

"I said, 'I want hard cider,'" Madison states again, without looking at Marshall or anyone else. Marshall pauses and realizes that it's his duty to fulfill this for her.

Marshall turns to Tyler. "Do you have any hard cider back at your house?"

"No, I only have beer and vodka," he says, trying to size up if this is going to be an issue.

"Shit," Marshall says. "Maybe we can pick some up at a store."

"Hard cider in June?"

"Yeah."

"After midnight? With a tux on?"

Marshall hypothesizes with Tyler and Madison's eyes beat down on him. Marshall lowers the divider and asks the limo driver, "Hey dude, can we stop at a convenience store in Briarwood?"

"Um, that's not really on the way back," the driver responds.

"I know, but it won't take too long."

"You know you only have me until one, right?"

"I'll pay whatever, if we go over."

"Fine, what's the address?"

The rest of us just sit and watch the exchange as Marshall gives him directions, sits back down and looks at Madison, who's not giving away anything.

"Briarwood?" Tyler sighs.

"That's always been my solid place," Marshall explains. "Sometimes they don't even ask for ID."

"Whatever. Just make it quick."

It's a good couple towns away, and as we arrive, Marshall shoots out of the car and enters the store. As we wait in uncomfortable silence, Jessica takes my hand and smiles at me. I smile back, as we hear the door open. Marshall reenters the limo with a brown paper bag, clinking relieving chimes of glass bottles hitting each other. Even Madison has a small smile forming on her face.

Marshall sits back in triumph, but then pulls out the bottles and says, "They didn't have hard cider, so I got hard lemonade." This would be a fine substitution in my book, but apparently not for Madison. She immediately bursts into tears, which induces hair-raising panic for everyone else, prompts Marshall to hit his breaking point, and prompts the driver to roll up his divider. "God! What do you want from me?" Marshall shouts at her.

"I'm calling my Dad!" Madison wails as she opens the limo door and storms out. Marshall follows, yelling at her, liquor in hand, as the rest of us peek out the window. The two of them have a shouting match in the middle of the parking lot, before continuing their argument behind a dumpster for privacy. We sit and wait while Tyler asks the limo driver to hold on. We all instinctively exit the limo, and overhear Marshall shout, "That's it. We're done!" He briskly walks past us, while Madison shrieks and continues crying at the dumpster, before chasing him with an open bottle of the hard lemonade. We collectively yearn to warn him, but are struck silent, as she pours it over his head. We watch in shock and horror as he catches her mid-pour and returns the favor, causing her to shriek louder. Just as all the juice runs out, they separate. The lemonade must be a strawberry flavor because both of their outfits now sport reddish streaks that kind of resemble blood. I can only imagine what it'll be like for Marshall trying to return his tux now. On the opposite end, Madison's dress would now make a good Halloween costume, like if you went as "Carrie" or something.

"How do you like it?" Marshall shouts at her.

Tyler tries to calm him down and offers, "Dude, lower your voice, or someone's going to call the cops." Marshall says he doesn't care, and vanishes down some residential street. The girls walk over to Madison and try to offer comfort in some way. No one asks her what happened, but through her sobbing she mentions Marshall not taking prom seriously enough, him hanging with friends too often, and him dancing with Mrs. Johnson too much. We all nod sympathetically as Tyler approaches the group.

"Where's Marshall?" Kelly whispers to him.

"I don't know," Tyler says, exasperated. "He just walked off."

"Well, then you need to go and find him," she instructs.

Tyler looks at the rest of us guys and sighs, "Can I get some backup?" Mark, Pete, Tyler and I start walking to find Marshall when a cab pulls up, and Monica and Courtney bail. The rest of us collectively say "Okay" and "Goodbye," but secretly resent how easily they were able to slip out of the situation.

Us four guys start walking down a dark street looking for Marshall, while trying to stay quiet and not scuff up our dress shoes. Marshall isn't answering text messages, so Tyler and I pair up and split off from Mark and Pete, who search off in the opposite direction. I would have never guessed that I'd be spending my prom night rambling around an unknown street in Briarwood with Tyler Chen, but here I am. I make some small talk about how the chicken at prom was bad, and we eventually find Marshall, sitting on the curb of a dead end street, near some bushes. His head is down, but he's aware that we're there.

"We got to head back," Tyler says.

"Alright," Marshall concedes. "Just one second." We wait, and Marshall takes it upon himself to open up. "It's just that we were looking forward to prom since we started dating."

Tyler takes it in. "Maybe basing your whole relationship on one night means it's not sustainable." I look over at Tyler, impressed with how insightful he just was. We eventually are able to corral Marshall up, and get him to walk with us back to the limo. Tyler adds that Madison and he will either get back together or he'll meet someone new in college. I text Mark and Pete to meet us back at the limo, and Mark says he's calling a cab for just MAP and its dates.

By the time we get back to the parking lot, the driver is arguing with Kelly about the time, and the girls are able to get Madison back in the limo. Our cab shows up and we say goodbye to Marshall, Tyler and Kelly, who understand why we're leaving.

"Sorry we have to bounce," Mark tells Marshall.

"No prob," Marshall says.

"We probably aren't going to go back to my house anymore," Tyler adds.

"Sounds good," I say.

Seeing an opportunity, Pete asks Marshall, "If no one else wants it, can I grab that hard lemonade?"

"Sure," Marshall responds, without a fight. Pete grabs the case from the limo and the six of us cram into the cab. It's a quiet ride back to Mark's house, and we sit in his backyard drinking and talking. I'm amazed as Jessica downs hers in two gulps. Content with the night, Mark drops each of us off. I walk Jessica to her front door, where she surprises me with a kiss. I think about it the whole ride home, and slink into bed as the sun begins to rise.

Chapter 5: Late June

It's the last Friday of classes, and all us seniors are wired to bolt from the school the second that we can. I have to come in next week for three finals, but even if I bombed them, I still wouldn't have to worry about graduating. At this point, it's a lock, so both teachers and seniors don't have to try or care.

Today, most of our morning is the Senior Breakfast where we receive our yearbooks. MAP finds a cafeteria table and grabs some bagels and orange juice.

"This may be the last time we eat in this cafeteria," Mark announces to us.

"That's a bad thing?" Pete says, with a raised eyebrow.

"No, but think of all the memories we've had here," Mark says.

"There was that time Kyle Ramirez threw up in Cheryl O'Brien's hair," I joke.

"There was that glorious food fight of sophomore year," Pete adds.

"There was that fist fight that happened during another food fight, junior year," I remember.

"Yeah, that was crazy," Mark says. "Everyone started throwing food at the guys fighting."

"Who won that fight?" Pete asks. None of us can recall.

Pete shoots me a grin, and just before taking a slow sip of orange juice, asks Mark, "So, what's going on with Emily?" Mark smirks, but doesn't give anything away.

"C'mon," I say. "I know that you guys were hanging out at prom a bit, even though you weren't each other's dates."

"Fine, we've been hanging out a bit," Mark relents.

"Nice," says Pete.

"And what about you and Jessica?" asks Mark, turning the tables on me.

I know better than to try and fight it. "We've been texting back and forth a little bit, but since prom, I've only seen her in the hallways."

"Well it's something," Pete offers. I had asked Jessica to meet up one night, but she said she was cramming. She said maybe after finals, so for now I figure I'll just enjoy the senior activities.

By now, our whole class is pretty much eating, and PTA moms start handing out our yearbooks. Once we all start flipping through the pages, the room's chatter dies down as we're all transfixed by the paper summation of our last four years, thirteen if you count kindergarten. My photo looks alright, but the guy whose photo is to the left of me has a patchy mustache, and the girl to the right of me looks a bit cross-eyed, so I guess it could be worse. I check to see if Mark and Pete are watching, and skip to the photos of the juniors to find Jessica. I make a mental note to tell her she looks pretty in it. Suddenly, Mark hits my arm rapidly, in excitement.

"What?" I ask to get him to stop. I see that he's ahead of Pete and me, on the Senior Superlatives page. At first, I don't understand why he's so giddy, because we knew who all the winners were a day after we voted. But then, he points it out.

"Look at the Cutest Couple," Mark gossips in a loud whisper. And there they are, Marshall and Madison. Madison's head is tilted, resting on Marshall's shoulder, and Marshall is kissing her forehead. They've been broken up since prom, with no visible signs of reconciliation, but I never considered the yearbook implications. No one ever tells the Cutest Couple candidates that they should be willing to stay together until Commencement, or face some embarrassment. Marshall and Madison were such a staple, no one saw it coming. MAP looks at each other and snickers, before we not-so-discreetly look to see if we can spot either of them in the cafeteria. I think I notice some other people doing the same. We shouldn't play into the drama, but I think MAP feels somewhat entitled to gossip because of the way our prom night ended.

We continue looking through our yearbooks and get to the blank pages around the same time. We take out our pens, swap books and write surprisingly forgettable messages in spite of having been best friends for thirteen years. As people start getting up and swapping, Mark disappears, and I ask Pete where he's going.

"Take a guess," Pete says, before mouthing "Emily." Pete goes over to his theatre group, which leaves me looking for someone who may want to write in my book. My eyes align with Stacy Silver, who I don't really need a message from, but don't know the etiquette of denying someone a yearbook exchange. Next is Tony Spiranti, and I write about him taking my place in beer pong.

I see Marshall sitting by himself at a table. I'm sure that he's had plenty of people signing his book, but now there's a lull. I get the sense he's isolated himself to this one table, to give Madison the ability to bounce around and revel in the last strains of popularity. I walk over to him and we both greet each other with a nod, and swap. I write, "Dear Marshall," and case my mind for some material. Our closest memories were all really negative for him. I jot down the most generic of generic, and as I'm signing my name, we hear the bell ring. We all seem to look around to see if we're staying in the cafeteria, or if the Senior Breakfast is over. We hear a familiar voice and see Madison standing on a nearby table to give us instructions. I'm not sure if she's actually a student activities coordinator, or if she just designated herself to be one.

"They need to clean up for the first lunch period, but your teachers in your next class should let you keep signing yearbooks." Madison glances at Marshall for a second, but quickly steps down off the table, losing her line of sight with him. Marshall lets out a big sigh, takes his yearbook, and slaps me on the arm.

"Guess I'll see you when I see you, Alex, my boy." I gain a better appreciation of what he's going through, but can tell he's going to be alright. I feel a wave of guilt for my prior snickering, before offering, "Right back at you." I don't see Mark or Pete, so I just shuffle out with the rest of the crowd. I start heading to my English class and see Jessica walking towards me. We're about fifteen feet away from each other, and I'm pretty sure that she notices that I'm holding my yearbook, but I make the split decision to just keep walking. She probably doesn't have the time to sign it right now and I don't want her to feel rushed anyway. I just hope that she doesn't know that I saw her too, and think that I'm purposely ignoring her. In English, Mrs. Johnson just lets us sign each other's books and talk, just as Madison prophesied. Farah Martinez is in my class, and I guess she was bursting at the seams trying not to gripe about the "Cutest Couple" superlative in front of Marshall and Madison, because now she's really letting loose. She doesn't care that everyone in class can hear her, including Mrs. Johnson.

"Of course I'm pissed off. Everyone voted for them, and no one voted for me and Ethan, and who's still together at the end of the year?" Farah complains. Some of the class nods with disingenuous agreement, some of us try to ignore her, and Mrs. Johnson just seems like she enjoys being privy to the student gossip.

The rest of the day breezes by, and when I get home, I see Diana in the kitchen. She's making a smoothie with her headphones on, so I have to get her attention in order to talk to her. I catch her by surprise and she uncovers an ear.

"Do you want to see my yearbook?" I ask her.

"Algebra final," she answers while putting the headphone back in place.

"Okay, I have work now, but let me know if you need help later," I offer.

"Yup," she chirps as she closes her door. I shrug off Diana's demeanor because I know she's always like this when she's cramming, and try to open my bedroom door. It's locked.

"Hey, Gerry," I call, already slightly annoyed. "Can I get in here?"

"Uh," he grunts. "One second." I figure he's either jerking off or rolling a joint, but don't care if I'm interrupting either.

"Gerry, I have to change for work. I need to get in the room," I say, more annoyed.

"Alright! Calm the fuck down," he answers back. He opens the door and we can both tell that we're about to get into it.

"You can't lock it when I'm home," I tell him.

"Fuck you. I'm supposed to memorize your schedule?" he snaps back.

"No, you're not supposed to even be here." I know what's coming as soon as I say it. Gerry charges at me, throwing haymakers, but I swing my backpack in front of my body so that only a few of his punches get to me. He mostly connects with my books, and after, he backs off and rubs the knuckles of his right hand. He's only an inch or so taller than me, but he's always been better at fighting, so I take moments like these as victories.

"You're such a little bitch," he whimpers.

"Whatever," I say, pulling out my yearbook, noticing a small dent. I grab my work shirt from my drawer and change into it. "Do you have the car keys?" I ask him.

"Yeah. Why?" he asks.

"I've got work. I need the car."

"Shit. Can I drop you off?"

"No."

"Alex."

"That's the house rule. Whoever's got work has first priority."

"Can you just let me drop you off?"

"What do you have to do that's so important?" I snap. I can tell that this one hurts him, too.

"Forget it," he resentfully scowls. I briefly revel in my minor victory, but then quickly feel guilty for putting him down.

"Fine," I relent. "But you're picking me up, too."

"Thanks," he begrudgingly says.

"Twenty minutes." We don't talk the whole car ride, and as we're pulling up in front of Pets Unlimited, Gerry breaks the silence.

"I would be home by this time anyway." I look at him confused for half-a-second, but then realize he's referencing our fight. He's trying to say that if he hadn't dropped out of college, he'd be home in June, and we'd still have to share a room.

"Sure," I shoot back at him, letting him know I couldn't care less about his comeback. "Make sure you're here at ten," I order him. I pause, but when I realize that he has no intention of confirming that he's heard what I've said, I just slam the car door and walk into work.

Abigail and Stephen come by early for Father's Day, and find Mom and me prepping food. "Hey, we're here!" Abigail announces as she walks into the kitchen. "Where's Dad?"

"He's picking up his mother," Mom says, while turning around with greasy, contaminated hands. "I'm still marinating," Mom says, as she kisses Abigail and Stephen, holding her arms away from them. I take a break from shucking corn and give them a fist bump.

"Where's everyone else?" Abigail adds.

"Gerry's working; Diana is studying," Mom says, finishing with the chicken.

"Whoa," Stephen says. "That girl doesn't slow down."

"I was the same way and look where it got me," Abigail tells him.

"She'll come out soon," Mom says, washing her hands. The conversation almost immediately shifts to Abigail's pregnancy, whose belly has increased a few inches. Mom talks about what it was like when she was seven-months pregnant with Abigail, while Stephen and I just nod to show we're listening. Eventually, Dad and Grandma arrive and Diana slinks out of her room. We head outdoors, and Dad starts grilling.

"Would you like some corn-on-the-cob?" Mom asks Grandma, fixing her a plate.

"No, just potatoes," Grandma says. As Mom places the plate in front of her, I know better than to start eating before Grandma takes her first bite, but God, she's taking a really long time. I finally dig in, and Abigail decides to break the food-induced conversation lull in the worst way.

"So, how's Gerry?" Abigail asks. Mom, Dad, Diana and I look at each other, knowing that Abigail brought up the topic that the four of us don't talk about, even when he's not around.

"Oh, you know," Mom treads carefully. "He seems to like work."

"I mean, how's he since…" Abigail leads on. We experience an awkward pause as neither Mom nor Dad is willing to take the bait.

"Abbie, let's talk about something else," Stephen offers, trying to save his in-laws from imploding.

"I just want to know what his plan is. Will he go back to college? Will he go locally?" Abigail continues. I have to hand it to Abigail because she's addressing our family's unspoken question. When Mom and Dad had their "talk" with me, I took it as a warning. After it, I just assumed they didn't have the money to give Gerry another shot, or were trying to gauge if he was worth it. Dad stammers for a moment, before abandoning the thought he was formulating. Abigail takes this as her cue to repress. "Should I ask him?"

"Honey, it's Father's Day," Mom begs. We're all surprised when Grandma perks up and speaks. I guess the conversational turn made us forget that she was there.

"I just think he's a bright, young man with so much potential," Grandma says. We pause for a moment, deferring to Grandma to add more, but when she doesn't, Mom takes the mantle again.

"Let's just talk about this later." Abigail reluctantly accepts, and Stephen looks incredibly relieved. The rest of the dinner is more pleasant, but it carries the strain of Abigail's inquiry. I think it took someone not in the house to bring it to light. I don't know if she would have raised it if she was living at home with the rest of us. The night winds down somewhat quietly, Diana retreats to her room and Gerry arrives home while Dad is dropping off Grandma. He meets us in the den, and when he says hello, our initial reaction tips him off that we were talking about him. He just shrugs it off and goes to the kitchen to heat up a plate Mom made for him. I give him a lot of credit for that; I'm not sure that I'd be able to do the same. Abigail turns to me, and brings up the subject that didn't come up at dinner.

"So, Alex. Saturday's the big day."

"Yes, it is," I smile back at her.

Chapter 6: Very Late June

I don't have any finals until Tuesday, so I tell Carla I can work the whole day Monday. She agrees quicker than I expect, and when I come in Monday morning I find out why. She gets a big delivery in, and I unload the truck while she delegates to me where to put the boxes. The plate glass is what makes it so heavy, and the heat isn't helping either. I soon regret offering to work the extra hours, but after we finish with the delivery, the rest of the day is pretty light, and Carla lets me slack off a bit.

I drive home, and as soon as I come in the door, I see Gerry walking towards me. For some reason, after everyone was talking about him yesterday, I feel I owe him some niceties.

"Hey, Ger. How is it?"

"Keys," he shoots back, looking through me. For a split-second, I try to process his response to my question as I look at the car keys in my hand. But then Gerry offers clarity by grabbing them and opening the front door. "Does it have gas?" he barks.

"Some," I reply, still somewhat dazed by the swiftness of the transaction.

"You got to fill it up. House rules," he says condescendingly, with his back to me. I stick my head out the door.

"Well then I'd be home later, and you look like you're in a rush," I shout back. But Gerry just keeps walking and pretends he doesn't hear me.

I go to my room and lay on my bed. I'm pretty tired, but know I should study a bit for my Statistics and English finals. I don't feel like sitting up, so I swat my hand at my backpack until I grab a hold, and pull it closer to my bed. I pull out a few folders with one grasp, and also my yearbook. I succumb to my temptations, and procrastinate before studying. I relook at Jessica's photo. I think about texting her, but tell myself to wait. I set my yearbook aside and crack open my Statistics review packet. I thumb through it, but halfway through, I begin to doze off. I try to stay awake, but lying down isn't doing me any favors.

I snap up in a sweat and look at my phone. An hour-and-a-half has passed, and I make a judgement call. I feel like I know Statistics pretty well, and my English final will be an essay on a surprise topic, so I can't study for it anyway. Plus, I'm exhausted. Saturday's still on schedule, so who cares? And I'm in good company. Since all the seniors are already admitted into their colleges, finals are pointless. With that rationalization in place, I get up to turn off the lights, and then collapse back into bed.

I feel pretty confident about how the Stat final goes, but finish the test with only a few minutes to spare. That's just me; I've never been a speed demon like Mark. As I hand Mr. Timberson the test, we exchange a nod and sly smile: him acknowledging that I'm no longer his student, and me admitting he was a cool teacher. I still have some time before my next exam, so I head to the cafeteria and grab a Snickers from the vending machine. If Mark were around, we could drive and get food, but neither Pete nor he had a final this morning. I stand and watch other kids hunched over the lunch tables, cramming before the afternoon block. Since I can't study for my English final, I just break out my phone. Anyone worth texting is either still in a final or studying for their afternoon one, so I look around the cafeteria to see if I see anyone I know. I spot Jessica pretty quickly and debate in my head if I should bother her. I figure I can just wish her good luck and walk away. I think she might like that.

"Hey," I say timidly as I approach her. She looks up surprised and half-fazed, as if her mind is still in her book.

"Oh, hey Alex," she responds deadpan. I can't read if she's up for talking or not, so I can give her an out.

"I can let you study. I just wanted to say hi."

"No, you're a welcome reprieve," she offers. "What's up?"

"Um," I stall. "What are you studying for?"

"We've got to work on you not bringing up the thing I'm trying to take a break from," she jabs.

"Just like prom again?"

"Mmmhmm," she says, rolling her eyes. "It's Physics. Do you have anything this afternoon?"

"Just an in-class English paper."

"And then you're done?"

"One more tomorrow. You?"

"Tomorrow and Thursday."

"Okay." We sit in silence for a painstakingly long number of seconds. I turn my head and look behind me, as if I heard something.

"Pete had me sign his yearbook. How come you didn't give me yours?" she asks. I'm embarrassed that I didn't, and excited that she wants to at the same time.

"Uh, we said we would meet up after the year was over."

"That doesn't mean you couldn't have come up to me in the hall."

"Oh, I just thought you were so busy."

"So, when are you going to let me do it?"

"Do you want to come over after your final on Thursday?" It just comes out of me.

"Sure," she says. I feel a ton of excitement in my chest and kind of want to leave to end on a high note, so I hightail it out of the cafeteria, and spot Pete in the lobby.

"Just sit anywhere," Mrs. Johnson says to everyone. "This isn't class anymore." Alison McDonald is somewhat thrown off by me taking her seat, and sits behind me. Mrs. Johnson is in her serious mood and kills the chatter pretty quickly with her body language. She hands me loose leaf to take and pass back, and does so for the other rows. She then heads to the blackboard and writes an essay question about "Love in the Time of Cholera" and magical realism. I remember skimming through the book, but feel like I can pull it off. I'm in the last third of people in class when I hand it in, and Mrs. Johnson doesn't even look up from her computer when I place it on her desk. I guess there'll be no goodbye for us.

MAP hangs out at night, under the guise of studying for our Economics final. Mark doesn't need to study, and Pete and I only care so much. We eventually just play "Halo," before Dad picks me up. We talk about graduation a little bit, but he really just wants to confirm the details of the ceremony. Gerry's locked the door again, but Dad backs me up when I yell that I have a test in the morning.

During the final, I take my time, but feel little to no pressure. I was never great on the global portion, but simple business economics feels pretty intuitive. I just relate everything to the pet store.

As I walk out the classroom door, I make sure to tell myself to take it all in, that I'm done now. As I make my final procession through the hall, I drag my fingers across the wall, and decide to go to my locker one last time, just for the hell of it. I look into its emptiness, feel satisfied and head home.

After work, I see Diana watching *Zoolander* in the den. I'm not sure if she's taking a break, or completely done with her school year, but I join her all the same. Even though she's way brighter than me, I feel like I've set somewhat of an example for her. Abigail's too much older than Diana to be a role model, and Gerry's a waste of space, so I'm the best she's got. She tells me she has her middle school graduation ceremony on Friday. It's kind of cool that we're both graduating a school at the same time, and I guess the same will happen when I finish college, and she high school. We're both half-asleep by the time it ends, but manage to make it to our rooms and say goodnight to each other.

Gerry wakes me up in the morning as he's getting ready. Usually, I'm the one that's up before him, but finishing high school makes me feel like I deserve to sleep in. He doesn't even attempt to be quiet, and when he sees me rustling in bed, he lets me know he's leaving in his own way.

"Dad left a note with some chores on it for us," he says, already instigating.

"What kind of stuff?" I ask.

"Pruning, mowing."

"Which do you want to do?"

"This is all you." I take the bait and snap up from my bed.

"You said he left it for both of us." Gerry walks to the doorway, and turns around.

"I'm working today; you're not." Before I can contest, he's closed the door. I know that if I get up and have it out with him, he'll count it as a victory on some level. So, I just let out a big breath, grab my phone, and lay back down. It's just after eleven, and I see that I have a text from Jessica.

Hey, I'm done. I'm getting lunch with friends, and then come by afterwards? What's your address? I scrape some gunk out of the corner of my eye and text her back.

61 Grove Street. What time?

Dunno. Maybe like 12:45? I will let you know.

Okay.

I realize that this doesn't leave me a lot of time, so I knock out the yard work and jump in the shower. I rush out, half-dry, and check my phone.

Maybe like 10 minutes?

The text is from seven minutes ago, so I haul ass throwing on anything, and try to pick up my side of the room as best that I can. She arrives ten minutes after that, but with that extra time I'm able to scarf down a bowl of cereal and brush my teeth. I hear the doorbell and let her in.

"Hey," she says.

"How's it going?" I ask, giving her an awkward hug. I hadn't planned what to do from here, so I kind of give an unnecessary tour, just saying the names of each room as we pass by them. I think we both knew that we were going to be the only ones at my house, but I can't tell if it's weird for her. At least she doesn't have to meet my parents right now.

"Do you want any food?" I ask.

"No, I told you I just ate," she says.

"Oh, yeah. Okay, just take a seat on the couch and I'll get my yearbook." I fetch it from my room, along with a pen. I briefly think that I should have just asked her to come to my room, but worry that would be too forward. I sit down next to her, and kind of just wait as she opens to the blank pages in the back, finds a spot and starts writing. When she's finished, she closes it completely, and slides on the coffee table towards me.

"Should I read it now?" I ask.

"You can if you want." I feel like it would be cooler to not immediately look, even though I really want to.

"I will, later. Show me your theatre photos." This gets her excited and she flips the book open again and slides closer to me. She tells me about playing Rizzo in *Grease*, her big solo and all the backstage drama. I can't really grasp everything she's talking about, but I nod along because she's so eager to tell me. After a while she runs out of things to say and we have a lull.

"Do you want to watch a show?" I ask her.

"Sure," she says. I can tell she's just about as clueless as me.

"You choose," I announce, handing her the remote, chivalrously. It may have not been the best idea because she's flipping through channels for ten minutes. We're mostly silent through the process, but murmur here or there if we've already seen something, or if the show isn't as good as it used to be. She finally settles on Fuse, and we just watch music videos.

As we sit back, it seems like we're further apart than when we were looking at my yearbook. I'm not sure how it happened, and want to rectify it, but don't know how to do so casually. I lean towards her, pretending to look out the window, and make sure to position myself so our legs are basically touching. She doesn't seem to mind and I breathe a sigh of relief. I'm not sure if she's fully focused on the Taking Back Sunday music video, but I'm personally pondering my next move. I don't really know what to do, but can't bottle the anticipation in anymore. I turn my head and look at her, and she instinctively does the same. We stare at each other for a second, and the eye contact on its own starts making my chest pound. I always thought she was pretty, but being this close sends me into outer space.

It feels like we've been staring too long, and like magnets, we both lean in to kiss. It reminds me of our first kiss, but we take a little longer this time. Pretty quickly, we're full on making out, and repositioning ourselves on the couch. Both of our eyes are closed, but every so often I open mine to check if hers are still closed. The TV's still going and gets especially loud when a screamo video comes on. It's hard to tune out, but I don't want to stop kissing Jessica, so we endure through it. We slow down after a few minutes and collectively decide to take a break.

We watch that new All American Rejects video, but once it's over, we're making out again. My brain suddenly deals me a scenario I hadn't considered, and now I'm struck with the debilitating fear that someone's going to walk in on us. It's very possible because we're on the ground floor, so I start hypothesizing each family's schedule and current whereabouts. I wish I didn't have to multitask while making out, but I can't keep my mind off it. I figure that we'd be able to hear someone turning a doorknob, so I relax a bit. Diana is really the only one that might pop in, but while we were watching the movie last night, I think she told Mom she was going to a friend's house today. I half-wish I hadn't remembered that, because now I'm just thinking about how Jessica and I are making out in the exact spot where I was with Diana less than 24 hours ago. You don't want to be thinking about your sister when you have your tongue in a girl's mouth. Jessica and I eventually sit back up, both seem satisfied with our session, and she puts her head on my shoulder as we continue watching TV. I lean forward for my yearbook, find what she wrote, and she watches me read it.

Hey Alex! Prom was so fun. I can't believe you're graduating and going to college! Be sure to stay in touch!
—*Jessica*

I could have sworn she had written more, and reading this now kind of bums me out because of how simple it is. I think she senses that I'm let down and takes it upon herself to explain.

"Well, I didn't know all this was going to happen when I was writing it," she says, gesturing her hand back and forth between us. We both laugh, and when Mom comes home, Jessica and she talk briefly, before I drive Jessica home. I invite her to Pete's pool party tomorrow night, and we make out in front of her house for a bit. Back home, I have dinner with just Mom and Dad, where Dad acknowledges the yard work Gerry and I did. I'm in too good of a mood to correct him, and for the rest of the dinner, they mainly talk to each other about work. "I've got some deadline," Dad keeps saying. He eventually resigns to his office, where he'll work until midnight like he always does when he has one of these projects. Mom and I sit and let our food settle a bit before we clean up.

"It was nice meeting Jessica again," she says.

"Yes," I respond, unashamed.

"Are you two a thing now?"

"We'll see."

"Alright." Mom changes tack. "We've got some exciting stuff coming up," she says with a proud smile. Now she brings up my graduation. I'm surprised she didn't bring it up on Father's Day. Her next question shows her priorities. "Are you excited to become an uncle?" I'm a bit disappointed, but I remind myself that she's becoming a grandparent for the first time, and this is a big deal for her.

"Yes, I am," I answer.

Mom drops me off a bit late for the pre-ceremony check-in, but it's mainly because of all the traffic. I'm a little bit nervous-excited, but playing with the zipper on my gown seems to keep me distracted. When we're a few blocks away, I jump out of the car and tell her I'll see her at the ceremony. Gerry's working and

Abigail was having bad morning sickness, so it will just be Dad, Diana and her. I see other kids in my class getting dropped off far away, too. It's funny to see dozens of black robes walking in one direction; we kind of look like a bunch of judges running late to work. I meet Mark and Pete by the baseball diamond, and we walk over to the sea of chairs on the football field. We sit about halfway to the stage and just review the party plans, waiting for it to start.

"Do you need me to bring chips or anything?" Mark asks Pete.

"Nah, my mom's got everything," he says. "You know what I'm most excited about?"

"What?" I ask, expecting some kind of joke.

"Never having to see half these people again," Pete laughs, snidely.

"You're such an asshole," Mark laughs back. It's kind of out-of-character for Pete to say something like this because he's the real connector of our group, but I just chalk it up to him being nervous, too, in his own way.

The bleachers look full of family members, but we're still waiting for the ceremony to begin. I overhear sprinklings of discussions: one about a party, one about a tray of eggplant parmesan, but everyone seems to be keeping their conversations brief due to anticipation. Finally, the moment comes when Principal Fanter and Dean Onk walk onto the stage wearing their own green, garish robes. If we look like pubescent judges, these two look like rejects from the Emerald City. Dean Onk approaches the podium as some of the underclassmen theatre kids file in and stand on risers next to the stage. I quickly spot Jessica and try to remember if she told me that she was performing at graduation, or if I just forgot.

Following the National Anthem, there's a parade of speeches from administrators I never met, teachers I never had or students I didn't have much of a connection with. It feels like one, last punishment for us to endure before we get to leave this place. Madison gives a speech for some reason, and the Valedictorian and Salutatorian speeches are equally terrible. One is delivered in a boring, rote monotone and the other has so many jittery "uh's" and "um's" that I'm waiting for a faculty member to swoop in and let her know it's okay if she doesn't finish. Mark is able to get a hand on one of the programs and we scope it out to see how far along the ceremony is. We see a librarian come up to the podium and Mark not-so-subtly lets everyone know that this is the last speech. I remember her once yelling at MAP when we were goofing around in the library, which doesn't help reverse my already high distraction level. As she begins, I look around to see if everyone else is feeling the same way.

"The following passage comes from "Song of Myself" by Walt Whitman." It already sounds boring and I start daydreaming of Jessica.

"...I know I have the best of time and space, and was never measured and never will be measured. I tramp a perpetual journey; come listen all!" I look into the bleachers and spot Mom, Dad and Diana. I can tell that Dad is on his blackberry, but Mom and Diana appear to be paying attention.

"...But each man and each woman of you I lead upon a knoll, my left hand hooking you round the waist, my right hand pointing to landscapes of continents and the public road." Pete has turned the program into a paper airplane and is making eye contact with me to see if I'll dare him to throw it.

"...Not I, not any one else can travel that road for you. You must travel it for yourself." I give him a nod, and he chickens it out by only throwing it knee level.

"...It is not far; it is within reach. Perhaps you have been on it since you were born and did not know." A security guard comes by to investigate and MAP sits straight up, fighting back laughter.

"...If you tire, give me both burdens, and rest the chuff of your hand on my hip, and in due time you shall repay the same service to me, for after we start we never lie by again." How much longer is this going to last?

"...You are also asking me questions and I hear you. I answer that I cannot answer; you must find out for yourself." Mark points out Tony Spiranti a row ahead of us. At first, I don't notice, but then see he's fighting off a nosebleed.

"...You must habit yourself to the dazzle of the light and of every moment of your life." What a time to get a nosebleed! He holds his head back, and wipes his nose on his robe, but is still left with a red smear above his lip.

"*...Long have you timidly waded holding a plank by the shore. Now I will you to be a bold swimmer, to jump off in the midst of the sea, rise again, nod to me, shout, and laughingly dash with your hair.*" She slows down at the end, and her cadence tells me the speech is over.

As she sits down, us seniors rattle around a bit as the security guards usher the first row to the stage. Tony seems to have stopped any blood flow in the nick of time, and after accepting my diploma, the ceremony is a blur. When Dean Onk sends off our class, we throw our caps and whoop while the bleachers applaud. Mom, Dad and Diana make their way down to the field, and Mom takes a photo of MAP, and then one of Diana and me. Mark and Pete find their families and we part without much of a goodbye since we're going to be seeing each other later.

"We had to park pretty far away," Dad warns.

Dad drops me off at Pete's house and Pete's mom answers the door.

"Hi, Ms...," I trail off, forgetting her maiden name. Luckily, she saves me.

"Alex, you're a high school graduate. I think you can call me Joanne."

"Thanks, Joanne," I say, feeling slightly awkward as the words come out of my mouth. I hand her the banana pudding I brought and head to their back porch. I lock eyes with a man I've never met before who's scraping their grill, and he extends a hand to me.

"I'm Joe," he says in a friendly and firm voice.

"Alex," I reply.

"Well Alex, congratulations and let me know if you want a patty, frank or both. I'm going to fire up the old smoke-a-roo in about fifteen." I translate his lingo in my head and decide to start off simple.

"I'll have a hot dog."

"You got it, brother." I catch Pete's mom beaming at who must be her new boyfriend, and head over to Pete, who's already in the pool. From Pete's facial expression and half-shrug, I can tell he didn't know Joe was going to show up, but isn't too bothered by it. I join MAP and Pete's cousin Fred for pool volleyball, and soon, Pete's theatre friends arrive. I notice Jessica right away, but feel I have to play it cool, and stay in while she talks to Pete's mom. We haven't really decided how to act in public yet, and I don't want to take any chances. I watch her smile and nod, exchanging pleasantries longer than needed. She's wearing a yellow sundress that ties at the back of her neck and has her hair in an orange scrunchy. I don't know much about fashion, but I think she looks prettier than she did at prom. BAM! I blink five times in a row as I touch the side of the pool and recover from the volleyball that was just pelted at my temple.

"Let's go, Romeo," shouts Fred, claiming his shot. Feeling a bit cocky, I smile at Fred and walk up the ladder out of the pool. "C'mon, we're in the middle of a game," he whines.

I grab a towel and wipe my face just in time to give Jessica a big kiss. She seems a little bit surprised, but I can tell it's well-received. I hadn't thought about other people watching and see that Joanne looks as though she's trying to readjust from the Alex she knew at five-years-old, while her boyfriend, Joe, gives me a not-so-subtle thumbs up.

Not long after, Pete's mom lights some citronella candles and everyone gathers around the picnic table as Joe sells his smorgasbord of salads, dips and sides to us. As we eat, the conversation turns to casual theatre gossip, like what the musical is going to be next year and who's going to be the lead. Fred takes one last bite of macaroni salad, shouts "Cannonball" and jumps back into the pool, which encourages the rest of the table to disperse. Most everyone else goes to swim as well, but I spot some noodles that must have escaped his mouth, floating near the filter, so I ask Jessica if she wants to lie in the hammock instead.

I stay there for a while with her. I feel every subtle swing and every inhale and exhale of her chest. I feel like I'm both completely alone with her and experiencing the rest of the world with her at the same time. I daze at the strands of her wavering hair, blurred out in front of the first, impatient fireflies sailing over a fading, sherbet sky. I hear a distant, doppler-effect-induced ice cream truck, accompanied by the ostinato of her continual breaths. I smell her smell, and I like it. I've noticed it before, but now it's more subtle, a bit masked by the chlorine on her skin, and the scent of the coals wafting our way. I don't mind; I'll smell just her again soon enough. Even though we both just ate, when we kiss, all I taste is her. I feel her eyelashes on my neck, as a few ambitious splashes of water cut through the breeze and reach us. We miniflinch with each drop, before settling back into each other's bodies. All these simulations meld into one moment and emotion, and I feel like I can stay here forever. I guess that's what summer can do to you.

The night ends with fireworks. Tony Spiranti lives down the street and we make our way towards him as he gleefully ignites all the contraband his uncle gave him. After Jessica leaves, I sit with Mark and Pete on the curb, and we revel in the falling embers, the humidity, and the night altogether.

Passage 2:

Summer before College

Chapter 7: Beginning of Summer

Nothing really has changed now that high school is over, but I guess I didn't expect things to. I'm still working, hanging out with MAP, seeing movies; it just feels a bit freer now. July is a blast just like other summers, and now I'm able to spend more time with Jessica. I know how to act around her parents when I go over her house, and score extra points when I entertain her six-year-old sister, Juliana. Jessica's mom keeps a watchful eye on us, but when she's not home, Jessica gleefully loosens up, like she's getting away with something, and leads me to her room. On these occasions, our makeouts are so much more passionate and unrestrained, and I usually get to second base, too. The downside is when Jessica hears the inkling of a car pulling into her driveway, I'm forced to dash to her living room in record time. One time she even pushes me off the bed, only to peek out the window and discover that someone was just using her driveway to make a U-turn. I guess it's better than my house because Gerry won't always knock if he sees the door is closed.

One afternoon, we're in my room when he knocks real quick and then shouts through the door, "Time to pull out!" Jessica and I aren't even doing anything and I don't say a word when he comes in the room a second later. He gives us a sarcastic nod, sits on his bed and makes comments about the music we're listening to.

"This song sucks."

"I think I better get going," Jessica tells me.

"So soon?" Gerry says. I've warned her about my brother, and she handles him by just leaving the room without responding. I glare at him and he returns the favor. "What? You want to go?" he asks with a sinister smile.

"Maybe," I reply, standing up. Gerry immediately jumps up from his bed, ready to answer the challenge. We stand nose to nose, staring each other in the eye, and just when it's its most tense, I turn around and leave the room.

"Pussy," I hear him moan as I close the door. I grin knowing that I got to him, but also know that we'll probably actually brawl sometime later tonight or tomorrow. I meet Jessica in my kitchen while she's talking to Mom.

"Hey Mom, can I use the car to drive her home?" I ask.

"Actually Jessica said she'd like to stay for dinner," Mom answers. I lock eyes with Jessica.

"Your mom invited me."

"Can you tell Gerry to come down in fifteen minutes?" Mom asks.

"Sure," I groan, my mind prepossessed on our last exchange. If I knew that Jessica would have to now share a meal with him, I wouldn't have pissed him off the way I did. Also, now delivering him a message from Mom kind of takes the shine off of my little triumph.

Dinner is quiet for sure, and Mom can't seem to place why Gerry isn't talking. "Was work okay?" she asks him, but he just murmurs "fine" through the chicken cutlets in his mouth. Diana is scarfing down her food, while glancing at a hardcover book open on the table. Jessica takes it upon herself to cut through the tension.

"Is Mr. Ryback working late?" she asks.

"No, he's visiting his mother at her senior facility," Mom answers, appreciating the question. "She had a fall today." My eyebrows must raise a few inches, because Mom looks at me and adds, "She's fine." A few more moments of silence pass, and Jessica tries again.

"Diana, how's your summer going?" she asks my unprepared sister. Diana stays perfectly still, but snaps her eyeballs away from the book to Jessica.

"It's good," she answers curtly.

"Dee-Dee, tell her what you do during the day," Mom encourages.

"Oh, I'm in a volleyball camp," Diana says.

"Do you enjoy it?" Jessica asks.

"Yeah. Most freshmen don't make varsity, but I'm sure I'll make JV."

"I think so, too. What are you reading?"

"*The Tempest* for Honors English."

"All my kids left their summer reading until the night before except for this one," Mom chimes in.

"Well, this isn't the only book I have to read," Diana shoots back at Mom. "And I have to do an AP Bio packet."

"It was a compliment, honey," Mom says, obviously annoyed that Diana is being short with her in front of company. After that exchange Jessica gives up, and Diana and Gerry both leave abruptly with Gerry leaving his plate on the table. I try to impress Jessica by doing the dishes, but Mom's surprised facial expression gives away that this isn't a normal routine for me. After I'm finished, I ask for Mom's keys again.

"I think Gerry is behind me. Can you take his car?"

"You mean the 'third car?'" I correct her. If there's one thing Mom knows, it's that we're meant to share it equally.

"You know what I mean," she answers with a big exhale, begging me to cut her some slack. I drive Jessica home, she kisses me, and before closing the door, says, "See you tomorrow."

I love summer.

July slides and meanders by like opposite ends of an ice cream cone melting at different speeds. Days fly by when I hang out with MAP or Jessica, but being inside the store on sunny days drags like nothing else. I'm a bit over the job, but I'll keep it until mid-August when I leave for school. Mom and Dad constantly stress to me not to burn bridges with Carla because she'll probably let me work over college breaks. It's getting harder to be around her, and I wonder if it's because she knows that she'll have to hire someone new in a month. She's been on my case recently, but it's warranted— I have been texting more now that I have a girlfriend.

Jessica often joins MAP in Pete's basement for its infamous drinking sessions, and quickly proves she can keep pace with the great Alex Ryback. I always pegged her for a bookworm like Diana, but am now discovering she also likes to party to release the school stress. One week, she's away as a counselor-in-training at a summer camp she used to attend. We miss each other a ton, but Jessica says this'll line her up to get a job at the camp next summer.

Abigail is getting bigger by the day, and Mom's worry level is commensurate with her daughter's size. She's always over their house and buying things like wall socket covers and baby books. She throws Abigail a baby shower, which banishes Dad, Gerry and me from the house for a day, but I'm working anyway, so I don't mind. I'd think Diana would now get a taste of middle-child syndrome, but she's so self-involved that I don't think it even fazes her that the house is always empty. Us two definitely have a special connection with each other, that no other sibling has. Abigail is a good deal older and always felt older. She has the classic oldest-child independence necessitated by Mom and Dad having had three more kids, but her own personality also made her super ambitious. She had her whole life planned by the time she was twelve, and I guess everything fell in line for her. The sibling disconnect was also exasperated by Gerry being a screw-up. Mom and Dad had such a different parenting approach with Abigail, that they were wholly unprepared for some of his antics. Gerry once skipped a week of middle school and they had no idea because he still got up early and went to the bus stop. He must have forged a note in advance because the school never called Mom or Dad. The disparate difference between them kind of just left Diana and me to be "also there" in the family dynamic. I unfortunately had to suffer through Gerry babysitting me, but after Mom and Dad came home to both of us having bruises, they never let him watch over her. I got to, and I think that's what instituted our unique bond. Diana is an overachiever and straight-A student, but I'm not sure if she'll be ambitious in the same way as Abigail. She doesn't care one bit about becoming an aunt, so I can see Diana not thinking about starting a family until she's fifty or something.

One night in early August, Jessica and I have a movie date. I shell out what feels like a whole week's paycheck on the restaurant, movie tickets, popcorn, and ice cream after the movie. I make sure to act like it's no big deal because Abigail always said Stephen was so chivalrous when they first met. We see that new one with Sophia Bush, which I don't mind because the last two movies I saw with MAP were terrible action flicks that made no sense. Romantic-comedies are good because they get you girlfriend points by just buying the ticket. During any schmaltzy, lovey-dovey scene, Jessica grabs my whole arm and rests her head on my shoulder. I'd feel close to her as well, but there's a woman behind us, who sounds like she may need CPR at any second due to her bronchial panting. After it's over, Jessica latches onto my arm again as we stroll to the ice cream shop. While we wait in line, there's a hush between us. As I ponder which flavor to order, I notice Jessica's merriness recede into melancholy. I ask her what's wrong and she says, "Nothing." Before I can press further, it's our turn to order. After she gets her cup of mint-chocolate chip and hands me my cone of the same, we walk slowly towards the parking lot, stopping at a mailbox along the way. Jessica rests her cup on top of it and swirls around her ice cream a bit, while I diligently lap up any drips coming off my cone. I can tell she's still thinking of something and it finally comes to a head.

"What are we going to do when you go to college in a few weeks?" I knew this conversation was coming, but am totally caught off-guard. I thought that a romantic date would be the last place it would occur, but I guess the tender feelings somehow made her worried, too. It's like she's wistful in advance. I think that once it was subconsciously established that we weren't just a summer fling, we each let our guard down a bit, and didn't think to consider summer would ultimately end.

Chapter 8: Middle of Summer

One night, MAP goes to a party a few towns over in Wattsville. Pete knows the kid from summer camp or something. I don't ask too much about him; I just think it's cool going to a party with people outside your high school. Jessica hangs by my side, a little less attached since our last date, but I can tell she thinks it's cool, too. After Pete jumps into Mark's car, Mark says we have one more person to pick up.

"I hope it's not Tony Spiranti," Pete snickers, as we pass by Tony's house.

"No, it's Emily," Mark answers coolly, without looking at us.

"Oh!" Pete and I vocalize in unison, as Jessica raises her eyebrows, still adjusting to our dynamic. Pete and I knew that Mark had been hooking up with Emily here and there this summer, but he'd been keeping it somewhat under wraps. This could definitely be a step forward for them, but it also may be nothing.

"Pete, jump in the back," Mark says, as we arrive at Emily's house. Pete obliges with an impish grin, and forces me into the middle seat.

Emily walks out, and Pete nudges me when she gives Mark a kiss before entering the car. We won't bust his chops now that she's here, but maybe afterwards. We arrive at the house, and when Pete knocks on the door, and I half-expect that it will be the wrong house or we'll be turned away. The door swings open in one quick motion, and we're greeted by a surfer-dude-looking guy wearing Mardi Gras beads and Aviator sunglasses. I question whether it's a costume party for a second, but then figure that this is the type of guy who wears sunglasses at night.

"Petey C!" the guy shouts, with his hands spread out in both directions. Mark and I look at each other, as neither of us has ever heard Pete go by "Petey."

"Johnny D!" Pete responds with equal volume. Johnny D. lets us in and gives all five of us an individual, unwelcome hug. There's about thirty people there and it doesn't appear that Pete knows any of them other than Johnny. I didn't think of it before we came, but figuring out how to fit in at a party full of strangers can be tricky. It also is more than just high school kids; some people look a bit older. We take in our surroundings before Mark takes it upon himself to get Emily and himself beer from the keg. A keg! This is a first. The remaining three of us follow, and somewhat nod in approval, impressed by Mark's pumping skills. After Pete takes a turn, I fill up two cups for Jessica and myself, but they come out half-foamy.

"You over-pumped, man," some random girl shouts at me, laughing.

"Oh, thanks for letting me know," I reply, embarrassed by my inexperience. "Do you want me to get you another one?" I ask Jessica.

"Don't worry about it," she says. God, she's the best. We wander outside, towards the beer pong table on the patio.

My heart sinks. No. I know it's him from fifty feet away and know that my night is officially ruined. Gerry is standing at one end of the table practicing throws, as some tall guy is refilling cups for another game. Gerry spots me right away, too, but remains completely unfazed. Jessica catches on and pulls down my arm so she can put her chin on my shoulder.

"We can leave if you want to," she whispers, sympathetically.

"No," I say. "It'll be fine." She nods and as we continue to the table, and Gerry knows just how to play it.

"Holy shit! Mark and Pete?" he exclaims in disingenuous delight, as he gives them both a half-hug. Mark and Pete fall for it and engage with Gerry, feeling like he's let them into the approval of the older crowd or the next level of coolness, or whatever. He chums it up with them a good bit, without a mention or glance at me.

"You know Alex is here, too, right?" Mark jokes with him.

"Oh, I saw that fucker at breakfast. I don't need to say hi to him," Gerry says, garnering a rousing laugh between the three of them. "Well, are you guys playing or what?" he asks them. Mark and Pete both offer a "Yeah," and as Mark and Emily square off against Gerry and Tall Guy, I watch from the side of the table, about three feet back. "This is where we separate the boys from the men," Gerry announces before they play. Jessica rolls her eyes and I motion that she doesn't need to try and cheer me up.

As soon as their game is over, Gerry eyes me and asks, "Are Romeo and Juliet up next?" As people turn their heads back and forth, I can tell that no one catches on to who he's talking about.

"No, we'll sit this round out," Jessica replies coolly.

"Okay, whatever you say," Gerry responds louder than he needs to. Pete and Johnny D. take the helm and start playing Gerry and Tall Guy. Jessica reduces my boiling blood by a dozen degrees when she pulls my neck down and starts making out with me in front of everyone. We only kiss for a few seconds, but I check to see if Gerry's watching. After, she takes my hand and says, "Let's go inside." I oblige, and we refill our beers.

We don't really know where to go, so we find some people in the den playing Xbox. We block the TV for a second, and are scolded by a "Move!" from one of the guys playing. Jessica and I quickly shuffle and squeeze into an empty armchair and watch the room transfixed on the TV. MAP definitely appreciates a good video game, but I would have thought it would be frowned upon at an actual party. The people in the room are still drinking, but the focus is definitely on the screen. The "Move" guy looks to be in his late-twenties, so I'm not surprised that he doesn't want to talk to us, and we leave the room. A punkish girl gallops down the stairs, two steps at a time, signaling that the second floor isn't out-of-bounds. I figure that if Johnny D. doesn't mind her up there, we can explore. It feels kind of strange, but once we're upstairs, Jessica just opens a door and walks into the room. It's instantly clear that it's the master bedroom, and I feel like I'm intruding upon Johnny D.'s parents, whoever they are. I figure that if they raised a son who was nice enough to let me into his party, I should give them a little privacy in return. I quickly look to leave, but Jessica lingers.

"Hold up," she assures me. "No one knows we're up here, and it's not like we're doing anything." I'm a bit surprised, but I don't want to come off uncool to my girlfriend, so I play along.

"Okay." I just stand and look around as Jessica walks up to the mother's dresser and vanity mirror. I don't say anything, but have to admit that I start to panic when she opens a drawer. Jessica finds a tube of lipstick, opens it up and observes the color. The room would be pitch dark if it weren't for the hallway light coming in, and Jessica takes it upon herself to lean towards the mirror and apply the mother's lipstick on herself. My panic switches to shock when I think of the germs, but I give a nod when she turns to me and smiles. This chick is unpredictable. Jessica leaves the tube on the dresser and walks towards me. She stares at me for a second with a half-loving, half-plotting smile, and then rolls up the sleeve of my t-shirt, kissing me on the arm. I just watch her with stillness as she pulls down the sleeve, and then repeats the action on my other side. She finishes with a kiss on my lips, and I oblige because most of the lipstick has already come off, but I can't help thinking that I'm kissing Johnny D.'s mom. Jessica walks out the bedroom, but before I follow her, I put the tube back in the drawer and check my face in the vanity to make sure there's no visible lipstick.

As I close the door, I see a punk guy coming out of another room and say to me, "It's not in there."

"Uh, what isn't?" I ask, thinking I've been caught.

"We're rolling up in this room," he says before he walks downstairs. Jessica and I consider that an invitation and walk into the room he's pointed us to.

It looks to be Johnny D.'s bedroom, and we're greeted by the punk girl, who's dragging a nightstand into the center.

"Have a seat on his bed for now," she instructs us, and we readily follow her instructions. Johnny D.'s bed is half-made and we sit down cautiously, trying to catch as much comforter, and as little exposed bedsheet as we can. I'm not sure if it would be more or less awkward if I knew him better, but I feel like I can't ask him to make his bed, and don't want to make his bed myself. The punk guy and Johnny D. enter, sitting on makeshift seats, before plopping a ziplock bag of weed and rolling papers onto the nightstand. I've never smoked pot before, but also never swore against trying it, so I guess this is as good of a time as any to get my beak wet. I'm pretty certain that Jessica's never smoked either, and from her recent lipstick probe, I assume she's in an adventurous mood. I glance at her and she confirms my suspicions with a wry smile. Just as the punk guy is licking the paper to seal the weed, I hear footsteps coming up the stairs, and he enters the room.

I should have known that I wouldn't be able to get away from him for too long, and my mind switches from excitement to defense mode. Mark and Pete follow Gerry in tow, and from the look on their faces, they both have a good buzz going, and have been enjoying hanging out with Gerry. I don't consider it a betrayal or anything; they just don't know him like I do. I think they feel that he's let them into the club, when I know in actuality he's just being nice to them to mess with me. Gerry gives me a knowing smirk and plops himself down uncomfortably close to Jessica, instead of next to me.

"Move down," he commands, bumping into her. "Everyone needs to fit." Emily sneaks into the room, equally buzzed, and Johnny D. motions for Mark to close the door.

"Alright, that's close enough," I warn Gerry.

"I just have to make sure you two aren't hogs, that's all," he replies sarcastically.

"Well, if this joint doesn't do it for you, I'm sure you've got plenty more," I shoot back at him.

"Son, this isn't a joint," the punk guy says to me as he lights it. "It's a blunt." Damn, there's a difference?

"Don't you teach him anything?" Johnny D. asks Gerry.

"Oh, every day is like amateur hour with this one," Gerry says, not looking at me, but pointing at me with his thumb, almost hitting Jessica in the face. She flinches back and knocks her head into my ear. I'm seething, but am able to contain it.

Johnny D. takes a hit and passes it to the punk guy, who does the same and passes it to the punk girl. I study how they hold it, their intake and reaction after they've inhaled. Johnny D. and the punk guy both say it's "good shit." As the punk girl passes the blunt to me, I figure I can't copycat with the same adjudication, and come up dry with a unique line to say. The game seems to be to just act like you've been in the room before. A few minutes ago, this was just going to be a new experience, something I could look back on with fondness or humor, but that all changed when he walked in. Now, I feel his eyes beating on me, waiting for me to mess up on some level. Luckily, I know what he's counting on. He expects me to take too big of a hit for my first time and have a coughing fit, for which I'll be ridiculed in front of everyone. I take a small drag on the blunt and watch the embers glow. I let the smoke fill my lungs, and exhale upward, looking at the ceiling. As I pass to Jessica, I hear the punk girl snicker.

"That's it?" she cries. The punk guy and Johnny D. join in the laughter. Shit, I overcompensated by undertoking. I guess too small of a hit makes you look inexperienced, too.

"Man, you must be flying high after that," the punk guy says. Gerry doesn't utter a word. He doesn't have to; they won for him. Jessica takes her hit and starts coughing up a storm. They all laugh, and Gerry leans forward to look me in the eyes.

"At least she didn't bitch out like you, Alex." I guess Gerry did feel the need to say something. His point of view generates another round of laughter from these pot veterans. Gerry takes a big hit, blows it into my face and passes to Mark. Mark and Emily both cough, but Pete doesn't. Maybe Pete's smoked before; he does have a hippy mom. The blunt goes around a second time, and this time I take a bigger hit, from which I do cough.

"There we go," he says softly, but still loud enough for everyone to hear. Great, he was able to burn me two different ways. The blunt makes its way to Pete again, and after he hits, it's pretty much gone. Johnny D. takes the end and puts it into a container with other ends, while the punk guy starts rolling another joint. Mark, Pete and Emily are giggling a ton; I guess the hits really took their beer buzz to a new level. I look at Jessica, who's a little glassy-eyed, but can't really tell if she's stoned. I definitely am feeling a little more mellow myself, but think my Gerry-induced anxiety has counteracted its full effects.

Johnny D. plays with his lighter, ready for the next round, but then we hear some yelling downstairs. As he gets up, Pete, Emily and Mark get out of his way so he can investigate what's going on. As the door opens, we can hear two guys cursing at each other. When Johnny D. says "Calm the fuck down or get the fuck out of my house," Gerry shoots up and dashes downstairs, with the punk couple right behind. Jessica looks at me, and her eyes tell me I should go down, too, because my brother is there. I reluctantly get up, and as we pass Pete, Mark and Emily, I tell them to stay where they are and not to worry about it. Jessica and I walk downstairs and hear that the argument is coming from that video game room. We walk in to find the "Move" guy and Tall Guy staring each other down. Johnny D. is trying to position himself between the two, and Gerry is a step behind him.

"Fucking do something," the "Move" guy says to Tall Guy.

"Why don't you?" Tall Guy replies. I can't tell what sparked the argument, but it seems like it doesn't really matter at this point.

"We're all trying to have a good time. Can you guys just separate or leave?" Johnny D. pleads to them both.

Gerry takes a step forward and stands in front of Tall Guy. I don't know if Gerry is really defending him, or even if they have much of a relationship beyond beer pong partners, but Gerry is now standing nose to nose with the "Move" guy.

"Listen up, dirtbag. It's pathetic enough that you guys can't find a party with people your own age, but don't start shit just to make yourself seem tough." Gerry hit it on the head. When he's not using his put-downs against you, one has to appreciate his skill.

"Back the fuck away," the "Move" guy says to my brother.

"Just leave and we don't have a problem." The "Move" guy takes a second, backs up slightly, and looks down. I can't believe Gerry's strategy actually worked. I was expecting a punch to be thrown at any second. Then the "Move" guy lifts up his shirt to reveal a knife clipped into his waist, which he removes, flicks open and points towards Gerry. Gerry instinctively jumps back and puts his hands up, palms facing his mortal threat. Dead air fills the room, and I feel frozen.

"Say what you said one more time," he says to my brother. Gerry stays mute with his eye on the knife.

WAOM, WAOM, WAOM! A siren starts blaring and everyone covers their ears including the "Move" guy. I jerk my head towards the source of the noise, and see the punk guy holding his lighter just below a smoke detector. My senses are stunned again, when I then see the punk girl hurl a candle towards the "Move" guy. She wildly misses, and the candle shatters on the wall behind him. I take this opportunity to grab Gerry's arm and Jessica, and we run out the back door into the backyard, jump over a chain link fence into a neighbor's yard, and find a gate to the street. Gerry leads us to the car, and we speed away.

After a minute of driving, our breathing slows down and Gerry asks Jessica where she lives. As Jessica gives him directions, I panic as I remember Mark, Pete and Emily are still in the house. I call Mark immediately, but get his voicemail. Pete calls me and says that Mark's driving, but they got out alright, and we'll talk tomorrow. I hang up and keep quiet so Jessica can keep giving directions. She still gives me a kiss when she gets out of the car, but I know she's shaken. Gerry and I stay quiet as he drives us home, and the silence remains as we walk into the house, enter our room and lie in bed. It takes some time for the adrenaline to wear off, and neither of us says a word while we lie there. I find it difficult to even close my eyes, but I eventually fall asleep.

The next day, Dad takes Gerry, Diana and me to see Grandma at the home. When we walk into her room, we find her contently watching TV at a blaring volume.

"Mom?!" Dad announces our arrival. She maintains her gaze on the screen. "Hey, Mom!" he tries again. Still, no reaction. "Mom!" he says one last time, waving his hand so she sees him.

"Oh, I didn't see you there," she beams with an oblivious smile as he leans down to hug her. As Grandma attempts to find her remote to lower the volume, Gerry instinctively does so from the set, so she doesn't have to. We mostly sit while Dad talks to her about Abigail and the goings-on in the nursing home. Then on cue, Diana, Gerry and I give her an update on our lives, for which she offers a "that's nice" to each of us. Eventually, she gets tired and dozes off right in front of us. We usually take this as a cue to leave, and Gerry places her remote on her lap for when she wakes.

While leaving the Burger King drive-thru, Dad zeroes in on me and asks, "Did you like seeing Grandma?" I try to decipher why he only asks me, and nod while in mid-bite, which is enough of a response to satisfy him.

Chapter 9: Late Summer

It finally happens. At breakfast, we get a call from Stephen that Abigail's in labor. Dad picks up the phone, and says, "Okay, that's great." That's all Mom needs to know to decipher the message, and she runs to their bedroom to grab a bag that she's already packed. Dad draws in a deep breath, readying himself for when Mom reenters.

"Abigail's water just broke," he exhales. The three of us smile back, sharing the moment with him, before Mom rushes back in, already half-harried.

"Do you have my keys?" she asks/demands of Dad.

"Stephen said to meet them at the hospital."

"That's ridiculous. Someone needs to park and someone needs to check her in."

"They're already on their way."

"Fine," Mom pouts. I think Mom was planning on relegating Stephen to being a chauffeur at the birth of his first child, so that she could bark orders at nurses, but he must have gotten wind of it and found a way to circumvent her scheme.

"Kiss?" Dad pleads as he hands her the keys. Mom delivers one reluctantly, and races out of the house. Dad knows that he'll be backup, probably fielding a dozen phone calls from Mom, and then bringing any supplies she deems necessary. He turns to us with a look of joy that he's about to become a grandpa, tinged with relenting acceptance to Mom's antics. "So, we have a little bit of time. You guys are all around this afternoon, right?"

"Work," Gerry says.

"Volleyball," Diana adds.

"Work," I say, as well.

"Ooh," Dad reacts. "I'm glad your mother left before she heard that. Okay, when do your shifts end?"

"Four," I say.

"Same," Gerry says.

"And when do you finish practice?" he asks Diana.

"Two-thirty," she replies. "I can hang out with Kaitlin until you pick me up."

"She's going to want me there sooner. It will have to be you two," Dad says to Gerry and me. "Don't even come home. Just pick her up and head straight to St. Mary's."

"I'm going to have fish guts all over me," I complain.

"Bring a change of clothes," he shoots back. "Today isn't about you."

"Did you tell that to Mom?" Diana quips.

"You're too clever for your own good," Dad grins, taking a giant slug of coffee. The four of us enjoy the rest of breakfast, with only two, consecutive phone calls from Mom, and then Gerry and I head off to work. We don't talk; it's been a weird few days. Between the party, Grandma and now Abigail, the usual tension between us is somewhat softened.

After my shift, I wait outside for Gerry. I jump in the car and he hands me a crumpled-up piece of paper.

"What's this?" I ask.

"Diana's friend's number. You got to call her."

"Don't you know where the house is?"

"Maybe. I don't know which friend is which."

"Didn't you ask her where it was?"

"I got the number. You call and tell me where to go," he says as he navigates in the general direction of our house. I take a look at the digits and inquire about a curly "four." "Is this a nine?" Gerry takes a glance, and returns an unashamed "Yes."

I speak with Kaitlin's mom and quickly call up the house in my memory. "It's two blocks after the Pickford Elementary school."

"Where we played soccer?" he asks.

"Middle school soccer," I confirm. Diana's waiting and jumps in the car. "How was volleyball?" I ask her.

"Good," she replies.

"Any crazy spikes?"

"No, but I did have a good dive."

"Is that when the other team spikes and you save it?"

"You got it," she laughs. I laugh as well, and then turn to see Gerry, stone-faced, staring at the road. I really feel bad for Diana, since she has to be alone with him all next year. Knowing Gerry, he'll still be in the house when she's a senior. "MMMBop" kicks on the radio, causing an immediate groan from Gerry and a gleeful squeal from Diana. Gerry instinctively reaches for the dial, but I block him long enough for him to give in. If we were alone, he'd have given me a punch in the arm or thigh, but he relents because of how much Diana is enjoying the song. Abigail's the one who introduced her to it as a kid, so it's completely appropriate for the occasion.

At the hospital, we navigate our way to the maternity ward to find Mom crying and a doctor smiling. We look at Dad who reads our faces as he hugs Mom.

"Abigail's just delivered. It's a baby girl." Diana covers her mouth in delight.

"Can we see her?" she asks.

"Probably in a few hours," Dad replies.

"And your sister is doing fine," Mom snaps at us for not asking the question.

"Does it have a name?" Gerry asks.

"No, Abbie hasn't chosen one for *her* yet," Mom responds. We sit in the waiting room for a while and I call Jessica to let her know. Stephen eventually walks out beaming in hospital scrubs, and gives everyone a big hug. He tells us that Abigail is on pain medication, but wants to see us all soon. He invites Mom back to the room with him, but tells the rest of us we'll have to wait a bit. When it comes time for the rest of us, Dad gives us a talk in the elevator.

"You know why this is such a big deal for your Mom right?" Gerry, Diana and I all nod, but he doesn't seem satisfied by the non-verbal response. "Abbie was kind of a surprise for your mom and me. We were kind of young," he says with a pregnant pause. "And Grandma Susan died about a year before." He gifts another confusing pause. I'm not sure if he wants us to revel in the supposed profoundness of these statements, or if he's having difficulty articulating what he's trying to say. Either way, we run out of time when the elevator doors open at the maternity floor.

We walk into Abigail's room to find Stephen cradling the baby, Abigail resting in bed with an IV in her arm, and Mom on the edge of her seat watching Stephen. Mom snaps her gaze towards us and says, "Wash your hands!" in a harsh whisper. I guess Dad's speech was more of a warning about Mom. I would have thought that she'd calm down now that the baby is born, but apparently not. We each get a turn holding the baby under Mom's watchful eye and how-to-support-the-head suggestions, and Gerry eventually re-asks his question.

"Do you have a name?"

"Oh, they've got plenty of time," Mom answers for Stephen and Abigail.

"Actually, the staff is asking us," Stephen says.

"We were talking," Abigail says, "and we do have a strong contender." This is news to Mom whose eyes go wide. "We're thinking of *Suzie*," Abigail says. Everyone immediately knows why, and Mom starts weeping again and gives Abigail a hug.

Abigail gives the okay for Jessica to come, who's thrilled when she gets to hold Suzie. As she does, I look my niece in the eyes and smile. I can't tell who Suzie looks like, but she definitely has that newborn baby smell. I make sure to bask it in because it's not a smell you get to smell every day. Diana takes a photo of Jessica and me, which causes one of Dad's eyebrows to raise. When Suzie needs to be breastfed, Jessica and I walk to the vending machine holding hands. We share a pack of M&M's as the sunset paints an orange glow onto her cheeks.

Things turn somewhat back to normal when Abigail is discharged and they bring Suzie home. Mom is at their house quite often, but she's calmed now that she can follow a schedule. Dad takes me to PC Richard to pick up a laptop, which depletes a good chunk of my savings, although Mom, Dad and Grandma help me cover the cost, too. As we're driving home, I receive a take-care-of-this talk from Dad. I'm sure that it's Gerry related, even though his laptop is still fine. I show Diana, who's a bit jealous, but then realizes that she won't be competing with me for the desktop anymore.

I work one more shift and then give my notice to Carla, who tells me to call for availability when I come home on break. Ms. Waters is throwing a going-away party for Pete before he heads to Chile, but it also feels like a last-party-of-the-summer for all of us. When Jessica and I arrive, MAP is already there drinking with Ms. Water's approval. I get Jessica a beer and we scope out the snacks that that boyfriend, Joe, put out.

"You gotta try my dip," he says.

"Okay," she complies. Jessica dips a potato chip into the bowl he's pointing to, and gives an exaggerated "Mmm," after her bite. Joe congratulates himself and we quickly scurry to people our own age. No one's really swimming in the pool yet, so we settle on talking to Ethan and Farah. Farah quickly turns the conversation into her complaining again about losing "Cutest Couple."

"But as we've talked about before," Ethan lectures her, "we're moving onto other things."

"Yeah, but people will always look back at the yearbook," she cries.

"There's nothing we can do about it. Why do you keep bringing it up?" he asks.

"Well now there's a new development," she says looking at me.

"What's that?" Jessica asks, intrigued.

"Here we go," Ethan laments. Farah locks eyes with Jessica and gives off the vibe like she's uncovered a conspiracy.

"Marshall and Madison broke up in June," she gossips.

"Yeah," Jessica follows her.

"I've heard from a very reliable source that Madison Solomon is now engaged." Ethan rolls his eyes.

"Really?" Jessica asks.

"Yup. And I heard she's engaged to a much older guy."

"But what does this have to do with the yearbook?" Jessica asks.

"Well, nothing directly," Farah concedes with a pause. "But it makes you think."

"Think what?"

"That they knew they were going to break up last fall, but stayed together just to be cemented in time as 'Cutest Couple,'" Ethan says, revealing Farah's theory with disbelief.

"I wouldn't put it past them," Farah says. "All I'm saying is, at the time of the voting, they didn't seem as happy as they did, a couple weeks prior, and I also noticed—" Farah stops mid-sentence with her eyes transfixed a few inches above Jessica's head, and her face struck with embarrassment. Jessica and I turn around simultaneously and quickly share the same emotion as we see Marshall Kinley standing near the snack table. I don't think he overheard us, but it's clear that he knows that we were talking about him when he catches our gaze and sees who we're standing next to. He takes it upon himself to avoid any more embarrassment by striking up a conversation with a much-obliged Tony Spiranti. Without missing a beat, Farah picks up the gossip where she left it.

"Can you believe how awkward that was?"

"Yeah, I guess it *was*," Jessica says irreverently, implying that it still will be if she keeps talking. Farah doesn't get the hint.

"I mean, he was staring at us for so long, like we did something." Jessica then points at something over Ethan's shoulder.

"Look, it's Mark and Emily!" she announces to me. "Let's go. I want to take a picture with them."

"Okay," I reply.

"We'll be right back," she tells Ethan and Farah, insincerely. You'd think Ethan would be sick of her complaining, but he just stands by his girlfriend. I guess they did deserve "Best Relationship," or whatever it was called. He just nods as I say "Catch you in a bit," and I don't feel bad about excluding them from the photo opportunity that they'll clearly be observing from a distance.

Jessica whips a digital camera out of her purse. "Joanne, do you mind snapping one of the four of us?" she asks our host.

It's funny how Jessica doesn't mind calling Pete's mom by her first name.

"Sure!" she agrees, with glee. "Right here?" she motions towards a bench. Jessica nods with a wide grin.

Jessica sits on my lap and Emily on Marks's, but I can tell he's a bit uncomfortable from his plastered-on smile. I'm not sure if they're not as much of a PDA couple as Jessica and me, or if Emily and he are going to split soon, but either way, it's clear he doesn't want much evidence of the two of them together. Pete ultimately ends the photoshoot by shouting, "Shots!" which draws a big, collective "Yeah!" from us kids, and a delayed, raspy "Yeah!" from Joe.

For the rest of the night, the party is the perfect mix of chill and raging. Jessica and I get some alone time, but I also make the rounds and talk with everyone, including Marshall, Tony and even Joe. I'm not drinking too hard so that I can focus on Jessica, and figure I'll indulge more once she heads home to meet her curfew. When her mom arrives, I tell her I'll see her tomorrow, and she nods, asking if we can "talk" then. I say, "Of course," but know that the word "talk" carries something ominous. We settle on getting lunch and I kiss her goodnight. I try to shake off what she said and head back to the party where I do my best to catch up with MAP by downing three shots in a row. At one point, Pete puts an empty case of beer on his head, and Mark and I smack the sides of it with our hands. He runs away for reprieve, but crashes into the side of his pool before he's able to remove the cardboard helmet. MAP rolls on the floor with laughter while Emily shakes her head.

The party eventually thins out as MAP sits around the deck table and picks at the now-decaying appetizers, while Ms. Waters asks Emily about college and Joe snores on Pete's living room couch. Since it's assumed that MAP is all crashing at Pete's house for the night, we really have no reason to slow down, although the depleted beer supply is sort of guiding us in that direction.

"We can do more shots," I suggest, still not as drunk as them.

"Fuck that; I'm done," decides Mark.

"Pussy," Pete says.

"Don't you have to fly tomorrow?"

"Not until way late at night."

"Can we see you before you leave?" I ask.

"Sure," Pete says with a droopy, flattered smile. We sit for a few minutes and kind of just drink in the moment and the night. I'm still riding my buzz, but feel the bittersweetness creeping in. Every other year of our lives, the wistful, end-of-summer feeling seamlessly rolled into the start-of-a-new-school-year excitement, filled with comparing class schedules and talking about the best movies of the season. This time it's different. As I think about it, Mark reads my mind and cuts the deafening silence.

"This will be our last sleepover."

"Some of us are already sleeping," Pete responds, his eyes half-closed.

"When are we all going to be together again?" I ask.

"You coming home for Thanksgiving?" Mark asks Pete.

"Probably," Pete answers. After a few seconds of nothing, Pete changes the direction of the conversation. "Yo," he shoots at Mark, sitting upright. "What's going on with you and Emily?" Mark shrugs it off a bit and looks to see if she's close enough to overhear.

"Uh, we've talked about it and we're going to end it when we both leave for school."

"Really?" Pete says.

"But it's mutual. I mean we aren't as serious as them two," he responds, pointing to me. "We're going to be a thousand miles apart, you know. What else were we going to do? But, it's good. Maybe we'll see where we're at during a break or something." Pete nods and takes one final slug of beer satisfied with both Mark's answer and his alcohol intake for the night. Mark comparing Emily and himself to Jessica and me gets me thinking for a second. I never really considered the future distance. When I'm with her, I just think about her. I wonder if that's what the "talk" will be about. "But speaking of," Mark pauses, dramatically. "I think I owe her a little more time before her pick-up." With that, Mark salutes us and heads inside. Pete and I sit awhile before it hits me.

"Holy shit, you're going to be on a different continent tomorrow," I say. Pete laughs.

"Well, by the time I land, it will technically be two days from now," he counters. "Actually, what time is it?"

"Quarter after two."

"Well then, yes, I'll be in Chile tomorrow." I realize I never really asked him about the specifics of his trip; I just thought he'd be hiking and rafting, if those are the types of things you do there.

"So why Chile?" I ask him.

"Why not Chile?" Pete counters. At my sobriety level, I can't fully decipher his tone.

"So where exactly are you going to be?" I ask, as if I could even find Chile on a map.

"Valparaíso." I nod again.

"Can you send me an email when you get there?"

"Not too many computers, not too much internet."

"What?" I stammer. I thought he would have told MAP this earlier. "How are we going to get in touch?"

"I'll log in here and there, but write me a letter. Old school."

"That's it?"

"Yeah, I'll write down my address tomorrow morning," he yawns. We take this as a cue to head inside to meet MAP, Emily and Ms. Waters sitting in the living room, laughing at Joe's snoring. Ms. Waters is sitting right next to him, talking at full volume, and he's still out cold. Around the same time that Emily's sister picks her up, Ms. Waters gently wakes up Joe and shepherds him upstairs.

"Can you believe Marshall showed up?" Pete says.

"Ah, he's alright," Mark counters.

"I think he's kind of a loser now, without his other half," Pete giggles, smugly.

"Who are you, Farah Martinez?" Mark jokes.

"I saw him talking with Tony," I offer to the conversation.

"He's a weirdo, too, but I had to invite him because he lives like five houses down," Pete says.

"When do you leave for college?" I ask Mark.

"Friday," he says. "What about you?"

"Wednesday."

"Why so early?"

"I haven't registered for classes yet." After another auditory gap, Pete stands up.

"Alright, boys, I'll see you in the morning," he says, walking towards the stairs.

"Not crashing with us?" Mark asks.

"Nah, I want to sleep in my bed one last night." As Pete disappears, I think about our sleepovers in his living room. Ms. Waters usually put sheets over each of the couches and inflated a blow-up mattress. Tonight, Mark and I just lie on the bare cushions in the clothes we partied in. We're too tired to care, but I have to admit I was expecting Ms. Waters to at least offer sheets and pillows. I guess she's tired herself, or figures Pete's old enough to get them for us.

When we wake up, I see that I have three texts from Jessica, dispersed throughout the morning hours.

What time can you pick me up today?

Are you even back at your house yet?

Let me know when you wake up.

I look at the time and see it's close to 1PM. I do some rough travel math in my head and text her that I'll be at her house in an hour. I sit up and look over to an empty couch beside me. I head to Pete's kitchen and find Mark buttering toast, with bedhead to the ceiling.

"I just beat you by like five minutes," he croaks, reassuring me I didn't sleep in too much compared to him.

"Good morning, Alex," Ms. Waters greets me from the kitchen table.

"Hey," I say, already feeling one foot out the door. Joe peeks at me from under his newspaper, and then disappears again.

"Come make yourself some breakfast," Ms. Waters says.

"Actually, I have to bounce," I tell her.

"Already?"

"Yeah, I forgot I have to do something." I know I'm coming

off like I'm hiding something, but I don't really want her to think I'm having relationship problems.

"Good luck, man," offers Mark, fully aware of my concern. I give him a nod as I rub flakes out of my eyes.

"Where's Pete?" I ask the room.

"Oh, he's still sleeping," Ms. Waters tells me. "I don't know if he'll get any sleep on the flight, so I'm letting him rest."

"Oh," I contemplate. "Can you let him know that I'll be back before you leave for the airport?"

"Of course. You just need to be here by five-thirty, if you want to see him off."

"I'll be here before that," I say. I feel bad not spending the afternoon with Pete, but my gut tells me this "talk" will be worse if I push it off.

I down a cantaloupe wedge before realizing I have no way back home. I look at Ms. Waters and Joe relaxing in their pajamas; I figure I can't impose on them today. I say goodbye, and break into a mild jog the instant my foot hits the pavement. Since MAP all attended the same elementary school, it's not too much of a stretch, but I still need to hustle if I want to shower and change.

As I approach my house, I only see the "third" car in the driveway. I expected Mom or Dad to be home so I could borrow their car, instead of negotiating with Gerry. I run upstairs to find the bathroom door locked and hear the shower running. I'm desperate, so I knock.

"Gerry?" I call.

"No, it's me," Diana answers.

"Are you almost done?"

"I just got in." Shit. I may have pressed more with Gerry, but I don't with Diana because we're close and she's the youngest. I have no choice, but to deal with Gerry. I pop into our room to find him reading *Rolling Stone* on his bed.

"Hey, I need the car," I blurt out.

"For how long?" he asks without making eye contact.

"Kind of the whole day. I'm meeting up with Jessica and then saying goodbye to Pete before he leaves for South America." Part of me feels that I don't owe him an explanation, but I know it may help.

"I'm working tonight," he says, unsympathetically.

"Shit," I say to myself, but loud enough for him to hear. "Where are Mom and Dad?"

"At Abigail's."

"They took both cars?"

"Yeah."

"What for?"

"I don't know." I realize my only option. I need to ask him. "Can you drop me off at Jessica's?"

"Uh, when?"

"Right now."

"No," he says matter-of-factly. "Maybe if you had given me more notice."

"Please, Gerry. I need to see her now, but can't explain," I beg him. He finally looks at me, semi-empathetically, and contemplates.

"Fine," he says, sitting up. As we walk to the car, I can tell he's not moving as urgently as my body language is dictating us to go, but we both know I don't have a leg to stand on. As we drive, I look at myself in the side-view mirror, lick my fingertips and try to pat down my own bedhead.

"Thank you," I tell him, as I close the door in front of Jessica's house. "I'll find my own way home."

"I don't care; I'll be at work," he says, and drives off. As I walk to Jessica's door, I tuck my nose underneath my shirt to see how bad my body odor is. It's surprisingly passable, considering my lack of shower and the fact that alcohol is still sweating out of my pores. She opens up the door with a half-happy, half-solemn smile, that I'm unable to interpret. I go to kiss her and she turns her head so that my lips land on her right cheek. I take this as a bad sign.

"I just had some of my Mom's scallion-cream cheese bagel," she explains.

"Aren't we getting lunch?" I ask.

"Yeah, but I was getting hungry."

"I don't mind tasting scallions," I say, leaning in for another try. Just as I do, I see Mrs. Connors walking towards us.

"Hey, Alex," she greets me with a big hug. "Where are you two going for lunch?"

"I don't know," I say. "Where are we going?" I ask Jessica.

"Oh, just the diner," Jessica says, coolly.

"Okay, I'll get out of your hair," Mrs. Connors says, getting the hint. Jessica and I walk down her street to the diner on the corner. It's only a five-minute walk, but the hush between us makes it feel like forever. She does let me hold her hand, and her grip doesn't feel any different, but I'm not sure if you can tell what's on someone's mind from their hand-holding form. The maître d' tells us to sit anywhere, and Jessica chooses a table in the corner, apart from other people. We both thumb through the menus, and eventually Jessica puts down hers and exhales.

"So, how was the rest of the night?" she asks me with a smile. I've never felt so relieved by the switch to small talk and suspect the silence was just due to her desire to be alone with me.

"Ah, not much happened. We just drank a bit more and then crashed."

"The last hurrah."

"Yeah, but MAP is going to see Pete off tonight." Jessica raises an eyebrow when she hears "MAP," but then nods when she remembers our acronym. We talk about Abigail and Suzie, but when our food comes, the conversation hits a lull. I figure it could be because we're eating, but Jessica is really just picking. "What's wrong?" Jessica raises her eyes to mine and draws in a deep breath.

"Let's talk after lunch."

"Okay," I reluctantly agree, even though the wondering is torture. We pay the check and start walking towards her house, but divert to Weatherton Elementary School. Jessica leads us to the playground and we sit on the swings.

"Now?" I finally ask. She takes a deep breath again.

"I'm going to visit camp friends tomorrow."

"Okay," I say slowly, guiding her to the next sentence.

"It just came together. My friend from Clarksdale invited me."

"Oh, that's far."

"Yeah, we're all spending the night."

"So you're coming back…"

"Sometime Tuesday." I scan what's left of the summer in my head. This means I have the rest of this afternoon and Tuesday night with her, before I head off.

"Well, I'll see you when you get back," I say.

"I don't think it's going to work out." Part of my brain tells me to ask her to clarify what she means, but the tone of the day has overridden any possible denial in my head.

"Why not?"

"You're going to be too far away, and we're both going to be busy."

"But earlier in the summer, we said we were going to try."

"I know."

"What changed?"

"I think it just hit me now." I don't know how to respond to this, so I go to give her a kiss, but she doesn't kiss me back.

"It's really that bad?" I say, admittedly surprised. I guess I make her feel guilty because she gets up and walks up the playground staircase to the platform at the top of the slide. "I'm sorry," I say. I can only see her through the slits of the plastic walls, but she's sitting down. As I ascend the staircase, my eyes lock with her sodden eyes, but neither of us looks away. I lower myself next to her, but have to put one leg down the slide in order to fit. She lets me put my arm around her. "Why did you come up here?" I ask.

"I don't want anyone to see me crying," she says.

"We've had such a good summer. It doesn't have to end. What makes you think it will go bad?"

"Because I feel awful now, and you're still here. If I missed you any more than this, it would destroy me." This is quite the mental gymnastics. I'm not sure how to comprehend this thought and certainly don't know how to refute it.

"What did you like most about the summer?" Changing the subject may not help, but it's the only move I got. She doesn't take the bait.

"I loved this summer, but I just know things will change. Can't you see it falling apart, when we're not together?"

"I don't know." I honestly hadn't given it much thought. I never had a girlfriend before, so I had no reason to consider distance being a problem. "We can talk every night on the phone."

"It won't be the same." I'm not sure if I'm just out of things to say, or if I'm finally picturing what the fall might look like, but I stay quiet after that. She does, too.

We sit for a while and watch a custodian mow the grass. He doesn't see us and we don't mind the distraction. I graze her eyebrow with my nose and she meets my eyes. We make out for a while, and it feels so passionate that I can't believe she means what she says.

I glance down at my watch and realize MAP is due at Pete's pretty soon to see him off. But with every one of her breaths, I feel Jessica's body and spirit anchoring me to stay. I have to make a tough call, but figure MAP will be fine with it. Plus, if I mention it to Jessica, she may get up and encourage me to see Pete, just to be nice. I just can't let her go yet. I text MAP that I won't be able to make it and Jessica doesn't ask who I'm writing to. We make out some more, but this time I can feel the melancholy in her breathing, and she starts to cry again. We both resolve on dozing off for a bit, and I'm awakened by orange rays illuminating my eyelids, as the sunset pokes through the tower's plastic barrier. I rub Jessica's arm until she wakes up.

"Hey, we were sleeping," I whisper to her. Jessica's eyes open wide as she takes in the time of day and remembers our location.

"I better get back," she concludes. "I need to pack for tomorrow." Part of me regrets waking her up, but I know it's inevitable. I honestly have to pack myself. We both stand up and I point to the slide. She chuckles and shrugs. "You first," she offers. I crouch down and launch myself into the darkness, but am jolted to a halt when my sneaker gets stuck in the turn. As I readjust, the rest of the ride is smooth, but slow. I wait for Jessica at the bottom, but don't hear her coming. I peek my head in, and then immediately remove it when I hear her whooshing towards me. Jessica zips out of the dark with a pink luminescence painting her beautiful smile. We walk back to her house holding hands, but I desperately want more time. There's more that I want to say, but I don't have the words right now.

"Promise me I can see you on Tuesday when you get back, and you won't make any decision until then," I beg her.

"Okay," she says. I can't tell if she actually wants to see me, too, but at least I still have a girlfriend for now. "I'll call you when we're on our way home." When we arrive at her driveway, her dad is doing yardwork, and I instantly know that I won't be getting a goodnight kiss. We hug and I intentionally breathe hard on the arch of her ear. It tickles her, and she giggles and gives me a look before heading inside. I wave to Mr. Connors, who waves back. I walk home, listening to the crickets and tracing my thoughts. I don't know how I really feel about splitting with her, because I'm also excited to go away. I figure I'll have tomorrow to sort it out in my head, and then one more night with her to find out where we are. Maybe she'll change her mind; maybe we can get back together during my breaks. When I get back home, I reluctantly start packing because there's nothing else to do, and text Jessica to have fun with her camp friends. She texts back a "Thanks," and I decide to give her some space. Maybe it'll make her miss me. Gerry gives me a perturbed look when he gets home. He knows that the room will be his in a few days, but still can't offer any semblance of kindness.

Dad wakes me up pretty early to start packing the car, and by midday it's half-full. We pick up a small handyman kit of screwdrivers and Allen keys at the hardware store, and then get lunch at Wendy's. We stop by Grandma's, who's happy to see us, but the conversation mostly revolves around Suzie. Dad took Grandma out of her home to see "the baby" when Abigail first came home from the hospital, but she hasn't brought Suzie to the home yet. I figure it's because Abigail is paranoid about old-people germs, and Dad says Mom was the same way with her.

"Next time you see Alex, he'll be a college man," Dad says, patting me on the back.

"That's so wonderful," Grandma says, with a heart-warming smile. I have to admit, it does light me up inside. "Maybe you'll meet your sweetheart," she adds, wagging her figure.

"Maybe," I say. I haven't told her about Jessica, and yesterday points to that being a good idea. Thinking about another "sweetheart" brings me down a bit. I still consider Jessica and myself as together, at least until I see her tomorrow night. I hope she feels the same way. I wonder if she's thinking about me, too, but know she's probably just catching up with her camp friends. I don't recall her saying if there'd be guys there; I just assumed it was all other girls. I hope she didn't say she wanted to break up yesterday just so she could hook up with someone else. That thought makes my chest drop to my toes. She was so upset yesterday, she probably wouldn't. But, would she? Maybe we'll decide to stay together after we've had the day to think about it.

Dad and I say goodbye to Grandma and meet everyone at Abigail's house for dinner. I get to hold Suzie, although Mom still keeps a watchful eye over me even though there are photos of me holding Diana when I was two.

"Don't grow too much before I see you again," I whisper to Suzie, as she sleeps. I know she'll be remarkedly different, so I try and memorize her face as it is now. As soon as I think about missing Suzie, Jessica pops into my head. I don't get much of a reprieve from her. Maybe that means something.

It sounds bad to say, but I'm going to miss Jessica and MAP more than my family. And of them, mostly Suzie, Diana and Abigail. No offense to Stephen, but I just don't know him too well yet. It'll be nice to be free from Mom and Dad's rules for the first time in my life. And I'm certain Gerry is counting the hours until he doesn't have to share the room or car. No one said anything about it being my last night with them all tonight, but I guess Suzie will be the center-of-attention for some time going forward, and I don't recall Gerry getting a big send-off either. I just thought there'd be something said.

When we go to sleep, Gerry is unusually friendly, giving me advice about college.

"You know the 'beer-before-liquor' rule, right?" he asks me, chuckling. I can't determine if he's trying to take me down a peg again or just wants to chat.

"Yeah," I say.

"Stick to it. You'll thank me."

"Okay."

"And watch out for girls wearing girdles," he adds. "You won't know what they really look like until it's too late." I wonder if that means he can tell I'm single again, but he's probably just trying to make himself laugh.

"Okay." I think he gets the point, because the advice ends after that.

Mark texts me the next morning about getting Vincino's with Emily and him. The car keys aren't on the hook, so I fish them out of Gerry's jeans, being sure not to wake him up. I don't care if he wants the car today because I know he isn't working and it's my last day home. In the parking lot, I break and decide to text Jessica.

Hope you had fun. What time are you back? When can I stop by?

I figure she's left by now or is leaving soon, so I shouldn't be coming off as the jealous boyfriend. Mark, Emily and I each grab a couple of slices and talk about Pete's party and college.

"What was it like with Pete at the airport?" I ask Mark.

"Ah, you didn't miss much. I just helped him with some luggage. His gate was switched at the last second, so Joanne and him were just focused on that." I'm sure there was more to it, but Mark knows how to make you feel like you didn't miss out.

"Who's your roommate?" Emily asks me.

"Some guy, Matthew Caron," I say.

"Have you spoken with him?"

"No, are you supposed to?" I ask them both.

"Yeah," they answer in unison. I feel dumb for not knowing that, but I guess Matt Caron didn't know either.

"It's not a big deal. I just called mine as an initial introduction," Emily says.

"Are you guys staying together during college?" I ask them both. Mark's taken aback, but Emily answers like it's nothing.

"We're breaking up now, but leaving it open ended. Touching base again on the breaks." Mark nods along as if he contributed to the conversation.

I give them each a big hug in the parking lot, and Mark and I agree to call each other sometime in our first week. I drive home to find my room empty. I check my phone and see nothing, and send another text.

Hey, I'm back from lunch with Mark and Emily. I can come by anytime.

I lay down on my bed and wait, but then decide to take Mark and Emily's advice. I pop up and ravage through my backpack for the letter with my room info. I find it and see Matthew Caron's phone number. He picks up surprisingly quick.

"Hello?" he says.

"Oh, is this Matthew?" I ask.

"Yeah, who's this?"

"It's Alex."

"How the fuck did you get my number?"

"On the roommate letter from Belston," I answer, now panicked.

"Oh! You're my roommate, Alex," he laughs, in a calmer tone.

"Yeah, Alex Ryback." I guess I should have led with my full name.

"I thought you were Alex Trebson. I fucking hate that guy."

"Well, I guess all Alexes aren't built equally," I respond, commenting on a person I know nothing about.

"Yeah. I'm Matt. So, how are you doing?" he asks, now in a genuine, happy voice.

"Good. Excited for college."

"Me, too. Where are you from?"

"Domport."

"Where's that?"

"It's near Briarwood."

"Oh that's like the other side of the state."

"Yeah. When are you heading up?"

"Uh, Friday. How about you?"

"Tomorrow."

"Cool. So, what kind of person are you?" I'm confused by his question and at the same time am wondering the same about him.

"Uh, I'm pretty chill, I'd say."

"Do you party a lot?"

"An average amount." I leave it vague so as to not to worry him if he's a bookworm, or make him think I'm boring if he's a party animal.

"Alright, we're going to get along." I still don't know which he is.

"Do you want me to save you a certain side of the room?"

"Yeah, that would be great. Give me the left."

"The left from the doorway, or the left from looking at the door?"

"You know, when you walk in."

"No problem," I confirm. I think I know what he means. We chit chat for a bit longer before hanging up. I don't have much of a first impression of him, and I don't think I came off too great either. I check to see if I got any texts while we were talking, but there's none. I turn on Gerry's boombox to distract myself from my thoughts, and lay down. I close my eyes, replaying what Jessica last said, and imagine what she'll say tonight.

I wake up to the sound of pounding. I squint and see Gerry standing in the doorway with his fist resting on the knob, and then look out the window to see the sun sitting just above the horizon. Gerry bangs again. He sees my pupils, and knows he can deliver the message, whether or not I'm awake enough to receive it.

"Dinner's ready," he barks.

"What time is it?" I ask. He doesn't answer. Having fulfilled Mom's request, he flicks the light switch on and off a few times and walks down the hall. I look at my alarm clock and see that it's past 7:30. I had no intention of taking a nap, but must have been out for at least four hours. I scramble for my phone and panic, knowing Jessica's probably home and wondering where I am. I flip it open and see that there's no missed calls. I go to my texts and see one from Jessica.

I'm not coming home tonight. I'm so sorry. Call and tell me about college.

My insides turn to knots and sweat starts dripping from every pore in my body. Why isn't she coming home anymore? There can't be that much traffic. I dial her number, and clear my throat as it rings. She doesn't pick up and I rack my brain trying to think of what I can say in a voicemail that doesn't reveal my crazed state of confusion.

"We're waiting for you," Diana says to me, suddenly standing in the doorway. I instinctively close my phone, hoping that the voicemail didn't pick up her voice.

"Okay, I'm coming now," I tell Diana. The fact that Mom sent Diana, too means that she's getting annoyed with me. Diana nods and flicks on the light. I stand up and open my phone again to text Jessica.

Why not? I can come over as late as you want. Just let me know when you're back.

Closing my phone with self-denial, I enter the kitchen and feel Mom, Gerry and Diana staring daggers at me. As soon as I'm half in my seat, Gerry grabs his corncob, and starts munching down on it ferociously, with his gaze still locked on me. It's not just for making him wait to eat. It's also for taking the car, using his boombox and probably going to college tomorrow, too.

"Where's Dad?" Diana asks Mom.

"He said he had to stay a little late in order to take off tomorrow," Mom answers.

"So, who will be here?"

"Just Gerry and you."

"Can I have people over?"

"As long as it's okay with Gerry," Mom says. Gerry shrugs to show that he doesn't care. I eat slowly and remain quiet while a whirlpool of agitation and heartache flood my brain. I'm not sure if they can read my emotions or just see me as woozy from waking up. My pocket buzzes and I meet Mom's eyes.

"I have to go to the bathroom," I announce to the table.

"Already? Why didn't you go before?" Mom berates me, as I've already turned the corner. I'm praying for some good news, but don't get it when I read her text.

Everyone else is staying another night, so...

That's it? That's all I get? Now the whirlpool in my head is filling up with incredulity and anger. I have enough cool to know not to text back right away and return to the table.

"Did you wash your hands?" Mom asks me.

"Yeah," I answer, coldly. Gerry catches a scent of my mood, and puts out the bait.

"So, who told you you could listen to your shitty music on my stereo?" he asks, smarmily.

"NOT NOW! OKAY?" I snap at him. I glance at Mom and Diana who are visibly taken aback.

"Tomorrow's going to go great, honey," Mom says. "No need to be nervous, and no need to take it out on us." I turn back to Gerry.

"Sorry," I offer to Gerry with rage cutting through my fake-penance. Gerry just pucks his lips and nods in satisfaction. God, I hate him. When he came back last fall, I didn't say a word to him. I didn't ask him any questions about it, didn't ask how it happened and didn't say anything about losing my room. Dinner is pretty quiet after that, and after I clear my plate, I grab the car keys.

"Don't stay out too late," Mom says. "Tomorrow is an early morning." Gerry also overhears the metal jingle and walks towards me.

"Are you serious right now?" he asks, in macho disbelief.

"Fuck off," I whisper to him, and leave before I can even see his reaction.

I pull out of the driveway, but park halfway down the block. I call Mark and he tells me generic stuff like "We'll pick up where we left off," and "I'll meet tons of girls in college," but none of it really helps. I get some ice cream and eat it in the car. I spill some down my arm, and out of laziness, just wipe it up with my shirt. I watch some high school kids go into the shop. Their summer is still going, but mine is officially over. I finish my ice cream, take in one last breath of the muggy, cricket-chirping air, and head home.

Passage 3:

Fall Semester of College

Chapter 10: Very End of August

The drive is pretty smooth and I sleep some of the way. When we're about forty-five minutes from Belston, Mom and Dad launch into the speech again. I'd been expecting it, but thought they'd save it until right before they left. I guess they want to get it out of the way, or are worried they'll miss the opportunity to remind me. I nod along and say, "I know," while they run through their spiel: the loans, my aid, minimum 3.0 GPA, studying, not going to bed too late. I just hope I don't get phone calls every week.

When we get off the highway, I roll down the window to see the town, before arriving at the campus. At least, they can't take this from me. Everything feels new because I only saw Belston when I visited last winter. It was pretty then, with its snow-covered pines and Christmas lights still up, but now the sprawling oaks and maples are in full green, just like in the brochure. I get a whole new flavor, and the excitement totally dissipates the funk from Mom and Dad's warning. I think they can sense how excited I'm feeling, which makes them feel better. At the entrance, some guy with a Belston shirt is shepherding cars, and when we pull up to him, he asks us which dorm we're looking for. Dad lets out a long "Um," and when I say "Parker," Dad repeats my answer just as I'm finishing with the word. The docent explains the path to us and we park at a lot just across the way from my dorm. At the front desk, I meet a busty RA named Becky, who greets me with an impossibly-wide smile and gives me my room number, key and meal card. There's a handful of other kids moving in, but Becky tells me Friday is the big day when everyone comes. We walk up a few flights and I open my door with Dad and Mom standing on my heels. It's about the size of my room at home, just a little narrower and a little deeper. After many trips of carrying my stuff up, I see Dad look at his watch. I know he's thinking about leaving and making good time on the drive back, which is fine by me. We grab a late lunch at a diner in town, and when they drop me back off at Parker, Mom asks if I want them to come up.

"Naw, it's okay," I tell her. I know it's supposed to be an emotional moment for us all, but I'm really just itching to go back to my room. Except for a few months last year, it will be the first time in my life I won't have to share a living space with Gerry. I know that I'll be sharing it with Matt Caron, but I get the feeling he's a chill guy. Even if we don't get along, I'm sure he won't put me in a full nelson every chance he gets or embarrass me in front of girls.

"Okay," Mom says. I can tell she wants to give me the speech one last time, but is restraining herself. This puts it over the edge for me, and I want them to leave so badly. I give Mom a big hug, and Dad a firm handshake. With that, they're off and I head back to my room to unpack. At night, I make my way to the dorm's common area, and find some people playing Scrabble. Becky's ordered a pizza for us, and I join in the game, but the stilted, forced-socialization coaxes me to duck out early. It's my first night sleeping alone in a while, and I don't waste the opportunity. I jerk off without the fear of anyone walking in, but afterwards still have Jessica on my mind.

My alarm clock drumrolls against my nightstand, and I see it's 9AM. I think about hitting the snooze, but I'm meeting my advisor in an hour and honestly don't know how long it will take me to get to Renard Hall. I dig for my toiletries, towel and clothes, and make my way to the guys' bathroom.

While in the shower, I hear someone else come in and go into the shower stall next to mine. I guess it takes me by surprise because I'm not used to being in the bathroom at the same time as someone else, and have never been one of two people showering at the same time. I guess Gerry and I used to take baths together when we were real little. We also didn't mind if one of us took a leak while the other was in the shower. That all changed when Gerry once opened up the curtain and threw a pile of my clothes at me. I tried to land a swing at him before he ran out, but slipped and banged my elbow on the sink. He defended himself saying I could just dry them, and Mom and Dad just chalked it up to typical, brotherly shenanigans. They were more annoyed that I pulled down the shower curtain and made Gerry and me install a new one. After that, I always locked the door.

While I'm shampooing, I hear a faint sound. At first, I figure it's an old showerhead squeaking a bit, but then words accompany the melody. I realize that the guy in the shower next to me is singing. I can't make out the song, but what kind of person sings in a public bathroom? Does he know that I'm in here, too? Maybe he does know and is singing to me. Does he expect me to sing along? I figure the best plan of action is to finish up and get out of here as quickly as possible. I dry off and start changing into my clothes. Just as I finish tying my first shoe, I hear the other shower turn off, and the song rings clearer, ending in a flourish. I grab my towel, soap and shampoo and exit the stall, to find him between me and the door. We look at each other, each a bit surprised by the other's appearance. He's obviously confused to see someone walk out of a shower fully clothed, and I've never met someone for the first time when they're only wearing a towel and flip flops.

"Were you just in there?" he asks me.

"Yeah."

"You brought all your clothes in here?" I suddenly realize how foolish I look, with my hair still wet, and blotches of my shirt soaked with water.

"Yeah, I didn't know if we're allowed to be in the hallway without clothes." Saying it out loud, I realize how stupid this sounds. Maybe I thought it was more sensible to get dressed in a stall instead of in front of a roommate you only just met. Maybe not. I guess I'll ask Matt Caron when I meet him tomorrow, although asking "Can I change in front of you?" doesn't give off the best first impression. "Do you know what we're allowed to wear in the hallway?" I ask the guy in the towel.

"I think it's whatever you want."

"Okay. Good to know." I wonder if girls walk out of their bathroom wearing only a towel. I think about making a joke to him about this, but worry he may figure me for a creep, and also can already tell that he's gay. It's not nice to say, and it's not just from him singing in the shower, but his mannerisms give it away. I don't have an issue, I would just feel awkward having a conversation with anyone in a towel. I'm afraid that if I leave, he may be insulted, so I stay and continue the conversation. "What were you singing?" I ask.

"Oh, just a little night music," he tells me. I stare at him, wondering if gay guys only listen to certain songs during certain times of the day. But it's morning. I think he senses my confusion. "Sondheim," he adds, not really clarifying. "It's a song from the musical, *A Little Night Music*," he finally spells out, clueing me in.

"Oh!" I say. "Sounded good. My girlfr—ex-girlfriend was in *Grease* last year."

"That's a fun one. I'm Antione," he says, pointing out that we haven't made introductions yet.

"I'm Alex," I say, extending my hand for a customary, cordial handshake. He offers his, but was obviously not expecting the physical contact. Right then, another dude approaches us and asks if he can use either of the showers that we're blocking. Antione and I take this as a cue to finally leave the bathroom. "Nice meeting you," I tell him. "I have to go register for classes for now."

"Me, too. Are you on Facebook?" he asks. I'd heard about it from Gerry, but he never showed me his because apart from people from his high school class, he was mostly connected with college kids he only knew for a brief time.

"Not yet," I tell Antione.

"Do you want me to help you set it up?"

"Yeah, that would be great."

"Okay, I'll come by tonight. Help you start looking for a new girlfriend," he jokes.

"Definitely."

I make a couple of wrong turns along the way to Renard Hall, but make it into the building with five minutes to spare. I pull out a form and see my advisor's name is Makena Carter. I use my remaining time, and then some, finding her office. I knock on the open door, and a hyper-focused woman diverts her eyeline from her computer screen to me.

"Uh, I'm looking for Mrs. Carter?" I half-say and half-ask.

"If you mean Professor Carter, then you've found her," she responds.

"Yes, I'm Alex Ryback."

"Have a seat, Alex," she instructs, pointing to an open chair across from her. "Welcome to Belston. How do you like it so far?"

"It's great. Really beautiful campus."

"Isn't it?" She opens up a folder and her face instantly switches from small talk to no nonsense. "So, let's get down to business. It looks like you're not coming in with a declared major."

"No," I confirm. I have no idea what I want to do with my life yet, and am astounded by anyone my age who pretends that they do.

"Do you have any classes that you're interested in taking?" she continues. I pause.

"I thought that you're supposed to tell me that." Professor Carter's face goes mildly stunned for a second, then droops with disappointment, like she's all too used to students like me.

"It sounds like you're still determining your interests and should take some Gen Eds this semester."

"Yeah!" I confirm, letting her know I couldn't have said it better.

"Alright, stand next to me and let's look at some courses," she says, pointing at a manual on her desk. I pick it up and stand beside her, looking at her computer.

"Well, you know you have me for Freshman Literature, right?" she asks me.

"I do?" I ask back in legitimate uncertainty.

"Yes, all freshmen take Literature taught by their first-semester advisor. You can find a description of it under E-N-G one hundred in the English section." I nod and flip through the book to find the right page. Since she's my teacher, I don't know why she can't just tell me about the course, but I go along with her instructions, so as not to make a bad first impression. I find "ENG 100" and it reads pretty generic, "novels, plays and short stories that shaped the world," and so on.

"So, it's like Language Arts," I say.

"At Belston, we call it Freshman Literature," she says coolly, calling out my high school speak.

"Oh, okay."

"This is a one-fifteen-to-two-thirty, Tuesday-Thursday class, here in Renard Hall," she says, pausing for an audible confirmation. Although I just did the walk, I pull out my campus map to review its distance to my dorm.

"Okay," I say.

"Next, let's do your Freshman Seminar." I nod and smile, because I don't need to ask what this one is. I remember Abigail telling me about hers. She spoke about it as an easy, introductory class, where she played in a drum circle. "Now, you're registering pretty late compared to other freshmen. The only class that's available is an eight-to-eight-fifty-AM, Monday-Wednesday-Friday." She pauses again. I think she's looking for me to say that I'll be able to show up on time, that early in the day.

"Sign me up."

"Great," she says, perking up. "You'll have Sally. She's excellent." We get in the rhythm of it, and I sign up for the final three classes: Physical Geology, Introductory Theatre and Sociology of the United States. She seems glad to be done with me and I thank her. "Now be sure to pick up your books," she reminds me. She analyzes my face and adds, "The book store's in the student union." I smile and nod to thank her for her kindness.

I head straight there, and when the clerk rings me up, the total shoots my eyebrows to the ceiling. Mom and Dad did warn me about this, but I wasn't expecting it to be over seven-hundred bucks. They told me paying for books would be on me, but I didn't think much of it at the time. I hand the clerk my debit card and shake my head in disbelief. She entertains my expression and offers a cursory head bob in return. This will clean me out of most of my high school scholarship money. I guess that's the game, but I'm already thinking about calling up Carla to pick up some shifts, and classes haven't even started yet. I lug it all back to my dorm and think of calling someone else, but brush the thought aside. Admittedly, I'm proud that I made it through the morning without thinking of her. I consider texting Mark, but email Pete instead.

Hola Signor. How's it down there? Meet any mami chulas, yet? Just got to Belston yesterday. It's pretty cool. I'm even taking a theatre class! I'll have to ask you for acting tips. MAP forever!
—*Alex*

I watch Youtube videos for a few hours and check my email to see if Pete responded, but there's nothing. I hear a knock on my door and see Antione.

"Hey, want to get dinner?" I say "Sure," figuring it's better than eating alone. We head to the dining hall and each grab a wrap and a soda. "Did you make your schedule?" he asks, after a few bites.

"Yeah, there wasn't much left, but I signed up for five classes."

"Same. What's your major?" I grimace, realizing I'm going to be asked this question a lot.

"I'm just undeclared for now, so my advisor put me in a bunch of Gen Eds."

"Oh, okay. I'm a Theatre major." I feign surprise, but it honestly would have been my first guess if you asked me.

"I'm actually taking a Theatre class for a Gen Ed."

"Really? Which one?"

"Something intro?" I guess, not knowing the specific title.

"Introductory Theatre?"

"Yeah, that's it."

"What time?"

"Uh, eleven AM on..."

"Monday, Wednesday, Friday?" he asks, with increased excitement.

"Yes."

"Oh My God!"

"What?" I ask in panic. "Does it have a bad professor or something?"

"No," he laughs. "We're in the same class!"

"Oh." I guess that's good news, but I don't think it's that big of a deal. Would he be equally distraught if we were in different classes? I did compare which classes I was in with MAP every year, but we didn't get this overjoyed. Also, I've known them my whole life, and this guy I only just met.

"And don't worry, I've heard good things about Livingston."

"Who's that?"

"The professor."

"Right."

"Well," Antione contradicts himself, "I've heard he's fair. It's a lecture class, so people say you can't really tell if he likes you or not." I nod, half-understanding what a lecture is, but don't want to come off any more dumb to him. We talk a bit about high school and the past summer before heading back to our dorm. Antione sets me up with a Facebook account and adds himself as my first friend. "I was going to go work out at the gym," he adds. "Want to come?"

"Nah, maybe next time." When he goes back to his room, I see that he immediately accepts his own request he made from my account, and writes on my wall, "First post! Good chilling with you again." I search for some other people from high school to add as friends, but MAP isn't on there yet.

With nothing else to do, I decide to practice my path to class and take in the fireflies. They remind me of graduation night. Same thing, different place, halfway different feeling. My pocket buzzes and I scramble to find a text from Jessica. I flip my phone open as fast as possible, and am flooded with an array of emotions before the message displays. I'm happy that she texted me first, but also feel stupid for having pride in such a petty victory.

Hey, Alex. How's college?

My chest pounds. I was hoping for more. I wanted an *I miss you*, *I want you*, or *I need you*. It's better than nothing, but it comes across more friendly than anything else. My insides are twisted, but my gut tells me to hold the line. I text back, *It's good*, with no follow up question. She doesn't text back either. Belston is helping keep her out of mind so far; I only pray for more of its magic in the coming days. I look back at the fireflies and try to recontextualize them in my mind.

Chapter 11: Just Before Classes

BANG, BANG, BANG! My eyelids leap off my eyeballs, and my mind spins. I hear the banging again and I sit up in my bed, trying to determine where the sound is coming from. I then hear the sound of metal grinding against metal and realize someone is unlocking my door. My eyes shoot back at my alarm clock and see that it's a bit after eleven. My head turns back to the door which is now opened. My eyes meet a middle-aged woman sporting a fanny pack, and her eyes meet a half-naked, half-asleep freshman.

"Oh," she gurgles, before closing the door to go back into the hallway. I figure it must be Matt's mom. He did tell me he'd be arriving today; I just figured it would be in the afternoon. If he's here with all his stuff, I've got no right stopping him from entering his own room.

"No, it's okay," I shout to her. "Come on in."

"Are you sure?" she asks.

"Yeah." She walks in and nods with some embarrassment, as she places a bag on Matt's barren bed.

"Are you Matt's mom?" I ask.

"Yes, I'm Debbie. Nice to meet you." She still keeps her distance. A few seconds later, Matt and his dad walk in carrying a big trunk, with equal surprise. I decide I can't stay in bed while they unpack, so I get up and walk over to Matt.

"Hey, nice to meet you," I say, shaking his hand, wearing only underwear.

"Likewise," he says. "Sorry, I should have told you we were coming early."

"It's not that early," his dad chimes in.

"It's fine. I shouldn't have slept in." No one says anything for a few seconds, probably because I'm still just in my drawers. "I'm going to get out of your hair and take a shower."

"Okay," he says. The "Can I change in front of you?" conversation will have to wait until tomorrow or after his parents leave. In the shower, I remember what day it is and smile to myself. Afterwards, I return, now fully clothed, and check my emails while they finish setting Matt up. Still no word from Pete, but I do get a text from Mark, who remembers like he always does. He's the first one to say it today, but honestly, it's nice to be surrounded by people who are in the dark. I tell him thanks and that I already have a funny story.

I excuse myself when Mom and Dad call, who offer the obligatory recognition and sentimentalism. When I come back, Matt's parents are gone and he immediately addresses the elephant in the room.

"Dude! I can't believe you were talking to my mom in your underwear."

"I didn't know what to do. I'm sorry," I say humbly. The last thing I need is to piss off my roommate for the year, on the first day.

"No, it was hilarious!" he laughs, to my relief. "We were joking about it before they left."

"Really?"

"Yeah, my dad asked her if you had any morning wood."

"I didn't, I swear," I stammer, in defense.

"That's not what she said," he jokes. We talk a bit longer, getting to know each other, and I hear the greatest hits. He's a Psych major, he played baseball in high school and he loves horror movies. I share introductory facts about myself before he changes tact. "You said you party, right?" My brain tries to remember what I said on the phone, without leaving too much of a pause.

"Yeah," I reply, hoping that would suffice as an answer.

"That's great, man," he says relieved. "I was worried I'd be with someone who'd rat me out if I came back hammered."

"Of course not."

"Beautiful. Do you want to go to a party tonight?" I had no idea that parties started this early in the semester; I thought only freshmen were around.

"Sure," I say, trying to hide my excitement.

"Cool. My friend from high school, Hunter, heard about parties at this frat house." He tells me the name of the frat, but to me it just sounds like he's trying to recollect a math equation. "Anyway, he's a good dude, and knows how to get there."

"You're friends with him from high school?" I ask.

"Yeah, I've known him since like seventh grade."

"And you didn't want to try and room with him?" I honestly just mean this out of curiosity, but realize it might have come off as me not wanting to room with him.

"We kind of just got close in the past few months, so it's like, whatever. Maybe we can all dorm together in a suite next year."

"Maybe," I respond with a smile. I'm kind of astounded by how welcoming and inclusive he's being with me. If MAP was going to the same school as me, I feel I'd make certain I was rooming with one of them. And I think for the first couple of nights, we'd mainly just hang out with each other. Matt's acting like I'm already in his friend group, which is awesome.

He shows me his DVD collection and we watch *The Texas Chainsaw Massacre*. After the movie, Matt proposes getting food at the dining hall, before going to the party and calls Hunter. It's awesome that I'm part of his crew, but as we're walking in the hallway I think of Antione. My gut tells me that he'll have nothing in common with Matt, and I'm worried that Matt will be annoyed with me for inviting him. But I feel guilty because he was so nice to me yesterday.

"Hey, can we ask this guy, Antione?" I ask Matt.

"Sure," Matt says with no resistance. I knock on Antione's door and his bored face instantly perks up.

"Do you want to get food with us?" I ask him.

"Yes," he responds with no hesitation, as he quickly grabs his wallet and keys. I look past him and see someone else in the room playing Xbox.

"Do you want to ask your roommate to come, too?" I ask, inferring who it must be. Antione disappointingly exhales.

"Hey, Heinz," Antione says. The roommate doesn't respond; he just keeps on playing. "Hey, Heinz," Antione says a bit louder with a slightly different pronunciation of his name. Heinz pauses his game, and looks at us wide-eyed. "Do you want to join us for dinner?" Antione asks, motioning by rubbing his belly. Heinz just shakes his head and returns to the screen. Antione doesn't need to be told twice and leaves his room. "He's a foreign-exchange student," Antione explains, obviously frustrated with his living situation.

"Gotcha," I respond with sympathy. I guess I hit the roommate jackpot, and he got the dregs.

I introduce Matt and Antione, and we meet Hunter outside the dining hall. My first impression of him is that he's a slightly different version of Matt. Not like a twin brother, but in a mannerisms way. They both talk, act and carry themselves with near-identical cadences. They also both sport short bangs, flipped up with gel. I guess it's not that strange; it probably adds to their friendship. When I come to think of it, it's probably stranger that MAP is so different, yet still so close.

After we grab food and find a spare table, and I try to keep pace with Matt and Hunter, who are devouring their fully-loaded plates. After they're halfway through their mounds, they take a break to digest. I'm a bit behind, so I keep eating while they start talking. I pray the conversation is any topic except for one thing.

"There's a lot of hot girls in our dorm," Matt says. My prayers are rejected.

"Yeah, in mine, too," Hunter agrees.

"Got your eye on anyone?" Matt asks me. I know how to answer this, but also feel like I should change the subject so that Antione doesn't get put on the spot.

"Um, there are some prospects," I joke.

"So no dibs, yet?" Matt asks.

"All's fair in love and war." This generates a laugh between the four of us, and when I see Antione laughing, I don't feel as bad. Luckily, he doesn't get asked about girls, because Hunter and Matt recount the queen bee from their high school.

I start to get the hang of their competitive dynamic even though it's somewhat foreign to me. I was only competitive with MAP when it came to video games. Growing up, we were so different that no one ever felt jealous. Mark was always heads smarter than Pete and me, and Pete was the only artsy one, so it's not like we were going out for the same theatre role. I played soccer as a kid, but when I think of guys being competitive, I usually get a bad taste in my mouth because it reminds me of Gerry. But Matt and Hunter's dynamic is different. They compete with each other more as a form of camaraderie.

MAP also never talked about girls we liked. Even though they were my best friends, it felt like if any classmate knew about a crush you had, the whole school would soon find out. I distinctly remember that happening to Tony Spiranti in seventh grade, and it served as a cautionary tale because of how Stacy Silver shunned him for like three years. I guess there's a big difference between the high school cafeteria and the college dining hall, because Matt and Hunter are talking about girls like they don't care who overhears. It feels like medicine because the mere idea of meeting someone makes Jessica seem lightyears away, if only for a moment.

We clear our plates and walk back to our dorm. The conversation turns to high school parties and Matt proposes his plan for the night.

"We keep talking about it; how about we actually get going?"

"Let's do it!" Hunter bellows with excitement. Antione and I offer a collective shrug and nod to Matt and Hunter.

We all change our shirts to appear more dressy for some reason. I wasn't going to at first, but Antione points out that my t-shirt has a hole in it and finds a better one for me in my dresser. Matt leads us to an off-campus, frat house with Greek letters that look like three zeros. As we approach, I question whether or not we'll even be allowed in, but Matt assures us we will because it's a pre-rush party.

"What's that mean?" I ask Matt, not realizing how naïve I'm coming off.

"A rush party is when you're checking out a frat to see if you want to join. You don't have to; it's just to check it out. Pre-rush is basically the same thing, but not as official."

"So basically, it's just a party?" Antione asks.

"Pretty much," Hunter confirms, laughing. One of the brothers lets us in, and says, "Welcome to Theta Theta Theta. Keg's in the kitchen." We give him a nod, and Matt leads the way to the beer. There's a good amount of both guys and girls, and I try to carry myself like I'm not a freshman and it isn't my first college party. I nod along to the DJ who's blasting that song "Tipsy," obviously trying to set up a vibe. We each grab a cup and head to a crowded room where the beer pong is happening. There's a chalkboard on the wall with about ten teams in line to play. Matt and Hunter immediately sign up, and I look to Antione to see if he wants to partner up with me.

"How long are you thinking of staying?" he asks. I think he's already discovered this frat isn't his scene, and his eyeline and the puzzled look on his face also tells me that he's done the math in his head, and that we wouldn't end up playing for a while. I'd like to play, but don't really want to stand around in this room for two hours.

"Want to check out the DJ?" I suggest, thinking it may be the best option.

"Okay," he says, with a tone that conveys he's just about ready to leave. It's too loud to talk, so we just bounce our heads to the music, pretending the frat brother who proclaimed himself DJ has exemplary taste. After a few songs, he plays "Yeah," and one girl starts going crazy for it. We both chuckle, and watch her as she starts dancing by herself. I'm not sure if she's just drunk, confident or just really likes the song, but she doesn't mind the solitude in the slightest. Antione and I look at each other and telepathically agree that we should join her. We start dancing next to the girl, who may or may not be aware that we're even there. I can tell Antione is a much better dancer than me because he's doing very little, but making it seem effortless. Eventually, she moves close to me and rubs her butt in my crotch. I know this is called grinding, but I've never done it before. I kind of just go with it, and pray that she doesn't realize that I'm starting to get an erection. She then pulls Antione towards her, so that he and I are now sandwiching her. I look around and more people are dancing now, and the wannabe DJ is basking in the credit. After a few songs, his song selection sucks again, and the girl walks away into the kitchen, while Antione and I retreat back to the speaker.

Matt and Hunter come by, and I can tell from the looks on their faces that they've surrendered to the reality of the beer pong wait. We make a collective decision to head out, and since it was the only party we knew of, we just go back to our dorms. Matt and I chat a bit in the room, but he conks out fairly quickly. I figure the night was alright, but wonder about the girl we were dancing with. We didn't talk to her; we never got her name. At least, she kept my thoughts at bay until right now. I guess that makes it a good party. Also, not a bad day for an eighteenth birthday.

Chapter 12: Start of Classes

On Monday morning, I make sure to leave myself enough time to get to Renard Hall by 8AM; I don't want to be the guy that walks in late on the first day. I find the room of my Freshman Seminar and arrive with a good ten minutes to spare. There's a few other kids scattered around the classroom, and I realize I have to make an instantaneous decision of where to sit. I pick a seat in the middle so I'm not a teacher's pet nor a loafer. I spot the professor on her computer, and look at my schedule to reconfirm her name: Sarah Le. If it was high school, I'd call her Mrs. Le, but as Professor Carter implied to me during my class scheduling, I don't think that's how students address teachers here. I assume I'll call her "professor," even though it makes me feel like I'm in *Harry Potter*. I also heard a lot of college professors are also doctors in their field, which makes me feel like I'm in an episode of *Scrubs*. Would she be offended if she's a doctor, and I only call her "Professor?" I guess I can play it safe by calling all my professors, "Doctor." But what if a professor is only a *professor* professor, and you call them "Doctor," and a real *doctor* professor overhears you and gets offended because they had to do more to earn their doctor title, and this *professor* professor is getting called "Doctor" for free? By the time I'm done debating it in my head, the class is pretty much full. There's at least twenty-five kids, and not everyone appears to be too enthusiastic. I remember this was one of the only seminars open and wonder if I've been lumped with the freshman dregs. Doctor or Professor Le faces us and beams a warm smile in our direction. This puts me at ease and I perk up with pen in hand.

"Welcome to your Freshman Seminar," she greets us. "I'm Professor Le." That settles that worry. "Today, we'll be going over the semester and what to expect. If everyone can pass around the syllabus." As she hands out a pile of papers, two stragglers sneak in, but she offers a kind nod and gestures for them to sit down. "I'm not sure if everyone here knows what this class entails, but basically, there'll be readings, discussions, projects and presentations, to familiarize you with the type of work you'll find here at Belston." I jot some notes, trying to write without looking down. "Today, we'll be doing an elevator pitch, where you'll partner up, introduce yourself, and tell your partner three interesting facts about yourself." This seems easy enough, and I pair up with a guy named Paul who tells me he likes being at college, he likes cars, and he likes movies. These three insights into Paul strike me as a tad generic, but I figure this activity is more about confidence when Professor Le reminds us to speak clearly and make eye contact. I tell Paul that I just became an uncle, I work at a pet store, and that I want to try that Kan Jam game. This sparks a conversation about his pet iguana, to which I nod along. At the end of class, Professor Le assigns us a reading and grants me another gracious smile on my way out.

Next is Physical Geology with Amir Laghari in Tapper Hall. This class is huge with at least eighty students, and I apply my same mid-depth seating strategy. As soon as he starts speaking, I get a read that he's not looking at anyone's face directly, more just at the mass of bodies in the seats. This feeling goes both ways because he's the epitome of nondescript. He then puts the syllabus on the projector and reads it line by line, while each of us hold our own paper copies. The top of the page says "PhD" next to his name, and I make a mental note. Already I can tell he won't be trying to get to know all eighty of us, and probably will never learn my name. I figure as long as I pay attention, I can stay seated in the middle of the class, or maybe even migrate further back. After he mentions the assignment due Friday, he reminds us of our lab portion of the class. I don't remember Professor Carter telling me about a lab, but I guess it makes sense for a science class. I pull out my schedule and don't see anything other than my normal classes, before I catch it in the bottom, right-hand corner.

PHYSICAL GEOLOGY (GEO 205) LAB
FRIDAY, 5PM-8PM

I get a panicked jolt when I see the length of the class and the time it's at. No one gave me an option about when my lab was. The worst is that my last Friday class ends before noon, and now I'll have to wait around until five. I try to sort it out in my head and say it won't spoil the beginning of each weekend, but can't imagine how it won't.

I hop over to Witz Hall for Introductory Theatre and join Antione in the second row. This class is even bigger, with well over 100 kids, and I think I understand what "lecture" means now. I look down at my schedule for the professor's name, and realize Antione can probably answer my perennial question.

"Is it Professor Livingston or Doctor Livingston?" I ask him.

"Professor," Antione replies in a whisper. I catch his tone and mouth "Thank you." This leaves only two more classes where I'll have to uncover the professor vs. doctor puzzle. Professor Livingston gives an overview of the class, and then runs through the syllabus. He really emphasizes the readings and the weight that each test holds. Antione diligently takes in every word, and after class we get lunch at the dining hall. We both know that I'll be leaning on him a good bit, but neither of us seems to mind.

My alarm wakes me up at 7AM, and I sit up only to remember that I don't have class until 10:30 today. I look over at Matt who's sleeping like a log. He didn't seem to writhe one bit yesterday morning either. This is a welcome change from Gerry, who actually had the gall to yell at me if I didn't turn off my alarm quick enough, when he came back home from college. Luckily, it

113

didn't last too long because Mom spoke with him about getting a job and working morning hours, too. I lie down and try to fall back asleep, but feel too awake. I get up and shower, and figure I can change in the room because Matt's out cold. With plenty of time to kill, I do my Geology homework and send another email to Pete. I wonder if the first one got to him successfully, or if he hasn't gotten to an internet café yet. Matt gets up in the middle of my email writing and rambles into the bathroom. He returns a short bit later in just a towel, and I turn to my computer to give him privacy.

"Yo, did you already have a class today?" Matt asks me, still audibly groggy. I turn to answer him, assuming he's finished changing, but am visually attacked by the live image of Matt drying his nether regions with his towel. He actually started a conversation with me while he was completely naked. I can't see his junk because it's covered by his hand and oscillating towel, but I have a perfect view of his hips. That's not a part of a guy you see very often. My head shoots up to his eyeline, and he seems unfazed by his lack of attire.

"Uh, no," I tell him, the words crawling out of my mouth with awkwardness. "My first is at 10:30."

"Oh, me too," he says nonchalantly. I nod for what I hope is a polite amount of time, and whip back around to my computer.

I'm one of the first people to arrive in my Sociology class and make eye contact with the professor at the wipeboard.

"Good morning," she addresses me. I wasn't expecting this, but luckily I remember her name.

"Good morning, *Doctor* Prescott?"

"Yes," she confirms, alleviating my title uncertainty. I exhale and sit down in the first row. Might as well keep the good relationship going.

The class has about thirty kids in it, and we jump right into a discussion about the state of affairs in America. I contribute a short thought about globalization that I remember from high school, but when other kids are called on, some go on rants. A redhead girl and a guy with purple glasses get into a lively debate about housing policy, while the rest of us sit captive to their opinions. Dr. Prescott tries to temper them a bit, but I can tell she's enjoying it. I bet they're already her favorite students, at least the one who she agrees with. She assigns a reading, but I can tell you can gain more favor with her by participating in class. I don't think I could go toe to toe with Redhead or Purple Glasses, but I figure if I chime in now and then, I'll get by.

After lunch, I have Freshmen Literature with Professor Carter. I can tell she remembers me from orientation, but her face doesn't give away much else. Our first book is by Kurt Vonnegut, and Professor Carter teeter-totters between softness and sternness as the lesson goes on.

Wednesday and Thursday are pretty much repeats of Monday and Tuesday, and I get the feeling that it'll all be doable. There are more readings and essays than high school, but you do have shorter days.

Matt informs me that Science labs are indeed three hours sessions, but only worth one credit. This sours me for the start of the Geology lab on Friday night, but seeing twenty or so other kids reminds me that I'm not the only one in this time slot. I see a few of them finishing off sandwiches before class begins and I wonder if I should have done the same. A girl stands up from her chair, walks to the front and faces us.

"Hey guys, I'm Alex. I'm your TA." She keeps talking, but I half-tune her out, confused by what her position is and why she's teaching the class, instead of a real faculty member. I gather her full name is Alexandra, but goes by Alex. I hate when this happens because growing up, someone like Tony Spiranti would start calling me Alexandra for a week. I can tell she's an upperclassman, but I didn't know teaching assistants taught labs. I feel somewhat resistant to the idea, because she's just another student at Belston, but now also determining my grade. I mean, what if right after class, I see her at a party? I get paired up with some guy named Jason, and our first lab isn't even hands on. We just fill out a worksheet and reference some tables in a textbook. Jason definitely wants to work by himself and is pissed off that I'm slowing him down by asking questions. TA Alex lets us go fifteen minutes early, by which time I'm starving. I scarf down two slices of pizza from this place, Sansone's, and head back to my room to find Matt, Hunter and another dude with a Fohawk in my room. All of them appear a bit surprised to see me.

"Alex! Come in, come in. Close the door," Matt quietly orders me. I follow his instructions, and their sigh of relief is followed by them bringing their beer bottles back into view. They're playing Higher or Lower with an Iraqi-most-wanted deck of cards, and Hunter hands me a bottle of Bud Light to join in. At first, I do pretty well, but then I start purposely guessing wrong so I can catch up to them.

When they decide we've got a good buzz, we head out for "Tri-Theta," as I've learned it's called. If they'd ask me my opinion, I may have steered us in the direction of a little more variety, as the frat was kind of boring the first time. The beer pong wait is too long again, and I let them know I'm going to head out after forty-five minutes. I walk around a bit and see a crowd of kids heading towards another frat house. The crowd has a good mix of guys and girls, so I assume the party will be more evenly mixed, too. There's a five-dollar cover at the door, which I reluctantly pay. The music is too loud and the beer is shitty, but I drink as much of it as I can to get my money's worth. I totally forget about Antione, but I know he wouldn't want to go back to that frat house, and probably wouldn't like this one either. The guy-girl ratio is more lopsided that I originally estimated, so I end up moseying back to Parker.

By Wednesday of the next week, I'm overdue to do some laundry. I'm down to two clean pairs of underwear and don't want to have to be doing wash on Friday, or go commando this weekend. I lug my hamper down to the basement and find a spare washer. Mom taught me how to do laundry at home, but her washer's a bit fancier, and these seem to be industrial strength, probably so college students don't mess them up. It's easy enough to work, and I pull out my Vonnegut to read while I wait. After a few minutes, a girl with dark brown hair and butterscotch skin comes in wearing a purple tank top and plaid green pajama bottoms. I don't know much about fashion, but I assume the color clash means those are the only clean clothes she has. I sneak a look as she bends over and takes her laundry out of a washer and puts it in a spare dryer. She's very pretty and I'm surprised I haven't noticed her in the dorm before. Then she goes into another washer and transfers another pile into a second dryer. I think she can tell I'm glancing at her and gives me a look as she leaves. Or at least I think she does. But something about her bothers me. I distinctly remember our RA Becky telling us we could only use one machine at a time, so one person doesn't hog the whole room. I thought this made perfect sense in the realm of communal laundry fairness, but maybe it was only a suggestion and no one is really following the rule? I go back to my book and hear my load click done. I fish out half the pile of wet clothes and lumber over to the one dryer that the pajama girl isn't using. I just finish putting the rest of my wet clothes in, when I see the "Out of Order" sign on the glass. I initially feel frustrated by my luck, and then look over to the two dryers that the pajama girl is taking up. Did she not see that the only dryer left for me was out of order? Or did she not care? My belief in the one machine per person rule is reinvigorated, and I'm slightly incensed. I don't want to leave my clothes sitting wet, but see one of her dryers only has fifteen minutes left on it. I guess I'll just wait it out until she comes back, but I'm considering saying something to her.

While those fifteen minutes tick, I keep rereading the same page, distracted by my plan of what to say. Her first dryer clicks and she's still nowhere to be seen. I settle on bold action. I decide to consolidate her laundry into one dryer, and put my wet clothes in the other. Then I'll go back to my room and hope that I don't see her when my cycle is finished and I come back down. It will send a suggestive message, but at the same time, not be confrontational. I just have to move fast. I open up the dryer and grab a bunch of her clothes. I realize I should have opened the other dryer door first, and dropped a few items before transferring them to the dryer still going. I pick them up, finish her clothing transfer, throw my wet clothes in the one she should have left for me, start the cycle and scurry out of the laundry room as fast as I can. I make it to the staircase before I realize there's something pulling at my foot. I look down to find a red thong wrapped around my shoe. I don't think I've ever seen one in real life before. I know Mom and

Diana don't wear them, and I never got far enough with Jessica to find out if she had any. I stop imagining and panic as I realize that I made an incomplete transfer. I pick it up off the ground and weigh my options. If I return it, I run the risk of seeing her. If I don't, she may think I stole it, which I guess I technically am doing. I could return it later tonight and maybe she'd find it next time she does laundry? But then it would be out in the open for everyone to see. I wouldn't like that if it was my thong. Maybe I should just leave it on her doorknob, knock and run away? If only I knew her room. I decide returning it now is the best course of action because she wasn't there when her first machine was up, so she's probably still running late.

Boy, am I wrong. I arrive into the laundry room to catch her shocked, appalled and offended reaction to my transfer, only to have those same emotions amplified when she makes eye contact with the perpetrator, and sees the smoking gun dangling from his hand.

"You've got to be fucking kidding me," she spews at my slack-jawed face.

"I just had to…"

"Give me back my underwear!" she demands, as she grabs it from my hand. "Why is it all dusty?"

"It fell on the floor."

"You threw it on the floor?"

"No, it just happened."

"Bullshit. You stole my underwear, you fucking creep."

"There was a mishap."

"You're damn right there was. You went into my dryer and touched my fucking clothes." Her dryer? After hearing her lay claim to the machines, and one too many "fuck"'s hurled my way, my backbone has resolidified.

"You were hogging all the machines!"

"There's a spare one right there," she defends herself, pointing to the broken dryer.

"It's out of order."

"I didn't see that."

"That's bullshit," I shoot back at her. "You just didn't care. Same reason why you weren't back on time to take out your clothes."

"What, did you have to wait an extra thirty seconds?" she counters.

"It was like ten minutes," I lie.

"No it wasn't."

"When the time's up, the time's up." She pauses, still fuming, trying to form her next attack.

"You're not allowed to touch other people's clothes."

"You're not allowed to use more than one machine."

"You violated my property."

"Well, get used to it. Because it's going to keep happening." She stands stunned, taking in my last statement.

"I'm getting Becky," she threatens me.

"I dare you," I say, with the most bravado I've ever had in my life. Without a response, she strides out of the room. I know she meant it and where she's heading, so I catch up to her and keep pace.

"You following me?" she snaps at me.

"I'm going to the same place as you," I respond, a few steps behind her.

The pajama girl raps her knuckles on Becky's door, and bounces her knee in place, waiting to explode. Our RA opens up, looking like she just awoke from a nap.

"What's up guys?" she asks cautiously, reading our faces. The pajama girl launches into her tirade, and I watch Becky's face as she takes it all in. Pajama Girl is sure to pepper in why she *needed* to step out of the room during her cycle and how she always is considerate of other people when their dryer loads are finished. I patiently wait for her never-ending tale to end, so I can tell my side of the story.

"He's just inconsiderate," she finishes, with a big exhale. Becky looks at me, and then back at Pajama Girl before speaking. I realize I may need to interrupt to get a favorable verdict.

"So, you're saying that you were using two dryers, and he took out your clothes without your permission, when they were done drying?" Becky asks her.

"Exactly," Pajama Girl says.

"And you're saying he's inconsiderate?" Ooh, I'm getting a good feeling.

"Yes," she mumbles, defensively.

"If it were me, I would have taken your clothes out mid-cycle," Becky says, to a shocked Pajama Girl. "He let them finish. That's pretty nice." It's hard to contain the smug smile that wants to blossom across my face. I watch as Pajama Girl tries to change tact.

"I had my delicates on low heat, and he threw them in with my jeans that were on high heat. If my clothes are ruined now, he's going to have to pay for them." This is a curveball for me, because in my short laundry career, I've only ever put everything in together on the same setting.

"No, he won't," Becky defends me. "You should have just done two different cycles, one after the other."

"You know it's very violating for a man to touch a woman's underwear and bras." Now she's going the woman-to-woman route. I don't know if Becky will empathize, but I still feel her on my side. "He even took a pair of my underwear and was holding it for some reason."

"Did you?" Becky asks me.

"It was an accident," I explain. "I didn't know I had it with me, and I came back to return it." Becky processes this and turns to Pajama Girl.

"You have to be less precious about things like this. The laundry room is the wild west. If you leave your detergent out, someone else can use it." Pajama Girl does not like what she's hearing. Becky turns to me again. "In the future, can you be more aware of which stuff is yours, when you go back to your room?"

"Yes," I confirm, knowing that it's a small concession, and the victory is ultimately mine.

"And you need to respect the one machine rule. We have it for a reason," Becky scolds Pajama Girl.

"Okay," she reluctantly accepts, before about-facing and storming back to the laundry room with the same speed she came from it. By the time I look back to Becky, she's already closed her door, probably to return to her nap. I head back to the laundry room myself, where Pajama Girl grabs all her clothes as quickly as possible and heads out, while never making eye contact with me. I finish a Vonnegut chapter and my load, and the next day receive an email from Becky to the whole Parker dorm. It's a reminder that we can only use one laundry machine at a time.

I get through Friday night lab, and shove two more slices down the hole. Matt, Hunter and Fohawk are all waiting in my room. Is it bad that I don't remember Fohawk's name?

"Dude, you ready to rush?" Fohawk asks me.

"I know it and you know it," I answer instinctively, as he high-fives me. I don't really know it because I don't remember what rushing means, but halfway into our pregame, I deduce it means applying to a fraternity. It sounds like a world of difference from applying to anything else, because instead of filling out an application, you're really just going to a party and saying, "I want to join your frat."

"First up, Tri-Thet," Hunter announces to us.

"No objections, here," Matt laughs. I laugh too, but I'm pretty sick of that place already. My best memory there was really dancing with Antione and that random girl. We finish our drinks, and head out to Theta Theta Theta, where they're doing their best attempt to spruce up the atmosphere. The beer selection has been refined with some name brand choices, there's a brother regularly emptying the trash, instead of letting it fill up and blossom onto the floor, and Tri-Theta's sister sorority is in attendance to provide a female allure. The brothers let anyone who's rushing have first dibs on beer pong, and some of the sorority girls really are knockouts. I talk with a banging junior named Tina, and have to remind myself that she's only flirting with me for recruitment reasons. I tell her I'm undeclared and she tells me she was too, freshman year. In high school, the difference between a freshman and junior felt mammoth, but Tina makes me feel like we're one and the same, even though she's got me shaking in my boots.

"Alright, I have to continue to mingle," she tells me, with a mock-pout on her face. "But, promise me that you'll seriously consider pledging. We'll have a lot of fun."

"I promise," I flirt back without realizing. A brother takes down our names and emails, and we check out two more frats. Both are a jumble of Greek letters, but one is similar to Tri-Theta, and the other is a damp and dimly-lit dump. Matt, Hunter and Fohawk end up submitting their name to all three we check out, but I skip out on the last one.

We follow the exact same schedule on Saturday night and I get wooed by a Tina look-alike, but it might as well have been Tina. On Sunday, I see that Hunter put up a photo of the four of us on Facebook. Mark had tagged me in some photos of MAP, but this is the first one from college. I sort of feel bad that Antione set it up for me and there's no pictures of us, but he hasn't been coming out to the parties with the rest of us. Before resigning to my readings, I call Mark, who's coming up dry with Pete, as well. He says that he'll get the mailing address from Ms. Waters, and we'll have to do it the old fashioned way.

The week rolls by at a normal speed, somewhere between used to and getting used to the groove. Professor Le goes over Belston's zero tolerance policy on plagiarism and has us do some teambuilding exercises as she floats around and observes. We're tasked with moving a golf ball with a ring and some string, and it's immediately clear it's about communication and not having too many chefs in the kitchen. I catch Professor Le smirking as Paul gets too eager and forces his team to drop theirs. Seminar serves as a great lead into Geology and Theatre, which are more about taking notes. I fulfill my prediction by moving back a row in Geology each week and wonder how Antione can find Sophocles so fascinating. Sociology feels well within my grasp. One day I not only give my thoughts on food availability, but also pose a follow-up question to everyone else. Dr. Prescott runs with it and the discussion lasts until the end of class. She compliments me with a "great question" afterwards, probably because I was kind of doing her job for her. I hope I'm starting to impress Professor Carter because I really did read the book, which I can't always say for high school. I submit my paper on Thursday and pray she'll agree with my viewpoint. I get through Lab without pulling out my hair, and find Matt and Hunter in my room dressed in slacks and button-down shirts. I remember it's bid weekend, so I'll have to dress up, too, to make the best impression. It's clear that they're hoping to receive a bid from Theta Theta Theta, and I can't imagine why the three of us wouldn't get in. Matt offers to style my hair and I realize how important this is for him. I oblige, and have to admit that the finished product does make me look quite dapper. I thank him, and after some insistence, also use some of Hunter's cologne.

"Wait'll Tina sees me now!" I announce, which cracks Matt and Hunter up. I think of Antione's bum roommate and again am so grateful for how I've lucked out. Maybe Hunter and Matt will be my college mini-version of MAP. Even though they can't compete with thirteen years of friendship, we're connecting at a quick pace. I'm not sure if we'll have an acronym, but if we did, it would probably be HAM. If Fohawk joins this mix, it will be something else, but I'll have to learn his real name before I can come up with it.

We leave our room and walk with swagger towards our first stop. Unfortunately, we hit up the dark and damp frat first, but at least we're getting it out of the way. Fohawk meets us outside and offers each of us a way-too-hard high five. It's pretty crowded, and kind of funny to see people wearing formal attire while chugging shitty beer in a dilapidated shack. There's a handful of non-rushers who are just here for the free booze, so dressing dressy is a good strategy for standing out. One dude wearing a tie is playing beer pong, and has the terrible habit of unknowingly dipping it into the cups. Every time he does, someone points it out and he laughs at himself. Finally, he takes the soaked end, plops it in his mouth and starts sucking. This causes the entire room to start cracking up, and the dank hovel suddenly has more charm.

Then I see her and my grin melts away instantaneously. We lock eyes right as she enters the room. Her expression of curious interest swiftly turns into a death glare, and it only takes her a second to about-face. Now, I'm ready to bounce, but my crew is still schmoozing with the brothers. My heart sinks again when she returns with a reluctant friend. She won't make eye contact with me, but her face says that she's not going to leave the party just because I'm here, and that her mere presence will make me want to ditch first. Her put-upon friend is flashing brief glances at me, obviously aware of the laundry kerfuffle, and obviously uncomfortable that she's being made to stand next to Pajama

Girl for support. I try to use this same tactic back, but I know this girl is destined to win this game of hate chicken. Whenever I'm not looking in her direction, I feel the pressing pulse of her eyes on me. The tension gets to me quick.

"Yo Matt, I'll meet you at the next one," I half-shout in Matt's ear. Matt gives me an agreeing pound, while nodding his head. As I pass Pajama Girl, I look her dead in the eye to let her know that while we both know that she won, I don't care. I hear Hunter ask "Where's Alex going?" as I step onto the porch, but I'm sure Matt will fill him in. I try to manifest my mood to change, but when I'm not even two houses away, I hear her shouting.

"HEY, THONG MAN!" I instinctively jerk my head back and see her hanging off the porch railing. She sees that she has my attention and yells again. "Yeah, you! THONG MAN." I look at her one more time, and also scan to see if the passerby know that it's me she's talking to. I reckon they could take it to mean that girls give me their thongs, but I'm more worried people are thinking that I wear thongs. "Why'd you run away?" she taunts, as a follow-up. I turn around and increase my speed. I hear rushing footsteps coming towards me, and maintain my pace. "Thong Man!" Ignore her. "Hold on." Ignore her. "Alex!" I stop in my tracks. How does she know my name? Oh right, Hunter. I turn around and see she's caught up to me, attempting to cover up her panting. She half-smiles when she sees that I'm engaging her and no longer walking away. "Why'd you leave, Alex?" she asks with a coy smirk.

"Why'd you think?" I say. She laughs and coughs at the same time. "Can I go now?" I plead to her.

"If you want to, THONG MAN!" she replies, announcing her nickname for me to the street. A few nearby girls laugh, and I look at her, begging for mercy. She wants a reaction, and I figure I can give one to her and be on my way.

"Well, why are you following me, Color Clash?" I know my comeback isn't as good, and she lets me know it.

"Color Clash?"

"Yeah, you were wearing purple and plaid that day."

"And you remembered?" she darts back.

"Yeah, I think I would when you were yelling at me and reporting me." This shuts her up, but only for a few seconds.

"Well, my name is Lily."

"Well, nice to meet you, Lily. Goodnight, Lily," I say, turning around.

"Wait!" she stops me, grabbing my arm. "Where are you going?"

"To a frat at the corner of the next block." Why am I telling her this?

"Oh, Beta Phi Sigma?" she asks. That name rings a bell now.

"Yeah, I guess," I tell her. "What, do you think you're coming with me?" I ask sarcastically.

"Okay," she responds, cheerily, as if it's an invitation. Her friend is nowhere in sight, and I figure that moments like this are the reason why. I relent and we stroll to Beta whatever together. "You never apologized, you know."

"If I apologize, will you stop calling me 'Thong Man?'" I beg.

"That can be arranged, Thong Man."

"I'm sorry for touching your stuff."

"That's a pretty weak apology. I'm not sure it counts." I realize she may be like this for the rest of the night.

We arrive at Beta Phi Sigma, and I make all the necessary courtesies with the brothers to show them I'm interested in their frat, before Lily and I head over to the bar. The bartender is just one of the brothers, but he's really taking orders, which is pretty incredible when all you're expecting is stale foam.

"I'll have a Sprite with vodka," I ask him.

"Really?" Lily judges me. This girl doesn't let up one second.

"What's wrong with that?" I ask her.

"I mean, it's okay. Just a bit boring. Especially when they have a full bar."

"Alright, what should I get instead?" This gives her an impish grin.

"Scratch that. Make it two whiskey sours," she instructs the bartender. I've heard of it before, but this'll be a new drink for me. She observes me as I take my sip, and I nod to let her know I like it. Honestly, I would have nodded even if I didn't. She flashes joy across her face, proud of the choice she made for me. In that moment, I remember how pretty I thought she was when I first saw her in the laundry room, before our fight.

Matt, Hunter and Fohawk eventually show up, and start schmoozing with the brothers way more than the bare minimum that I put in. Lily must have texted her friend because she shows up, too, and is genuinely shocked that we're seemingly getting along now. Lily and I tell the group the story of our laundry argument, each interjecting with our perspective and version of events. This garners a big laugh from everyone, and the dread I felt just an hour ago is now just part of a funny memory. Man, if I could get over Gerry stuff this way, he might actually feel like a brother to me.

Matt and Hunter play a round of Flip Cup and Fohawk drunkenly hits on Lily's friend, allowing Lily and I to talk more. It's strange to delve into superficial niceties after seeing someone at their angriest, but I also just learned her name, so maybe we're destined to go out of order. Lily tells me about being an Architecture major and doing dance since she was six. Her Freshman Seminar sounds similar to mine, and I tell her about Abigail's wedding after she mentions her sister being engaged.

"Is that girl your roommate?" I ask, pointing at her friend, who's still entertaining Fohawk.

"No, she's in my Architecture class," Lily says. "I hate my roommate."

"You seem to have problems with a lot of people here," I tease. "Maybe it's not your roommate that's the problem."

"No, it definitely is."

"What's her name?" I ask.

"Martha," Lily groans.

"That's kind of an old fashioned name."

"Well maybe that's because she's forty-five."

"What?"

"Yup."

"How is that allowed?"

"Anyone of any age can go to college here. So, anyone of any age can dorm here."

"Fuck, what's that like?"

"It sucks. She gives me a curfew."

"No."

"Yeah, she complains that I wake her up if I come back after midnight." Damn, this makes even Antione's roommate the coolest guy in the world. I'd rather room with someone who ignores you than someone who's basically your college mom. "I actually had to have Becky talk to her. I feel weird being in my own room."

"Well, you can always chill in the laundry room like I do."

"Shut up!" she laughs, pushing me.

Matt, Hunter, Fohawk and Lily's friend watch us like we're in a fishbowl, half-hiding their raised eyebrows, while whispering asides. Lily blushes when she makes eye contact with her friend, and I do my best to distract her from being so self-aware. The night flies by when you're partying with good company instead of standing around, nodding and waiting for something to happen. Then I see Matt signal me and tap the imaginary watch on his wrist.

"We still have one stop to go, possibly the best stop," he announces to everyone.

"Let's roll out!" Fohawk says.

"Alright," I echo my boys. I look over to Lily, whose expression tells me she doesn't want to end our conversation just yet.

"Where are you guys heading?" she asks me.

"Uh, Theta Theta Theta," I recall, with less enthusiasm than I should have for my number one choice.

"Tri-Thet!" Hunter roars at a volume that startles Lily's friend.

"Do you want to come with?" I ask Lily. She looks back at her friend, who without uttering a single word conveys she's done for the night.

"Um, I should probably just head back," Lily whimpers with a flirty frown. "My den mother is probably waiting to scold me."

"Sure," I say insincerely. I'd really like to say "Screw your friend," or directly tell the friend to "Buzz off," but I know social etiquette dictates I can't.

"Well, it was nice talking to you," Lily says, in an overly cordial tone, that wildly deviates from the chill vibe she was putting out seconds earlier. "I have to say it was a better conversation than the first time we spoke. Maybe I'll see you—"

"Actually, let me walk you guys back," I say.

"Sure!"

"I guess so," her friend chimes in, less enthusiastically. I smile at my second chance, but then Matt pulls me to the side.

"Dude, I get where you're coming from, but it's bid weekend," he says to me. "Tri-Thet is our number one pick. You've got to impress the brothers."

"I know," I say, his rational argument conflicting with my sex drive. "We still have tomorrow night though. I promise to do extra impressing then."

"Alright man, your call," he says, understanding, yet somewhat disappointed. We say goodbye to the guys and I let the girls lead the way back to the dorms. As we walk, the friend is standing between Lily and me, and I'm kicking myself for not positioning our order better.

"Uh, let's go to your dorm first," Lily suggests to the friend.

"Why? Parker is closer," she says, willfully ignorant. I've never heard of girls cockblocking their friends, but now I'm experiencing it live in person.

"I just want to walk a bit more," Lily says, saving the situation.

"Fine." We drop the friend off at Syle Hall, and once she's inside, I consider taking Lily's hand for the walk back. It's a risk, but if she rejects, it'll only be awkward for a few minutes. I lightly tickle my fingers against her palm, to test the waters. She takes my grasp and our fingers interlace. When we're outside her room, the desire to linger is palpable to both of us.

"I guess this is goodnight," I say, after some silence lives too long.

"Okay, goodnight," she coos. She stays in place and doesn't turn towards her door, like her parting words imply she would.

And then, we're making out. I was definitely hoping for a regular kiss, but we really just launched right into it. It kind of feels like the natural thing for both of us. Since she's only the second girl I've kissed, I don't really know how long it's supposed to go on for, but we take a couple of breaks to catch our breath, open our eyes and stare at each other. Every time we start kissing again, I wonder if it's going to be the last, hope that it's not, but know one time it will have to be. The universe makes the decision for me when Lily's door swings and a middle-aged woman wearing a teal, old-lady rag, brushes past us, and steps on my toe.

"Excuse me! You're in my way!" she barks at me. As she passes, I stand astonished, and then look at Lily.

"That's her," Lily says plainly. When we see that she's entered the bathroom, we crack up laughing.

"And I thought your pajamas were bad," I add. This sends Lily into an overtired, giggling frenzy, which may be the most beautiful I've seen her yet. We make out one more time before saying goodnight. I walk back to my room walking on air, barely registering Martha grumbling as I pass her.

The next morning, Matt tells me he vouched for me at Tri-Theta and asks what happened after the girls and I left.

"If you're going to ditch me on bid weekend, I got to hear the details," he argues. It doesn't take much convincing for me to recount the evening. In fact, I'm pretty much bursting at the seams, wanting to tell someone. I could call MAP, or well Mark, but it feels more fun in person.

"We walked her friend back, then we walked back here, we held hands, and we made out a bit," I reminisce.

"Nice," he responds with a slight nod. I guess they all saw the writing on the wall, because he doesn't seem surprised. In high school, you were so invested in the gossip because you knew everyone for over ten years. Maybe in college there's less chatter because half your classmates stay strangers. "That's it?" he asks, after a few seconds.

"Uh, yeah."

"Alright, cool."

"I didn't ask for her phone number. Do you think I should have?" I ask him, still wanting to chitchat.

"I don't know. She lives in this building. You could always just go see her."

"Do you think I should?"

"Not today. You don't want to come off desperate."

I agree and try to not get ahead of myself, deciding to swing by her room tomorrow. I keep my phone call with Mark brief, and try not to sound too much like a babbling schoolgirl so Matt won't think I'm naïve.

I see Antione at brunch and feel bad for not really hanging out with him anymore. I rationalize it in my head by saying that it's bid weekend, and he's not rushing. Plus, he's sitting with some theatre kids, and I figure he's found his pack. While we're on the omelet line, I do tell him about Lily, and he provides the jovial interest, feedback and questions that I'm ultimately looking for.

"Give it a day, but if you like her, hang out with her more," he advises. "Wouldn't you kick yourself if she got with someone else because you didn't show interest?" I nod, realizing he makes perfect sense. I guess it's a delicate balance of how eager to be.

Hunter and Fohawk are soon over in ties and sport coats, and I suit up to match them. Hunter has some vodka and we each take three shots before nursing Matt's treasure chest of Bud Light. We're about forty minutes from heading out and repeating the previous night's itinerary when we hear a knock on the door. We all panic, get real quiet, turn down the music and hide the booze. I heard that Becky wasn't too strict about people drinking in their rooms, but had to bust one room for blasting music and shouting. Matt takes it upon himself to creak open the door, as Hunter, Fohawk and I stay stone silent, knowing that this could ruin our night. Matt peeks his head out, and returns with a half-relieved, half-annoyed expression.

"Alex, it's for you," he says, without revealing anything else. I get goosebumps, wondering why Becky would want to just talk to me.

As I slip outside my room, I breathe a sigh of alleviation when I see it's Lily.

"Hey, how's it going?" she asks.

"Good!" I say, catching a beer burp, looking to escape.

"You look like you're busy, so I'll come back another time," she says, reading that I'm already drunk.

"No, no, no, no, no, no, no, no," I plead, not wanting her to go. "What is it?"

"I was going to ask if you wanted to go to a party with me."

"At the frats? Yeah, that's where we're going."

"No, it's a house party."

"Oh."

"There's supposed to be this reggae band there, but no one really wants to go because it's in Bicksdale."

"Where's that?"

"It's the town over, but there's so many rush parties tonight that people don't want to make the trek."

"Oh." I see that she's resigned herself to going solo. I desperately don't want her to leave, and a creative idea pops in my head. "Hold on a second," I tell her and zip back into my room. Matt sees my face and knows that something's coming. "Is it alright if I chill with Lily for a bit?" I ask him.

"Uh, we're just about to leave," he says.

"Yeah, but I figure that since I'm not really rushing the first place, I can just meet up with you guys at the Beta house?"

"Why doesn't she just come with us?" Hunter asks.

"She wants to go to a thing," I say, leaving out the details.

"Okay, but just make sure to bounce when I text you," Matt says.

"Got it," I say.

"Tonight is it," he reminds me. "We get our bids tomorrow, so this is our last chance." I bob my head conciliatorily to demonstrate that I understand the stakes.

"Thanks guys," I say to the three of them, and sneak out to Lily. "Let's get our reggae on." I say to her.

"Really?" she says, with a bright smile.

"Totally. I'm just going to have to cut out a bit early," I tell her, pointing to my formal attire.

"Sure, just leave whenever you need to."

We have a good walk to the party, but the thick, night air, budding chrysanthemums, paling hydrangea and captivating company make it all feel effortless. We follow some hippyish upperclassmen down a cellar door to see the band still setting up to a somewhat sparse audience. We grab beers and Lily talks up the band. I nod along, searching for something to say other than "Remember when we made out? I can't wait to do that again," which is what I'm primarily thinking. The band starts playing, and as she grooves along to the trippy guitar, my eyes magnetically follow the outline of her swaying figure. I catch myself and look back at her face. She definitely wasn't lying about being a dancer and I worry because I haven't danced since prom. She slowly floats closer to the band, into what she's declaring to be the dance floor, and I know that I have to join her and try to hold my own. I reluctantly do, and she sets me at ease as she moves into my immediate space, and I into hers. Pretty soon my hands are around her waist, and she runs her hands up and down my arms. I let myself go to the ethereal vibe, look into her eyes, and it's magic. I don't know if it's the music or if I'm just totally lost in her, but either way, this may be the longest I've ever held eye contact with a woman. I feel my pocket buzz and know it's Matt telling me that time is up. Luckily, Lily doesn't notice and we maintain the energy between us. I already know that I won't be meeting up with them, and try to form the seeds of my apology to Matt. This may tank my bid, but maybe I can rerush next semester. I just can't lose this moment. I lean in to kiss her and it's like we're the only people there. We stroll back towards campus around 2AM, stopping at that pizza place, Sansone's, along the way. I check my phone and see that Matt only texted me once, probably assuming early on that I was bailing. The night ends with another make out session at her door, although this one is briefer. We're both pretty tired, and I'm also just plain dizzy from Lily.

Matt isn't as upset with me as I thought he'd be, but I think it's just because he's anxious to find out what bids he'll receive. I'm certain my chances are shot, and I tell him that maybe I can rerush in January. He replies with an apathetic "Maybe," showing some annoyance. We're both doing work at our desks, when he gets the calls, all between 3PM and 4PM. I can't help but eavesdrop. He easily gets into the damp frat, for which he shows little excitement, followed by the Beta whatever, for which he breathes a sigh of relief, signaling he'll be alright with it. Tri-Theta finally calls and Matt's tapping his foot about fifty times a second before he pumps his arm in the air, and accepts their bid on the spot. He seems to appreciate the hug I give him, so I'm pretty sure we're cool. Hunter calls to say he got into Tri-Theta as well, but all Fohawk got into was the damp frat. They're nice enough to invite me to their celebratory dinner at the dining hall, and I'm genuinely happy for them.

The next day I see Matt after classes, but he has to leave for the frat house by 5PM to start pledging. I've heard of the chores and hazing that can come with the process, but know that Matt can take it. Hell, I take him for the type that will enthusiastically carry on that tradition. He doesn't come back until after 10, and although he's hiding it, I know he's exhausted. Tuesday's the same and I take advantage of his absence by inviting Lily over. It's super convenient that the only place we can both sit is on my bed, and we cuddle while watching a rerun of *Friends*. I wonder if she's aware of my erection, but luckily she doesn't protest. On Wednesday night, Matt drops the bombshell that he'll be sleeping at the frat house for the rest of the semester. I'm initially shocked, but then settle into the thought of having the whole room to myself. That Thursday night does feel a little weird at first, but I tell myself to enjoy it because I'll be rooming with Gerry again when I go home for break. I guess I'm just a tad disappointed because Matt's been an awesome roommate so far. Just my luck that the roommate I like has pretty much moved out, and the one I hate is waiting for me at home. The one good thing is I'm able to jerk off without any apprehension.

My pocket buzzes and buzzes during Lab, and I panic that something's happened to Suzie. I tell Jason I need to use the bathroom and he just shrugs, signaling that he's going to continue without me. I pull out my phone in the hallway and see I have three texts from Lily.

I hate her.

Becky isn't around tonight. I don't know what to do.

I'm sorry. I forgot you had class. Can you call me when you're out?

I call her right then, with a pretty good guess of what's going on.

"Hey," Lily answers. "Are you out of class?"

"No, I just stepped out for a second."

"Okay. It can wait," she whimpers, disappointed.

"Well, I already stepped out and we're talking, so why don't you tell me about it now, and we'll talk about it more when I get back?" She doesn't need to hear the offer twice, and launches into it.

"I hate Martha!" I guessed right. "She's impossible. Anyone else would have exploded at her by this point; I think I've been pretty nice. All I was doing was listening to some bachata while writing a paper, and she told me to turn it down. I did, but then the next song was naturally louder on its own. She told me to turn it down again, but really nasty this time. I turned around and said, 'You always play your Joni Mitchell music and I don't complain.' Guess what she said back to me? You'll never guess what she said." I don't guess. I just stay silent, and she doesn't give me much time to respond anyway. "She said 'My music is relaxing. Yours is aggravating.' So I said, 'If you can play your music, I can play mine.' Then she threatened to report me to the Dean of Housing, and I just left the room. I mean, I can't even be in my own room. I can't pregame, I can't have friends come by, I can't watch TV when she's around. This is like the last straw." It sounds like Lily's done talking, but then she starts right back up. "And Becky just tries to smooth things over. She has no problem overseeing students younger than her, but Martha is so much older, and she doesn't know how to handle her. I'm sure Martha has threatened to report her to the Dean as well. It's just so frustrating. They figured someone had to room with this old woman, and I got stuck being that person." I wait for more, but nothing comes. Now she's done.

"That sucks," I say. It's the best I can come up with on the spot. "I'm almost done here. I'll call when I'm out and we'll meet at my room. Okay?"

"Okay."

I head back to the lab to find Jason already gone. TA Alex takes some mercy on me and comes over, probably because she's noticed Jason basically ignoring me as a partner, as I try to copy and comprehend what he's left on the table. She helps me orient the sample map, and I thank her as I'm the last person to leave and she's had to stay late on a Friday night. I had thought about grabbing a sandwich on the way back, but go straight back to the dorm because I'm already later than Lily expects. She's waiting outside my door, and the lack of loudness tells me that my room is no longer pregame central, as Matt, Hunter and Fohawk are likely pregaming at their frat houses. Can you call it pregaming if you're not going anywhere else different from where you started drinking? I guess they're just gaming.

Lily lays a soft kiss on my lips, and I fold her into a big, long embrace. I let her in my room and we cuddle on my bed. I wait for her to tell me more, but her eyes and breathing reveal that she's emotionally exhausted. We turn on the campus movie channel and watch *Mean Girls*. This seems to make her feel better because she laughs more and more as it goes on. *School of Rock* follows immediately after, and I try to hide my stomach's grumbling. At about 10:30PM, I notice that she's dozed off and wonder if I should turn down the TV. When I do, she tells me to keep it on and that she won't stay too much longer, although she just falls right back asleep. I'm able to free my arm without waking her when I have to go to the bathroom, and when I return I decide to turn off the light and let her sleep a little more. I'm able to guide her under the covers, where I join her. About an hour in, we're both getting hot and uncomfortable in our clothes, and we kind of naturally just slip them off. This helps us settle into each other more, and I chuckle to myself when I see she's wearing that red thong that was caught around my shoe. I know I'll offer to walk her back to her room when she wakes up and wants to leave, but she never does.

In the morning, one of our writhing bodies wakes up the other person, but I can't tell who woke up who. We're still spooning with our bare legs touching, and I just hope my morning wood wasn't the thing that ended her slumber. Lily sits up a bit, making sense of her surroundings, with slow, full-extension blinking. She looks over to see Matt's bed empty, and then over at my alarm clock to see it's almost 9AM.

"Today's Saturday?" she confirms with me. I just nod and she settles back into cuddling with me. We lie in silence, but neither of us is able to fall back asleep. Our minds are now fully aware that we spent the night together, and a bit of awkwardness and excitement are driving around in our heads. Well, at least excitement for me. "I should check my phone," she eventually says. She slips out of the covers and I get a brief glimpse of her legs and underwear before she quickly puts on her shorts.

After I zip up my own pants, I suggest we get breakfast, but it kind of reinforces the awkwardness by making us feel like a real couple. Luckily, we see Antione with some theatre friends, and we join their group. Antione's a real mensch because he doesn't give me a gossipy look or ask what happened.

On the way back to Parker, Lily has the idea of having dinner at this fancy restaurant, Bressel's, and I make the reservation. I recruit Antione to help me with my evening attire and spill my guts out to him about Lily. I try on a couple of outfits at his instruction and command, and he reaches and retracts two different ties to my neck like he's swimming laps, before throwing them both on my bed and just unbuttoning my collar.

"You're golden," he says. "Let me know how it goes." I thank him and have Heinz take a photo of us together, doctor and creation.

I knock on Lily's door and the vision of her fires right to my core. She's wearing a red and white sundress with her hair done up. I can tell she's wearing makeup because her face is gleaming and her lips are especially shiny. We both smile at each other.

"One second," she retreats, closing the door just as quickly as she opened it. As it's shutting, I catch a glimpse of Martha, whose mug tells me that the feud isn't over and I shouldn't ask about it.

Lily returns and somewhat slams the door, denying Martha any more of the night that's just meant for us. I ask Lily if we can make a pit stop and knock on Antione's door. Heinz takes two more photos: one of just us and one with Antione. Lily probably gathers that he completely cultivated my look, but I don't mind. Credit is given where credit is due.

Dinner goes perfectly, and without question Lily stays the night again. On Sunday, she initially feels strange using Matt's desk to do some homework, but I assure her that he's not coming back since he's taken all of his books and laptop to Tri-Theta. Admittedly, it feels like we're playing an unspoken game of chicken of who'll bring up whether or not we're having another sleepover. I guess it's because it's a weeknight and we both have class in the morning. When Lily yawns and says she's tired, I involuntarily say, "Go lie down, then," and that's all she needs. In the morning, she has to leave extra early to go back to her room to get changed and pick up books, but as the week winds on, more and more of her books, clothes and toiletries inhabit my abode. She still pops in her room once every other day or so, but I can tell there's no love lost between Martha and her.

Antione puts up both pictures of us on Facebook. He writes "The cutest pair!" in the comment section, which pretty much forces our hand into becoming an "official" couple. When we change our statuses to "In a relationship," Lily dances with glee, and I receive friend requests from some of her high school friends, whom I've never met.

It turns out fooling around progresses a lot quicker when the person's in your bed every night. I've been turning my back whenever she's changing, but when I accidentally catch a glimpse one morning, she just elicits a "we're-being-naughty" giggle. So that night, it only feels natural when she takes my hand and places it on her bare chest.

It doesn't take long for my hand to migrate south, but I almost dash my chances when I reposition myself and almost knock her off the bed. Her forehead hits the bedpost and she gives me a look that makes me think I've ruined the mood. I improvise by climbing off the bed so she has the whole space to herself. Standing up next to her, I make another attempt. She gets very quiet, so I stay quiet, too. She slowly lets out some subtle moans, and I feel relieved and excited that I'm making her feel good. Her auditory feedback doesn't deviate that much, so I don't alter my technique. I'm not sure how much time has passed, but my wrist starts to cramp up. I know I have to grin and bear it, but it really is getting sore. I wish I could use my other hand, but the logistics would be tricky because the other side of my bed is against the wall. I figure the only possible way would be for her to swivel to the other end so that her head is where her feet are. Her air increases in volume ever so slightly, and I know I'm stuck like this. When I'm practically wincing, she lets out a big exhale and pulls me in close for a big kiss. The whole next day my wrist clicks, and that night, I implement my swivel strategy so that both of my hands can share in carpal tunnel damage.

Lily surprises me one night when she kisses me on the lips, then my neck, then my chest, and further down the line. It's like nothing I've ever felt. I don't last very long, but she's not disappointed in the slightest; she actually seems proud. After I catch my breath while saying "Thank you" ten times in a row, I know it's my turn to pay her back. Thank God I remembered to brush my teeth tonight. I don't really know what I'm doing, but I employ the same strategy with my tongue that I use with my fingers, and it seems to do the trick. Actually, after a minute or two, her pipes tell me it's working better. Maybe my fingers need to take a few pointers from my tongue. Or maybe the tongue is just naturally a more sensual tool. I guess French kissing someone is really hot, but you'd never want them to put their fingers in your mouth. I start to feel a crick in my neck and wonder if that'll be clicking all day tomorrow, too. I remember learning some neck rolls in high school Gym; maybe next time, I'll do those beforehand. After one, melodic rise and fall, I swear I hear some words inside one of her gasps, but just keep going. She then grabs my hair, and I look up to see her whispering something again.

"What?" I ask, stopping only to get out that single word, before returning to the action.

"I love you!" she shouts while panting. I stop dead in my tracks and feel a rush of emotion that makes my heart pound a million miles a second. No girl has ever said this to me before, and I had no idea a string of words could swirl inside your chest so hard. My response comes without thought.

"I love you," I answer back in a muffled tone, my mouth suppressed by flesh. The emotion is so strong, I only then realize my head is still situated at her waistline.

"What?" she asks, desperately wanting to hear my response. I can't believe that the first time I told a girl "I love you," I said it into her vagina. I raise my head and we look each other in the eyes.

"I love you, too," I say, softly. She pulls the back of my neck down for a deep, passionate kiss, and we feel the pulse of everything we just said to each other. I'm also a bit surprised she wants to kiss me, knowing where my mouth was just five seconds prior. Then I remember where her mouth just was, and am mentally repulsed for a second, before quickly not caring.

With being around each other so much and feeling the way that we do, it's not much longer before we go all the way. We gradually get closer every day, and then one night, it just feels right. Afterwards, we remove ourselves from each other and fling the sheets off my bed to cool down. Our eyes scan my ceiling in a wide-eyed stare, as if it's full of constellations and shooting stars. Maybe we need some silence to process what we've just taken from each other, but that's actually a terrible way to put it. People always say "take." This felt divine. There's got to be a better phrase. We lie there with some space between us, and I study her body until the sweat and stickiness has receded. When it does, I retrieve the sheets and we fold back into each other's arms.

Passage 4:

Rest of the Fall

Chapter 13: Midsemester

An autumn chill saturates itself into one October weekend, ending the Indian summer in an abrupt halt. It's rainy, windy and cold, and we're suddenly in sweaters, corduroys and coats for the rest of the year. Classes continue pretty well. Having Lily around kind of motivates me because I feel like I can't slack off while she's working in the same room. Freshman Seminar is turning out to be a cakewalk; there's usually no homework and I'm able to half-wing most of my presentations. Freshman Literature and Sociology aren't bad either; I just don't do that good on the papers. I read the books and am alright at writing, but I think I'm getting B's because some of the other kids in class are crazy eloquent at making their points, and my papers pale in comparison. Professor Carter puts up an example of one student's paper and it's so verbose and highfalutin that it's like hieroglyphics to me. I try to write a little fancier, but mostly pick up the slack with class participation. Theatre is just five big tests, but they're really hard. It sucks that none of the material is popular stuff like *Sound of Music* or *Oklahoma*; it's all old, foreign plays and acting theory. Antione is godsend in this class. He reminds me of small details that sneak their way into trick questions. Geology is probably my toughest class. On test days,

I try not to get distracted as everyone else leaves before me. I have to stay the whole class length and usually still run out of time. The lab is hard, too, because I'm really doing it with no help. TA Alex knows Jason is blowing past me, but she doesn't say anything to him about being a better partner. I feel dumb for asking her so many questions and she doesn't really explain anything; she just reiterates.

Mark talks to Lily a couple times on the phone, and tells me he's planning on visiting Emily one weekend coming up. He never receives a letter back from Pete, but says Ms. Waters says Pete sends his best. I get the full update whenever I call home. Mom sounds like she's more involved with Suzie than she was during the pregnancy. Abigail doesn't plan on going back to work for the full six months, and Stephen's teaching again at his college, so I guess it makes sense for Mom to be over their house a lot. Dad has a handful of business trips, so Mom brings Suzie over to see Grandma now and then to give her some company. I have to really grill to find out Diana didn't make the JV volleyball team and is down about it. I call to console her, but she doesn't want to talk. I give unsolicited encouragement anyway, knowing that it will ultimately make her feel better. I tell her that Domport is in a really competitive volleyball division, and there's even some junior girls on the JV team, so there's less space for freshmen. She agrees, but tells me that some freshmen did get on, and thought she'd be one of them. Since Diana is such an overachiever, she's not used to rejection. I know it screws with your mind when you're not rewarded for what you've worked so hard on, but she'll find a way to overcome. I mean, I'm pretty used to missing the mark, and I usually find a way. My final attempt to cheer her up is to tell her about Lily. I wasn't planning on telling any family about her yet, but always knew Diana would be the first one to know. Diana perks up and we gab for a good half hour. Diana offers plenty of cute date ideas, and I swear her to secrecy until I'm ready to tell the rest of the lot. I'm glad I got her to feel better. Lily does tell some of her family about me, but I haven't spoken with anyone on the phone. She invites me to her sister's wedding in January, and I revel in her anticipation for a few seconds, before confirming, sending her over the moon.

Matt drops in now and then, and doesn't mind in the slightest that Lily's taken over his desk and closet space. I sometimes see him in the dining hall with his brothers or doing volunteer work for his frat's community service. Since the frats' pledge season started, most of their parties are Greek only. Lily and I stay in most nights, but whenever we get tired of TV and fooling around, we scavenge for a house party. As Halloween approaches, I take one of Diana's suggestions, and ask Lily if she wants to wear couple's costumes that correspond with each other. She jumps a foot in the air, shouting "YES!" and I take all the credit for the idea. Lily decides upon Tony and Maria from *West Side Story*, and when Antione hears this, he takes me to a shop in Bicksdale to get a 50's outfit. On Halloween, he invites us to a theatre party, where we're a big hit, to the point that his friends are singing songs from the movie, right in our faces.

Sometimes Lily and I go for walks. I would have never thought in a million years that I could get tired of fooling around, but there are times when we're both feeling stuffy and need to leave my room for a bit. We stroll around the campus and take in the charm of the new season, with its fiery sweetgums and scarlet sycamores. Lily usually wears her heavy, maroon Belston sweatshirt, and I wear my grandpa's Harrington jacket that Dad gave to me. Sometimes the wind howls so hard that Lily buries half her face into my chest while locks of her hair wildly whip me in the face. There's one particular canopy of oaks and maples just off the Green, and sometimes we lie beneath it just to watch the branches dance. We hear every scrape as the leaves rustle against the sidewalk. Often, I take the canopy cuddling as a cue to suggest a retreat back to my room, where we usually get at it pretty quickly. Weekend mornings are the best. Sometimes we'll just lie around for hours, fully awake, just communing with each other.

In early November, we get an email to register for classes for the Spring semester. It feels so far off, but people really seem to analyze the offerings and devise their next schedule as soon as it's announced. Lily makes a grid of her ideal semester, asks around about Architecture professors and ranks them based on her preference. The academic corner of my brain is solely focused on my current classes, and when I look at her chart, I feel far behind. Freshmen need to confer with their advisors before registering, although I don't want to come off like a blubbering idiot to Professor Carter again, I figure I'll lean on her.

I sit in the same place I was in late-August, which now feels like two years ago.

"Do you have your proposed schedule for me?" she asks quickly.

"Yes," I murmur, slowly handing it to her. I'm expecting some praise for actually having a plan this time, but her face gives nothing away as she scans my sheet and then her computer monitor.

"You can't take Sports Management because it requires a prerequisite class." I guess I didn't read that part of the coursebook. "Are you interested in taking some business classes?" I know I can't say that I don't know.

"Yes," I perform with certainty, while in reality not knowing anything about business other than it being Dad's college major.

"Alright, then let's put you into a business class you're able to take." I nod. "And you still haven't declared yet?" This is too big of a decision to fake.

"No, not yet."

"That's okay; you have another year," she unexpectedly comforts me. I feel like I'm in a good cop/bad cop interrogation scene, but she's both cops. "But, if that's the case, you should really just take more Gen Eds."

"Okay," I say, now just wanting the meeting to end. I end up taking Introduction to Business Management and Statistics II with Professor Le. Both are prerequisites to the interesting-sounding business classes, and Statistics will take care of my math Gen Ed requirement as well. There're slim pickings for my other Gen Eds, but I'm able to get into this political science class, United States Elections, with Dr. Prescott. I'm doing alright in her sociology class, so I figure I kind of know what I'm getting into. I knock out my history requirement with Early-European History with Neal Spetato, and my foreign language requirement with Spanish II with Jorge Molinero. I thank Professor Carter, and return to my room where Lily grudgingly gives me the kudos I don't deserve over an achievement this small.

I hand in my *Twelfth Night* paper, and immediately after class run back to Parker to finish packing, and get one last session in with Lily before the break. It's only five days, but it'll be the longest I'll have gone without seeing her since we got together. Antione knocks on my door to let me know that he'll be ready to leave in twenty minutes. I give Lily one last big kiss and she laughs, assuring me it'll go by quick. Antione and I aren't going to get in until mad late, but leaving on Tuesday allows us to miss the Wednesday-before mega-traffic. He puts on a showtunes mix, and is happily surprised when I actually know some of the songs. Over the course of hours it gets old, but my hand gets patted away when I reach for the radio dial.

He drops me off a bit before 2AM, and I thank him profusely because he's gone out of his way and still has forty minutes to drive. I creep up the stairs, so as not to wake anyone, and undergo an instantaneous mental shift the second my hand touches my doorknob. All it took was one minute, and I'm transported back to our old dynamic. I try to mask my frustration and say his name at a reasonable volume, so no one else will be bothered.

"Gerry," I call out, estimating it's loud enough for him to hear. "Gerry, I need to get in the room," I repeat, still maintaining my cool. I wait fifteen seconds, and then my patience is up. BANG! BANG! BANG! I repeat the knocking until I know he's gotten out of bed.

"What the fuck?!" he shouts.

"Open up!"

"Calm down, you fucking psycho," he says, as he unlocks the door without opening it. By the time I enter the room, he's already back in his bed, not even looking at me.

"What's going on?" Dad asks at the doorframe, with heavy bags under his eyes.

"He locked me out," I inform Dad.

"How was I supposed to know you were coming home in the middle of the night?" Gerry snaps back at me, now looking at me with exhaustion and vitriol.

"You knew I was coming back for Thanksgiving."

"Not at two in the fucking morning!"

"What does the time matter?"

147

"Guys," Dad says, trying to smooth things over with one, useless word.

"You're the asshole, waking everyone up," Gerry fires at me, ignoring Dad's attempt.

"I tried being quiet, but you wouldn't open the door!"

"Then, sleep on the couch!"

"I'm not doing that."

"Well a decent fucking person would, instead of waking the whole fucking house."

"CAN YOU GUYS SHUT UP?!" Diana shouts from across the hallway. This somehow deflates the tension ever so slightly, and Dad nods and goes back to his room as if he actually contributed to any type of resolution. My blood is boiling and all my fatigue has been robbed by the panting streaming through my nostrils and the adrenaline coursing through my veins. I know for a fact that Mom or Dad told him I was coming home tonight. I don't know if he forgot or locked me out on purpose, but either way, don't care. No one even said "Welcome home." I know they might say it in the morning, but the fact is, the first thing that happened was a fight. I know he's probably used to this being just his room again, but Mom and Dad should have told him that he can't lock the door whenever I'm coming home. I know seeing me now probably delivers an extra sting to him because it proves that I didn't mess up. Last year, he was back home way before Thanksgiving, but it's more than me surpassing that date. Seeing me now, means he'll have to endure a Thanksgiving where I actually might receive praise, attention and interest in my first semester. Well, if he can't handle that, fuck him. He's the one that screwed up, not me.

I get up around ten to find some pancake batter left near the stove and Mom at the kitchen table. She usually takes the day before Thanksgiving off to shop for last minute items, but the packed-to-the-brim fridge and her relaxed posture convey that we're totally prepped for the big day. I make some flapjacks and join her while she nurses her tea and reads the paper. She invites me to go over and see Suzie, to which I happily oblige. I'm sure I woke her up last night, but know she won't bring it up, preferring to act like it didn't happen. Their sore-subject-avoidance is convenient when you're the one that screwed up, but annoying when you feel you were wronged. She mentions Gerry working a double shift today because of early Black Friday sales, which mildly taints my self-righteousness in waking him. I ask if Diana will come with us to Abigail's, but Mom says waiting for her won't work with Suzie's nap schedule, whatever that means. Plus, she says Diana hasn't shown much interest in visiting lately. We pause for a minute or two, and I decide to bring up the thing about Diana that Mom's circumventing.

"So, is Diana feeling better now about the volleyball team?"

"I hope so," Mom replies, plainly. "She didn't really want to talk about it too much. I'm sure she'll make the team as a sophomore." After thirty seconds of silence, I gather the topic has concluded, and we leave for Abigail's.

Abigail gives me an enormous hug, and I still feel weird coming in contact with her stomach, having to remember that there's no baby in there to consider anymore. I hold Suzie for a bit before one of her naps, and afterwards try to make small talk with Stephen. Abigail fills me in on having taken extra time off beyond her maternity leave, but she may go back to work at some point. Mom makes a face that says "If I could retire, I would this instant and nanny for you," to which Abigail's face says "I know." Back home, Mom makes the cranberry sauce and sets the table for tomorrow. We usually get a pizza the night before turkey day, but I bounce for dinner with Mark.

When he opens the door, I put out my hand, but he doesn't take it.

"Dude," he says, defensively, as if the gesture's insulted him.

"What?" I ask. Mark spreads his arms and gives me a bear hug bigger than Abigail's. We've never been the hugging type, but I guess we are now.

"How's it been, man?" he asks.

"It's great. You?"

"College is so awesome." It's a unique state of mutual euphoria. It feels like we never missed each other, but are still happy to see one another after too long a separation.

"No Pete?"

"No, he's still down there, but apparently says 'Happy Thanksgiving' to us. He says that he probably won't even come home for Christmas."

"What?!"

"Yeah, maybe flights are too expensive or something."

"God, maybe we need to fly down to him."

"I know, right?"

While in mid-laugh, I walk down his basement steps and am a bit surprised by who's already in the room. I guess I should have expected Emily would be joining us tonight, and should be happy for Mark that they're able to maintain their arrangement. Maybe I assumed it would just be a him and me night, but also present are Marshall Kinley and Tony Spiranti. I assume Marshall is with us tonight because his main high school friend group is still fractured from the Madison debacle, but Tony was never really in our friend group. Maybe Mark invited him to be nice? I adjust easily enough and everyone shares their college stories over pizza. All of the tales pretty much revolve around parties, and have similar plotlines, just with different names and locations. I tell them about Lily, and Emily is especially happy that I've gotten over Jessica. She talks about wanting to get a fake ID, to which Marshall responds to by whipping out two twelve packs of Heineken.

"For when you can't get into your hometown bar yet," he says. Tony takes out some playing cards and we each get a turn explaining the drinking games we've learned. I get a text from Lily, who's having a similar evening, and we make a plan to talk Friday.

Mark drops me off the next morning and I find Diana watching the parade on TV, and Mom checking on the bird. Dad asks Gerry and me if we want to throw around the football in the backyard, something we haven't done for at least eight years. Gerry and I look at each other and decline Dad's request.

"C'mon, guys. I want to talk to you about something," he adds. This postscript stirs enough intrigue for us to comply without further protest. We lace up and watch Dad rifle through the garage, looking for the pigskin, that's probably deflated anyway. He must nick his hand on something in the search because we hear him shout "Fuck!" before licking his wound. Gerry raises his eyebrows because we rarely ever hear Dad curse. When it's discovered, we form a triangle and toss around the ball in silence for a good five minutes. I'm bubbling with anticipation, waiting for Dad to say what he wants to say. I figure it can't be about Gerry and me getting along; he gave up on that years ago. Maybe he was just bluffing about the talk portion. Gerry throws a rocket that I need to take to my chest, but I don't give him the satisfaction of reacting like it was an especially hard throw.

"After this, I want you guys to come with me to pick up Grandma," Dad says, out of nowhere. Gerry and I give him full attention, expecting there to be more. When there isn't, we both say, "Okay," and keep throwing. Then he starts up again with a melodic, "Um." We can see he's processing by a pair of ill-fated throws that land at Gerry's feet. I see Gerry considering holding the ball, but he just floats me a lob to let me know to relax the pace. "Grandma's getting older," Dad finally says. I half-chuckle because Grandma was always older to me, but I know what he's getting at. "Alex, you're at college, and Gerry, you're working a lot these days." He takes another pause. "I just want you to spend some time with her today." Gerry and I nod, and the catch lasts just a bit longer. Dad finds his rhythm again, obviously glad with what he said. I wonder if he gave the same talk to Abigail and Diana. Maybe he didn't want to worry Abigail with Suzie and everything, and figured that with no volleyball, job or driver's license, that Diana will be around.

The three of us walk into Grandma's room and she gifts her usual ear-to-ear smile. Gerry and I walk with her while Dad idles in the car, and she is significantly slower than I remember. She always said that she never wanted to be in a wheelchair, but in moments like this, it would be convenient. When we return, Abigail, Suzie and Stephen are over, and Mom is bouncing around the kitchen like a pinball. I wonder why Abigail isn't helping out, because she's usually Mom's sous-chef on Thanksgiving. The reason is made apparently clear when I enter the living room and see Abigail nursing Suzie. I turn my head and cringe, rationalizing to myself that I didn't catch any nipple, so it doesn't count as seeing your sister's boob. Grandma's a little too weak to hold Suzie, so I hold her and sit right next to Grandma. I think about them both, and for some reason Lily, too.

"You're so good with her," Grandma says to me. I feel golden.

"I forgot the pickles!" Mom shouts from the other room. With the amount of food she's making, it's a really minor concession, but knowing Mom, it's deemed a necessity. Gerry and Diana offer to pick up a jar, while the rest of us veg out to football. Mom calls us to our seats at ten minutes to four, although Gerry and Diana aren't back yet. Mom's flustered, because of course we'll wait for them, but 4PM has always been our Thanksgiving dinner start time. They roll in and plop the pickles on the table in the nick of time and we lower our heads for Grandma's prayer. Suzie is bubbling her lips a bit, and Grandma waits for a lull to begin.

"Lord, bless this food. Amen." We open our eyes and hesitantly start passing around the food, confused by the brevity of Grandma's grace. Usually it goes on so long that we get squirmy, so this is a welcome change, although out-of-the-ordinary. I wonder why Gerry and Diana took so long, thinking maybe they had to go to a couple of stores, but then see Gerry's eyes and his appetite, which are ruby red and ravenous. I hate him so much. He took a long time just so he could get baked out as much as possible. And he probably did it in front of Diana, and drove her back while high. All while I was spending time with Grandma, which Dad told us to do. He really is a piece of shit. Diana would never say anything either. I feel bad for her, but at least she doesn't have to share a room with him.

As the tryptophan sails through my body, I lie in my bed thinking about Lily. I wish she was here with me. I'm still not ready to tell my family about her. I guess I just miss her even though we've only been apart a few nights. I've spent every night with her for the past few months, almost since we first met. I don't know if you'd consider that living with someone, but it sure brings you close to them. I've gotten so much of her. I know her schedule, her food preferences, how she brushes her teeth, how she chooses an outfit, how she acts when she's diligently working, how she acts when she's fried from studying, how she acts when she's horny. All of our free time is with each other. It's like we're living *in* each other. For me, in more ways than one. I guess it took her being gone, to really see that. I tell her all this on the phone, and momentarily panic when I don't hear an immediate response.

"Alex, you're going to make me cry," she finally says. I gather this is a good type of cry. Antione has us leave crazy early Sunday morning, so I get back to Parker hours before she does. When I do get a knock on my door, I'm barely able to open it before she jumps onto my chest, with her legs wrapped around my waist. She lays a string of long kisses on me, and I return the favor until my oxygen level collapses from holding her up. We make love that night like we hadn't seen each other in forty years. "How are we going to get through Winter Break?" she asks me, pensively. We both crack up.

"Only until your sister's wedding," I say.

"Yeah, maybe we can find a broom closet or something." I know she's joking, but just her saying it turns me on, and we're back at it again.

Chapter 14: End of Semester

There's only a few weeks of regular classes before finals begin, and it feels like the semester has ramped up into third gear. All of those long term assignments that seemed far off before break are starting to become due. But with all the sudden stress, there's a commensurate desire to party on the weekend. Paul from Seminar tells me about a house party on Friday with a Christmas theme. He said you just need to wear red or green to get in. This sounds like another matching-couples event that will delight Lily, but she informs me she's got a group project for her Seminar, and Friday is the only night everyone can meet up. She gives her blessing for me to attend alone, and after getting through my habitual Jason-lab-abandonment, I'm ready to get blitzed.

Antione joins me, but I quickly lose him when he sees a guy he made out with a few weeks ago. I've never been to this house before, probably because it's filled with mostly upperclassmen. I nurse my beer and look for Paul, but he's nowhere to be found. I decide to poke my head into different rooms, hoping to find a face I know.

"Hey, are you in?" I hear from across the hall. I turn around to find where the question's coming from and if it's directed at me. I enter a room with a few upperclassmen in it, one of them staring at me with a Santa hat, green eyes and a five o'clock shadow.

"Are you talking to me?" I ask him.

"Yeah, De Niro. I am," he jokes, casually. "Are you smoking with us?" I look to see the girl next to him rolling a blunt. Never have I been invited to get high with people without knowing them at all. Now this guy asks me to smoke just because I'm in his vicinity.

"Sure," I say, sitting down next to him on the bed.

"Simon, we're good to go," says the girl rolling, as she passes him the blunt. Simon takes a long drag and passes it to me next. My mind replays all the fears I had at that summer party. I try to match Simon's intake, and my lungs give me a millisecond notice, before coughing my throat out. I instinctively look at Simon, knowing that I've disappointed him and that he'll spread word throughout campus to not party with me. But when we make eye contact, he has the same demeanor as when he extended the invitation.

"Nice," slowly pours out of his mouth. When I see that no one else cares, I relax and just listen to the scant conversation. I just nod along even though I don't know what they're talking about. When it's my turn again, I cough again, but not as much. It's not until the third round that I really start to feel the THC take hold of me. I feel time ticking slower and everyone in the room holds a warm glow. Without thinking, I lie back on the bed. I don't know if it's Simon's bed or anyone else's, but no one complains. The blunt chain just passes over me and no one cares that I've tapped out early. The room is such a mellow place, and I feel so at ease with these people that I don't even know.

We eventually go downstairs for some beer pong, and everyone starts singing that Mariah Carey Christmas song at full volume. I see Antione roll his eyes with how offkey everyone is, but he sings along, too. At the end of the night, Simon and I are sitting on the couch and Simon turns to me, strangely pensive.

"You're a cool dude. What's your name?"

"It's Alex." He nods five times in a row before saying anything.

"Alex," he says and rests. "Simon," he says, pointing to himself. I mirror his five nods back to him. Out of nowhere, a girl wearing a green miniskirt and reindeer antlers plops down next to us. She kind of sits on me, so I scooch over a bit.

"Where were you all night?" she mock-interrogates Simon.

"I was right here!" Simon defends himself.

"Liar!" she laughs. Eventually, someone calls for a photo and everyone crowds around the couch. Another girl with reindeer antlers plops down on my lap and swings her legs around so that her boobs are right in my face. I smile for the picture and wait for her to get off of me. After the party, I walk back with Antione, who just rehooked up with the guy, both of us high on life and other substances. I find Lily already asleep, so I crash in Matt's bed to not wake her.

I'm working at my desk, when I hear Lily call my name from Matt's.

"Alex?"

"Yeah?"

"What's this photo?"

"What photo?" I ask getting up to find her on Facebook. I look at her screen and see the couch picture from last night. I guess someone already posted it. There I am, surrounded by strangers, with an ear-to-ear smile, and some random girl sitting in my lap. It doesn't help that she's also smiling, my arm is resting on her bare legs, my chin is practically nesting in her cleavage and my eyes are pointed down in the same direction. I look back at Lily, who's very still and quiet, but in a hyperaware kind of way. She looks at me, but doesn't say anything, and I know I have to speak first. "It was just for a picture."

"Who is she?" Lily asks, still stealthily calm.

"I don't know."

"You don't know?" Lily pauses, but keeps an eyebrow raised that's half perplexed, half furious.

"I didn't pull her down," I try to explain. "I was looking at the camera, and suddenly she just sat on me."

"And you just kept smiling?"

"They were taking a picture."

"That you knew I would see."

"No, I didn't."

"Oh, so you were hoping that I'd never see this?"

"No, I didn't think about it. It's not like she grabbed my dick or anything." Lily just shakes her head and stares me down. I fear an explosion is coming, but don't know the best way to diffuse it. Maybe some rationality. "What was I supposed to do, push her off?" I say.

"No, you were supposed to say 'Excuse me, can you get up?' and get up yourself."

"You weren't there; it happened so quick."

"And, you should have told me about it the first chance you got."

"Well, I don't know. I probably would have."

"But you didn't." I don't know how to counter this and let out a big breath that quivers a few strands of hair on her forehead. Lily ends the uncomfortable silence herself. "Well, why don't you think about why you didn't, and then we can talk?" Lily darts up and I back away as she gathers her laptop and books and walks out of the room.

I lay on my bed and review what just happened. I guess our first fight had to come eventually. I just don't know why she can't see that I didn't do anything, and that it just happened to me. I don't even know the girl. I watch some TV to try to distract myself, but when that doesn't work, resign to my Geology homework. If I'm miserable, I might as well be productive. Midway through, she calls and I pick up my cell as fast as I can.

"Hey, um, I just wanted to say—"

"I'm still not talking to you, yet," she cuts me off.

"What?" I ask, confused by the contradiction of her statement and the fact that she called me.

"I need to get some things from the room. Can you leave for a little bit?"

"What do you need to get?"

"None of your business."

"Okay, I guess. Do you want to get dinner?"

"No, I'm going to eat with friends."

"What about afterwards?"

"We're going to a party." I know the answer to my next question already, but have to ask.

"Can I come?"

"No, it's only Architecture people." I reckon I've mucked up worse than I thought. I'll give her what she wants for now.

"Okay, I'm leaving the room now for like thirty."

"Thanks," she reluctantly says.

"Will I see you later tonight?"

"I don't know." We live in a long pause that feels like an eternity. "I have to get going," she finally says. We hang up without saying goodbye, and I head into town to grab a burger and eat by myself. She never comes back that night, and I never text or call her. My gut tells me you can't in situations like this. I look at the photo again to see how bad it is. I look at the tagging notification for the first time and see that Antione tagged me. I knock on his door and apparently wake him up. I don't care how late it is. He opens up his door, squinting at the hallway light.

"Why did you tag me in that picture?"

"What picture?"

"The one from last night, with the girl on my lap."

"Um, because you were in it."

"You didn't think of running it by me first?"

"No, why?"

"Because you've fucked things up with Lily and me."

"How?"

"Because there's another girl on my lap! Didn't you see that?" I see Heinz poke his head up, and say "Sorry" to him.

"I'm sorry, man?" Antione squeaks out, looking to return to bed. His intentions may have been genuine, but his apology's not.

"Well I'm fucked," I throw back at him, as I return to my room. MAP would never stab me in the back like this.

I wake up alone the next morning and think about Lily the instant my eyes hit the ceiling. I hope I don't have to wait too much longer for her to come back. With her roommate drama, I bet it won't be long at all. I plan on finishing up my Geology work until then, but I procrastinate first and go on Facebook. It's the first post on my wall, and the heart sink that I know all too well returns with a vengeance. Now I know what she got up to last night. And to top it all off, they're her photos; she uploaded them herself. It's like a lance in my chest, but I have to view each one.

There she is at a party with her Architecture friends, looking like she's never been happier. Even though it's December, she's got on a skirt and a tube top, two items I've never seen her wear before. The photos start with group photos with people I've never met, but then evolve to her with her arms around two of the guys from the group, and of course, her sitting in the taller one's lap, his hand on her thigh. Lily, can you be any less subtle? I get the message loud and clear. There's another with her head resting on the shorter one's shoulder, and then, the KO: Lily kissing him on the cheek. I think she took more photos with these guys than there are of us together. They haven't been up long, but they already have a ton of likes, one of which is from Antione. Bastard. I close my laptop and pace back and forth between my bed and Matt's. I see a few passerby staring at me through my window, so I close my blinds and lie down. I consider calling Mark, but don't. My brain tells me there's only one person that can make me feel better right now, and mercifully, she answers.

"Wow! Hey, Alex. It's been too long. How are you?"

"Hey, Jessica. I'm good. What's new with you?"

"Senior year!"

"I know, is it crazy?"

"A little bit, but hopefully the worst is over. I've gotten all my recommendation letters, and applied to all my schools."

"Excellent. What's your top choice?"

"That would probably be Yabely, followed closely by RQU and Cheps Institute." I feel like I should know more about these, but never heard of any of them.

"I think those are great choices for you," I say. "Do you know your major?"

"I'm thinking about Osteopathic Medicine or maybe Radiology."

"Yeah, I could see you doing those things," I say, while not sure what they are either. "Are you still doing the musicals?"

"That's in the spring. Maybe. I've been doing cheerleading since September."

"Really?" I ask. I can't picture her being one.

"Yeah, it's actually loads of fun." We talk for a full thirty minutes, and it really does make me feel better. I don't mention Lily at all, but why would I with what she did to me today? When Jessica says, "It's nice that we can talk and catch up," I know the conversation is almost over, and I have one last chance to do the thing that I've been thinking of since I saw the photos.

"Yes," I reply. "Hey, do you have Facebook?"

"No, just a Myspace, but I don't go on it too much."

"Oh, okay. Would you mind if I put up those pictures of us from my graduation? The ones in Pete's backyard."

"Um," she contemplates. "Sure, why not?"

"Great, can you email them to me?"

"Sure, I still have them on my desktop." She still has them on her computer!

"And you can put them on your Myspace, if you like," I add.

"Okay," she responds, in an indecipherable tone that doesn't necessarily point to her doing so. We talk about maybe meeting up over Christmas break and then say our goodbyes. The pain and stress have substantially subsided, and I can finally take a breath that doesn't feel like the air is lacerating my lungs.

Soon enough I get the photos, and go through them. I won't put up the ones with Mark and Emily because I have enough sense to know they're not together right now. I pick out two near-identical photos of just Jessica and me on the bench, and then one of MAP as well. I put them up on Facebook and tag myself in all three. This somehow makes me feel a bit better, but to be honest, part of me still feels hurt by Lily. I'm able to go back to Geology, while returning back to Facebook, now and then. When I do look, I get a lot of likes and comments, including from both Ethan and Farah. I would have never expected this from them because we purposely excluded them from our couples photos that night. I forget that I'm Facebook friends with Madison, but see that she comments, "You two are so cute. Can't wait to see you both over break!" Why does she have the impression that we'd ever meet up again? The last time I saw her was when she ruined our prom night. I click on her profile to see if she's really engaged like Farah said. Her profile photo is her with some guy, but neither of them are wearing rings or anything. It's that moment that I hear a pounding on my door, and I know it's Lily. She's come home to roost. I know she was waiting for a reaction from me with her photos, so I just gave her a taste of her own medicine and knew that she'd blink first.

I don't know if I was expecting an apology, or an argument and then an apology, but when I see her face I instantly lose half my self-righteousness. Her hair is matted, her make up from last night is smudged and streaking down her cheeks, her entire face is swollen and puffy from the tears, and she's wheezing shallow gasps from her mouth, like a little kid hyperventilating. I wanted to make a point and ended up devastating her. She walks in without either of us saying a word, and as I close the door, I remind myself that I was justified, even though I still feel rotten over how upset she is.

And then we get into it. We spend forty-five minutes hashing out the past 24 hours. 24 hours. Who knew a relationship could get completely demolished in that amount of time? She's pretty defensive about what she did, which she equates to my offense.

"How is it the same? A girl sat on *me*. I didn't do anything!"

"You allowed it to happen," Lily fires back.

"You, on the other hand, initiated it with those other fucking guys."

"If you can be handsy with other girls, I can do the same with other guys."

"Are you crazy? It's nowhere near the same thing. I wouldn't have done what you did if some guy was in your lap for one picture."

"Well I guess we'll never know." This comeback doesn't make much sense to me, and I don't know how to respond. "Well isn't it better that it's guys I know, and not some random bimbo?"

"No, it's worse! Those are guys you're still going to routinely see. It makes me think that you're trying to get with them."

"Then how do you think that I felt seeing you post a photo with your ex?" Shit, I fell for the trap.

"All it is, is a photo of me with my arm around her. I'm not kissing her on the cheek; there's no sexiness to it. We were at a graduation party."

"But apparently you're meeting up with her for Christmas." I glean that she assumes that from Madison's comment.

"No, today was the first time I spoke to her since our breakup."

"You spoke with her today?" This one wasn't a trap, but I still fell. Why did I just say that?

"Who else was I supposed to call after what you did?"

"So you're running back to your ex, a high school girl?"

"No! How can you even compare talking with someone else versus kissing someone else?"

"Because you dated her! You obviously still have feelings for her, and are planning to meet up to do who knows what, while I'm not around." I don't have an immediate response, which she interprets as an admission of guilt. "Wow. I guess that means you're really thinking about it."

"How can you not see what you did was worse?" She ignores my question.

"Did you meet up with her during Thanksgiving break? Don't lie to me."

"No." We argue for a good while longer, most of it just recircling the same arguments. Neither of us gets what we want out of it, and I leave my room for a while so she can bring her stuff back to her own room. Not long after, we decouple our relationship status on Facebook. Here ends the ballad of Alex and Lily. Part of me feels bad that she has to live with that Martha again, but most of me just doesn't give a flying fuck.

Chapter 15: Finals Week

The silver lining in my atomic bomb of a breakup is that I'm completely inundated by finals week, so Lily only takes up so much of my headspace. Freshman Lit doesn't have an actual final, just a ten-page paper on *Beloved* that's due by midnight on the Friday of Finals week. This is the longest paper I've ever had to write, but I know I'll be able to break it up piecemeal. I don't know if there's an unofficial rule on when you can round-up the last page of a paper, but for me, if you get past four lines, you can count it as a whole page. Sociology's also got a paper due at the end of the week, but it's only three pages. The annoying thing is that we also have an in-class essay during finals week, too. Theatre is a 75-question test. I may have studied with Antione before all the Lily stuff, but seeing him like all her pictures was the nail in the coffin. Plus, he only could really help me with assignments; he doesn't really need to study for the tests. We briefly make eye contact when he walks out of the final twenty minutes early, but I quickly dart my eyes back to the page. Geology is the same scenario with a final test, but the pisser is the work for the Geology lab. The TA Alex must not have allotted time well throughout the semester because she gives us two labs to do on the last day of class. Jason doesn't even make an attempt to engage with me, and just rifles through both so he never has to see me again. With ten minutes left, I'm only halfway done with the first lab, so I abandon it and start the second. TA Alex lets us stay fifteen minutes late, but then she kicks us out, saying she has somewhere she needs to be. I'm not the only one that doesn't finish on time, so I don't feel as dumb. She says we can come back the following Friday night, but I know I'll be finishing up other stuff then and won't be able to. With no access to the rocks, scale and litmus paper, I end up making up a lot of data, and just hand the labs in, hoping for the best. Freshman Seminar is just a presentation on the last day. I give mine on managing stress, which is pretty ironic because Seminar is my least stressful class. I actually end up feeling really natural and confident during my speech, and even get a "Great job, Alex," from Professor Le when I hand in the written part. It figures that my best class is the easiest one. Too bad you can't major in Seminar. I submit my *Beloved* paper with about an hour-and-a-half to spare and go for a walk to blow off some steam. Most of the other students left sometime today, but there are a few other stragglers ambling around town. When I get back, I pack before falling asleep with all the lights on. As soon as Dad picks me up Saturday morning, he says, "One down; seven to go." I'm so wiped, all I can do is roll my eyes and turn on the radio. I dread the thought of having to do finals week even once more, let alone seven more times.

Passage 5:

Winter Break

Chapter 16: Holidays

When we're about an hour from home, I call Carla and pick up a couple of shifts before Christmas. It'll be busy enough that she can use the help, and I can certainly use the cash. I think I've got just enough for next semester's books, and don't know if Mom and Dad will float me if I come up short. Plus, I still need to buy gifts for Abigail, Gerry and Diana. And maybe Suzie, too? Mom and Dad's rule is that you don't need to buy gifts for them two, but if you're working, you have to give something to your siblings. Diana is still exempt, and Gerry and I have always had a mutual, bottom-of-the-barrel, barely-a-present exchange, but Abigail has always been tremendously generous with us, even from when I was very young. Being the oldest, she's been giving for so long, and hasn't had that much getting. I don't know how Suzie factors into the rules, but my gut tells me I have to treat my niece like a sibling, and the gesture will go way further if I don't ask Abigail. Now, I'm basically getting Abigail two presents. I guess that's her way of evening the score.

Mark, Emily and I see *Blood Diamond* at the Domport Arthouse and get burgers afterwards. It's been less than a month since I saw them, but it feels like a lifetime has passed since then. I'm pretty amazed and impressed by how they reconnect over breaks, and don't want to become their sad sack third wheel who's always lamenting over exes. Pete would round us out, but we won't be seeing him until June. I'm thinking about Lily a lot, but not as much as I did with Jessica. Probably because there was so much left unspoken with Jessica, and Lily and I ended so ugly.

I get all my grades on Christmas Eve, which is a really terrible system because you're either filled with impending doom or you're blindsided by a class you didn't do as well in, as you originally thought. Either way, it can ruin your holiday. Some alarm sets in when I see the B- I get in Geology. It wasn't my best class or anything , but I honestly thought I did better. Did I bomb the final or was it those dumb labs I had to half-ass because the TA didn't give us enough time? I guess I'll never know where I screwed up, which is kind of shitty. I could email Dr. Laghari about the last two labs, but it probably wouldn't change anything and I'm never going to take another class with him, so what's the point? I know a B is a 3.0 GPA on the dot, which is what I need, so starting with a B- is bad news for me. I decide I can't bear viewing my grades piecemeal, and just scroll to the bottom of the webpage to see my overall GPA, and whether or not I've lost my scholarship.

Semester GPA: 3.2
Overall GPA: 3.2

"WHOO!" I shout out loud, jumping up from my chair. I feel such a relief and an adrenaline rush that I can't sit down just yet. I walk into Diana's room, give her a full-windmill high-five, and shout "WHOO!" again. She looks at me as if I've gone mad, and I return to my room. *Now*, I'm ready to look at the rest of my grades. I get an A in Freshman Seminar, but don't congratulate myself too much, because you'd have to be an idiot to screw up that class. Theatre is a B, which is fine. Sociology is a B+, which is what I was expecting. And, Freshman Lit. is a B+, which is what I was hoping for. It sucks that Geology was my one four-credit class, that counts the most towards my GPA, but it's whatever. This is my Christmas before Christmas, and it'll help keep Lily out of my head for the rest of the day. I go to Mark's for his family's Christmas Eve party and can't contain telling him my grades. He's already pretty drunk, so he just smiles and nods. I know a 3.2 doesn't merit this much excitement for him and his GPA is probably higher, but I just wanted to tell him.

Christmas morning is pretty routine. I get a lot of winter clothes, including a pair of really good winter boots from Mom and Dad. Gerry gets me a pocket nail clipper, and I don't do much better with the mini-screwdriver set I give him. I write Gerry and Diana's names on my present for Suzie as well, and when Abigail thanks us, they both glance at each other and me in confusion, but don't give it away. Abigail puts the Christmas-themed bib on Suzie for brunch, and I'm proud of myself for not just gifting diapers as a present. Lily texts me *Merry Christmas*, which is the first communication we've had since the breakup. I text the same thing back, and the exchange ends right there. For some reason, I text Jessica *Merry Christmas*, too, and get the same response. Dad, Gerry and I replay the retrieve-Grandma routine, and she's somehow even slower and frailer than Thanksgiving. Dad imposes on Mom's dinner-planning dominion and insists that it include pierogies and stuffed cabbage. Mom says it doesn't go with everything else, but still picks up some from the deli. Grandma appreciates the gesture, but is only able to pick at the specialties. Dad looks a bit disappointed and I imagine Mom is mildly annoyed, so I make sure to overstuff myself with both the Polish food and Mom's traditional fare, so neither party is slighted. Abigail doesn't even stop me from spoon-feeding Suzie a few dollops of sour cream.

"You're going to have to change her diaper," she warns me.

"It's just dairy," I say. "You should be thanking me; I'm sparing you a nursing session." Grandma lets out a silent laugh and that's all I need.

Pets Unlimited is busy with returns the day after, probably because parents realize their kids are too young or uninterested in lizards and gerbils. Handling them is the most interesting part of my day. Mark texts me about a party at Nicole Bryant's house tomorrow night. He doesn't have to tell me that Jessica will most likely be there.

Since Nicole's house isn't too far off, I just walk there, so I can put together what I might say to Jessica. It's cold enough to see my breath, and there's a leftover crunch from yesterday's dusting. I'm wearing the waffle knit shirt and corduroys that Abigail got me, and the winter boots from Mom and Dad. I just hope it doesn't come off like I'm trying too hard. I think about Jessica's camp friends screwing up our goodbye. It really bothered me at the time, but at least it wasn't a meltdown breakup. I guess this'll be a fresh start. She seemed happy when we spoke on the phone, so there's a potential something could happen. And then, we'd have a few weeks together. I know I'll be leaving again in a month, but if Mark and Emily can do it, Jessica and I should be able to, as well.

Nicole leads me to her basement, and I recognize some faces from the theatre crowd. Mark and Emily are already there and I join them on the couch. Just as I plop down, Jessica walks out of the bathroom and our eyes meet. I get up to give her an awkward hug and all the room's eyes are on us. It may have been too much, but I feel like a "Hey," or a wave would have been too little. She goes back to her seat across the way, and I retreat back to mine. It turns out to be a more chill type of party, because people are really just sipping and chatting. There's no pong or drinking games going and we're cruising at a one-beer-from-the-mini-fridge-at-a-time pace. Most of the conversation is insular, but they also mention teachers I had, so I'm able to offer useless agreement and commiseration. I purposely try not to look at Jessica too much, and when I do steal a glance, she always catches me.

We all chip in for a couple of pizzas, and when Nicole says that she forgot to toast some garlic bread to go with it, I take it as an opportunity to volunteer my chef capabilities, just to give myself a break from the crowd. I go upstairs, put the loaves in the oven, and hang out in the dark for a while. About five minutes in, I see a figure approach and not bother to turn on any lights either. She came up so we could be alone.

"Hey," Jessica says.

"Hey," I say. This is definitely a more natural reintroduction than that hug.

"So, how's college?"

"It's fun," I say, trying to expand while only bringing up things that don't involve Lily. "I rushed a frat, but didn't end up joining."

"Cool."

"Classes are good. You have more free time, but finals week is nuts."

"Fun parties?"

"Yeah, and the cool thing is, no cares that you're a freshman. A freshman can go to a senior party."

"God, it would be so weird if ninth-graders were here with us," she laughs. I remember that laugh. The lifetime that passed since I saw her now feels like a second.

"Did you guys all just do a play?"

"They all did, but I did cheerleading." Still can't believe that.

"That's right. Are they all pissed you didn't do it?"

"Some were surprised at first, but it's nice to get a break from the *drama* drama. Now I have *cheerleading* drama," she laughs. There it is again. There's a lull. I guess the silence comes because it's tricky to bring up the stuff you did when you were dating. You can't say "Remember when we swapped spit?" I fantasized about us making out tonight, drawn back together by some primal, unresolved feelings, but they're not materializing for me here in this dark kitchen, while we're talking about cheer routines and waiting for bread to toast. I get the sense that she may be waiting for me to make a move, and I don't know why I don't. We bring the garlic bread down to the basement, and the rest of the night has the same vibe as before. I cut out early, and Jessica and I share an equally awkward goodbye hug. I try to process the night and the state of my head on the walk home, and settle on feeling a little bit disappointed and a little bit sexually frustrated. Jerking off can help cure one of those.

Marshall is hosting New Year's Eve, which is great because I'll go anywhere that saves me from just watching the ball drop at home. I've never been to his house before, and am surprised when it doesn't look much different than mine. I had assumed he was rich because he was popular in high school, but it's just like any other house. There must be over fifty people, and the faces I recognize are intermingled with Marshall's family and

171

other old people. I weave my way through the crowd and give big hellos to Alison McDonald, Hector Allen, Tyler, Kelly, Tony, Mark and Emily. Even Ethan and Farah are here. Maybe they put their cutest couple gripe to bed. Or just came to make a point. It's funny that our whole prom limo is here, except for the orchestrator herself. Maybe Madison really did get engaged, or maybe everyone eventually chose to side with Marshall. We all decide to do a shot of tequila together, followed by some cheers from Marshall's parents.

I get a text from Antione wishing me a happy new year, and I text him back the same, just to be polite. In the middle of talking to Tony, I feel my pocket buzz and see I'm getting a call from Lily. I panic, not knowing if I should let her go to voicemail or answer it right away. I sneak out to the back porch and take the call, not knowing how to begin.

"Hello?" Lily says. "Are you there, Alex?"

"Oh yeah. Just needed to get outside," I finally respond. My mind is racing, trying to determine what she wants, and why she's calling now.

"Can you talk?"

"Yeah, for a little."

"Great. How was your Christmas?"

"Pretty good, spent it with family. Got to hold my niece again."

"Aww," Lily coos. With this one cute verbalization, I'm transported back to my time with Lily: working side by side, lying in bed all day, fooling around. I remind myself that this same thought process just happened with Jessica and to not get too swayed by it. After a second of silence, Lily gets to the reason why she called. "Do you remember when I asked you to accompany me to my sister's wedding?"

"Yes, but you said you'd find someone else, after we, you know…"

"I know, I did say that. I just haven't been able to find anyone on short notice."

"Oh."

"I was wondering that since you have the date open, or had it open, would you still want to go?" I'm still really hurt, and want to fire something back at her like "Well, you should have been nicer to me," and hang up, but that's not how I respond.

"When is it, again?"

"Oh, it's the Saturday of MLK weekend. And it's in Arbhorsville, so it's kind of in between us."

"Is that near that big amusement park?"

"Same town." It's not as close as she's selling, and it's right before classes start back up.

"That's on the way to Belston. I'd have to drive two hours and back, and then drive past it again twenty-four hours later."

"I guess so; I just thought I'd ask. Happy new year." I know this tone. She's genuinely disappointed. She wouldn't have called me if she wasn't really running the risk of going stag.

"Wait," I say. "I'll go."

"Really? Thank you so much. I'll text you all the details again. You just need to show up to the church by four."

"Okay." It's nice to hear her happy, and even though I didn't foresee our demise, I did say I'd go with her. We chat for a bit longer, but I start to get cold, so I wish her a happy new year, suppress the kneejerk "I love you" signoff that I guess my brain is still deprogramming, and hang up.

Inside, I do a couple more shots with the guys, but have her in the back of my mind. Maybe we shouldn't have broken up. I mean, she doesn't hate me enough to not ask for help when she's in a pinch. I don't know, maybe I'd still reach out to her if I needed her help with something. Who knows, maybe it'll be an opportunity for us to reconnect.

When midnight comes, we all sing the song, and Alison McDonald and I kiss. We barely know each other, but it's the thing you do at midnight. She's got a great rack, but I don't see anything for us beyond that peck. I feel guilty because I'm not sure if Lily and I are making moves to go out again, but I tell myself that our conversation was too hazy to glean that, and that Lily may have just kissed someone herself. I shake my head. I don't even want to imagine that. It feels like that girl Antione and I grinded with. I kind of forgot about her, but kissing Alison brought up the same confusion. I go back to talking to Tony to distract myself. Goodbye to the year that ended high school and started college, and hello to whatever's next.

Chapter 17: January

I work a lot the next couple of weeks, not just for books, but now for the wedding, too. Mom says I have to give at least fifty bucks, but I wasn't planning on giving anything since I'm going as a favor. I remember Abigail complaining after her wedding about a friend who gave too little. I guess it's something that brides talk about, so I'll have to cough it up, so it doesn't get back to Lily that I'm a cheapskate. I'm not getting a hotel room; that would break the bank. If Lily wants me to crash with her I totally will, but I don't know if she has her own room or if she's sharing with family or something. If not, I could see her asking me to stay with her. We did it all fall, and didn't have sex every single night, so I don't think it would be weird. She told her family about me, but not that she was staying in my room. I figured they must have assumed so, when she stopped griping about Martha. They must know we broke up, so I wonder what they make of me coming to the wedding.

One day, I bring in the mail and see a letter addressed to me from Belston. I figure it's something financial, but when I open it, I see it's about my grades. I feel myself beam ear-to-ear when I look over the words.

Dear Mr. Alex Ryback,

We are pleased to inform you that you're maintaining the GPA requirements necessary for your participation in our Arthur Academic Scholarship program. Please continue to monitor and maintain your GPA in order for your scholarship to continue to be honored.

Sincerely,
Marion Syle
Dean of Students

It's funny that they sent a letter to just say "everything's fine." I know the Dean doesn't get any specific info from the professors, but you'd think it would be a little more personal. I bet he didn't even write it. His office must just look at the GPA's of all the scholarship kids, and send the one I got to everyone that made the cut, and a bad letter to those who didn't. I put the letter back into its torn envelope and leave it on the kitchen counter with the rest of the mail. By the next morning, Mom and Dad haven't said anything and it's still there. I take it back out of the envelope, but still no word. By the third day, I'm getting annoyed, so I show it to Mom, who says, "Good job," and then goes back to cooking. Maybe Dad will have a lengthier response when she tells him.

Apart from work and hanging out, I chill with Mark as much as I can. We go see *Borat*, even though we both already saw it at college. It's the type of movie that MAP would have gone to together, so it's nice to have that experience, even though we've already talked about our favorite parts.

Then one day, it finally happens. I'm in the breakroom and get a call from Abigail.

"Hey, what's up?" I ask her.

"Where are you?"

"I'm at work."

"You're working right now?"

"I'm on my break."

"When do you get off?"

"Maybe nineish?"

"Okay, I'll see you when you get home."

"You're over?"

"Yeah, we all are." This is unusual because when the three of them visit together, they've usually left by now.

"What's going on?" I ask.

"Um," she hesitates.

"Now you have to tell me," I tease.

"Grandma died," she reluctantly reveals. I was expecting it at some point, but am still blindsided.

"When?"

"This morning. The home called Dad about her having a slow pulse, and she died just after he came. But he got to be there."

"Everyone's home except me?"

"Gerry's working, too. I asked him to pick you up since Dad is you know…"

"Okay." I finish my sub and head back to work. It's slow, which is good because my mind is elsewhere. I think about the last time I saw her; I think it was the weekend after New Year's. Nothing too significant, just a normal visit. I believe the last thing I said to her was, "See you later." Not a terrible goodbye, I just didn't know it would be the last one. I guess you never do. It's funny that Dad didn't say anything this morning, tell us where he was going or asked anyone if they wanted to come. I don't know how he was thinking; his demeanor didn't show anything was off. It's also weird that he found out this morning and wasn't going to tell me until I got home tonight. I can tell they didn't want Abigail to tell me over the phone. I don't know why. I try to remember where I was when they told me that Grandpa Ryback died, but don't have a strong memory of it. All I can call up is Abigail being in tears. I remember being sad that she was crying, but too young for it to really hit me. I imagine she wasn't as fazed by Mom's dad because I have no memory of him at all. Gerry picks me up just after nine, and we sit in complete silence as he drives. It's a lot like the drive home from that knife party over the summer. When we walk in, we hear Suzie crying upstairs and Stephen trying to pacify her with some offkey lullaby. Gerry and I find Mom, Abigail and Diana in the den and give them each a hug. They don't need to tell us that Dad's in his office, and when we file in, he barely looks up from his monitor. We offer our sympathies, and he just says "Thank you." When we join the girls in the den, Abigail reads our expressions, and explains he's probably contacting people, organizing the funeral and writing his eulogy. Diana pops in an old home movie, and we go through photo albums.

Chapter 18: End of Break

There's a rush of planning and prepping in the days before the wake, which perfectly coincides with the wedding. When Dad tells us that the wake is on Saturday and the funeral is on Sunday, my stomach drops. I'll have to cancel on Lily again. I would never try to skip out on Grandma's services; I just feel bad for leaving Lily hanging because it's so last minute. I look at her last text about one of her sister's bridesmaids suddenly dropping out and now she's filling the spot. She sounds so excited and I know she's going to be crushed. Before I can phone her, Mom brings it up.

"You have that wedding Saturday night, don't you?" I'm surprised she remembers. I felt I had to tell her about it because I asked for the car and said I may stay the night in Arbhorsville.

"Yeah, I'm about to call her and tell her I can't come," I say.

"Not so fast. Maybe you don't need to go to the second wake at night."

"Really? Do you think Dad'll mind?"

"I'll talk to him. Could you leave straight after and make it on time?"

"Probably. I'll be wearing my suit, so I should be able to just go."

"But you can't stay the night. You'd need to be back for the funeral. Even though it starts at ten, we're showing up early."

"Of course. I'll be back."

"I'll talk to him."

"Thanks," I say, giving her a big hug. On Friday, I deposit my last check and work one last shift before coming home, helping finish up the photo collage and ravaging through the takeout scraps. On Saturday morning, Gerry and I pick up bagels while Diana and Mom dominate the bathroom. There's dead air in the car ride to the funeral home. I don't know if I was expecting Mom or Dad to say something before we go inside, but there's just an absence of sound. Now I can see where Gerry and I get our quiet-car syndrome from. I look at Grandma for the first time since the last time I saw her, but stand five feet back. I don't know why, but it takes a few minutes for me to get to the kneeler. I don't remember Grandpa having this much makeup, but they say it's to make them look presentable and lifelike. I mentally chuckle to myself. It's a funny concept to act like something's still going on, when it's clearly over. I mean, I don't think anyone's going to say, "She looks so good! Are you sure she's dead?" I hear Uncle Clark and Aunt Kate walk in, and embrace each. I walk around saying hello to some of Grandma's friends and the nursing home staff that liked her, but also keep an eye on the time. I hold Suzie for a little bit, but after I'm unable to soothe her crying, Stephen smells her diaper and takes her away. I check my suit for baby crap and am relieved to find no streaks. I can't imagine what Lily would think if I showed up with actual shit on me.

Mark and his parents come to pay their respects. His parents talk to mine, while he and I struggle to start a conversation. He already said, "Sorry about your grandma," so we talk about the wedding and the coming semester.

"When do you go back?" I ask him.

"Monday."

"Me, too," I say, leaving another lull.

"Did you know Pete was home during Christmas week?"

"What?"

"Yeah, apparently he was."

"He said he wasn't coming home for Christmas."

"I know, but Tony said he saw him."

"Why would he see Tony and not us?"

"No, Tony just saw him on their block, one day in passing." I'm reeling with incredulity to fully process this.

"Do you think Tony's making this up to screw with us?"

"Maybe. I don't know. But I don't think so." We just stand there for a minute or so. I'm pretty stunned, but Mark appears more matter-of-fact about it. After the first wake, we head back home, and I'm ready to bolt as soon as Mom gives the okay. When she hands me her car keys, I wait for a nod from Dad for final confirmation, and I'm on my way. I sing along to that new Red Hot Chili Peppers song and tap my breast pocket for the wedding card laying just behind Grandma's prayer card.

I'm a little late to the church, but it hasn't started yet anyway. I sit in one of the last pews and wave to the flower girl as she walks down the aisle. She looks like what I imagine Lily looked like as a kid. The wedding party starts to process out, and I spot Lily with a goateed groomsman. She looks like an angel. Even though I've seen her naked so many times, something about her look now totally stuns me. She makes eye contact with me and raises her eyebrows in a super cute way, to let me know she's excited and glad I'm here. When her dad walks out with her sister, everyone stands and I follow suit. Laura is a hair shorter than Lily, but you can tell they're family. Lily's dad looks at me, but his expression isn't as warm as Lily's. I figure that she probably showed him a photo of me. I knew I'd have to meet her parents when I agreed to this, but am worried about the first impression since they probably know about our catastrophic breakup. The ceremony is pretty typical, but nice and not too long. Afterwards, everyone shuffles out, but the wedding party stays inside the church for photos. Since I'm her date, I don't know if I'm meant to enter the reception without her. I guess I'm just meeting her there because everyone else is driving off.

I walk into the venue and slip my card into some cloth sack. It's funny that for such a fancy occasion, the gift deposit looks like a loot bag from some sort of cowboy, bank robbery movie. I'm relegated to a table of strangers, and watch as the DJ plays the wedding party in with pump up music. Laura and the husband dance to a Shakira ballad, and eventually, the DJ invites other couples to join, but I just stay in my seat and watch because Lily's dancing with the groomsman she was paired with. I think the reggae party was the only time we ever danced, but it was more swaying. When the music gets livelier, I mosey to the dance floor and stick to some basic moves. Lily comes over and gives me a big hug, and we dance face-to-face a bit, but then it kind of morphs into a circle with everyone else.

"Let's see some salsa!" announces the DJ, transitioning to the next song. There's a big "Woo!" from everyone except me, who apparently is also the only one who doesn't know how to dance this particular dance style. Lily's kind and teaches me at half speed, while everyone else is having more fun. It's really just moving your feet back and forth, but I don't really get the hang of the hip part. Not long after, the DJ announces that the dinner is coming out, and to return to our seats. On the way off the dance floor, we bump into Lily's parents, and I'm faced with the inevitable. We say hello, shake hands, and they're very cordial, but another family friend grabs their attention, and I'm released from the pleasantries. Lily returns to the bridal party dais, and I back to the strangers. I gobble up some amazing pork and rice dish, and listen to the toasts. One of the speeches is overly schmaltzy, but the other is funny. Lily laughs and chats a lot with her sister, brother-in-law and that groomsman. Some old couple across from me start gossiping, and I can't help but eavesdrop because I'm certain they're talking about Lily.

"That's the sister," the woman says to her husband, pointing towards the dais.

"La chica?" the husband asks, with his own immodest, fully-extended point.

"Sí," the wife hushes him, swatting down his arm.

"¿Cuántos años?"

"Universidad."

"Oh. Buena." he says with a pause. "¿Novio?" he asks, pointing again at the dais. This is the one word I can't translate, so I discreetly lean in to see if I can infer. The woman pushes down her husband's hand again.

"Tal vez. He's a friend of the groom. They were put together for the wedding."

"Well, you know how these things work," he chuckles.

"Rhumba time!" the DJ shouts, blasting the music again. I hesitate as I stand up, because it's another specific dance that I don't know. The whole bridal party sprints to the dance floor, and Lily dances with her groomsman. The moves look pretty complicated and not something I could fake, so I sit back down to wait for the music and dancing to go back to a more freestyle feel. That moment never really comes, and I watch Lily and that groomsman have another romantic, slow dance. I don't know what to make of it because I'm technically her date, but he's her bridal party partner. They're holding each other close, but I guess that's just the gist of the dance. They're still talking and laughing a lot like they were at the table. I don't know if it means anything, I just wish I was holding her. Some of those laughs she's having remind me of our reggae date.

As the cake comes out, I look down at my watch and realize I need to leave. I'm still not going to get much sleep, but I can't be comatose at the funeral. I take a few bites of my slice, and say goodbye to Lily. She gives me an obligatory hug, but doesn't seem too concerned that I'm leaving early.

I make good time home, and sneak into the house as quietly as possible. I try to take off my suit and hang it up in the dark, without giving it any new creases. As I slip into my bed, I hear Gerry rustle and feel guilty.

"Sorry, did I wake you?" I whisper, hoping not to hear a response.

"Nah, I was already kind of up," he answers.

"Okay. How was the second wake?"

"Pretty much the same."

"Oh."

"How was your thing?"

"Uh, it was okay." Gerry doesn't say anything back. I know he's not asleep; I just didn't say anything he could respond to. "I actually didn't see much of her at all," I continue. "She was a bridesmaid, so she had to do a lot of separate stuff. I didn't know anyone else there, so it felt like I was by myself the whole night. She asked me to come as her date, but she was pretty much bound to the bridal party. I don't know, the whole thing felt like…" I don't know how to articulate it, maybe because I'm still processing. I probably put Gerry to sleep anyway with my grumbling.

"You're a loser," Gerry labels me. I launch. I'm on my feet and at his bed in less than two seconds. I rage. Our room is pitch dark, but I start wailing haymakers on any limb I can find. "What the fuck?" he screams. "Get the fuck off of me!" I don't say anything, just keep swinging sloppily. Gerry's able to lay his feet on my chest and catapults me across the room. I slam on the ground and bang my back against his dresser. His boombox falls, crashing on my head. Being thoroughly dizzy, I know it's over. I rub my head, knowing there'll be a welt there in the morning. I'll probably have a sore tailbone, too. "Get the fuck out of here!" Gerry yells at me. He thinks he can kick me out of my room?

"I'm not a loser! You're the fucking loser," I shout back at him. He doesn't immediately respond, and I'm confused why. He's not the type to get hurt feelings, especially when he used the same words against you.

"I wasn't calling you…" he starts, but then trails off.

"What?" I question him, still half-riled.

"Never mind." In that moment, I realize what he meant. He wasn't name-calling, he wasn't bullying me, he wasn't trying to make me feel worse when I was down. He was offering empathy. The one sentiment I have no memory of him ever lending me. I don't blame myself for misinterpreting it when he's never given it before; I just feel bad for pounding him when he was trying to be nice. We may never have that opportunity again.

The door flies open and Mom is furious. She must have heard my thud, or the cursing and shouting. Probably all of it.

"What the hell is going on in here?" she hisses in a seething, loud whisper. Mom never curses, so I know she's livid with us.

"Nothing," Gerry responds, coolly. "Alex was just going to sleep downstairs." Mom looks at me on the ground, and I don't say anything.

"Listen," she continues to both of us, "tomorrow we bury your father's mother. We need to be up in a few hours. Will you let the poor man sleep?" I nod, although she probably can't see me doing so. "I don't care what's going on with either of you right now. Figure it out on your own and be ready." Mom closes the door and we sit in silence. I get up, grab my pillow and blanket, and sleep in the den.

The funeral is sad, but no more sad than anyone else's. Abigail cries a little, but not as much as Grandpa's. Uncle Clark reads a passage from one of Paul's letters, and then a priest from Grandma's church talks about how wonderful a woman she was, how she loved her Creator, and how she's with Him now and that kind of stuff. Dad goes up after and hesitates for a few seconds, shuffling his papers around. I wish I could say or do something to help him ease into his speech, but all I can think to do is to stare at the ground so that he has one less pair of eyes on him.

"Love must be sincere. Hate what is evil; cling to what is good. Be devoted to one another in love," Dad reads. I'm guessing he's starting it with another passage. "Never be lacking in zeal, but keep your spiritual fervor, serving the Lord. Be joyful in hope, patient in affliction, faithful in prayer." Dad was never as religious as Grandma; he just played it up when she was around. Maybe this is a verse that had an impact on him. "Bless those who persecute you; bless and do not curse. Rejoice with those who rejoice; mourn with those who mourn. Live in harmony with one another. Do not be proud, but be willing to associate with people of low position. Do not be conceited. Do not repay anyone evil for evil. Be careful to do what is right in the eyes of everyone." Dad pauses. It is a very beautiful passage, and I know Grandma would like it. He takes a deep breath, and I wait to hear his take on it.

But he doesn't say anything more. Dad just sits down and the priest goes back to the lectern. I thought Dad was working on his eulogy in his office these past few days, but apparently, he had only ever planned to do a Bible reading.

The priest says more at the gravesite, and that night is just packing. Dad drives me back to Belston the next morning, and we don't mention one word about the funeral.

"Thanks for bringing me back with everything going on," I say. Dad nods, with his eyes fixed on the road.

"That was always the plan."

Passage 6:

Spring Semester

Chapter 19: Beginning of Classes

I thought I'd see Matt the first day or two, but we either didn't cross paths or he never came back to the dorm. The great thing about this semester is that all my classes start a bit later. On Tuesday, I show up for my Spanish class in a new building, Calib Hall, and I sit in the middle of the pack. Professor Molinero appears nice enough, but I fear that if I sit too close to the front, he'll always be calling on me to answer questions. I did alright in Spanish in high school, but dropped it after the state test because I sucked at the speaking part. I know that I'll probably have to do some speaking for this class, but prefer to keep it to a minimum. After Spanish, I have Statistics II in another new one, Weston Hall. Professor Le greets me with a nod that says "Yes, I remember you from last semester, but this is a new class and any good report we had in the fall, will have to be reproven now." The class has less than twenty kids in it, and most must be sophomores and older. I was able to use some math credits from high school to place out of Stat I, so I'm less intimidated and feel I deserve to be here. Most of that assuredness evaporates when Professor Le starts the class. Her tenor is stricter and more formal than last semester. Maybe the professors are told to go easier on students in Seminar. There isn't much introduction, and we launch right into normalizing outliers in data sets. I jot down her notes from the wipeboard, but she also says some stuff that she doesn't write down. I don't know if that means that that info isn't as important, but I try to catch everything she says while simultaneously copying the board. The worst part is you have to take notes at a mad rapid pace because she erases what she writes as soon as she's out of space. This results in a constant flicker of head bobbing, and I often have to take notes without looking down. I review my notebook afterwards, and deem it legible enough, some letters just intersecting with others. I'll have to get better at this no-look writing.

My history class starts at 10AM on Monday-Wednesday-Fridays. I arrive a bit early, and hear some other kids talking about the professor.

"Yeah, he's brilliant."

"I know, he wrote his dissertation on Charlemagne."

"Have you taken Mass Migration with him?"

"No, is it good?"

"You have to take it—so interesting." I reckon they're history majors and they've had him before. It's funny how you wouldn't be caught dead praising a teacher or class in high school; people would think you're a nerd. But in college, it's actually cool to be passionate about your major.

No one really notices when Dr. Spetato walks in. He just takes out a stack of syllabuses from his bag and places them on an empty desk before approaching me. He has gray hair, a short beard and is wearing a basic, button-down shirt with slacks. I don't know if I was expecting a pipe and monocle from the "brilliant" description, but he's pretty regular looking to me.

"Do you mind handing these out?" he asks me in a soft-spoken tone. He turns around before hearing my response and I realize it wasn't a request. I start handing a paper out to each student in class, and without introducing himself, Dr. Spetato just starts lecturing about the serf economy in the dark ages. I panic because everyone else has started taking notes, and just split the stack in half for the last two rows to disperse themselves. I dash back to my seat and am further delayed when the first pen I retrieve decides to conk out on me. When I find a working one, I try to remember what he previously said, while still listening to what he's saying now, while trying not to wonder what I missed. He doesn't write anything on the board; he just talks. Some kids are taking notes, but a good bunch are just listening, and maybe jotting stuff down here and there. When he's flipping through a book, I look down at my notes to see if everything I wrote is necessary or even makes sense, and I decide that I'll just keep the guy next to me in my periphery and write notes, whenever he does.

Dr. Spetato dismisses the class five minutes late, and when I leave I hear one of the history majors say, "I'll finish all those chapters tonight." I wonder what he's talking about because Dr. Spetato didn't assign anything. I go to check the syllabus only to realize that I didn't take one for myself. I return to find an empty classroom, but find him in the hallway.

"Dr. Spetato," I call, panting and panicked.

"Yes?" he asks, still walking.

"I handed out the syllabuses—"

"Syllabi?"

"Syllabi, but didn't get one for myself."

"Oh," he says, not fully concerned. "Take this one," he offers me.

"Thank you," I say in relief, watching him use eye contact to signal the conversation is over, before walking away. I catch my breath and look down at the syllabus. There is a reading assigned for the week. Thank God I caught him. He must expect us to just hand things in when the syllabus says so, with no verbal reminders. I don't know anyone else in the class yet, so this piece of paper is my only resource.

I'm a few minutes late to Introduction to Business Management, but so is someone else and Professor Le doesn't mind too much. She seems a bit more laid back in this one, probably because it's a 100-level class. I settle in and am more at ease because she actually goes over when the big stuff is due, and it's all relatable. She teaches a lesson about "vampire marketing" and a bunch of us recollect commercials that were so good that you forgot what they were selling. I know it doesn't sound very academic, but I find it fascinating when we go over ways to combat it. She mentions how memorable those Geico commercials are, and the concept is cemented in my brain.

I leave Weston Hall, just to go right back to Renard for US Elections with Dr. Prescott. She displays her teaching style again with group discussions, and I can tell it's going to be another paper-heavy class. It'll suck, but I figure I should be able to pull another B+ with her.

I never see Lily, not in Parker, or even on campus from a distance. It's for the best, although I wouldn't act weird to her if we bumped into each other. I'd just have nothing to say. I spend the first weekend or so alone in my dorm, leading me to realize that I have to reform my social circle since Lily and Antione are out. I consider rerushing Matt's frat, but it doesn't have the same draw as it did in the fall. Maybe that's because back then I felt the camaraderie of doing stuff with the guys. Matt or Hunter might put in a good word for me, but also may be resentful that I bailed last semester. Also, since they're already in, they'd be doing the hazing. It would be too weird for your roommate to be a notch above you and mess with you. One weeknight, I'm walking back from Walmart and see Simon sitting on his porch.

"Yo!" he shouts towards me. I stop and look at him. "Yeah, you. How do I know you?"

"I was at one of your parties. The Christmas one," I respond. I'll never forget that night, but not for any good reasons.

"Oh yeah. We smoked together." I unconsciously look around as if there's a cop behind me before I confirm.

"Yeah, that was me."

"Get over here, man," he signals. I have nothing else to do, so I join him on his porch and he hands me a beer. "You still smoke?"

"Yeah, sure."

"Nice. Yo, you were fucking good that night."

"You were, too?" I offer, not knowing what to say.

"Of course, I'm always good! Yo, what are you doing Friday?"

"You tell me."

"Nice. It's going down here, boy!" He gives me an overly-enthusiastic pat on the shoulder, but it makes me feel so welcome.

While working at my desk, I get a call from Abigail that Stephen was in a car accident, and I assume the worst. She says he's alright, but has a shattered knee that will require a lot of physical therapy. She informs me that without asking, Mom's been coming and staying over twice as much, which I didn't know was even possible. She also mentions Diana missing half of a midterm because she couldn't get a ride in the middle of the day, but Dad is trying to call her teacher so she can retake it. I thank her for telling me and make a note to call Diana and give her some brotherly encouragement.

Simon's party is pretty identical to the one in December except without the holiday garb. This time I hold my own a bit more when smoking with him, but it's hard because Simon's got lungs of steel. I wonder if I can train mine to match the tolerance level of my infamous Ryback liver. In the meantime, I realize I can slow Simon down with conversation.

"Simon," I say when I know I'm about two draws from tapping out.

"What?" he asks, after an extended processing pause.

"So, what dorms did you use to live in?"

"Uh, Parker and then Tealy."

"Cool! I'm in Parker now."

"No shit. What year are you?"

"Oh, I'm a freshman." I answer without thinking, and hope it won't change how he thinks of me.

"Cool." Another relief. I had eighteen years of Gerry taking me down a peg even though we were only a grade apart. This sort of thing doesn't matter to Simon.

"What about you?" I ask.

"Oh, I'm a senior." Since he lives off campus, I knew he was either a junior or senior. It's just awesome that he's not talking down to me. "And, I was a senior last year," he adds, followed by a self-deprecating laugh. I'm not sure if it's a "I don't even care" laugh, or a "I'm depressed about it laugh." "Yo, turn that up!" he yells in the stereo direction. Before he can repeat his request, some jam band is blaring, and Simon stands up and dances with himself. I watch him and laugh, amazed with how confident he is.

"Do you need me to chip in for the weed?" I ask.

"No, man. It's a party. Throw in like five if you want."

"Okay," I shout over the music. I put a five on a table, and he gives me two wavering thumbs up, as he continues dancing.

"Just let me know if you ever need any, just for yourself. I'll give you a good price."

Classes are somewhat similar to last semester. Statistics is pretty hard, but I'm able to comprehend any tricky concepts after attending Professor Le's office hours. For one Stat Excel project, I'm there four times in a single week, but I get an A on it, so I don't feel as stupid for needing all the extra help. I don't know if you still call it "extra help" in college, but that's what it basically is. It's funny how people like Mark are just so naturally smart that it makes you feel dumb by comparison, but at the same time, you can get an A on a project if you work for it. Sometimes that means it was easy for everyone else and it was just hard for you, and sometimes it just clicks and you're in the zone. What really sucks is when you're graded harsher because everyone else is better. In a way, that's how history feels, especially when I get my first paper back.

Dr. Spetato puts all the graded papers on the front desk after class and just leaves. I'm in the middle of the pack and am already stressed because everyone else can see how I did. I see my name inching out of the middle of a now undone pile, slip it my paper and scurry away from the crowd. I got a D. My pulse races. How is this possible? I didn't phone it in; I actually tried. I was at least expecting a B+. I scan through his notes to see where I went wrong, but there's not much to go off of.

Specious argument
Unconvincing
Needs more

And then there's his KO summary:

Many logic and coherency issues

I stand there stunned, unaware of the other kids, until I overhear two talking.

"What did you get?"

"An 'A.' You?"

"A minus."

"Yeah, it's a cake class."

"Totally." Literal sweat drops down my neck as I hear this, and I pull my paper towards my chest as if I'm exposed, and the two of them are looking at me. They aren't, but I leave the room so I don't hear any more gloating. I go back to my room and read the syllabus to see how much this puts me in the hole. 20% of my final grade. Fuck. But, recovery isn't impossible. I can't recall if I ever bombed a class in the beginning and then leveled out. Even if I did in high school, I had a whole year to improve. Each class in college is only a couple months, so every test or paper carries more weight. I take a breath and figure the best thing to do is be proactive. Dr. Spetato doesn't have office hours listed on the syllabus, so I email him and ask him if we can meet to go over my paper. He replies within the hour, saying that he's available between 12PM and 3PM. This kind of sucks for me because I have class until 2:45, but I'll take what I can get. I tell him 2:45, knowing that I'll have to leave Stat early.

I give Professor Le a heads up before class, and luckily she's fine with it. I sneak out, and my mind is racing the whole way to Renard. I wonder if he'll let me rewrite it. It'll add to my load, but I don't really have a choice. Maybe he'll bump up my grade just because I'm showing effort. As I get to his office and knock on his door frame, I see that he's putting on his winter jacket and zipping up his briefcase.

"Dr. Spetato?" I call, meekly.

"Yes?" he answers, still buttoning his coat.

"It's Alex from History class."

"History class?"

"Sorry, Early-European History. I wanted to talk to you about my paper."

"Okay," he says sitting down and motioning me in. "Good thing you caught me. I was on my way out." Seriously? I emailed him I was coming yesterday! I decide it's not worth it to remind him, and take out my D paper. I place it on the edge of his desk and his blank stare lets me know I'll have to end the silence.

"I just wanted to talk to you about my paper about the history of the English language."

"What about it?" I guess he doesn't remember my specific paper. I know he's got loads of students, but he could throw me a bone.

"I just worked really hard on it, and did a lot of research for it, and don't know why I did so poorly." He yanks up the paper and begins scanning it. After fifteen seconds or so, he lowers the page so his eyeline is just above the edge.

"You argue here that the results of the Battle of Hastings birthed the English Language."

"Yes, I tried to focus on that event."

"Well, that's incorrect." I don't know what to say to this.

"Um, in the book for this class, it says it was a very important battle in European history."

"It was very important, but that's not what your thesis is. The Battle of Hastings was instrumental in terms of change in monarchy, migration and feudalism, but the English language existed long before the Normans invaded." I gather my thoughts.

"I thought it was why we have so many French kind of words in our language, like the word 'dough' and stuff like that." I know I'm not coming off smart, but he's really fighting me on what I wrote.

"Old English existed before the Normans invaded. The aftermath of the battle may have influenced the transition to Middle English, but you didn't write that." I'm blanking on how to answer again, and I see he's getting antsy.

"Okay, but other than that point, was the rest of the paper really that bad?"

"Well that was your thesis," he counters, unsympathetically. "If your central argument is incoherent, that negatively affects everything else."

"Oh." I literally can't muster any other way to respond. He hands me back my paper and I know that any chance of a rewrite or extra credit work is out the window.

"I do need to get going," he says, standing up.

"Okay." When he stands up, so do I. For some reason, I feel inclined to shake his hand, as if I'm apologizing for botching the paper. Displaying an impatient expression, he entertains my gesture, but pulls away before we even really grasp. I exit his office, and in the hallway put my forever-D paper back in my backpack. With my back to him, I hear his office door slam, the lock click and feel his coat chafe the back of my ear as he whizzes by. There was no "Here's what you can do to improve," or "Come to me while you're working on your next paper," or even "Now you know what I'm looking for." Just that encounter, whatever that was. I had to put aside time just to get the specifics of my failure. It's like giving the details of his criticism was a courtesy to me.

Chapter 20: February

Simon lets me in just as Billy Joel is finishing up the National Anthem, and laying on his coffee table are wings and a two-foot tall, electric blue and green bong. With the week I had, I couldn't ask for a better combination. Simon's quite proud of his bong, and I can tell he doesn't take it out at every party, just for smaller gatherings. This'll be my first time using one, and I try to observe everyone else's technique. When it's my turn, Simon senses that I'm hesitating and teaches me.

"First you put your mouth on the glass penis," he instructs, completely deadpan. I follow his lead and take the lighter. "Then, it goes: light it, tilt it, bring the flame to the bowl and start sucking a bit." It hits me immediately. The room is suddenly in slow motion, and he has to tell me twice to blow out the smoke. I accidentally blow it in his face, before crashing down on his couch.

I'm living in a warble. I feel Simon pat me on the head and say, "Ricky, you're next." I look over and see a dude with a short ponytail, and realize he's the guy that Antione made out with. I feel anxious about that joke Simon said earlier, but my mind is eased when Ricky says, "I'll show you how to suck a glass penis." The fabric of the couch feels scratchy against my neck, and I rub my fingertips against the armrest for a few minutes to confirm that it's the material and not just me. The game is only registering as noise and colors for me right now, but every time the ref blows his whistle, it's like a needle pricking my brain. I renotice wings in front of me and grab a mini-drumstick, mashing it in my mouth. My mouth is a volcano and I drop the remains in my lap, while scooping up a dollop of blue cheese with my finger, and transporting it to my tongue. I say "hot" to myself about fifty times, imagining it'll help. I panic again because I'm sure that everyone saw me handle the dip, and wants me to leave because I'm being unhygienic. When no one says anything, I inconspicuously gather the wing scraps from my shirt and put them in a napkin.

The halftime show vibes with my high way better than the actual game. I bounce my head as Ricky sings along with Prince, and after another bong hit, descend back into the couch at my own desired speed. Ricky and I lock eyes and a conversation feels inevitable.

"Have we met before?" he asks me.

"Yup," I answer, before realizing I should elaborate. "The Christmas party."

"Right. That was a chill night."

"I know Antione."

"Oh yeah?" he says, downplaying their interaction.

"Are you guys a thing or something?"

"Uh, we hooked up a couple of times, but he's a freshman."

"What's wrong with freshmen?"

"Are you one, too?" he laughs.

"Yeah, what's the matter with that?"

"Super nice guy, but I don't know, he might be too young for me."

"He's a great guy."

"I know."

"Listen, the only time we have with each other is the amount of time we see each other. And if you don't make the effort to see each other, then you won't have any more time together. And if you have good times with someone, then you want more good times with them." I hope my unsolicited advice comes off as profound as it sounds in my head. Ricky is straight-facing me, so I don't know if he's ignoring me or taking it in.

"Maybe you're right," he finally says.

"Yes! He lives in my dorm. Do you want me to say something?"

"Uh, dorms! I want to be done with dorms." We laugh and I can see why Simon gets along with him. Everyone here is really cool. I shoot the shit with some couple, Stephanie and Bobby, and their friend Neil.

Neil is the only one who's really following the game. He gets really pumped when the blue and white team does good, but yells at the TV when they do bad. "Godammit Scott, this is your second one," he yells after one of his team's linemen goes to block too early. Neil's team has to move back one green row and he shakes his head at anyone who'll give him attention. I fear he's staring at me, so I shake my head overenthusiastically to let him know I agree with him.

"False start. Offense. Number sixty-five. Five-yard penalty. Remain second down," the ref announces.

"Dammit!" Neil stews. It's the same kind of mistake as before, but now it's a different guy. I feel bad for player Sixty-Five. I know he doesn't know Neil is upset, but he probably knows fans like Neil are mad at him. He's probably remembering that the Superbowl is one of the biggest events of the season, so it gets more scrutiny. I think Neil just really hates that kind of mistake, and is still mad at the other teammate for making it earlier. But, that's not fair to Sixty-Five. He doesn't have anything to do with the other guy. Neil shouldn't put that on him.

I suddenly feel a wave of panic and stand up. I must look pretty weird because everyone is staring at me, waiting to see what I'm going to do. Now I'm worried that I'm blocking the TV or being a distraction.

"I got to go," I tell Simon.

"You feeling okay? Why don't you stay 'til the end of the game?" he asks, trying to get a read on me.

"No, I got things to do."

"Now?"

"Yeah, I have homework."

"Alright man, thanks for coming." I nod and give everyone a big wave before bolting out the door. I buy a slice from Sansone's and eat it while jogging back to Parker. I throw my crust in my trashcan and watch the rest of the game in the dark, with no volume. The blue and white team end up winning, so I don't feel as worried about Neil getting upset.

I wake up in a panic, somehow knowing I'm late. I look over and see it's 10:29AM. Shit, so much for History. I skip my shower, but make it to Business alright. My missed History class stresses me out a good bit, but I stay proactive and keep up with the reading.

On Wednesday morning, I figure I'll show up early and apologize to Dr. Spetato, although he probably didn't even realize I was missing. He's not there yet, but I see an upperclassman girl and am able to coax her to remove her earbuds.

"Hey, I was sick on Monday," I lie. "Can I borrow your notes from last class?"

"Oh, I don't really take notes," she says with a tone that could either be dishonest or indifferent. "But you didn't really miss anything. We just went over the reading."

"Great, thanks."

"Yeah," she mumbles as she puts her buds back in. Phew. I did the reading and am pretty sure I understood it, so I should be alright.

Dr. Spetato walks in right at 10AM, and immediately starts speaking.

"As I mentioned last class, going forward there will be the possibility of unannounced, in-class essays. Today is one of those days. Put everything away except for some loose-leaf." He starts writing a prompt on the wipeboard, and I shoot a look at the girl who told me I didn't miss anything, but she just ignores me. I scramble to pull out some paper, and squint to decipher what he's scrawled.

Illustrate how 17th century colonialism relates to the Reformation and their effect on each other.

Shit. I know this, but some of it I read yesterday and some I read over the weekend, before I got really high. I close my eyes and try to remember the main points of each and come up with a thesis statement. I try to block out everyone else, but can hear that most of them are already writing their essays, and at a brisk rate. I never understood how other kids can come up with their ideas so fast. I've always have had to recollect, and it makes me feel so dumb or late to the game. Alright, refocus, Alex. 17th century means 1600's, I remind myself. Reformation. Thirty Years War! I basically know what to argue, and start writing fervently, as if I'm behind. I write about the Protestants and the Catholics fighting, how it weakened the Holy Roman Empire and how other countries got stronger. Other kids finish when I'm only halfway done. I'm used to this, but it still drives me nuts when they brush past you loudly and tell you to push in your chair. If I was them, I'd slink by as stealthily as possible, or just stay in my seat for the extra ten minutes.

It's another buzzer beater, and Dr. Spetato takes my paper just as I'm reviewing it. I leave with test PTSD, but remind myself that I could have overslept today instead of Monday. Thank God. I click my wrist all the way to Business, trying to cure my hand cramp.

"Alex, are you feeling okay?" Professor Le asks me, when she catches me running my hands through my hair.

"Yeah, I'll be alright," I respond, somewhat embarrassed. A lot of the History stress is still with me at the top of Business, and I remind myself I need to get over it, or at least hide it better.

Professor Le is still harder in Statistics than Business, and today is definitely one of those days. She's going over set theory, but booking through it at a crazy pace. She takes brief pauses for us to do each problem, and whatever amount of time she leaves us seems to be plenty for everyone else, but never enough for me.

"This next one's a bit tricky, so I'm going to give you a few minutes to solve it," she announces. I take a breather, and squint at the overhead projector. I'm only just done drawing the Venn diagram, when she speaks up again. "Alright, everyone finished? Let's review it." That wasn't even one minute! "A couple minutes" means at least two, but "a few minutes" means at least three. You can't tell people you're giving them three and then cut them off at one. And worst yet, she didn't wait for anyone to say if they needed more time. Why would you ask people if they were done, if you didn't really care? It's like a rhetorical question in the cruelest form. I swivel my head around my neck to see if any of my classmates share in my fluster, but all their faces are composed and unfazed. I remind myself to pay attention and write down whatever's on the projector without really grasping it. There's got to be someone else in the class who thinks she's going too fast, but I can't get a good read. Maybe she overplanned for class and is trying to get through the lesson so the homework makes sense. Whatever the reason, I know I'm going to have to go to her office hours to make sense of some of this stuff. I wish I could go today while it's still fresh in my head, but I've got to finish up that Poli-Sci paper on the 17th Amendment, plus do a History reading. I would skip the reading, but I can see Spetato giving a surprise essay two classes in a row. I'm in bed by 1AM, and promise myself I'll go to her office hours next week.

Luckily, there's no essay in History, but I'm still mentally spent. My mind meanders to the weekend, which'll commence in two hours with a big lunch and an epic nap. At the end of class, Dr. Spetato leaves Wednesday's in-class essays out front again, and I'm smart enough this time to grab mine first and leave the room so I don't have to hear any gloating.

How I get to the hallway, I don't know. All I can see and think about is the grade. An "F." I stand there baffled. All he wrote as notes are "conjecture" and "tepid reasoning." He's already out of sight, and I'd have to work around his schedule to have his ridicule translated for me. The thing is, I didn't BS this paper. Yes, I could have done better if it was assigned, but I did the reading and knew what I was talking about. I'm in a daze throughout Business and Poli-Sci. I keep sneaking looks at the grading rubric on the History syllabus. I do some rough math in my head and think about how it's going to affect my semester GPA, and my total GPA, and my scholarship's 3.0 requirement. Shit, one class can really drag you down. I try to configure a pathway forward in my head, but I honestly don't know if there is one.

After my nap, I pull open my dresser drawer and count my cash. Since I came up underbudget with books this semester, I have more to throw around, and reckon I can indulge. With the week I've had, I definitely deserve it. I call up Simon and he's down to chill. When I turn into a customer as well, he takes to me even more, and he brings me to a party hosted by other seniors. Saturday night, just he and I hang out, and we get baked while watching some *Freddy Krueger* DVDs I borrowed from Matt's collection.

When Monday comes, I skip History again, but don't go to Business or Poli-Sci either. On Tuesday, I miss Spanish and Statistics. Wednesday and Thursday: repeat, and I stop going altogether.

Passage 7:

The Trench

Chapter 21

The Sopranos really is an insane show. Matt never told me that he pretty much has all the seasons on DVD, up to the current one. I've blown through his horror collection pretty quickly. *Halloween* is great; *Rosemary's Baby* was weird; *Hannibal Lecter* was great; *Friday the 13th* is good; *Freddy Krueger* is good; *Scream* is terrible; *The Shining* is amazing. I figure I'm pretty desensitized to the jump scares now. I don't know why Matt never mentioned *The Sopranos*, but after a few episodes, I figure it's better to watch all by yourself. Horror movies are better with other people because they're usually a simple story and you can talk while you're watching. I feel like you got to be more focused with HBO shows. And you can watch as many in a row as you want. I usually can do four or five episodes in one session until my laptop starts burning my chest, or its fan is spinning too loud, or both.

It's funny how my *Sopranos* break time is kind of like my new alarm, but instead of it getting light out when I get up, it's just starting to get dark. I don't know how I got up for an 8AM class last semester. I don't know what time the sun currently rises, but it definitely isn't really light until like 10AM or something. And then it starts getting dark by 4:30PM. If it weren't for food, some days it's not even worth it to leave the room. I make myself shower at least every other day, every three days at my worst. But of course, if I'm meeting up with Simon and them, I'll shower. I used to get up extra early just to be sure I'd get one in before class. And I'd hurry up, too, so I wouldn't screw anyone else over that was waiting. That's the best part of waking up in the middle of the day: I can take as long as I'd like and no one's there.

A couple nights a week, I'll smoke with Simon, and then we'll get dinner afterwards. Simon takes me to this insane BBQ restaurant, Bonesie's, in Bicksdale. First of all, they give you unlimited cornbread. They also have entire paper towel rolls on the table. We never went to places like this growing up, maybe because Mom was too fancy for it, or something. I've had pulled pork before, but this is my first foray into ribs. Simon says you can get a spicy sauce on the ribs, but it's not traditional. He recommends a sweet and smoky flavor, and it doesn't disappoint. We both end up with BBQ sauce on our cheeks, noses and even eyebrows, but you can just wipe it off at the end, unless it's really bothering you. Growing up, we ate things with bones, like a rib roast or turkey, but if Mom ever caught you licking the actual bone or sucking it, she'd have your head. It would be like the ultimate bad manners to her. At this place, it's pretty much encouraged, which is awesome.

Porn is so much different now. It was pretty much impossible growing up because the family computer is off the den in full view of everyone. Even if I was home alone, I'd feel like the neighbors could see or someone would walk in at any second. When Gerry got his laptop for college, he started locking the door more. I was so mad at the time, but I told myself I'd only have to put up with it until he left. I don't remember if it was two months or just under, but I was in jerking-off heaven while he was at college. And when he came home, sharing everything again sucked, but the jerking off part was a big subconscious frustration. I had to go back to doing it in the shower, which gives you some privacy and is the simplest cleanup, but Dad's always been a czar about hot water and not taking too long. You had to be efficient with your time or else you might hear a bang on the door, which totally kills the mood. Most days I was able to pull it off and still have time for the showering part of the shower. I could never do it in the shower at Parker, although I bet tons of guys do. With toilets flushing and Antione singing, I could never get in the right headspace. Matt moved out just around the time I started seeing Lily, during which I had no need. I had a hard time doing it after we broke up just because of processing her and finals stress, and then was right back home with Gerry. I didn't do it too much in January either. I must have still been ruminating because of how the wedding went down. For a while, the back of my head told me that she might come around my room, thank me for attending the wedding again, and something could happen, but I haven't seen her around Parker at all. I was able to do it thinking about Alison McDonald a bit, but am not really into her. At the very beginning of college, they warned us about unapproved sites and illegally downloading songs and movies, and I heard rumors of guys getting busted and having to go before a review board. Can you imagine having to admit using porn in front of a bunch of old administrators? Antione's roommate, Heinz, told me he was able to get around the college monitoring software and was ripping movies, so I'm starting to take more risks every night. A lot of the well-known sites are blocked, but you just have to do a little more digging. When only left with my imagination, I spend so much effort purposely trying to not think about Lily, but she's the only girl I've ever been with, so it's hard. Now these sites make it easy, and I don't think about her at all. And I can do it whenever I want: as soon as I get up, right before an afternoon nap, while high. I haven't gotten blocked or emailed by the college yet, so Heinz must be right.

I try to avoid going on Facebook, just because I know I'll be tempted to look at Lily's profile. Once she pops up on my newsfeed with that friend who hates me, but another time I succumb and look at her sister's wedding photos. I see her with that groomsman and it still stings.

One day, I get a text from Simon about some alcohol obstacle course he's designed. It's a forty dollar buy-in, but there's a $100 jackpot. I text him "Yes!" and the next night, I show up at his place at midnight, with the backpack he instructed me to bring. There's a handful of people including Bobby, Neil and Ricky. Them three seem to have banded together as an unofficial team, which I didn't know you could do, but that also means they'll have to split the winnings three ways if they win. Simon stands on his porch, while the rest of us stand on his lawn and listen to him explain the competition in mock-grand fashion.

"Tonight's contest descends from the German game of Kastenlauf, where participants must run a race, whilst drinking." This already sounds awesome. Simon is so worldly, but about actual cool shit. "Thus, this tournament is titled 'Belstonlauf,' and it is not for the faint of heart. If any of ye are not up for the challenge, please relinquish yourselves now. No refunds." This garners a raucous laugh, and everyone stays put to hear more. "Excellent. First, ye must all drink a can of beer and do a Jello shot." Simon opens his cooler and we each grab a Bud Light and a technicolor, plastic cup. I down my bright yellow Jello, which is less potent than a regular shot of vodka, but really sweet. Other guys chug their beers, but there doesn't seem to be a reason to rush yet, so I sip mine. "Here," Simon announces, holding up a stack of papers, "is a list of locations you must visit, with the tasks you must perform at each. You must bring back all of your empty cans. First person or team back here is the winner. Begin!" Simon throws the instructions in the air, and all of us jump in a melee to grab a copy. Other people run towards the spots right away, but I stay on the lawn, continue to drink my beer and strategize.

> *Simon & Bobby's house – beer & Jello shot*
> *Beta Phi Sigma – beer & luge*
> *Sansone's – beer & wing*
> *Steph's house – beer & salon*
> *Witz Theater – beer & sing "Twinkle, Twinkle, Little Star"*
> *Juge Hall – beer, flip off and shout "Fuck You" at*
> *College Green – beer & do a cartwheel across Green*

Eight locations with a beer at each. That's a fair amount of drinking, and even just a fair amount of liquid. But that's not what's going to get people. It's the running around that'll fuck you up. I can't make sense of everything on the list, but I think my best shot at winning is to do the campus stuff first because it seems more physical and there's a chance the University Police might get tipped off later in the night. My plan'll make my overall route longer, but I'm willing to bet it'll pay off.

I finish my beer, throw the empty can into my backpack and lookup to see Simon staring at me, trying to size up whether I know what I'm doing.

"Where's Steph's house?" I ask him.

"38 Tulip." With that, I make a mental note and I'm off. I do the cartwheels on the Green, palms crunching on the forming frost, and discover a stash of Millers in a bush. I grab one and make my way into Witz Hall, towards the theater. I wonder if the entrance is always open at night or if Simon orchestrated it to be open somehow. I sing the nursery rhyme and grab a Coors Light near the curtain. I chug the Coors and the Miller in the dark auditorium at a moderate pace. It's way less conspicuous than the Green, and it allows me to warm up a bit. I know I'll have a love/hate relationship with my jacket by the end of this because I need the insulation now, but my pores will have drenched it with beer sweat and regular sweat in a short amount of time. Even though I've never been there, I find Juge Hall and spot the Busch behind the bush. I down it, and offer a middle-finger gesture and salutation to the building, before viewing the remaining list.

Beta Phi Sigma – beer & luge
Sansone's – beer & wing
Steph's house – beer & salon

That frat sounds familiar and I realize it's the one I pledged where Lily and I first really talked. I jog at a decent pace, beer sloshing around in my stomach, and make my way to the backyard and a crowd surrounding some ice sculpture. As I get closer, I see it really is just a tilted block of ice with a canal carved down the center. I watch as some girl crouches down and opens her mouth at the bottom, while a brother pours Jägermeister from the top. This must be the luge. The pourer makes me down a can

211

of Keystone Light before it's my turn, and when the syrup hits my tongue, it's freezing, sweet and has that nasty licorice taste you always hated as a kid.

As I dash towards Steph's house, the sloshing continues, my coordination is starting to falter, and the sugar intake is definitely getting to me. I feel the acid reflux coming and stop dead in my tracks, remembering that "beer before liquor" rhyme Gerry mentioned. I throw up in my mouth a bit, but force it back down, and continue at half-pace.

"So, you're the last one?" Steph asks/tells me. I panic, wondering if I'm way far behind, but figure most of my competitors probably went here first because it's close to Simon's. Steph hands me a Rolling Rock and instructs me to sit down, while she paints my nails a shade of magenta. This must be the salon. After it's over, I take a leak in her bathroom, and stumble into Sansone's where I'm recognized and handed an "incendiary" buffalo wing.

"No napkins, no drinks until you're done," the employee instructs. It's their spiciest wing and I'm practically crying as I force it down my throat, trying to make the sauce avoid my tongue on the way down. Once satisfied, he hands me napkins and a Natty Ice. I chug it down and trudge back to Simon's, only able to speedwalk at best. Now the inside of my jacket is soaked with my own poisoned perspiration, I'm starting to stumble, blood is rushing to my head, and my vision is getting blurry. I knock on Simon's door, and when he opens it, I can see he's alone. Has everyone already left?

"Are you really the first one?" he asks me with a grin.

"I guess," I slur. I dump out my backpack, presenting the medley of beer brands and can't believe what Simon says next.

"Great, you're almost done."

"What?"

"Last you have to drink a Bud and do a Jello shot."

"That's the first thing we did!"

"That was before I handed out the instructions; that was the audition."

"Fine!" I put them both down, I don't know how, and Simon lets me in, placing the $100 in my hand. I take another piss and collapse on his couch, begging for the world to stop spinning. As it does, Bobby, Neil and Ricky stumble in, and Simon informs them I won. They groan and then give me kudos, before recounting their own exploits of Simon's game.

Antione is seeing Ricky now. He's not in Parker too often, probably because he's at Ricky's place. Whenever I see them walking around, Antione gives me the backwards head nod and I return the gesture. Ricky must have told him I encouraged them to reconnect. Because of my matchmaking, Antione and I are cool with each other now, but not close like we were last semester.

Simon, Bobby, Stephanie and I go on a daytrip, 30 miles away, to an old-timey bar. Simon must know the owner because no one checks our IDs. The four of us do a couple rounds of whiskeys, and I grimace when I see the price tag for the round I'm paying for. I've been dipping into my bank account a lot with weed and days like this, but I figure I'll just work more over Spring Break. I tell myself that this is what my throwing around money is for and then overhear them talking about classes.

"I only have one class today and my group has already finished our project. So, I know how *I* can justify driving across the state on a Thursday," Stephanie proclaims, "I just don't know how *you* two can."

"Hey," Bobby mock-defends himself, "when you load up as a sophomore and junior, senior year can be a shit show."

"And I'm only taking one class this semester," Simon announces to a loud, communal laugh. Thank God the question isn't posed to me.

A few minutes into our drive back to Belston, Simon turns to us. "Hey, do you guys want to see something?"

"You bet your bottom dollar, I do!" Bobby replies, overenthusiastically.

"Alright, a small detour then." He takes us through some neighborhoods with really nice, landscaped houses that have a lot of property and upper-end cars in their driveways. Simon stops in the middle of the street and doesn't say anything.

"This is it?" Steph laughs.

"What's the big deal?" Bobby asks.

"See that house," Simon says pointing out his window. "That," he pauses for dramatic effect, "is my house."

"I live with you! That's not our house," Bobby jokes.

"Correction," Simon says. "That's the house I grew up in."

"Oh, how cool," says Stephanie. I look over at what looks like a mini-mansion. It's got a long circular driveway, giant trees, loads of rooms and two balconies.

"That's a nice Mercedes," says Bobby.

"Yeah, it's my Dad's, but he lets me drive it whenever."

"Then how come we're not using it at Belston?"

"I don't want some college dirtbags messing it up."

"True."

"Your parents still live here?" Steph asks.

"Yup. And after graduation, it'll be my address again," Simon says.

"Quite an upgrade from our shitty, plywood walls," Bobby says.

"Yeah," laughs Simon. Simon puts the car back in drive and starts to roll.

"We're not going inside?" I ask, honestly stunned. Simon stops the car and looks back at me.

"No, do you want to go inside?" he asks, with a perplexed face.

"No, I just mean that since you brought us all the way here, I thought we would."

"Why, do you want to meet my mom?"

"Oh, I didn't know anyone was home," I say, now noticing the SUV in the driveway.

"No, she's definitely home now," Simon says.

"Oh, okay," I say, wondering if I was out of line. We drive away, and I speculate what would have happened if Simon's mom saw his car and came outside.

On the highway, Steph's face lights up with an idea. "You know what we're near?" she asks.

"What?" Bobby slurs, with fries in his mouth.

"Blue Silk!"

"Oh, Jeez," he moans. Simon just smiles.

"Do you know what it is?" she asks me. I give her a momentary, blank stare, which she takes as a no. "It's a dance club! Would you want to go?"

"Uh, sure," I say, not wanting to spoil her excitement.

"Babe, it's way too early, and we don't even have the right clothes," Bobby argues.

"Then let's go back, change, and come back." She doesn't hear any immediate rebuttal, and adds, "I promise it's going to be fun."

I pretty much wear the exact same outfit that Antione picked out for my fancy date with Lily, and show back up at Simon's. He asks me to drive. Even at 11PM, the dance club is pretty packed and each of us pays a ten-dollar cover. I get an X on each hand for being under, but once in, Stephanie tells me to lick off the marker. I wonder if I'll have to get a round of drinks for everyone and mentally tally how much I'll have spent by the end of the night. Shit, this might be a $100 day. Simon hands us vodka-Coke's to start, and he and I size up the dance floor, while Stephanie drags Bobby right on.

"You heading out there?" Simon shouts to me.

"I don't know," I admit, bobbing my head to the music.

"Why not? What did you pay for?" I nod and shrug. I look out on the dance floor and see pockets of guys trying to dance with girls, but not having much success. A lot of the girls on the dance floor are really just dancing with each other, in closed-off, impenetrable circles. The guys try to inch their way into the girl circles, but rarely have success. At one point, a girl circle all leaves at once to go to the bathroom, and those guys have to awkwardly dance with each other for a bit to not look rejected or desperate, before ultimately leaving themselves. I don't want to be one of those guys. If Stephanie brought some female friends, it would be different.

"I think I'll hang back," I finally tell Simon.

"Want to know my secret?" Simon offers, yelling in my ear. It's amazing how he knows what I'm thinking. "Just look around at the girls within our eyeline and shouting distance," he instructs, while purposely looking at the ceiling so they don't know we're talking about them. "At some point, the DJ is going to play a song that they like, and they'll throw their hands up and get excited because it's 'their song.'"

"Okay," I say intrigued.

"Make sure you're looking at them and do the exact same thing," he finishes, with a proud look on his face.

"That's it?"

"Well then you go up to them."

"What if they don't see you react?"

"Try again next time."

"Well, every song can't be 'your song.'"

"Just don't let them catch you."

"But what if I actually hate the song?"

"Dude, if it's *their* song, it's *your* song." I think on it for a bit, and watch the girl circle return to the dance floor, followed soon after by the lingering guys. The DJ changes the song to "SexyBack," and the place goes nuts. One of the circle girls performs the excited hand motions and facial expressions just as Simon forecast, and within a split second, he does the same. He points to her, she nods, and he plows straight through the lingering guys and into the circle.

Now I'm really by myself, but I inch my way towards the start of the dance floor, bounce in place and scan the crowd. Then I hear some PVC-pipe-sounding thuds, I know the song instantly. Out of the corner of my eye, I see a girl perform the motion, and I lock eyes with her while mirroring her. She points at me, and we're on the floor. Thank you, Simon. Thank you, Whitney Houston. It's pretty dark, but I can tell this girl is cute every time the light hits her face. She's got braids and is wearing a black mini-skirt. I put my mouth at her ear and she instinctively pulls back her hair.

"My older sister introduced me to this song," I half-shout.

"Mine, too!" she screams with a smile. That smile is everything and my insides are fireworks. "It's not right, but it's okay," she sings, acting out the lyrics towards me. It's funny because it's an accusatory song, but she's wagging her finger at me in a flirty way. The DJ switches to that Brian McKnight ballad, and it's clearly a 90's set. The song calls for a little less distance, and the braids girl naturally comes closer and slides her legs around my knee. She leans her forehead against my chest, and I lay my hands on her bare back, while trying to force my sudden erection in a direction where she won't notice it. I can't help thinking about the times I danced with Jessica and Lily, too. I try to stay in the moment. The braids girl smells amazing. Maybe with women, the motions repeat, but things like their smell change from one to the next. My fingertips graze her shoulders, and she doesn't mind. It's not long before we're in each other's mouths, but when she hears a familiar voice, her lips leave mine, and her head swings towards the direction of the call, her hair whipping me in the face. She squints, and then turns back to me.

"Hold on, my friends are calling me. I'll be right back," she says, about-facing.

I never see her again.

Heinz sets me up with his old Xbox, and lends me a stack of games. I start with *Elder Scrolls III*. It's kind of like *Dungeons & Dragons* and *Lord of the Rings*, typical fantasy stuff. You can get pretty lost in it. I'll turn it on for a second, and the next time I look up it's been five hours or something. That's usually a good stopping point, because I can go smoke and get food. You could play video games stoned if you really wanted to, but some of these missions really do require your full attention and coordination. The need for button-pushing dexterity is the only reason I'm still trimming my nails. Well, for video games and jacking off. Thanks for the clippers, Gerry; your shitty gift helps in a small way. I also like smoking after gaming because it's like rewarding yourself for your hard Xbox work. If you really stay focused and play every day, you can beat a game in not too long, but then there's "completing" a game, after you beat it. With beating a game, you just have to defeat all the bad guys, but "completing" a game requires you to find every item, accomplish every achievement, beat every side quest. There's usually a tracker in the menu that lets you know how far off you are from 100%, and what else you need to do. If you really enjoy a game, it's a way to keep it going, but it's guys that are really obsessed that go for it, like Heinz. I crap out after doing just a few extras; I don't need video games to start feeling like school.

When I'm not smoking at Simon's, I just smoke in my room and blow it out the window. Since I get up around noon most days, my sleep schedule's a bit wonky. Sometimes I walk around the campus at 2AM or 3AM, even though it's freezing. When I do it on weeknights, there isn't a soul around, so I can pretty much smoke a joint without concern. I pass by spots where Lily and I sat or laid, and I think about how it's both different and the same, at the same time. We were there during the day, and now it's night. It was sweater weather; now it's twenty degrees. We were dating then, and now I haven't even seen her in passing. But it's still the same spot.

St. Patrick's Day is fucking insane. Simon has us meet at his house at 6:30AM, where there are Guinesses waiting for us. He fries up some eggs to go along with them, and we nurse our stouts while watching *The Boondock Saints*. At 10AM, Simon presents the main feature. He goes into the kitchen and brings out a small Tupperware container, scanning the faces of Bobby, Neil and me, back and forth, back and forth.

"Boys," he finally announces, "there comes a time in life when you're presented with a challenge." He pauses with his usual, dramatic effect. "And you can either face that challenge down with courage, or you can turn away. Today, right now, you'll have to make that choice." Bobby and Neil are nodding with conviction, so I follow suit. "What I have here is the first of five trials that I will present before you."

"No way!" Bobby says. "No fucking way! We're actually doing it?"

"What I need to know," Simon continues, "is are you up for the 'Far Out Five?'"

"Yes!" Bobby shouts, more in excitement than confirmation.

"Yes," Neil adds, immediately after, acting like he's in on it, too.

"What's the 'Far Out Five?'" I ask.

"Alex, my boy, can't you see that I can't tell you until you accept?" he answers me in an Irish, wise-old-elder tone.

"Perhaps, I do," I reply in my best brogue. Seeing that I'm aboard sparks a warm, almost proud look on his face. His reaction is everything I want.

"Gentleman," he whispers, peeling back the Tupperware container, "I present to you, the first trial." Bobby, Neil and I lean over the container, and they softly sigh in awe. Inside are tiny, brownie squares and I instantly know what's in them.

"They're first?" Bobby asks. "How long do they take to kick in?"

"Hour-and-a-half, two," Simon shrugs.

"Just in time for lunch?" Bobby deduces.

"Irish nachos and ribs from Bonesies." Bobby and Neil sigh again, and I join in this time, too. I don't know what weed, nachos and ribs have got to do with St. Patrick's Day, but Bonesies was incredible when I had it sober with Simon. My mind reels with the anticipated sensation. "But first," Simon says, "you have to make it through the 'Five.'" We each devour a brownie square, which is pretty yummy on its own, and await the next instruction.

Simon then whips out a standard joint and warns us to "pace ourselves." I've heard weed brownies are strong when they kick in, so I take a miniscule puff, kind of like the one I took my first time smoking at the knife party last summer. The rest of the guys take small hits, too. Third is a blunt. I take a medium toke, and for the fourth round, Simon takes out a bright yellow, glass pipe, which I've never seen before. The technique isn't all that different from a bong, and I start to feel it and eye his couch. I know the fifth round will be his pride and joy, so I'm not surprised when he brings down the blue/green bong from his room. Although we said we'd pace ourselves, we wordlessly signal to each other that we're feeling competitive, and take huge rips. That competition manifests in an additional, massive rip, which wasn't something that was originally planned. Number "Five" will go down in history as double-layered.

Now sufficiently high, each of us collapses onto a piece of furniture and Simon pops in his *Anchorman* DVD. Again, not much to do with St. Patrick's Day, but it totally vibes with my vibe. I laugh louder than when I originally saw it, and towards the end I'm both really hungry, and the brownie is kicking in, in full force. The entire room is oscillating, but in a good way. I've never been this high before.

The doorbell startles me, but my body doesn't show it; I'm only able to move my pupils. Simon plops down tortilla chips smothered with cheese, bacon and sour cream on his table, and

I have to consciously stop myself from drooling. He adds the ribs, more Guinness, and paper towels for good measure, and inserts *The Matrix* into his DVD player. We dig in, and I swear on my life that I will never question the genius of Simon ever again. Even though I can barely hold my beer, the experience is pure heaven. The high lasts the entire movie without needing another hit, and by the time the credits roll, we're somewhat functional. We help Simon clean up, drink a bit more, take turns taking dumps, and share a collective nap in his den.

We wake up around dusk, and Simon announces we've got to start prepping for the party. I initially look at him confused, wondering what he'd call what we just did, but then figure he's inviting a ton of people over like he did just before Christmas.

Bobby and Neil make a run to pick up some special whiskey they like, and Simon and I grab the keg, and a ton of cheap beer because he figures it'll go fast. I'm still pretty full, but I order us some egg rolls in place of a dinner.

"Dude, today," I pause, not knowing how to articulate my appreciation more.

"Day's not over," he says.

By 10PM, the party is roaring. End of the world in full effect. I know that St. Patrick's Day is a huge party day on its own, but for these seniors, it's their last St. Patrick's Day at college.

Antione and Ricky roll in and it's hugs all around. We all do a shot of that special whiskey and Ricky makes the rounds catching up with other juniors he knows, one being Tina from that rush party a lifetime ago.

"What do you think of your boyfriend macking on that girl?" Antione teases me, looking over my shoulder. I turn confused to find Simon chatting up this super hot chick. I try not to stare, but she could easily be a model. She's just about as tall as him, blonde, sporting a green crop top and skintight leggings. Simon's an alright looking dude, but she's lightyears away from any guy at Belston.

"I don't know, he's the best," I say.

"Maybe he's just got a good flirt game."

"Throwing the party doesn't hurt either."

"Oh! I forgot to tell you," Antione changes tact. "Guess who's got the lead in Gilbert Livingston's self-written play next month?"

"Heinz?"

"Fuck you," he laughs. "I'm telling you, he's a great professor once you get past the lecture. Your classes good?"

"Yeah." The lie comes so naturally.

We play a game of beer pong, smoke a bit, sing some U2, and by 2:30AM, the party really thins out. I suppose everyone started partying early like we did, but I think that brief nap gave our crew some extra life. Antione and Ricky stroll home together, Stephanie rides on Bobby's back, back to her apartment, and Simon is still talking to that girl.

I'm on Simon's back porch, finishing up a joint when I hear the commotion. I run inside to find Simon dashing up the stairs, and I follow him up. A bunch of people are standing outside the bathroom with a pair of legs lying on the ground, heel up. We find Neil face down on the tile, soaking in a good amount of his vomit that didn't make it into the toilet.

"Wake up," some guy says, kicking Neil's side.

"Dude!" Simon yells at him. Simon kneels down, flips Neil over and starts patting his face and talking to him softly.

"The ambulance is on the way," some girl says.

"Don't call a fucking ambulance!" Simon shouts.

"I already did," she says, indignantly.

"Fuck!" Simon looks at me. "Help me carry him down the stairs." I do so without question, but am admittedly grossed out by touching Neil's vomit, where Simon isn't fazed. We try to get Neil to drink water on the porch, but he's still out. When the ambulance arrives, they do a quick assessment and decide to hospitalize him.

"Is anyone meeting us at Teaf Medical Center?" a paramedic asks.

"Alex, you got to go," Simon tells me.

"What, why?"

"I'm hosting. I got to watch the house. You can take my car."

"I can't drive," I tell him, equally bombed from both booze and weed.

"You can come along with us in the ambulance, but we've got to go now," the paramedic informs us, just as Neil is being placed in the back. I look at Simon.

"Thanks, man," he says, determining my fate. "Call me when it's over and I'll pick you guys up." I climb in the back with Neil and two other EMT's, and watch in sheer horror as they pump his stomach. At the hospital, I wait in complete fear for this guy I hardly know, and when he's conscious and semi-coherent, they let me in his room. I make small talk with Neil who tries to recollect which drink did it, and only get Simon's voicemails when I call him. As the sun rises, Neil and I are left with no option but to call a cab, and I have to throw in because he doesn't have enough cash to cover the ride. I make sure Neil is settled in his bed, but just leave when he asks me to pick up some breakfast for him. I walk back to Simon's in a zombie state to grab my jacket, but discover that his front door is locked.

I slip in through a back window, grab my jacket, and observe the mess.

"Simon?" I call up the stairs. I don't want to wake him, but feel obliged to let him know that Neil didn't die. Bobby's room and the bathroom are both empty, and Simon's door is closed. I approach and knock. Nothing. "Simon?" I call again, somewhat softly. I knock one last time.

"Yo," I finally hear him say. "Who is it?"

"Alex."

"Alright, come in, but be quiet," he whispers. I open the door to find Simon, barely awake, with one arm making the "shush" gesture. The other arm is trapped under a mop of blonde hair. I guess he pulled it off, even with an ambulance call. "Neil okay?"

"He's okay," I tell him.

"Great. Do you mind?" he asks, gesturing for me to scram.

"Sure."

One day while heading back from Sansone's, I pass through Witz Hall. As some kid is leaving his lecture, I see some old, black-and-white movie playing in what must be a film class. I can't tell you why, but I catch the door and take a seat towards the back. It must be an early foreign film, because there's not much talking, and there's no subtitles. It's really just a man and woman walking around different locations, doing everyday stuff in a weird way. It's probably one of those movies where the story's not very good, but the professor admires it because it was innovative for its time or something. No one is vigorously taking notes and the professor is catching up on emails himself, so it can't be that deep or entertaining. I don't have a reason to, but I stay the whole class and watch the whole thing. This must be one of those once-a-week classes because I'm sitting there for at least two hours. I don't mind because even though it's mostly boring, it's different from whatever's on TV. When the lights turn on, no one gives me a funny look, but I don't expect them to because it's a lecture and people don't really concern themselves with classmates. The professor assigns an analysis of the movie, and I shuffle out with everyone else.

Everyone's talking about going home for Spring Break, but Becky says we can stay in the dorm for the week if we want to. I always planned on going home, but figure I'll be back there indefinitely in a month, so what's the point? Simon, Bobby, Steph and some other seniors are doing a Spring Break trip like you see in movies, but they planned it before I got to know them, and even though we're tight, I'm sure it's just a seniors thing. Neither Mom or Dad has called about Easter, so I don't know if they're expecting me. I at least thought Dad would have called to see if I needed a ride. I figure I'll initiate since Easter is Mom's big holiday and I could see her being upset if I didn't show. I dial their landline and am surprised by who answers.

"Yeah," Gerry starts.

"Oh, it's me."

"Oh, hey. What do you want?"

"Nothing really." It's terrible that I can't even make small talk with him, but he didn't really begin the conversation in any way that you could. "Is Mom there?"

"She don't live here no more."

"What?"

"No, she's not here. Since Stephen's thing, she's at their house a million times a week."

"What time does she usually get home?"

"I don't know, she usually stays over."

"Oh."

"Is that it?" he asks impatiently, trying to rush me off the line.

"No, wait. What about Dad?"

"M-I-A."

"Stop talking like they're dead. Where is he?"

"Accountant? Lawyer stuff, figuring out Grandma's will? Just working? Take your pick." I don't ask when Gerry expects he'll be home because I'll get another cheeky response. "Alright," Gerry says, impatiently.

"Can I talk to Diana?" I ask.

"Sure." A second surprise comes when she answers the phone almost instantly. She must be right next to him.

"Hello?" she answers, in a lethargic and croaky tone. My heart sinks. I know what causes someone's voice to sound like they're both hoarse and confused. She's high. She's getting high with Gerry.

"Diana, it's Alex," I say, still processing what I'd never expected my overachiever, little sister to do.

"Hey."

"How's school?"

"It's whatever. It's good."

"Able to keep all the plates spinning?"

"Yeah."

"Okay." More silence and I panic, fearing she'll rush me off the phone like Gerry. "Did everything work out with that midterm?"

"What do you care?"

"I just know you didn't have a ride that day and were going to try for a redo."

"So?"

"Well, did it work out? Did Mom or Dad talk to your teacher?"

"Why are you trying to stress me out right now, while…"

"While what?"

"Can't I have a break from school for one second?"

"I didn't mean to upset you. You're just so smart. You're like the smartest one in the family, and I don't want you to squander any opportunities."

"Fuck you, Alex." I don't know how to respond to this, but don't have to because I hear a click and the dial tone immediately after. I can't believe he did this to her. All I can think is, "Fuck you, Gerry." I'm pissed at Mom and Dad, too for not being around and not catching on, but so much of this is him. He knows how naturally smart she is and how hard she works. School could be cake for her, but she's always pushing her limit. Or at least she used to. He's corrupted her. When Mom and Dad are absent, he's decided to take her under his wing in the worst way. I don't know if starting to smoke weed in ninth grade is young for girls, but it's young for Diana. I don't even think he started until junior year or something. Fuck you, Gerry. At least now I know I won't be coming home for Easter.

It's a weird Spring Break week because there isn't a soul in Parker, not even the RA's. I could basically walk around naked if I wanted to. I see a few maintenance trucks around campus, but it's pretty much dead as well. If something happened like the power going out, or there being no toilet paper, I don't think anyone would come. The one good thing is I don't have to blow smoke out the window; I just lay in bed and get super high, letting the clouds waft around like it's a sauna or something. How many people can say they've hotboxed their dorm room? I get a call from Mom on Palm Sunday, but I don't answer. Five minutes later, I listen to her voicemail and am surprised that she's not pissed.

"Hey Alex, it's me. I'm just picking up some diapers and Stephen's prescription. I don't know if you're coming home next weekend, but we'll be eating at four like we usually do, except it'll be at Abigail's because of Stephen and the baby. I can't remember if you said you were coming home. Have a good week at school."

I don't know how I feel about her message. I'm glad she didn't order me home, but the tone of her invitation sounded indifferent, like she couldn't care less if I was there. So that makes three of them. I decide not to call her back. They'll figure out I won't be there.

I spend the rest of the week smoking, playing Xbox, jacking off, drinking some vodka Simon got for me and getting over twelve hours of sleep a day. It's funny that I'm not seeing much sunlight, but I figure for the amount of days in my life I had to wake up early, or stayed up late to finish an assignment, I deserve some days that skew more asleep than awake.

Stephanie puts all their Spring Break photos on Facebook, and I'd be lying if I said I'm not jealous. Simon tells me all about the beach, the girls, doing mushrooms, and I nod in fascination while in my head regret not begging to come along. Since the weather's getting warmer, they do invite me on a camping trip an hour outside of Belston.

"What time can you get out of class on Friday?" Bobby asks me.

"Whenever."

"Cool, let's try to leave by three." The park is nice, and the first night we set up our tents, grill chicken, have a campfire, and just drink, smoke and listen to music. Even from our site, you can see the reflection of the moon shimmering on the lake. It's so chill, and just then it hits me. In two weeks' time, I'll never see them again. Even if I stayed at Belston, they're still graduating, but maybe they'd come back to visit in the fall or something. It just makes me think about what my life is going to be like back home. Mark will be around during the summer, but then he'll just go away in late-August. I'll be sharing a room with Gerry again. I'll be leaving my three favorite people and returning to a family that doesn't even want me around. I grab another beer and try to shake it out of my head. Bobby and Steph go into their tent somewhat early, and I try to keep Simon awake with meaningless conversation as long as possible, just cause I won't be tired for a few more hours. He eventually collapses in our tent and I tend to the fire until the last coal dims out.

We go for a hike the next morning, and we stop at this overlook that's about two hundred feet above the lake. There's no railing or anything, and Stephanie screams as Bobby pushes her closer to the edge of the boulder. Simon and I stand half-a-foot from the drop, and I feel chills as I look down. We hike back down to the bottom of the lake and borrow some canoes. That night we have another campfire and I listen as Simon, Bobby and Steph recount their entire college experience. I don't know most of their references or half of the people they're talking about, but it's fascinating watching their faces and reactions. It's like they're swimming in the bliss of a four-year long birthday party. I feel lucky to see them like this, and wish I could have it, too.

Sunday is basically a repeat of Saturday, but we hike to a different part of the lake and go out to dinner. When we get back, it's starting to rain and we run to our tents. I hoped that I could have had a chance to tell Simon what's going on with me, just to tell someone, but he dozes off pretty quickly, so I just lie and listen to the patter.

For some reason I wake up early the next morning and feel like going for a walk before we leave. The rain's stopped, but there's still droplets on the tent cover and the ground is pretty damp and smushy. The sky is overcast, but the slight light pushing through tells me it's around sunrise. Simon asked if it was okay that we didn't get back until midday, and I guess he believed me when I said I didn't have any classes on Monday mornings.

I sift through the mist to try to get one more look at the lake, and stand atop a boulder about thirty feet above the shoreline. It's really hazy, and I inch forward and try make out anything on the horizon.

Shit.

My right foot slips on the boulder, and I career off the edge.

Shit!

A rock scrapes the back of my right leg, my left shin slams into another rock halfway down, and my fall ends when I faceplant into the bank.

"Fuck! Fuck!" I'm face down in about three inches of water, so my swearing comes out garbled, and I know no one can hear me. I feel a stinging pain in my shin and side, and for some reason the right side of my face as well. I take a couple of forceful, shallow breaths to manage the pain, inadvertently blowing bubbles in the water. I place my palms in the lakebed to get up, but am restricted by an excruciating pain in my cheek.

"Fuck!" I slam back down into the bank. My face is in the water again, but luckily one nostril and half of my mouth are above the surface. I slowly turn my head so the cheek that's hurting is fully above water, and bring my hand to it. There's something sticking into it. I try to pull it out, but the agony returns instantly. I pull my hand away and see that my fingers are painted red. Along with some lake water, there's a thicker liquid churning in my mouth as well. My tongue slowly sails through the slop until I taste a tiny, rough, metallic ring. Something's punctured my cheek, all the way through to my mouth. I can tell I'm bleeding a lot, and need to get it out as quickly as possible. I try to get up again, but the pain shoots me down. I softly touch my face again, and as I pull away, I feel the object is attached to a thin, synthetic string. My fingertips follow it from my cheek back into the water, where it disappears into the bed. It's definitely wedged under something that stays taut when I try to get up.

It only just hits me then that it's a fishing line, and that I've got a hook in my face. I try to lift and push off whatever's keeping the line down, but any mere movement increases the pain.

"Help! Help!" I shout. I don't know why I didn't shout that before, instead of "Fuck" so many times, but quickly learn it's in vain. It just comes out as a jumble of noise paired with tiny splashes. No one's there, and my calls are completely lost in the lake. I remind myself that I'm still bleeding and have to do something. I put my finger in my mouth and feel the exposed hook. I pat the tissue and feel that the barb is still in my cheek. Fuck. I fell so hard that the hook went through my cheek, into my mouth and back into my cheek. Double fuck. That's two separate puncture wounds.

My mind flashes back to a fishing trip where Uncle Clark taught us that the barb is the pointy part on the inside of the hook that goes in the opposite direction to prevent a fish from wiggling free. It's why you can't simply pull a fishhook out. It's what's keeping me stuck in place, face down in the muck.

I wonder if they'd know to come looking for me. They're probably still sleeping and I didn't tell them where I was going. I don't think it's a big enough wound for me to bleed out, but it is getting harder to breathe. And I'm really cold. Shit. My only option is tearing the hook out. It's going to hurt like hell and I'll probably fuck up my face for the rest of my life, but it's looking to be the only way. I just wonder if I'll be able to do it. Or if I'd bleed out faster from the resulting gash. I need to act fast because I've already inhaled a couple of tablespoons of lake water.

So here it goes, the moment that determines whether I make it out alive. If I do, I'll remember this exact morning for the rest of my life. I'll have to explain the scar to everyone I ever meet. If I don't—Wait! I pat my pocket and feel the bump of my keys. I snake into my jeans and pull them out. And there it is. What dumb luck. It isn't a guarantee, but it's a godsend compared to what I was planning to do.

I open up the nail clippers Gerry got me for Christmas and clamp them down on the fishing line. Nothing. The line is too strong, slippery and bendable. The clipper is really just squishing it. It'll have to be the hook. With the barb still nestling in my cheek, there's only one pathway forward. I'll have to push it back to the outside of my face. I yank at the line one last time to make sure it can't be freed. Fuck, the bed's really got a hold of it. Here we go. I take a deep breath and drive the hook through my cheek tissue, screaming through my teeth. It sprouts an inch away from the first hole and starts gushing blood. I line the clipper up just below the barb and push the clamp down like hell. I keep clenching, and crying, and writhing, and pushing, until the clipper snaps in two. One piece hits me in the forehead and I drop the other. I put my fingertips to the hook and feel it's hanging by a sliver. I rip out the barb end with my fingernails and unthread the remainder of the hook from my face.

"Fuck!" I shout into the lake, in both anguish and triumph. I crawl out of the bank, take off my shirt, and apply as much pressure to my face as I can.

As I get back to the campsite, I see Simon, Bobby and Stephanie are up. They react with expected panic and horror when they see the blood and my face, and I assure them the worst is over. I sit on the ground as they pack up in a flash, and Simon drives me to Teaf Medical Center in record time. Simon says he's dropping off

Bobby and Stephanie, but to give him a call when I get discharged. I give him a thumbs up.

Triage places me towards the top of the list and I see a doctor fairly quickly. The bleeding has pretty much stopped, and when I tell her what happened, she's not too fazed. I'm sure they've seen everything.

"How old are you?" she asks.

"Eighteen," I slur through the left side of my mouth. You'd think she'd spare me from speaking, but I'm sure it's a liability thing.

"Do you need us to contact anyone, like a parent or guardian?"

"Nah, my friend's going to pick me up and bring me back to Belston." She nods.

"Did you ingest any water?"

"A little."

"Any idea how much?"

"I don't know, a cup?" She scribbles something down and moves onto her next question.

"Was the fish hook rusty?"

"I think so."

"Have you gotten all your tetanus shots?"

"I think so."

"And you're a full-time student?" I panic. Is this lady a psychic, too? How does she know I've been skipping? It must be because it's Monday morning. I decide to lie.

"Yeah," I say hesitantly. "Why does it matter?"

"I'm just wondering for your health insurance."

"What do you mean?"

"Usually, you only have health insurance if you're a full-time student." Shit, if this happened two weeks from now, I'd be screwed even more. "Do you have your insurance card on you?"

"No."

"No problem. We'll just call Belston's Health Services department and have them fax it over."

"Thanks." With that, the questions are over, and I become a lab rat. I hear terms thrown around like "subconjunctival hemorrhage" and tell myself I'd rather not know. My back leg and shin get patched up, I test negative for secondary drowning and an x-ray reveals a fractured rib that'll heal on its own. I get four stitches total: one for each puncture on the outside of my cheek, one for each on the inside. She says there won't ever likely be noticeable scars on my face, but I might have some residual roughness in my mouth. I guess I can live with that forever.

After I'm cleared, I put my muddy, bloody, smelly shirt back on and check out with some accounting clerk. My health insurance goes through, but I still owe a small copay. I hand over my debit card and thank the heavens when it doesn't come back overdrafted. I pull out my phone and even before I try to turn it on, the fact that the button creases are still oozing lake water tells me it's not going to work. I'm able to get the clerk to let me borrow her phone, and scan my mind. There's only one non-family phone number that I have memorized, and I'm going to have to call her.

"Hello?" Lily answers, surprised.

"Hey, it's Alex," I say, self-consciously by both ex-boyfriend awkwardness and my new slurring condition.

"Yeah, what's going on?"

"Uh, I actually need a favor. Do you have Antione's phone number?"

"Yes."

"Great, can you call him and ask him to pick me up from Teaf Medical Center?" I know what's coming.

"Oh my God! What happened?"

"Nothing. Everything's fine. Can you just ask him for me and say that my phone is broken, so to just come to the front?"

"Okay, are you sure?"

"Yeah, I have to go, though," I beg for some release.

"Okay, I'll call him now." I can't be in that hospital for any longer, so I stand outside in my still-damp clothes and wait for Antione. When he arrives, I have to admit that I'm not totally surprised to see Lily in the passenger seat. As they pull up, both their mouths gape open wide when they see my appearance. Lily jumps out the car and gives me a gigantic hug. I appreciate that she doesn't mind my dirtiness, but she catches me just at that bad rib, and I wince. They can read that I don't want to talk about it, so we just sit in silence in the car for a good few miles.

"Did you have dinner?" Antione asks me.

"Not yet." We stop at some remote Taco Bell. It's completely empty inside and we scout out a corner booth. As we nibble, Antione and Lily exchange looks, and I decide to fill them in on what they desperately want to know. I tell them about this morning. And then I tell them about the other thing, too. I don't know why; it just comes out. There may have been more conversation if I only told them about the accident, but once they learn the state of my semester, the dead air returns. Lily buys me a bag of ice at a 7-Eleven, and when I get back to my room, I strip naked, throw my putrid clothes on the floor, lie down, rest the ice on my face and pass out.

Chapter 22: Mid-April

I wake up around 9AM, and get some looks in the bathroom when I take a piss. I look myself in the mirror for the first time since my accident and don't blame the guys at all for their reactions. The right side of my face is bright pink and slightly swollen. Sleeping on it probably didn't help. I also notice a quarter-inch slack of stitch string sticking out of my cheek, which'll probably bug me to death until it comes out. What no one told me is that my left eye has been repainted. The white part is now a deep red. The straining from removing the hook must have burst some blood vessels. I'm starting to look like Frankenstein's monster, but the doctor didn't say anything about my eye, so I'm assuming that it will heal on its own, too.

I go back to sleep, unsure which side of my face I should avoid more, and wake up midday. I decide to smoke a joint before lunch and halfway through, hear a knock on my door.

"One sec," I shout, overly loud. I lick my fingers, pinch it out and stash my contraband. In the middle of opening the window all the way, I hear her call.

"Alex, it's me," Lily says. It's a relief and an annoyance because I know she can't be here for anything good. I open up and let her in. She takes a look at me, takes a seat on Matt's bed and waits for me to close the door. I take a seat on my unmade bed and realize the last time she was in my room was our breakup. Let's hope this conversation goes better than that one. "How are you feeling?" she asks.

"Better than yesterday," I say, honestly.

"Do you need anything like Advil or Neosporin or band-aids?"

"Nah, I can just get that stuff at the Student Health Center."

"Okay."

"Don't worry about me, I'm fine."

"Alright." She pauses. "I want to talk about your classes, too." I knew it was coming.

"I don't really want to talk about it."

"Maybe you need to."

"It's fine."

"You can tell me what happened." Jesus, she's relentless.

"I have— had, a really tough History class this semester, and after bombing two papers, I knew I wasn't going to pass it. I'm here on a partial scholarship with a GPA requirement. When I found out I was going to lose it, I figured what's the point?" Lily takes this info in.

"Just one bad class?"

"Yeah."

"Was it a weed-out class?"

"What's that?"

"It's a class that's unnecessarily difficult to discourage some people from declaring that major."

"Dumb people?"

"Just so that it's not considered an 'easy' major," she clarifies.

"So they make it hard just for the prestige?"

"Basically."

"Maybe that's part of it, but everyone else in the class is smart, and the professor's really smart and scholarly, and everyone else thinks he's brilliant, so it's probably just me."

"Well, a professor can be smart and still be a shitty teacher." I hadn't thought of this. My mind reviews that brief office hours session I had with him and how unhelpful he was. "And if it was your only bad class, why didn't you just withdraw?"

"What?"

"You can drop one class a semester."

"I thought you can only do that in the first week?"

"That's more for switching around classes. This is like a mulligan where you bail on a class you're not doing well in, to save your GPA."

"Oh, no one ever told me that." I feel like an idiot. My semester could have turned out completely different if I knew this.

"I know, they don't tell you. I found out from Martha of all people."

"How is that old bag? I still feel bad that you had to move back in with her."

"No, I don't live with her anymore."

"Really?"

"Yeah, I got a transfer at the end of the year. I live in Syle now. I didn't tell you?" This explains why I haven't seen her around the dorm at all.

"No, we really didn't talk after we, you know." She nods. "Except for the wedding. Well, we really didn't talk then either."

"I know," she acknowledges. "Did you leave early because I was ignoring you?"

"No, I just had a long drive. And the next day was my grandma's funeral."

"Oh my God! I had no idea."

"It's fine. You were busy with the wedding party anyway. It looked like you were having a lot of fun with them."

"Yeah," she says, looking at the floor. We both know that I'm talking about that groomsman, but the tone in her voice tells me that whoever he was, it didn't work out. "Sorry I didn't spend more time with you."

"Next time." I don't know if she expects me to throw her more of a bone or is just still processing that night, but after some quiet, she takes it upon herself to leave.

"Promise me you'll let me know if you need anything, okay?"

"I know where to find you now." I don't mean any offense, but she may have taken some because she just gives me one last look and leaves.

Passage 8:

End of Freshman Year

Chapter 23: The Scheme

I wake up Wednesday morning, stash depleted, and head up to Simon's house to refill my prescription. It's raining, so I walk through the academic halls where I can. While passing through Witz, I stop by the lecture hall from that film class I sat in on. It's completely empty and for some reason I go in, close the door behind me and sit down. The lights are off and it's almost pitch black. I don't remember exactly which day of the week that film class occurred, but I remember it being a long class. The projector screen is down, so maybe it's today. It's starkly quiet. I don't even hear footsteps in the hallway. I'm surprised there's not a class in here right now. Maybe finals week has already started. I wonder what that film professor would have thought of my analysis of his foreign movie. I wonder if anybody is going to come in and kick me out. And somewhere in there, I see a spark of what still may be possible. It's preposterously insane, but I still wonder. My core cajoles me up, and I have a change of plans.

I dash back to my room and pull up my first semester's grades on the student portal.

Physical Geology – B-, 4 credits
Freshman Seminar – A, 3 credits
Introductory Theatre – B, 3 credits
Sociology of the United States – B+, 3 credits
Freshman Literature – B+, 3 credits

Semester GPA: 3.2
Overall GPA: 3.2

I scribble this info down and look up how GPA is calculated. Each letter grade has a number equivalent which is multiplied by how many credits the class is, and then everything is averaged. I check the math against my Fall classes and it works out. I got a 3.23625. I write down my classes for this semester.

Introduction to Business Management
United States Elections
Spanish II
Statistics II
Early-European History

All are three credits. If Lily is right about withdrawing, I can forget about Early-European History. I take extra satisfaction in crossing it out over and over again. This would leave me with twelve total credits, which is good because then my Fall semester's grades would weigh more heavily into my overall GPA. Now it's time to speculate. How shitty can I do in my remaining classes and still maintain that 3.0 overall GPA? Let's try a C in every class. That'd be a Spring GPA of a 2.0 with twelve credits. I factor that against my Fall GPA and the result is an overall GPA of 2.70643. Shit. I'd have to do better than all C's.

I spend the next half-hour trying out different outcomes and come to the conclusion that I'd have to basically get a B- in three classes and a C+ in one to end up with an overall GPA of 2.96357. That'll round up and I'd be golden. I put the least amount of faith into Spanish, but other than that, all the classes pretty much have the same amount of weight. This'll force me to grant equal focus on them all, since no one is a guarantee. I overlook my plan.

Introduction to Business Management – B-, 3 credits
United States Elections – B-, 3 credits
Spanish II – C+, 3 credits
Statistics II – B-, 3 credits
~~*Early-European History*~~

Semester GPA: 2.6
Overall GPA: 3.0

I think I can do this. I hope I can do this. Today's already the last day of classes, so I'm really behind the eight ball. It's a long shot, but I've got to try. I just need to meet with each professor. I could email them, but I feel I'll be able to evoke more sympathy if it's face-to-face. First'll be Professor Le since I'm taking two classes with her. When I knock on her door, her eyebrows shoot to the ceiling and I initially interpret it as an immediate rejection, but then I remember what my face looks like. My right side has actually started to swell more than before, and my left eye is still ruby. She's in the middle of grading an assignment, probably one that I'll have to make up, but she graces some time and allows me to sit down. As I explain my situation, her face emanates a wave of understanding that lifts my spirit.

"So, do you think I can do it?" I ask. She takes in the question and thinks. Uh-oh. I may have overestimated her empathy. "I mean I know I'm allowed to take the finals, but will you let me make up the work?"

"Yes, of course, I just think it will be difficult for you. You're in Statistics-Two?"

"And Intro to Business Management."

"I see. You missed two tests for that class, but I'll allow you to make them up."

"You will?" I beam.

"And there's also a final presentation."

"I know, I'll be ready for it."

"Perhaps, but you missed quite a lot in Statistics. I would recommend withdrawing, but you've passed the deadline."

"There are deadlines for withdrawing?"

"Yes, I don't know if we can get around that."

"Oh, I was planning on withdrawing from a different class."

"One you can't salvage?"

"Definitely not. And I need Statistics so I can keep my scholarship. And for health insurance."

"Oh, dear."

"Yeah."

"Well maybe you can pass-fail Statistics."

"What's that?" I feel like these two words are becoming my catchphrase.

"It's pretty self-explanatory: if you pass the class, you get the credits, but it doesn't affect your GPA. If you fail, you don't receive any credits and it also doesn't affect your GPA."

"Yeah, I'll do that!"

"Okay, you're also past the deadline for pass-fail, but professors can override it." I take this to mean she'll do it for me.

"Thank you a million percent. Are there any tests I have to make up for it?" Instead of answering, Professor Le turns to her computer to look something up.

"You actually did pretty well before you stopped coming. I'll make you a deal. If you pass the final, I'll pass you for the class."

"Yes! Thank you, thank you, thank you so much!" I run out of her office to the Registrar where I pick up a pass/fail slip and a withdrawal slip, too. I run straight back to Professor Le who signs off. With the empty withdrawal slip, I know who I must see now, but I don't feel ready for him. As I approach his office, my anxiety is going haywire, and I kind of wish I had replenished my stock with Simon. Luckily and unluckily, his office door is closed and I'm sure I'll have to arrange a time for me to grovel for release.

Dr. Prescott doesn't show as much concern for my injuries and situation as Professor Le, but luckily my Elections class with her is all papers, plus the in-class Final. She says she'll let me hand in the four papers I missed during the Final, but she'll have to take off some points for lateness. I thank her and repeat the motions with Professor Molinero. He also isn't as sympathetic, but offers a deal of his own.

"You can make up the assignments, but I won't let you retake any of the tests you missed. It wouldn't be fair to the other students."

"Oh." My heart drops, but his inflection tells me there's going to be a "but."

"But, I will take into account extracurricular participation if you'd be so inclined."

"What's that?"

"There's a Hispanic and Latino Heritage night this Sunday and we desperately need male participants. The scheduling is unfortunate, it being Finals Week, so we're a little short on people." I'm not really sure what he means, but my gut tells me to respond with enthusiasm, because this might be the only thing that keeps me afloat.

"Sure, what do you need me to do?"

"Have you ever done any Latin dancing before?" My mind flashes to Lily's sister's wedding.

"Yes, I have," I say, just a notch above lying.

"Great, meet at the Student Union Ballroom Friday night at five." I nod in agreement and am out the door before either of us can change our minds.

I do a couple loops around Syle Hall before I find Lily's room and give her door a knock. Her friend from that original frat night opens the door, whose face matches my level of surprise, but also has an added twist of friend-solidarity-hatred towards me, along with what-the-hell-happened-to-your-face?

"What do you want?" she asks. Lily leans her chair back, flashing her wicked eyebrows, and saves me.

"Alex, you remember Penelope, right?" Lily asks me. Penelope? With a name like that, I'd thought I'd stop referring to her as "Lily's friend" much sooner.

"Of course, Penelope!" I glance at her briefly and then snap back to Lily. "Can I talk to you for a minute?"

"Sure." Lily meets me at the doorframe, and Penelope sits down and goes back to work, although I'm positive she's got an ear crooked to eavesdrop.

"I would have called, but my phone's still on the fritz."

"Did you try putting it in rice?"

"That's a thing?"

"Yeah, it'll absorb the water."

"Great, I'll try that. Do you have any rice?"

"Actually, I do," she says, retrieving a mostly-empty bag.

"Great, I'll return this when I'm done."

"Please don't. Why would I want lake-water rice? Just chuck it."

"Right. I also wanted to tell you that I'm going to try to do it."

"Do what?"

"Finish the semester."

"What do you mean 'finish the semester?'" she asks completely perplexed.

"Hand in what work I can, take my finals and hopefully get a B-minus in all my classes." She takes it in and doesn't say anything for a second.

"That's insane."

"I know."

"The semester is basically already over."

"I know."

"You missed so much."

"I know, but I got to try." She takes another beat.

"Good luck, I guess?"

"Thanks. I guess I'll need it, right?" I want to tell her something more, but know that Penelope may still be listening in. I know I'll be holed in my room this whole next week, and this may be the last time I ever see her, so I suck it up and say it. "I also wanted to say 'thank you.'"

"For the rice?" she jokes, not yet realizing I'm trying to be sincere.

"That, and also other stuff. For what you said the other day, for everything. I'm sorry for being mean to you." Her face morphs as she senses my tone.

"You're welcome. And, sorry for being mean, too." I just nod. I don't know what else to say, so I give her a kiss on the cheek and retreat to Parker.

I immerse my soggy phone into the starch and then decide to get the worst out of the way first. I open up my laptop and begin typing.

Dear Dr. Spetato,

Do you have time to speak with me in person tomorrow in your office? I know you're very busy, but it's of the upmost importance and won't take long at all. Please let me know as soon as you can.

Sincerely,
Alex Ryback

I hope that sounds professional, but still urgent and not too presumptive. He was impossible to get a hold of when I actually attended class, so what can I expect now? I click the "Send" button with trepidation, knowing that it's now out of my hands. I hope he responds quick. I whip out my GPA worksheet to adjust it, now that I'm pass-failing Statistics. The math stays the same, and I take a tack and stick my plan on the wall as motivation, a reminder, my flexible fate, whatever you want to call it.

Introduction to Business Management – B-, 3 credits
United States Elections – B-, 3 credits
Spanish II – C+, 3 credits
Statistics II – Pass/Fail, 3 credits
~~Early-European History~~

Semester GPA: 2.6
Overall GPA: 3.0

All of this hinges on that withdrawal, but I have to make a leap of faith and assume it'll go through. I rack my brain trying to think of how to triage the mountain of work and studying before me. There are entire pages of syllabuses I have to cover and hundreds of textbook pages I need to read in order to learn the material I missed. I decide to start working on one of the four Elections papers I have to write and hear a knock on the door. I know I shouldn't be surprised when I open up to Simon's grin, but two days ago now feels like a lifetime ago.

"There he is!" Simon says walking in. "How's my boy feeling? I never heard back from you."

"I know. My phone wasn't working and I got a ride with someone else."

"That's what I figured. Feeling better?" he asks, eyeing each side of my face.

"A little."

"Well, take it easy then. I've got big news."

"What's that?" I ask, admittedly intrigued.

"Tomorrow night: last house party I'll ever be hosting. It's the end of an era. There's a Senior Bash on Saturday on the Green, so—"

"Simon," I stop him. "I can't. I'm sorry, I just need to be in finals mode this weekend."

"Totally cool, but if you need a break—"

"Thanks, but I can't."

"Alright. Also, I brought a little medicine in case you were still recovering, which from the look of you, you are." He whips out a dimebag, and the universe is taunting me.

"No!" I unintentionally shout. "Sorry, not now." I try to think of how to put this. "Simon, I need you to do me a favor."

"Shoot."

"Please don't come here or contact me until after Finals Week. Nothing against you; I just got to study." I expect him to be offended or disappointed, but he just nods, tousles my hair and leaves. Whew! Temptation averted. Back to Poli-Sci.

I decide to begin on the women's suffrage paper. I dash to the library, take out some books on the topic and grab a tuna fish hoagie from the café. As I get rung up, I eye my food balance, which is just under eighty bucks. I probably had a bit more this time last semester, but I did go through a pigging out phase during my class lapse. I do some rough math in my head and wonder if I'll be able to survive on that for the next week and change, but then put that thought on the backburner. Back in my room, I scarf half the sub down, but force myself to leave the rest of my dinner to the side as motivation. I take a break and check my email, but still no response from Spetato.

Protests, Temperance movement, opposition. I pace around my room a bit, go to the bathroom and splash water in my face. Its passing, women being reluctant to actually vote once it was passed, and its effect on the country and politics today. Done. It's just shy of four-and-a-half pages, but I've rounded up with much less on the last page. That's one out of four Poli-Sci papers down. It's just a dent in my workload, but it's a start. I close my laptop and go to bed at 3:10AM.

I wake up just after 8:30AM, and instinctively think about what class I have, only to remember that the next two days are designated study days. I roll over wanting to give myself some more, much-earned sleep, but grab my laptop and lay it on my chest. I log into my email and see a response from Dr. Spetato within the past hour.

Dear Alex,

A meeting is very unlikely. I will be in my office this morning between 8 & 9, but have meetings after then. I won't be back on campus until Monday for Finals and won't have time to meet then either.

-Dr. N. Spetato

My eyes dart to the clock. Fuck! Fuck! Fuck! I hastily slip on the nearest pair of jeans and shoes, leave on the shirt that I slept in, grab my backpack and gallop out of Parker. It's kind of chilly out, but I didn't have time to find a jacket and am already starting to sweat anyway. As I'm sprinting, I'm hacking up my entire throat and my backpack is swinging in rhythm, slamming into my fractured rib every time it shifts to my right side. I recite a canticle of "Fuck"'s every time it connects, but don't readjust or reposition my backpack; I don't have the time. I momentarily ponder why I brought my whole backpack, but then remind myself that the withdrawal slip is somewhere in it. Wait, did I put it in my backpack? God, I hope so.

Once in Renard Hall, I keep up my pace, avoiding pedestrians, and come to a sudden halt when I'm outside his office door, which thankfully is open. I rub the morning gunk out of my eyes, which probably doesn't improve my presentation much, considering I also have bedhead, a smelly shirt, sweat pouring out of my pores, a cherry red eye, and a cheek that's now more swollen than ever.

"Dr. Spetato?" I knock on his door. He lifts his head from his desk and his gaze is unforgiving. After a second it's clear that he's not going to verbally respond. "I'm Alex Ryback. I sent you that email yesterday."

"Yes, did you not receive my response?"

"I did, and I—"

"Did you not comprehend my response?"

"I did, but I needed to come anyway. I'm pretty desperate."

"I'm very busy and will be leaving momentarily."

"This won't take long, I promise," I say, willing myself into his office and into that dreaded seat.

"Fine," he relents. "Proceed." It's only then that I realize I hadn't prepared anything to say to him. My other professors lent me an ear, but I always knew he wouldn't grant me that. I'm here now and don't have time to craft it or polish it. I just have to say it.

"I need to withdraw from Early-European History. I know I'm past the deadline, I know the semester's over, but I'm not going to pass the class, and I'll lose my scholarship if I can't withdraw." He doesn't immediately respond, but maintains the stare. I don't know what else to do, but keep telling him my account. "I really tried in your class. After I did bad on my first paper, you barely gave me any time to discuss it. You just discouraged me more, and I did just as worse on the second paper. I didn't know students were allowed to withdraw from classes after Drop-Add. If I did, I would have. I think you should have even suggested it." He shoots upright in his seat. That last part may have been a little too presumptuous, but I did mean it.

"Mr. Ryback, it is not my duty to personally inform you of vital academic dates or hold your hand throughout your entire college career. The onus is on you to grasp the material of my class, stay informed and make any necessary academic decisions on your own. I outrightly deny your request."

"Please," I make one last attempt. "I won't be able to attend Belston without my scholarship. I'll have to drop out."

"No. This is all of your own doing and you need to take responsibility." He motions his hand towards the door and I know it's over.

It's over. I ponder that reality, walking aimlessly towards the other end of Renard. Back to Domport, back to a shared bedroom. I'm just like Gerry. None of this year matters because of one class, one professor. It's completely over and there's nothing left to do, but—Wait!

I spy an office down the hall that looks familiar. One more idea before I call it quits. It's a longshot on top of my Hail Mary, but I've got nothing to lose. I remember that I still have an academic advisor and thankfully, her office looks open. I stand in her doorway, trying to plan my words ahead this time, but she realizes I'm there before I can.

"Alex!" Professor Carter replies in the to-be-expected shock, after seeing my face. She remembers me! And my name! "Is everything alright?" This question lights me up like one of Professor Le's beaming smiles or like Lily in her entirety. I spill my guts out to her, and observe the wheels turning in her head. "This isn't likely, but I can make a call to the Dean, and maybe he can push that withdrawal through." I hadn't thought of going above his head.

"Yes! Thank you so much!" I tell her.

"It's not a guarantee, Alex. Keep doing what you're doing and I'll be in touch." I nod and walk briskly back to Parker, still kind of achy from those backpack slams. I fish my cell phone out of the rice and miraculously, it turns on. I don't expect anyone to be home, but I leave a message for Mom and Dad, reminding them to pick me up a week from Saturday. I spin the wheel of undone work in my head, and land on that pile of Spanish homework.

Mi hermano corta su pollo con su tenedor y cuchillo.

A good chunk into the mound, I break for lunch, wince when I see my balance, binge and find two emails waiting for me when I get back. The first is from Professor Carter.

Dear Alex,

*I spoke with Dean Syle and he has granted you "an audience,"
to consider your request tomorrow at 2PM in Juge Hall. Like
I said, it's not a guarantee. I will accompany you as a liaison.
Be sure to be on time and clear your afternoon of any other
obligations. Also, wear something presentable.*

See you tomorrow,
M.C.

I write her a quick confirmation, and process the information.
Dean Syle? I never heard of him. I wonder what a college dean
does. I guess stuff like this. I wonder if he's related to the guy
they named Lily's dorm after. I remember that I have that dance
rehearsal at 5PM tomorrow, but there's no way this meeting will
go that long. Right? I reread the "presentable" sentence and dig
in my closet for dressy clothes and a tie. There's nothing I can
do about my face, but the rest of me can play the part.

The next email is from Professor Le asking to arrange a time to
take my makeup Business Management tests. I scramble this added
info into my mind and ask to take the first test tomorrow morning
and the second anytime on Monday. I receive a confirmatory
email not long after, and tomorrow's schedule becomes clear.
Well, clear based on one, big condition. Tomorrow night, I'll
either be dusting off my limited salsa skills, or preparing to
leave forever. I push my Spanish stuff to the side and take out
my Business textbook.

I finish the test just before 11AM and give a half-hearted
smile to Professor Le. She arches an eyebrow, probably assuming
that I found it difficult, but that's not it at all. The test itself was
straightforward enough, just microeconomics and entrepreneurial
questions, really exactly what the syllabus said it would be.
Breezing up on the readings and cramming until 2AM was
definitely necessary, but it's such a breath of fresh air when a
teacher tests you on stuff you were actually taught, instead of trick
questions just to make the class seem hard. I don't know why they

do stuff like that; maybe so they're not thought of as pushovers or a cake class. But the expression that confused Professor Le was one that converged onto me the moment I finished the last question of her test. It isn't one of fatigue, it's one of impending doom and dread. The next thing will determine everything.

I go back to my room, knock out some more Spanish and put on my best dress shirt, slacks and tie. I look myself in the mirror and notice that both my shirt and pants are a little wrinkled. I wouldn't think much of it, but Professor Carter did go out of her way to tell me to look decent. There's only one man I can think of who can help me right now. I knock on Antione's door and regurgitate my spiel, before he cuts me off.

"I know."

"How?"

"Lily told me."

"Right. So, do you have an iron I can borrow and also, do you know how to iron?"

"Of course. Alright, strip off your clothes and follow me." I do as I'm told and follow him to the laundry room. Along the way, I get a few glances walking in my underwear and untied dress shoes. I don't know why I couldn't have disrobed once we got there, but then see Antione reading the tags. Antione pulls down an ironing board I never knew existed, as I pace around the laundry room.

"Who's the meeting with?" he asks.

"Dean Syle." Antione stops ironing for a second and takes in the name.

"Good luck." I guess there's not much more to say.

I get to Juge Hall with time to spare, and use it to empty my bladder and give myself a look over. Professor Carter arrives not long after, and before I know it, we're in the Dean's office and she closes the door. Dean Syle looks every bit as scary as I thought he would. He's got shoulder-length silver hair with matching eyebrows and beard. I don't know how they make scary old people. As a kid, the old man you knew best was your grandpa who'd treat you to ice cream and stuff. And all your friends had nice grandpas, too. And with his white beard, I'd expect more of a Santa Claus vibe, but this guy gives off the air that he'd be the judge that imprisoned Santa Claus. Maybe it's his suit, maybe it's his oak desk, maybe it's the fancy books on his multiple bookshelves. Whatever it is, his initial demeanor sparks a fear that fills me with doubt, knowing that I'm at his mercy.

I don't waste much time and explain my situation. When I'm finished, to my surprise, he doesn't take any time to mull it over and just asks me to step outside while Professor Carter and he discuss. I do as I'm told and purposely leave the door a crack open, hoping they don't notice.

At first I think they're talking very softly, but as I press my ear closer, I realize they're not saying anything. Finally, Dean Syle breathes an overexaggerated exhale.

"What do you want me to say, Makena?"

"I believe this young man should be able to withdraw from that class," Professor Carter responds, calmly.

"Hmm. One of my duties as Dean is to maintain the Belston standard. Should we let every failing student drop a class during finals week?"

"I believe this was just a hiccup for him."

"Makena, we've both seen the trajectories of his type; they drop out sooner or later. What good does it do us to keep a student here that can't pass muster? Shouldn't that scholarship go to a kid who actually performs well here?"

"Dean Syle, my duty as an academic advisor is to advocate for a student when I see potential. We both know this isn't the first time that this Spetato has been inaccessible to students. What good does it do us, to set students up for that?"

"Hmm."

"And doesn't granting some amnesty create an opportunity for a higher graduation rate?"

"At the expense of our resources? We can't afford to teach down to students that aren't of Belston caliber."

"Well, we accepted him, didn't we?"

"Alright, now you're just perturbing me." I hear a paper rustling. "This isn't going to be a regular occurrence." I hear a scribble. "It's not a good use of my time coddling a kid, just to delay the inevitable."

"Thank you, sir," Professor Carter says, conciliatorily. I'm trying to analyze what happened, but am receiving conflicting cues. I think he signed my form, but did so while insulting me. He clearly has no faith in me, but I'll be damned if I don't prove him wrong. I don't expect him to keep track of me, or even know if Deans do that, but maybe he'll recognize my name at Commencement and have to eat his words. Or maybe I can approach him, just at the end of my senior year and tell him that—

WHAM! The office door hits me right in the fish-hook-wound part of my cheek.

"Fuck!" I say to myself, covering that side of my face. I look up and see Professor Carter chidingly staring at me with inked paper in hand. She definitely encountered my expletive, but I have no idea if the Dean heard.

"Don't make me regret this," she says, handing me the slip.

"I won't!" I promise her. I give her an unwanted hug and race to the Registrar's office. The clerk must have never processed something like this before because there's a lot of back and forth and explanation on my part. She must take Dean Syle's signature as a forgery, because she keeps conferring with other employees and eventually calls him to confirm the validity of the document. Before she relents, she forces me to fill out an extra form, and then processes my withdrawal. I don't mind; by the time I walk out of the office, I'm walking on air. Neal Spetato no longer has control over my future, and I never have to see him again.

All this takes so much time, that I have to go straight to the Student Union for the dance practice. I walk into the ballroom and spot a group socializing near the stage. I don't know a soul, so I collapse in a chair some distance away from them. I try to mind my business, but then notice a figure within the group, one that keeps weaving herself into my life. Maybe she can feel my eyes or maybe someone else tells her that I'm checking out her shape, but Lily turns towards me and offers a surprised glance before returning to her friends. I should have guessed she'd be doing this event, and have the same thought again when Antione walks in.

"You're good, man?" he asks, massaging my shoulder.

"Yeah," I say, putting no effort into hiding my exhaustion. He joins the rest of the group and soon enough Professor Molinero has us sitting on the floor, stretching. As he goes over the routines, I quickly realize that he's really going to make me earn this extra credit.

The next three hours are full of seniors teaching us dance routines. I do my best to fake a semblance of technique and keep eyeing the clock. I get roped into a partner dance with some girl with a nose ring, named Maya, an all-guys dance and the big, group dance at the end. The partner dance is a bachata which thankfully isn't too fast, but Maya's body language tells me she wishes I was better at leading. Ironically, Antione and Lily are partners and practically float to the song.

"Pay attention!" Maya yells at me, after I step on her toes for the third time. The just-guys dance is macho casino salsa, and the just-girls dance is a "lyrical," which just looks like ballet to me. It's very elegant and serene, and my eyes latch onto Lily. I also constantly check the clock. When we get to the mambo finale, I'm relieved that it's just a basic step. We're all sardined on stage together, and they stick me in the back anyway, so I don't sweat it too much. Professor Molinero calls us together at the end for a recap, and my mind is already out the door.

"Muy bien, everyone. Now I know that some of you have individual performances that we haven't gotten to tonight; Carlos has the Neruda poem, Maya has a folk song, Lily and Antione have the Argentine tango. We'll have to get to these tomorrow morning. Now..." Tomorrow morning? He never said anything about two rehearsals. Shit. This really eats into my time. I reanalyze in my head and remember that he's not letting me retake any tests, so I need this and must adhere to his excessive rehearsal hours. "So be here, nine o'clock tomorrow morning..." Fuck that's early. "And I'll remind you of this tomorrow, but the ladies' attire for Sunday is any solid-color dress. Muchachos: comfortable, black pants and a white top. Pretty much what Alex is wearing, except without the tie." Everyone's eyes snap to me, and I'm pretty sure I look like a bum because I'm sweaty, my back is hunched and my tie knot is loosened to about three buttons down. I'm ready to limp back to Parker when Professor Molinero stops me. "Alex, I know you're trying your best up there, but I'm going to need you to do a little extra practice before the big show." Are you fucking kidding me?

"Uh-huh," I slurringly confirm.

"We can help him," Lily offers for both Antione and herself. Professor Molinero seems satisfied by this and finally releases me. I'm so fried that I can't possibly see myself doing any work between now and tomorrow morning's practice.

"Sansone's?" Antione suggests, reading my need for some alleviation. I just nod and the three of us walk into town. Antione's nice enough to treat and starts offering dancing pointers to me. Lily eventually gives him a look to ease up, because she knows when I'm really spent. On the way back, we pass some bars, hearing the "Woo!'s" of rollicking seniors. I wonder what Simon's up to. Campus on the contrary, is altogether tranquil, and I can't help noticing the moonlight on their faces, and the wind blowing Lily's hair.

"See you in a couple of hours," she jokes, as we split. I smile for the first time all day and wonder how she was able to induce that expression from me, when I haven't been able to muster it myself.

I swing by the library before dance practice and take out two books on different kinds of voting systems around the world for my second Poli-Sci paper. While other groups are practicing their routines, I arm myself with post-its, and implement my strategy of scanning and marking any good points or quotes. I consider my dancing as improving because I only step on Maya's toes once today, but still get a reminder to practice from Professor Molinero. When the rehearsal is through, he asks us to arrive tomorrow by 4:15PM, and I don't even bother wondering how long it will go. I'm out the door without any goodbyes, my food balance dips and I'm back in my room. I read the Poli-Sci book for a little longer, before deciding to finish up the last of my Spanish homework. One particular assignment is especially difficult because I have to write out conditional-subjunctive statements which sounds like totally made-up, gobbledygook, but it's a real thing, basically like math-if/then problems, but with words.

If I come to school, I see my teacher.
Si yo vendría a la escuela, yo vea a mi maestra.

If I am hungry, I eat food.
Si yo tendría hambre, yo coma comida.

If the weather is hot, I will drink water.
Si clima haría calor, yo beba agua.

My phone rings, and I see that it's Mom.
"Hey, Alex. How's it going?"
"Uh, good," I respond, trying not to lose my work stride.
"So, we're picking you up one week from today?"
"Yes."
"Dad and I are planning to get to you around ten."
"Sure."
"You sound distracted."
"Mom, I got to go."
"Alright honey, love you."
"Love you."

I read this chapter on pluralistic voting, which they do in some states, and make a note of how it's good in some ways and bad in others.

I once remember someone asking Simon if he had any Adderall, but he said no. Simon only really dealt the chill stuff like pot and 'shrooms. Adderall is antithetical to his MO. I have a faint memory of him referring the guy to someone else who dealt it. I could ask Simon, but I can't risk any side effects this week and I'd probably just waste my time tracking down the possible dealer. I need all the time I can get. I scribble down one last tilde, and this semester's Spanish homework is complete. My wrist is throbbing, the side of my palm is blotchy with ink, and I rush over and knock on Antione's door.

He eagerly helps me polish my casino salsa and mambo. Lily walks in on us mid-routine, and we switch to bachata. She gives a playful kick to my shin whenever I make a misstep, and isn't fazed when I remind her it's still healing from my accident.

256

Chapter 24: Finals Week

I force myself to study for Business all day Sunday until the Latino Heritage event. My first makeup test contained some material I remembered from before my lapse, but this one'll cover all new stuff that I wasn't in class for. Some of it's actually interesting, and I have to remind myself to only grasp the gist of each topic and move on.

I pull my Dean-dress clothes out of my hamper, steam them in the shower, and go to check my email before the event. I get frustrated when the webpage won't load and continually open and close the browser before restarting my whole computer. When that doesn't work, I unplug and replug both ends of my ethernet cable before submitting that it actually might be a technical issue. How can this happen now? I'm momentarily beside myself until remembering that I have been watching a lot of porn. Thankfully, the IT Center is open, and I'm able to drop off my laptop before the mini-rehearsal at the Union. Professor Molinero is either satisfied enough with my improvement or just apathetic because there's no more time for me to get better. Lily's wearing a sexy, red dress, and I momentarily steal a glance at her legs, before forcing my eyes down into my Business textbook. A fairly decent crowd of professors and students show up, and I peruse the tables I pass for their chips and salsa. The lights go out, and the darkness banishes my textbook to the floor.

Thankfully, the event goes smoothly. I don't step on Maya's toes at all and us guys get a lot of "Oohs" from female students for our macho number. Antione and Lily's Argentine tango is incredibly elegant, and I wish I was holding her instead of Antione, although their routine looks like it's the calculus of dancing. I'm completely transfixed by the girls' number. I knew it was pretty from the rehearsals, but seeing Lily illuminated in the dark takes it to a whole new level. She moves like a vapor across the stage. A strange cocktail of schoolwork anxiety mixed with longing for her churns in my chest like a jagged arrhythmia. Two things that I want that may soon become out of reach.

The mambo is actually a ton of fun because everyone's on their feet cheering, and the crew turns the house lights on, somewhat masking any mistakes. When it's over, all the performers give each other hugs. Maya gives me an especially long one, thanking me for learning my steps because her family's here, and by the time she lets go, the group hugging is over and Lily's in her seat with the other girls. I sit with Antione and descend upon the rice, beans and tacos, happy to refill on much-needed carbs and also happy that it's free. For potential brownie points, I make sure Professor Molinero sees me help clean up and break down tables, before returning my sweaty clothes to the hamper. Since I still got two Poli-Sci papers after this one, I force myself to handwrite an intro for the international voting one, before polishing off the Business textbook.

It's Monday, I tell myself the instant I wake up. On the way to Renard, I recite some Business terms I crammed into my head yesterday and knock out my second make-up. It is admittedly more difficult than the last, but I'm fairly certain I did well on the short essay about "wasted reach." I pick up my now-functioning laptop from the IT Center, trying to avoid eye contact with the Tech that now likely knows my porn preferences. As I inhale a burger from the Union, I notice I have just about fifteen bucks left in my account. That definitely won't last me until the end of the week. I read and write more Poli-Sci, getting to about a page-and-three-quarters of my International Voting paper.

I should be worried about my paper pace, but push it to the side of my brain for now. I shift to Spanish for the rest of the night, since the final is tomorrow, and text Lily to help me practice for the spoken section. She's not fluent or anything, but she took it in school, too, and it's also an excuse to see her.

She gives me a short window, and when she walks in my door, it's the best part of my day. The speaking portion is using the past, present and future tense in a conversation with Professor Molinero, and I choose the "describe a vacation" option. Lily shows some skepticism when I say, "Me gustan las vacaciones, mis últimas vacaciones fueron buenas, tendré vacaciones el próximo año," in one breath, and reminds me that Professor Molinero will probably throw some curveballs, to which she's most likely right. Antione pops in and asks if we want to split a pizza. I only have three bucks to chip in and promise to throw more in next time. I get the vibe that Lily and Antione want to chill a bit longer, but ask them to leave so I can study, to which they're mildly impressed. I practice a little more Spanish, before falling asleep with all the lights on and my voting book on my face.

It's Tuesday, Alex. When I walk into my Spanish exam, I sit where I normally used to and get a few looks from classmates in my area. At first I attribute it to my face, which is actually healing, but then realize they probably are wondering what I'm doing here since I haven't been to class in months. The test is by no means easy, but I hand in mine to the proctor with confidence, and wait in line for the speaking portion with Professor Molinero. That confidence is instantly shattered when I overhear the kids in front of me discussing the multiple-choice section, saying it was easy, making me realize I got more wrong than I thought. For my own mental health, I retreat away to the nearest vending machine and slurp down a bag of M&M's. I don't come back until I'm the last one in line, and Professor Molinero compliments me on my dancing as I hand in my stack of missing homework.

"Bueno," he says. I see him switch out of small talk mode and pull out a blank grading rubric, so I sit up straight and try to use my tongue to clean any lingering chocolate out of my teeth. "Let's do the 'restaurant' conversation," he tells me.

"Oh, I was going to do the 'vacation' one," I respond, now startled.

"No, I choose the example. You were supposed to prepare for all of them."

"Oh." Fuck, this is off to a bad start.

"Do you need me to read the prompt?"

"Yes, please."

"Alright, 'Using past, present and future tenses, call a restaurant with the intent of altering your reservations.'" I glanced over this one, but didn't consider it, because it sounded too hard. "Are you ready?" Not in a million years.

"Yes."

"Hola," he begins the mock-conversation. Here we go.

"Hola."

"¿Cómo puedo ayudarte?"

"¡No me gusta tu restaurante!" I don't really know where I'll go with this, but I can cross off using the present tense.

"¿Por qué no?"

"¡Ayer, la comida era fea!" I don't know why I'm shouting either, but maybe it goes along with my character in the story.

"¿Fea? ¿No te gustó la presentación?" Presentación? Shit, I think I said his food was ugly. In my book, that's good enough, but he's toying with me. I can see Lily smirking when I tell her she was right.

"¡La comida era mala! ¡Y fea!"

"Siento escuchar eso." Past done, future to go.

"¡Yo no vendré al restaurante mañana!"

"¿Debo cancelar tu reservación?"

"¡Sí, por favor!"

"Tu reservación ha sido cancelada."

"¡Muchas gracias!"

"Adiós."

"Adiós." With that, I check off Spanish in my head, and expand the stress of Statistics, Poli-Sci and Business into its resulting space.

I don't have any time for Poli-Sci today and know there's no way I'll be able to hand in all four papers Thursday morning.

I'll have to beg for an extension then. Since I'm pass-failing Statistics, I need to devote the entirety of tonight to studying for the final. I sandwich my studying around one last sandwich from the dining hall, tabling the inner-worry of how I'll eat the rest of the week. I calculate and speculate how much money I'll need versus what I have in my debit account. If I had a giant pack of granola bars or ramen that might do it, but there's no time for a Walmart run. It's the same as the Adderall possibility; with this crunch, I've got to just go with what I know I can do with what I've got.

Wednesday. The Statistics final is hard, and I pat myself on the back for devoting the whole night to it. I've been getting about four hours of sleep a night, and I'm definitely starting to feel it, but last night's studying was worth the deprivation. All the surveys, tables and plots were easy, and I'm certain I got the boot latching question correct, but am less sure about the one for hypothesis testing and confidence intervals.

I go to the bank to see what I've got left and am both pleasantly surprised and disappointed to see $33.74 blinking back at me. I'm glad I've got some dough, but hoped it would be a bit more. The disappointment overrides the pleasantness when the teller informs me I need to keep twenty dollars in my account for it to stay open. There's no use in arguing, so I withdraw my measly seventeen dollars and immediately wipe half of it out at Sansone's. I get to page three of my International Poli-Sci paper, before cracking the syllabus for the Final, which could be on anything. Antione and I grab burgers for dinner, and he covers me when I come up short. He sees it coming when I ask him for some more money, but is confused and mildly alarmed when I ask him to pick up three bottles of soda for me, too.

"Three bottles? Why don't you just get a two-liter size?"

"That's what I mean."

"What?"

"I want you to get three, two-liters of soda." His eyes go wide when he realizes I'm serious.

"What type?"

"One Mountain Dew, one Dr. Pepper, one Grape Soda."

"You sure about that Grape?"
"Yeah. Thanks, I'll get you back."
"That's a lot of Grape."

Thursday, I think? The lack of sleep is fucking with me because I sleep through my alarm. Terror spikes through my body, but some sixth sense, grace of God must have intervened because I have a solid half-hour before my Poli-Sci final. No time for a shower, brushing my teeth or brushing up on the material, but I am blessed with a self-reminder to bring the one makeup paper I completed. I wish I could have finished the one I'm halfway through, but I'm still going to have to grovel either way.

I hand Dr. Prescott my Women's Suffrage paper and immediately launch into my extension plea before her reaction sets. She makes this one last concession, saying she'll be in her office at 9AM on Saturday and if she doesn't have my last three papers by then, she'll have to count the assignments as incomplete. The final itself is on direct democracy overturning a legislative body's law. I sit there for a good ten minutes trying to decipher the meaning of the question as my classmates rifle through their blue books. I try to drown them out, combing through my memories of last night's cramming, and finally find my thesis. I write about recall elections, combatting lobbyists and even about some of its downsides. As per usual, I'm the last kid in the classroom. I'm in the middle of my very last paragraph when Dr. Prescott pulls the blue book from my hand and a streak of ink goes through the bottom of the page and onto the desk. I feel an urge to protest with indignation, but Dr. Prescott just taps her watch, snaps a rubber band across the essays and leaves the classroom.

I'm just about junkfooded out, so I blow some of Antione's money on a salad and look at the Intro to Business Final assignment on the syllabus.

Create a short presentation based on a topic covered in class this semester.

That's pretty broad. I'm sure that Professor Le gave some pointers on how long it should be and suggestions for good topics, but I missed all that. I'll just have to go with my gut. I comb through the textbook, searching for something from the beginning of the semester, but it all seems so basic and not something I could make a compelling presentation out of. I scan more.

Business insurance – What could you say about that? You should get it?
Fulfilling contracts – Same. You should do it?
Business cycles – Boring.
Overexpansion – This catches my eye.

There's not much written about it – *Overexpansion is an error in which a business attempts to grow itself too quickly and is therefore unprepared for future developments and unforeseen issues*. It reminds me of when our family would summer vacation at that same lake. We always loved this restaurant, Jack's Grill, that had air hockey and skee-ball. The owner told Dad he was opening a second location, but the next summer we saw that not only did it not materialize, but the original restaurant had closed, too. One day, we saw the owner while we were mini-golfing and I overheard him saying to Dad, "termites, the IRS and a divorce." Gerry asked what he meant by that, and Dad explained it to us the best that he could, saying sometimes things are different the second time you do them, it's hard to start a new thing while still maintaining the old, and sometimes things just fall apart. No offense to the Jack, of Jack's Grill, but I think his troubles just gave me my presentation. I do some research online, forage the library for the one relevant book and map out my outline in my head.

Antione and Lily come by to check on me and Lily treats us to one last pie from Sansone's. It feels like a last supper of sorts because Antione's leaving in the morning, Lily in the afternoon, and I might be leaving Belston forever. They mainly try to keep the conversation away from school, unsure of how I'm faring, so I decide to assuage their fears by explaining my presentation idea. I go through the big points to which they reflect blank stares and offer disingenuous support. Shit, they either don't get it, or it's a shitty idea. It still feels good in my gut, though. This is the first time at college where I feel passionate about a project. No time to change course; their feedback just tells me I need to find a way to make it clearer.

Lily tags along back to Parker and Antione ditches us to finish packing. She sits on Matt's bed like she did in her interrogation/pep talk that launched this whole scheme, and I wish I had time to be with her, just her, no distractions.

"You want me to leave, don't you?" she asks, reading my mind.

"Not want…"

"Okay, I'll go. I just need to fix one thing."

"What?" I ask, with intense curiosity. She chuckles and declares herself my surgeon, taking out my stitches with a tweezer.

"Better for your speech," she says. When she leaves, there's a sudden surge of awkwardness, and we say goodbye from a distance, no hug, no handshake, nothing. It's hard to refocus on Business, knowing that could have been our last interaction, but I think about her laugh and tell myself that at least I got that.

The Mountain Dew hisses open. I mark up the library Business book with post-its, and at 1AM, I have my concept and the project takes form. I realize that I need supplies that I don't have. I rifle through Matt's remaining stuff and text Antione who's dead asleep, before just catching a bus to Walmart. I pick up some index cards, construction paper and a bunch of dice, leaving me with four, borrowed bucks. The wait for the next bus is too long, so I just hightail it back to campus, hoping that no cops see me, wondering why a guy is jogging at 3AM with office supplies. I spend the rest of the night doing meaningful arts and crafts and rehearsing. I only drift off for an hour or so, before polishing off the Mountain Dew so I don't oversleep.

I take a shower, put on my dressy clothes, and take a gander at myself in the bathroom mirror. I haven't done a facial readjudication in a few days, but the swelling is mostly gone and my eye is only slightly pinkish. The lack of sleep isn't showing in my eyelids either, which is icing on the scraping-by cake. I practice my presentation one last time in my fancy clothes, gather my materials and make sure I'm at Weston early.

As we enter, Professor Le shoots her trademark kind smile towards each of us, but gives me a particular look of both hope and worry. As she calls up the doomed-to-always-be-first girl with the last name at the top of the alphabet, it becomes clear that this final is going to take the full three-hour block. Most people do PowerPoint presentations, which eats up extra time, finding their file, reconfiguring the computer, adjusting the projector and all of that. When the lights go out, it's hard to stay awake, so I continually pinch my thighs. What makes it even tougher to keep my eyes open is that so many kids hand out a printed copy of their PowerPoint for you to read, while they're displaying it on the projector and reading it word-for-word, in a monotone voice, from their own printed copy. One girl has an interesting presentation on supply chain management, but there are way too many ones on business ethics, which is basically just hearing 'be nice' over and over again, and one guy just talks about supply and demand, like we never heard of the concept before.

When I go up, I turn on the lights and everyone's eyes go wide, and not just from the brightness adjustment. Of all my classes, this is the one where people are most surprised and confused to see me, probably because I'm presenting. From their sea of faces, you'd think it was the end of a magic trick. I overhear one guy actually ask another, "That guy's still in this class?" I just take it in stride, and when I see I have Professor Le's attention, I begin.

"Who can tell me what overexpansion is?" I ask my peers. Crickets. "Overexpansion is basically when a company tries to grow its business before it's ready. The best way to illustrate this is through an activity. Turn your desks and break up into groups of six to eight." No one initially moves, but when Professor Le gives a harmonious nod, metal desk legs screech against the tile and I regain their attention. "Each group represents a restaurant," I tell them, handing out a die and fake construction-paper money. "Business has been going well for all of you in the past year, although you only have so much cash on hand. The restaurants on my left want to open a supplemental spot to grow their business, while the ones on my right are more cautious." I have the left groups split in half, turn away from each other, divide their cash and give me some back, to represent construction expenses. "Now let's roll the dice," I instruct, to the sound of plopping plastic against wood. "Raise your hand if you rolled a five or six. You've capitalized on a recent food craze, increasing your normal revenue." I hand out two green bills to each of those groups. "Three or four? Your business did just as well as last year. Restaurants with one location receive ten-grand. Restaurants with two locations break even due to permit and contractor issues." I can tell I have their attention as I hand out more fake money. "Now, who rolled a one or two? Hurricane season did a number." I take money from them and continue the game for several more rounds, citing investor rescission, getting audited, repeat business dwindling, broken equipment, pretty much anything that could go wrong. In the end, the tortoises fared better, although one dual-location group did defy the odds and survive. I explain that the sole-location groups were now ready to expand, and summarize that a company needs to be able to weather Murphy's Law at its harshest. I don't get applause or anything, but feel ecstatic with myself as I sit down. I take a peek at Professor Le who's scribbling on what must be my grading rubric, but can't tell if it's good or bad.

I endure the boredom of the rest of the class and can't believe who I bump into on my way out.

"Dude, how's it going?" Simon asks me. This must be his one final for his one class. I guess I never asked his major, but assume he's Business if he has Professor Le.

"Hanging in there," I say.

"Dude, you missed it. It was a bacchanal to end all shitshows."

"Well, maybe I'll have my own, my senior year."

"Tell me, and I'm there! Do you need a little something, something?" he asks, putting his thumb and middle fingers to his curled lips. I envision that dimebag, but don't even have a dime.

"I'm not out of the woods yet," I say, signaling I need to leave.

"Alright, peace brother." I give him a pound and notice Professor Le eavesdropping with a stunned look on her face. Shit. She probably had Simon for the past five years and now thinks I'm his apprentice or something. I just smile and dash out of the classroom, hoping it won't affect her previous sympathies towards me. Off to the library.

I must be the only student in the school who's checking out books on the last day of the semester. I take out two books for the 17th century voting paper and a couple of journals for the one on constituency trends. There's more parents and minivans than this morning, and as I scale the Parker staircase, I dodge rows of faceless bodies, heaving crates and bins.

The Dr. Pepper two-liter fizzles. I immediately return to the International Poli-Sci paper I was in the middle of, and when I have one page left to go, Matt walks in with his parents. They're not alarmed by my face, which tells me it's healed enough for my parents to not notice either. I take the sudden clatter as a sign to take a break and retrieve a Snickers from the vending machine. Matt and I say goodbye to each other, which feels wholly unnecessary considering this is the first time I've seen him in six months, and by 5PM I've finished both my second Poli-Sci paper and the Dr. Pepper. That's two out of four Poli-Sci papers, and two out of three two-liter sodas.

As I read, I thumb through the new library books I just took out, I quickly surmise that I won't be able to research and write both outstanding papers before tomorrow morning. I make a judgement call in my head and decide to put all my effort into one of them, and take the hit for the other. I figure one good paper is better than two shitty ones. "17th Century Voting" sounds more boring, so I pack those books away and start reading the journals.

An hour or so later, I hear a knock and there she is. I apparently wasn't the only one who wanted a better goodbye because all she does is plant a peck on me, and then goes on her way.

"Wait!" I plead.

"What?"

"How were your finals?"

"Now you ask?" she laughs, turning right back around.

"Better late than never?" I shout as she disappears into the stairwell.

I choose to write about dealignment and realignment, which is basically when people don't act like they used to when voting.

There's so much soda running through my veins that the instant I feel an inkling of a sugar crash, I crack the Grape bottle. I'll have to drink it lukewarm since Matt took back his mini-fridge, and after two gulps concede that Antione was right about two liters being a lot of grape soda for one person.

By 10:30PM, I've got everything marked up and treat myself to a Milky Way after the first page is done.

The Federalist party opposed the War of 1812, which turned out to be popular. This caused many of its supporters to vote for James Monroe in 1816, instead of their candidate.

Many people who voted for Herbert Hoover in 1928, voted for Franklin Delano Roosevelt in 1932 because of Hoover's handling of the Great Depression.

In 1976, southern Democrats voted for Jimmy Carter because they were registered as Democrats, but in 1980 the same people changed parties and voted for Ronald Reagan because their viewpoints were more aligned with his platform.

I blow the last of my money on some Twizzlers and Peanut M&M's, and the warm Grape, as gnarly as it is, doesn't last much longer either. I'm definitely past forty hours without any real sleep, but am unsure of the exact duration. I finish my bibliography just as the birds start chirping and the sky warms from pink to orange. As the printer ink dries, I consider writing a note about the one missing paper, but knowing Dr. Prescott, the gesture wouldn't garner much. That's three out of four papers done: one already handed in on Thursday, two in front of me and one forever forsaken, whose absence I'm gambling won't hurt me too much. The plastic at my feet displays a slightly better record of completion. That's three out of three sodas downed, which I'm certain are currently corroding my insides.

When I get to Renard, I discover the door is locked and am instantly and completely beside myself. I must be cracking up because I just giggle. I've come too far just to be stopped by a fucking door. Am I really going to have to smash some fucking glass? I seriously consider it, but circle the building until I find the unlocked door of an old freight elevator. My starved muscles somehow slowly heave the rusty, metal door open, paired with throat-scraping grunting, every yank of the way. There's no car, so I just scale the shaft, singing "Motherfucker"'s throughout the entire climb. I pry open the metal gate, hoist my body onto the floor, and reorient myself until I find Dr. Prescott's office. I wipe and lick the residual grease from my hands, slip both papers under her office door and walk out that damn, locked main entrance. It's finished.

With the library books dropped in the bin, I'm still too wired to go to sleep, but am also too dazed to start packing. Weird combination. My bones carry me into Witz, which *is* unlocked, and I find myself in that same dark, empty film class. Sitting in about the same seat where it all began, I start laughing, howling like a madman, which ultimately gives way to something else. I don't know if I'm crying because it's over and there's no one around to see or hear me, or if it's just some chemical necessity that my body is exerting, but either way, I don't have much choice in the matter. Maybe it's everything. A lamentation of the sleep deprivation, frustration, anxiety, depression, despondence, dejection, despair, disappointment, expectation, failure, comparison, constriction, impermanence, instability, ineptitude, isolation, insolvency, injury, technology malfunction, sucrose excess, substance withdrawal, people withdrawal, faculty indifference, faculty callousness, heartache, horniness, hopelessness, loss, anger, guilt, regret, mortality, self-loathing and self-forgiveness. I just accept the tears and let them come, and when my eyes are dry, I leave the dark room and walk outside to a bed of tulips that I hadn't noticed before.

Before I return to my room, I decide I owe one more person a proper goodbye, and when I get to his house, Simon, Bobby and Steph are standing outside in their caps and gowns. There's hugs and smiles all around, and I take a photo of the three of them, one normal, and one where Steph's face sports mock-shock, Bobby is sticking out his tongue, and Simon is sticking out his tongue and flipping off the camera. Simon gives me some ganja, gratis, and I return to Parker for the last time.

Mom and Dad are pissed when they find I haven't started packing, illustrated by their lack of care in depositing my stuff into the car. Dad fires up his Hendrix, as I watch Belston fade away in the side view mirror. I barely comprehend Mom informing me that we'll be stopping at a state park. My brain and my mouth are no longer working in conjunction, but I think I say, "Okay," before passing out.

Chapter 25: Going Home

"Alex?" The vocal vibrations pierce through my dozy daze. My eyes open to complete pitch darkness except for sets of headlights flashing past my face. "We're stopping for dinner," Mom adds when she sees I'm awake. All I can muster is a nod.

"Late night?" Dad asks with a grin. I nod again. He assumes I was partying, which is fine. The less they know, the better. As we exit off the highway, the realization that I can step outside of the zeitgeist of the past week begins to bubble in my brain, although my cortisol levels probably won't dissipate until I get my grades and know for certain whether or not it was for naught. I remind myself that no matter how it goes, my next immediate struggle is financial. I call up Carla and let her know I'll take any shift, every shift. We park at a Roy Rogers, and Dad gives both Mom and me a knowing smirk. There's really no story there, it's just that they're so rare and that the only time we'd eat at one would be on a family road trip. Gerry and I would go nuts, chanting "Roy Rogers!" like we were motivational speakers at a corporate event. Abigail would get so miffed until Diana would join us, which she thought was cute. Although I haven't been there in years, I still remember my usual, and we're about the only people there.

"We tried to wake you up at the park, but you were so knocked out, we just left you," Mom tells me.

"That's fine," I say.

"Was it a difficult semester?"

"Uh, here and there."

"Have you declared a major yet?" Dad asks, with a casual cloak over true inquisitiveness.

"I'm thinking of Business." If I go back, I really am, just so I can take more classes with Professor Le.

"Like your old man."

"I suppose so." A lightbulb flashes above Dad's head.

"I should see if I can get you an internship at my company this summer. What do you think?"

"Um, maybe next summer. I need to make some money for books next year."

"Really? Can they really be that much?"

"Yeah, it's like almost a grand each semester."

"Are you serious?" Mom asks.

"Wow," Dad says. "When we were in college, they weren't that steep."

"We really just had to write compositions," Mom adds. Another nod from me.

"But maybe Gerry would be interested in that internship," I offer to Dad. Mom and Dad stammer as if I suggested Dad try to get a job for a goldfish.

"Um, I'm not sure if he's on the right path for something like that right now," Dad assembles meekly.

"Why not? He does sales at his tech store. From what I hear, he's pretty good at it. If you bend the truth and say he's taking a marketing class in the fall, your company would probably accept that, right?"

"Maybe," Dad replies, mulling it over in his head. Another beat of silence.

"How was Easter?" I ask, only to quickly surmise that this wasn't the question to ask to quell the familial awkwardness.

"Oh, it was okay," Mom says.

"Did you do the butter lamb in memory of Grandma?" I ask, to ease them into the conversation.

"Oh, no," Dad says. "Not this year." I can't stand the conversation cessation.

"Did something happen?" I finally ask. Mom hesitates, but then lets it out.

"Well, Abigail and I had a small disagreement." I know I'll have to nudge more.

"Over the food?"

"No," Mom says. "Over Suzie."

"Oh." Her tone tells me it was a cataclysmic clash. And with her golden child. This must be earthshattering Mom, so I don't ask more. Unbelievably, she continues on her own.

"I just feel I do so much for them and they should be more appreciative, even if my way is slightly different. I mean, I do have twenty-five, twenty-six more years' experience than she does. I know she wants to do it on her own, it's just that my mother was already gone when I had Abbie, and that was really hard. I just want her to have what I didn't. We haven't spoken since, and tomorrow is Mother's Day." Oh my God. I've never heard Mom open up and confess like this. That was there my whole life? All I had to do was press a bit more? I make a mental note to ask Dad about Grandma's passing to see if it yields similar results. I don't really know what to say to Mom because I never knew her mother and don't know squat about babies, so I take an alternate route.

"Well, you do have another daughter." Mom laughs, and this is the first time I've seen her acknowledge her favoritism. "Wasn't getting cut from volleyball a big blow for her?"

"I think so."

"Well, maybe do some Abigail stuff with Diana instead. Show her there's more to her than just academics and hobbies, but also that she can try again or something." Now Mom just nods. I take a look at both of my parents and suddenly see them in a new light: they're spent. I consider what one week of hell did to me and then imagine the chaos of their lives in the past year: jobs, house, kids, grandkid, ailing mother. I'm lucky I got a pick up.

As we pull into our driveway, I can tell they're exhausted and let them know I can just unload all my junk in the morning by myself. Gerry's already asleep, and I do my best to sneak into bed quietly, although I won't be able to conk out for a while. I bet there'll be a dash of the usual room-return resentment in the next few days, but maybe less so now that it's becoming routine. I look at Gerry and think about that nail clipper. I laugh to myself because if he decided to buy me a comb or pens, I might not be here right now. I don't know if I'll ever tell him. I think about Gerry's own time of turbulence and wonder if he felt the same things I did. Maybe he's still in it and maybe he still does. Brothers are different from parents, so I don't know if there's anything I could ever say to him. And if my plan doesn't pan out, we'll really be in the same boat. Maybe we'll be able to talk then or maybe there'll just be more tension and resentment. God, I hope it worked. Either way, I reckon he and I will each figure it out in our own way.

Passage 9:

Summer after Freshman Year of College

Chapter 26: Mid-May

Carla returns my call just after 10AM, asking if I can come in. My cycadean rhythm is midway recovered from its wonkiness, but I jump at the shift because I need it. Turns out, Carla's hoping to spend the day with her mom, so she leaves me at the store alone for most of the afternoon and has me lock up for the first time. When I get home, Abigail, Stephen and Suzie are over, and although I sense a small amount of coarseness, whatever happened between Mom and Abigail is pretty much patched. I surmise that Stephen and Abigail have both returned to work, are putting Suzie in daycare, and that Mom is able to withhold any criticisms of the service. Diana is chilly towards me, but not completely cold. I imagine she's suspicious that I've ratted her out to Mom and Dad, although her eyes are all the evidence they need. I pick up Suzie and immediately sense that she's remarkably bigger and her hair's grown back a ton. She flashes me a big smile, and it's like I never left her. Her eyes stare into mine, and I feel perfect and worthwhile for just existing and making her happy. I consider what the world brought my eyes to, just yesterday morning, and meditate on how these two visions could be so incredibly different.

I wake up and immediately ponder checking what I'm dreading, although Monday is probably too early for all of my grades to come in. Just after Carla calls me for another shift, Mark texts about dinner. I ask Gerry for twenty bucks and unbelievably, he lends it to me, no questions asked. I don't want to ruin my shift, but my curiosity overcomes me and I log into my student portal.

Statistics II – PASS, 3 credits
Early-European History – WITHDRAW

Semester GPA:
Overall GPA: 3.2

Phew. It's both relieving and a small let down. I was pretty certain I'd cross the threshold to pass Statistics, but I was hoping for more good news. I also see that I have an email from Professor Le.

Dear Alex,

I'd like to compliment you on your presentation in Introduction to Business Management. Overexpansion! Obscure, but great topic. You were the only student to make their presentation interactive. Way to think outside of the box! I hope to see you in the fall.

Have a great summer,
Sally

I'm walking on air. My risk paid off. I wish she told me my grade, but this sure makes it sound good. I've been praised by teachers before, but this feels different for some reason. Maybe it's because it contrasts with everything else, or because I worked really hard on something I was passionate about.

I revisit the presentation in my mind my whole shift, and wonder what other classes I can take with her, or if there's another Business professor like her. I make a mental note to register for

Fall classes once I receive the final verdict; I think everyone else did that in the middle of the semester.

Texting Lily gets me through the rest of the day, and I meet Mark and Emily at the diner. Upon seeing him, I burst into laughter at the beard he's attempting.

"Shut up, man," Mark says, rubbing it.

"Did something happen to your cheek?" Emily asks.

"Why, does it look like something did?" I return, jokingly.

"Uh, it's just a little discolored." We catch up on everything and for some inexplicable reason, I feel they're a bit different, too. The distance between January to May has been lightyears longer than August to Thanksgiving. I consider telling them about everything, but then decide against it. I figure if I do, it'll be once I know. For now, it's nice that only a few Belston people are privy to my lapse.

Tuesday morning provides no update in my student portal. Dad takes the day off, and Gerry and I join him to view Grandma's headstone.

"Do you like how it came out?" I ask him.

"Yes," Dad says, with an indecipherable tone and facial expression.

"Do you miss her?"

"Yes." He may be a harder nut to crack. Gerry gives me a look, and I abandon the "opening up" inquiry. We grab a late lunch at a burger joint with an arcade, and Gerry and I take turns beating Dad at air hockey.

With my laptop on my chest, I check the student portal one more time, just before bed. Still nil; still in limbo. Gerry is frantically trying to make a call, but something is obviously off.

"Goddammit," he curses himself.

"What's wrong?" I ask.

"Nothing, someone's just not getting back to me."

"Dealer?"

"Yeah," he admits, reluctantly. I go into my backpack, fish out Simon's parting dimebag.

"Consider yourself half-paid back," I say, flinging it to Gerry, who catches it with a surprised look on his face.

"Thanks," he says with a smile, leaving the room.

I'm admittedly running a little late Wednesday morning. Gerry's dropping me off before his shift and his "Let's fucking go!"'s aren't as motivating as he thinks they are. I don't really have time to check the portal, but I can't stand the wondering. If it's up, I have to know. I log in standing up so that I can run out the instant I get the update.

As soon as the page loads, I can tell everything's in, just from the volume of text.

Introduction to Business Management – B, 3 credits
United States Elections – C-, 3 credits
Spanish II – C, 3 credits
Statistics II – PASS, 3 credits
Early-European History – WITHDRAW

Semester GPA: 2.2
Overall GPA: 2.9

2.9 GPA. No. Fuck. No, no.

"I'm leaving!" Gerry shouts. I close my laptop and meet him in the car. As he backs out, he curses at me more, but I just stare ahead in a fog. I didn't consider how I'd react if it didn't work out, and am surprised that I'm not feeling any anger or any intense emotions whatsoever. I'm just in nothing. I've sunken into a sedated state. I don't even notice that we're stopped in front of Pets Unlimited until Gerry barks "Can you hurry up?" at me. I momentarily snap to reality, gazing at the brother that I've become, and step out of the car. Carla has me moving around and opening up a lot of inventory in the basement. This is probably best for my disposition right now. Alex Ryback has been reduced to a zombie, heaving boxes around, probably all he's good for, while his mind is both floating and imprisoned two feet above his body. In the afternoon, Carla has to run to the bank and leaves the store to me, although no one really comes in. Sitting in one place just makes me feel like I'm being buried deeper and deeper in the ground, so I drift around the tanks, watching the fish stray in circles.

The car ride back with Gerry is silent until he turns on the radio. He's probably the first person I should tell, although I don't know if he could say anything to make me feel better. I wish I could open up to him right now, but can't. I tell Mom I'm not feeling well, skip dinner and go straight to bed. 2.9. I missed it by that much.

Chapter 27: The Scaling

I wake up Thursday morning and the leech comes rushing back to my brain. I wish I could turn myself off so I wouldn't have to think about or deal with this. Substance might do the trick, but I'd have to go find dealers, probably through Gerry. I remind myself that problem postponement has never served me well, so I get out of bed to face my family. I dread the look on Mom and Dad's faces, but it has to come. I'm not sure which is worse, the imaginary horror movie in my head, or swapping it for the real life version that will replay for eternity.

A quick sweep of the house tells me I'm the only one home. I'm not sure if that's a good thing. I lap our first floor with yesterday's same dreary pace before sitting at the kitchen table and taking out my phone. I need to break it to Mom or Dad to release this weight, even just a smidge. Maybe Lily first. She'd listen, but I can't take any more pity right now. I just need that reality smack to hit me already.

My brain sparks, and I contemplate one last possibility. It could just be a delay, or maybe a chance. I look up the number on my computer, dial it, but don't press the "Call" button. For some reason, I can't do it here. I open my backdoor into a chilly, overcast day, and walk into the farthest corner of my backyard, staring at the fence post from one inch away. I peek over at the neighbor's yard behind us, whose pool is still covered and whose grass needs a mow, and then to the backyard of the house beside us, whose dog is staring at me. I turn around facing the house, and press the "Call" button.

"Belston Bursar's Office," a man responds.

"Hey, I'm a student. Can I talk to someone about my scholarship?" I squeak out.

"Sure, I can help you. Which scholarship do you receive?"

"Uh, I don't know the name. It's one where I'm supposed to have at least a three GPA, but I just got back my grades and only got a two-nine. Does that mean I get kicked out of the program and don't get the money next year?"

"Uh, what year are you?"

"I just finished Freshman."

"And you received an overall GPA of two-point-nine for the year?"

"Yes."

"Okay. The Arthur scholarship does stipulate you need to maintain a three-point-oh, but we have had situations like this in the past. We generally revoke scholarships from students when their GPA disparity is especially egregious, like below a two, but in cases like this, there can be some leniency. I think you'll just have to bring it back to a three-point-oh within the next two semesters."

"Does that mean I'll get the scholarship next year?"

"Unofficially, yes. Once we get your grades, we'll send you a letter basically stating what I told you." If Mom or Dad get to the mail first, I can totally handle explaining that to them. "Anything else I can help you with?"

"No, that's great."

"Have a nice day."

"You, too." My face floods. The dog is still staring at me, but now with some bewilderment. When it's done, I lay my wrists on my forehead and drag my sleeves down to my chin. I walk back inside and call Lily.

Chapter 28: Release

Gerry, Diana and I drive to the lake to smoke a blunt before Abigail's dinner. We all get the sense that she's trying to establish a new dynamic with Mom, trying to prove she can cook and host all of us, on her own, even with a baby, to which the three of us smell disaster, or at least moments of discomfort. It'll be hard to focus on the meal itself, when Mom may lose her restraint from giving pointers, or Abigail may overcompensate as a preemptive strike on those very possible pointers, which inspires us to imbibe some medicine that'll dim the drama.

"Which of you is driving us there?" Diana asks croakily, passing to Gerry.

"Whoever's the least high?" Gerry decides before taking a giant hit. Guess that means me. I glance at Diana's glossed-over eyes and disposition, and gather that Gerry and she must be spending a lot of time together because she's got a pretty high tolerance for a ninth-grader. I may have been a little too hard on him. She is his sister, too, and he wouldn't let anything bad happen to her. I'm not sure if he does coke anymore, but tonight I'll make him promise me he'll never introduce her to it. Diana will be alright. She's kind of too smart for any of us to screw her up. She's just going through her own thing like I did. And if

Mom gets Abigail's message tonight, maybe her parental focus will shift.

We watch the lake, glassy and serene, but with faint ripples cooing over the sand. The sound reminds me of Suzie attempting to talk. I let them finish the rest of the spliff. I only had two hits, but I'm content with that. Since the call, I'm pretty cool with everything.

I spent an hour on the phone with that overly-bureaucratic Registrar's Office, just to get them to agree to let me register outside the normal window. I still have to look up Business courses, to see what I can take.

Antione told me that one of his suitemates for next year is actually going to transfer, so there might be a chance I can room with them. It would be all theatre guys, but that's okay.

Marshall invited Mark, Tony, Tyler and me to his family's Memorial Day party this weekend. It'll be good to see those guys.

Antione and I are driving up for Lily's birthday in June. I'd love to have them down here, too and meet Mark and Emily. It's funny that I don't have a new nickname for either trio. ALA and EMA don't really flow off the tongue. Maybe we can form a super group called LEAMA. Or maybe we'll just stick to regular names.

"I've got one," Diana announces out of nowhere.

"Let's hear it," Gerry says.

"Would you rather fly away or swim away?"

"Easy," he says. "Definitely, fly away. Air has less resistance than water."

"Yup," Diana agrees. The two of them high-five. "And you get to fly."

"Yeah, anyone can swim. Who gets to fly?"

"And maybe you can go all the way into space."

"Awesome!" Gerry says. I chuckle to myself, amused by my siblings. In a way, it's an interesting conundrum, although "fly away" and "swim away" are really just out-of-the-way ways of saying "run away." Personally, I'd pick "swim away." Flying means you're in full view. A hunter could spot you and pick you right off. With swimming, you could venture into the murky depths of the ocean floor and hide, so that no one could ever find you.

Acknowledgments

I'd like to thank the following people for their particular support and guidance in the writing and publishing of this novel.

To my marketing coach, Meg Calvin, my most encouraging supporter and social media sherpa: Thank you for teaching me how to take this book to the finish line and thank you for enduring my endless questions and bullet-pointed emails.

To my friend and writing confidant, David French: Thank you for listening and advising whenever I'm tossing an idea around, and thank you for helping me arrive at answers before I even know which question I'm asking.

To Marc DiPaolo and Ian Shane: Thank you for taking the time and taking a chance on my book, and for offering kind words.

To my cover designer, Luisa Galstyan: Thank you for your gorgeous artwork, and for offering the perfect balance of listening to my ideas while suggesting your own.

To my interior designer, Nicole Hayes: Thank you for making the inside of my book look beautiful and for enduring through my flourish pickiness.

To my beta readers, Alicia Whavers and Tianna Bays: Thank you for providing so much insight and confirmation in my book's early stages.

To my marketing street team, Chris Bartow, Hope Bartow, Leanne Boller, Cara Boyd, Mallory Boyd, Meg Calvin, Jillian Canning, Lynn Canning, Olivia Canning, Greg Condon, Jim Downing, Max Downing, Robert Downing, Samantha Downing, Stevie Downing, Sue Downing, Ted Downing, Molly Glass, Jessica Johnson, Melissa Lucenti, Erin McGuinness, James McGuinness, Owen McGuinness, Marie Montondo, Rory Zebrowski and Sara Zebrowski: Thank you for being early readers and early supporters.

Made in United States
Orlando, FL
01 March 2022

15263844R00176